Praise for *The Pilot's*

D0187023

"Jaeger's latest is a beautifully rendered ode to New York City, as well as an engrossing family drama. In Ellie and Iris, she's created two compassionate, conflicted heroines whose search for the truth resonates in all the best ways. Stirring and powerful."

—Fiona Davis, *New York Times*
bestselling author of *The Lions of Fifth Avenue*

"Wow, wow, wow. What a page-turner. *The Pilot's Daughter* is the story of two women over two time lines, and the combined secrets that haunt them. I gasped. I cried. I cheered. *The Pilot's Daughter* is one of the few books that truly earns the descriptor 'unputdownable.' Iris's and Ellie's stories will stay with me for a long time."

—Sally Hepworth, *New York Times*
bestselling author of *The Good Sister*

"Meredith Jaeger proves, yet again, that she is a brilliant storyteller. Layered with drama and danger, *The Pilot's Daughter* is historical fiction at its finest. Jaeger masterfully alternates between 1945 San Francisco, where a talented and determined young woman struggles to find her place in a man's world, and New York City's glamorous Ziegfeld Club, circa 1923, where a riveting, decades-old mystery is finally unraveled. *The Pilot's Daughter* is a timeless, multigenerational masterpiece that will leave you breathless, hopeful, and deeply satisfied. A triumph of hope and love, forgiveness and empowerment, Jaeger weaves a beautifully rendered tale of romance and redemption that will linger long after the last page is turned. If you're looking for the perfect blend of history and mystery, look no further than Meredith Jaeger's *The Pilot's Daughter*. You won't be disappointed!"

—Lori Nelson Spielman, *New York Times*
bestselling author of *The Life List*

"Shifting effortlessly between two time periods, Jaeger weaves a poignant and suspenseful tale, building a layered mystery while she draws us deep into the deliciously glitzy and often dangerous world of Jazz Age New York. But it is the tender and endearing bond between Ellie and Iris that is the beating heart of this propulsive novel. Their connection is so heartfelt and authentic that it makes it easy to root for both women as they journey to find answers—and forgiveness. I won't soon forget Ellie or Iris, and though I raced through the pages to the satisfying end, I did so conflicted—I so didn't want to give up their company!"

—Erika Montgomery, author of *A Summer to Remember*

"Meredith Jaeger's two previous novels sparked my love affair with historical fiction. *The Pilot's Daughter* once again showcases her remarkable talent in creating stunning worlds that are so enticing you'll never want to leave. Blending fact and fiction and alternating time lines between the glittering backdrop of the Ziegfeld Follies and the devastating reality of those left behind in World War II, *The Pilot's Daughter* takes us on an enthralling journey of two women determined to live by their own rules despite the strict societal expectations placed on them. Expertly written with compelling characters and an intriguing mystery begging for answers, this luminous, captivating story inspires, entertains, and completely satisfies."

—Samantha M. Bailey, *USA Today* and #1 national bestselling author of *Woman on the Edge*

"With a delectable mastery of not just one time period but two, Meredith Jaeger spins a tantalizing tale of two determined women searching for the truth. Jaeger moves effortlessly between the glittering Jazz Age and the final months of World War II in this richly detailed, propulsive, absorbing read that brings early-twentieth-century New York to life on the page. From the glamour of the Ziegfeld Follies, to the despair of a daughter whose father is missing in action, Jaeger transports us back in time and straight into the hearts of two conflicted women—Ellie and her aunt, Iris—as they untangle the threads of a complicated past— and an uncertain future. You won't want to put *The Pilot's Daughter* down until you reach the satisfying end."

—Kristin Harmel, *New York Times* bestselling author of *The Forest of Vanishing Stars*

"I've long been a fan of Meredith Jaeger, and her latest, *The Pilot's Daughter*, is her best work yet. Ambitious Ellie is looking for clues that her missing father, a WWII pilot, is still alive. But amid her search, she discovers he may have harbored a dark secret. Ellie's search begins to intermingle with the scandalous history of her aunt, Iris, whose former experience as a showgirl brings us straight into the heart of the 1920s Jazz Age—rife with its own unsolved mystery. In this layered tale of mystery and discovery, Jaeger masterfully develops the characters of two brave women who ultimately find closure by way of determination, self-empowerment, and forgiveness."

—Sarah Penner, *New York Times*
bestselling author of *The Lost Apothecary*

"*The Pilot's Daughter* is a captivating, richly detailed historical novel, following Ellie's journey as she travels to New York with her aunt, Iris, to attempt to find out what happened to her missing pilot father in WWII. Meredith Jaeger artfully weaves the glittering but also dark Jazz Age of Iris's New York with Ellie's search for answers there during WWII. An emotional and gorgeously woven story of strong women fighting for the truth and, ultimately, for themselves. I could not put this book down!"

—Jillian Cantor, *USA Today*
bestselling author of *In Another Time* and *Half Life*

"Jaeger has crafted heroines worth rooting for in Ellie, a resourceful young journalist, and Iris, a danseuse, who ignore the conventions of the day and strike out on their own journeys only to uncover a link between their family and a cold murder case that rocked the nation. An engrossing and addictive read with glimmering details of the Jazz Age and the war years, *The Pilot's Daughter* is one of my favorite books of the year!"

—Heather Webb, *USA Today* bestselling author of
The Next Ship Home and *Meet Me in Monaco*

"From the first chapter of Meredith Jaeger's *The Pilot's Daughter*, I plunged into a mystery that wouldn't let me go until the final page. But it's the two troubled heroines—Ellie and Iris—who pulled me into the heart of this rich, multigenerational family drama. Readers will enjoy the vicarious journey to both 1920s Manhattan and 1940s San Francisco, as they root for Ellie and Iris along the way. And they'll keep turning the pages to find out what happens next."

—Laura Morelli, *USA Today* bestselling author of *The Night Portrait* and *The Stolen Lady*

"Packed with dark family secrets, the drama and glitz of the Ziegfeld Follies, and a World War II mystery, *The Pilot's Daughter* is Meredith Jaeger at her best."

—Elise Hooper, author of *The Other Alcott*

Also by Meredith Jaeger

The Dressmaker's Dowry

Boardwalk Summer

The Pilot's Daughter

A Novel

Meredith Jaeger

DUTTON

DUTTON

An imprint of Penguin Random House LLC
penguinrandomhouse.com

LIBRARY OF CONGRESS CATALOGING-IN-PUBLICATION DATA
Names: Jaeger, Meredith, author.
Title: The pilot's daughter: a novel / Meredith Jaeger.
Description: [New York] : Dutton, 2021. |
Identifiers: LCCN 2021011289 (print) | LCCN 2021011290 (ebook) |
ISBN 9780593185896 (paperback) | ISBN 9780593185902 (ebook)
Subjects: LCSH: World War, 1939–1945—New York (State)—New York—Fiction. |
GSAFD: Historical fiction. | Suspense fiction.
Classification: LCC PS3610.A35697 P55 2021 (print) |
LCC PS3610.A35697 (ebook) | DDC 813/.6—dc23
LC record available at https://lccn.loc.gov/2021011289
LC ebook record available at https://lccn.loc.gov/2021011290

Printed in the United States of America
1st Printing

BOOK DESIGN BY ELKE SIGAL

For my mother, Carol, and my sister, Carolyn. I love you both.

You always are seeing her where the lights are bright. . . . Not the first Broadway Butterfly. Those wings are long since dust. . . . Many recall her dancing feet . . . her hair like copper. Even today's playgirls know her story. What happened to Dot King can happen to anyone who lives by the lights.

—*The Philadelphia Inquirer,* January 19, 1941

Prelude

NEW YORK CITY, MARCH 15, 1923

He liked her in yellow. He always told her this, and she'd become aware of how she felt whenever she wore it—like a kept woman. Her silk chemise, the exact shade of a canary, barely reached her knees, and she shivered as a bitter-cold draft blew through the open window. Did she leave it like that? She lay tangled in her bedsheets, listening. The sounds of the city had quieted—no nighttime whoopee, no honking automobiles. The apartment itself was silent, save for the squeaking ropes and pulleys of the dumbwaiter, which had woken her with its rattling—normally she'd never be up at dawn. What fool would carry hooch up to the fifth floor at this hour?

She'd forgotten to take off her diamond and pearl bracelet, and it sparkled in the early morning sunlight like a handcuff. Her world had grown smaller in these past few months, tightening around her like a snake. This room! She couldn't stand it. Secrets bubbled up inside of her, daring to spill out. But she'd never betray him. He had too much power. She touched her pillowcase, last night's lipstick smeared across it like a bloodstain. Then the dumbwaiter stopped and a terrible feeling came over her. Something wasn't right.

Chapter One

Ellie

Ellie wanted answers. She wanted witness statements, mission documents, aircraft records, and every single piece of classified information that the army refused to give her. As she climbed the stairs to the *San Francisco Chronicle* newspaper office, tears pressed against her eyelids. She had been unable to get through to the army officials in charge, the same men who'd sent her mother a Western Union telegram six weeks ago, blowing her life apart like a grenade.

MRS CLARA MORGAN 1944 DEC 15

 THE SECRETARY OF WAR DESIRES ME TO
EXPRESS HIS DEEP REGRET THAT YOUR HUSBAND
FIRST LIEUTENANT WILLIAM P MORGAN HAS BEEN
REPORTED MISSING IN ACTION SINCE FOURTEEN
DECEMBER OVER THE ADRIATIC SEA IF FURTHER

DETAILS OR OTHER INFORMATION ARE RECEIVED

YOU WILL BE PROMPTLY NOTIFIED

THE ADJUTANT GENERAL

Ellie had clutched that yellow envelope with shaking fingers, a scream scraping up her throat while back in the house, Bing Crosby crooned on the radio, "I'll be home for Christmas. You can plan on me." She'd sunk to her knees on the front porch, an icy feeling rendering her breathless, like the time she'd plunged into Lake Tahoe in early spring at age ten to prove to her father she was no sissy. Her heart had been beating too fast then too, the shock of the cold water almost unbearable.

Now, fourteen years later, she was determined to find out what had happened to her father and his crew. She'd written and called the adjutant general's office, requesting the operational details of her father's mission report, the government photographs that had been taken that day—any piece of information that could help her. But she'd received nothing in response.

The last thing Ellie wanted to do was speculate—she was terrified it would lead her down a dark hole from which she'd never return—but she needed to start somewhere. She had to assume the Germans had shot down her father's plane in a hail of bullets before he could return to his Italian base, so she'd marked up a map in blue pen, making *X*s along the beaches of the Adriatic Sea. *No one is a better pilot*, Ellie reminded herself. *Father could survive a water landing.* But her letters to the army, insisting her father could still be alive, received no reply.

She climbed the stairs two at a time, afraid to be late. Ever since the telegram, she'd moved about the world grief haunted and numb, but she'd returned a few days later to her secretarial position at the *San Francisco Chronicle*. Her mother, on the other hand, retreated to her bedroom with a bottle of pills the doctor had prescribed.

Ellie collected herself as best she possibly could, repinning a strand of auburn hair into her Victory rolls and smoothing her green wool cardigan over her white collared blouse. Ellie noticed her brown velveteen skirt had a stain on it and chided herself for not choosing differently. She would have much rather worn trousers, but as a secretary, she wasn't allowed to. Secretarial school had taught her to always look beautiful, to always please her boss, and to refrain from smoking—yet her boss, Frank Hardcastle, smoked like a chimney and looked like a bum, as did most of her male colleagues.

She wanted to go home, to change into one of her father's flannel shirts, and to curl up in bed. Her lip trembled, remembering how when she was eight, she'd ridden in her neighbor Billy Zubritsky's orange crate on roller skate wheels down Lombard's famous curves. She'd skinned both her knees bloody when she'd toppled over and ruined her Sunday dress. Her mother had screeched like a banshee and given her a night without supper, but her father had secretly given her a dime. *God, she missed him.*

A dark part of her wanted to say to hell with it all, and to drown her grief in a bottle of vodka, just as Mother drowned hers in pills. But unlike Mother, Ellie had hope—a dangerous, slippery thing.

She pushed open the door to the newsroom. Cigarette smoke and the smell of ink hung in the air around the horseshoe of battered desks where the copy editors huddled together, clacking away at their typewriters. The familiar scent of Lucky Strike, her father's brand, hit her like a sledgehammer. She would not cry. Not here. Ellie made her way toward the kitchenette to brew coffee for Frank, the managing editor.

"Where the hell is my Page One copy?" Frank yelled over the noise. He popped out from behind the glass door to his office, and Ellie quickly ducked into the kitchen, a small room with a sink and a hot plate. Though he wasn't the editor in chief, Frank oversaw all the day-to-day operations at the paper. Balding and potbellied, with a cigarette constantly dangling from his lips, he wore ill-fitting suits and a tie so loose that Ellie wondered why he bothered with one at all.

She brewed his coffee, then hurriedly poured a cup, adding powdered milk, just the way he liked it. She was almost to Frank's office door when she stumbled over a black briefcase. "Damn!"

Immediately, she slapped a hand over her mouth. "I mean, darn." But it was too late: Rick Johnson, one of the reporters, glared at her.

"Be careful, will you?"

"Forgive me." Ellie used a napkin to wipe away the droplets of coffee that had spilled over the rim of Frank's mug. Then she smiled apologetically at Rick. Never mind his misplaced briefcase had nearly caused her to break her neck. But Rick had received his press accreditation from the War Department and he'd already served overseas, reporting from the front lines before taking a job with the *Chronicle*. He carried himself with an air of importance—after all, he'd ridden in jeeps with officers and witnessed enemy gunfire up close.

Frank's shiny head was flushed from stress when he stuck it

out from behind his office door and grabbed his coffee mug. "Took you long enough. Now hang up my coat."

Ellie's hands shook with frustration. "Yes, sir."

She transferred his hat and coat from where he'd tossed them on his desk to the coat stand in the corner. Pinning a tight smile of compliance on her face, she turned to him. "Sir, is there anything else?"

"When's the traffic commissioner here for our meeting?"

Ellie bit her lip to hold back from pointing out the appointment was written in his diary, right in front of him. "Eleven this morning."

She returned to the din of the newsroom, shutting Frank's office door behind her. As she busied herself with filing, she thought of the wives and mothers of the airmen in Father's crew. Following the telegram, a woman named Catherine had written. Ellie's throat tightened, remembering the letter.

Dear Mrs. Morgan,

I would like to offer my sympathies because I understand how you must feel. Everything is so uncertain, and I just don't know what to think. All we can do is pray and hope we'll hear good news of our loved ones soon.

Knowing Clara wouldn't respond, Ellie had written Catherine back, the widow of Father's radio operator, and learned that Catherine wrote regularly to the other families of the missing airmen. These distraught relatives mailed letters from Arkansas, Minnesota, and Ohio, asking what news the army had sent and what personal effects they had received.

Catherine shared these details with Ellie, and her letters became a kind of life raft. A woman named Diane had gotten two bundles of her own letters, her husband's fountain pen, his pipe, and his hat. Ellie asked Catherine to share her address with the other women, inviting them to write her directly.

I believe Diane got more of her Jimmie's things than I got of my Ted's, a woman named Wilma had replied when Ellie asked what objects she'd received. Ellie hadn't gotten any of her father's belongings yet. She pushed that thought from her mind, remembering the most promising letter, which had come from Melba Doyle of Texas, the mother of Father's bombardier.

> *Dear Ellie,*
>
> *Though my Tommy is gone, he spoke highly of your father in his letters home. He said Lieutenant Morgan was a fine pilot who the whole crew got along with, and they sure trusted him up in the air. I am heartbroken at losing my Tommy, and I still can't believe my boy is gone, but I pray you'll receive good news soon . . .*

Tommy had parachuted out of the plane and had been rescued by local fishermen who didn't speak English. Ellie wished she could ask him what he had seen and where Father's plane had gone down. But Tommy Doyle had died that day, succumbing to his injuries. *Had others parachuted out too? Had Father?*

Ellie wrote regularly to the women of the missing airmen. All of them had one thing in common: hope. But they were paralyzed by uncertainty, unable to move forward with their lives—a feeling Ellie knew all too well. Their loss became a shared connection, and their wounds remained fresh. It was as if they shared a story with no ending, which only compounded their grief.

There was a chance—however slim—that Germans had captured the men, or maybe they were in hiding somewhere. If the army couldn't provide answers, then Ellie was determined to. She had access to breaking news, to the *Chronicle*'s team of factcheckers, and she was no stranger to late nights spent at the library. Unlike Mother, who had become a shell of her former self, Ellie wasn't going to give up hope that easily. She owed her father and his crew more than that.

Returning to her filing, Ellie felt a sharp twist of envy as she looked over at the reporters, thinking of her notebooks full of stories she kept stashed away in a drawer. She was determined to be more than Frank's secretary—to have a column of her own someday; but right now, her father gone and her spirits sunk, she lacked the courage to try. Ellie mustered just enough energy to make it through her workday, but that was all. Never had January felt so desolate.

WITH CHRISTMAS DECORATIONS taken down, San Francisco had returned to its cool gray state. Ellie rode the Powell-Hyde cable car, shivering in the fog. Both tough and elegant at the same time, Frisco was a city of sailors and reporters, well-heeled secretaries and operagoers in fur coats, jazz clubs and narrow alleys, windswept seascapes and impossibly steep streets.

The trolley grip clanged the bell. "Hyde and Lombard!"

Ellie stood up and stepped off. Beyond the redbrick Ghirardelli Chocolate Factory, Alcatraz Prison sat in the distance, on a rocky island marooned in the deep blue waters of the bay. Ellie clenched her fists, picturing its notorious criminals safe in their cells while good men were overseas fighting. She pulled a Chesterfield from her purse and then lit the cigarette, taking a long drag—a dirty little habit her mother didn't approve of.

She stared at the dark windows of her narrow Victorian home, its blue paint flaking. Before the telegram, the lights would have been on and a casserole would have been in the oven. Clara had once seemed to enjoy cooking, though she reminded Ellie to eat small portions, no matter how delicious the dinner, in order to maintain her figure. Did her mother say these things out of concern or spite? Ellie frowned. *Some people show love differently than others.*

She yearned for the strong embrace of her fiancé, Tom, a sergeant in the Harbor Defenses of San Francisco. He was stationed at Fort Winfield Scott in the Presidio, where he commanded a crew of soldiers who manned guns and antiaircraft radar along the California coast. Though she couldn't see his battery from where she stood, Ellie pictured his foggy barracks near the base of the Golden Gate Bridge, and she felt comforted knowing Tom was nearby.

Ellie longed for the companionship of her childhood friends too, Betsy and Mable, who'd married and left the neighborhood. Growing up, Betsy Gibbons and Mabel White were trouble, but the good kind. In high school, they painted their nails daring colors while listening to jazz records and sneaking nips of sherry. They were the bane of Ellie's mother's life, or, as she liked to say, "bad influences." Back then, before the war, the once-formidable

Clara Morgan had been an organizer of church potlucks and neighborhood committees.

Now she refused to leave the house, bathe, or even eat. Ellie had tried showing her mother the letters from the wives of Father's crew members, but she was met with a withering look accompanying a voice low and dangerous. *Don't speak of those letters again. Your father is dead.*

"You're not dead," Ellie whispered, standing at the crest of Hyde Street Hill and looking out at the bay as if she could see all the way to Europe. "I know you're not."

She stubbed out her cigarette and trudged up the creaky steps leading to her front porch. A box waited on the stoop. Had Aunt Iris brought by a meal for supper? Iris had no children of her own, and she lived alone in North Beach, in an apartment above an Italian restaurant. In the awful weeks since the telegram, Ellie had grown even closer to her beloved aunt, who came around with spaghetti marinara and comforting hugs.

But as Ellie climbed the stairs, she saw the foreign postage plastered on the battered cardboard box. Her breath caught in her throat. She tore through the tape holding the box together and tugged open the flaps. Inside was a woolen, olive field jacket. Tears clogged her throat. The army had finally sent her father's belongings. Ellie took out the official letter inside and read.

Dear Mrs. Morgan,

These are the personal effects of your husband, Army Air Forces First Lieutenant William P. Morgan. We offer our sincerest condolences.

Ellie wiped away her tears, pulled out his army-issued jacket, and brought it to her nose, longing for the scent of her father's cologne. But his jacket only smelled of mildew. In the bottom of the box, a cigarette lighter, a ballpoint pen, and a hair comb rolled around. Did these things mean anything to him? Ellie felt a renewed wave of frustration at the army. Where were the missing aircrew reports she had requested? What was the tail number of the plane her father had flown on the day of his disappearance?

Still clutching his jacket to her chest, Ellie felt something bulky in one of the breast pockets. She unfastened the button with her unruly fingers, stiff from the cold night air. When it finally came loose, Ellie reached inside and retrieved a stack of letters. They were tied together with twine, the blue and red striped airmail envelopes gossamer thin and smudged with dirt, as if her father had carried them with him everywhere.

Ellie's heart thumped as she untied the twine, removing the first letter. She didn't remember sending this many. Had her mother written him so often? Ellie had written to her father last when she'd gotten engaged to Tom, but she'd never heard back. She wasn't concerned at first, wartime mail and all, but then two weeks later, Father had been declared missing, and her world had gone into a tailspin.

Ellie blinked. She didn't recognize the name of the sender. *Miss Lillian Dell, 48 Bleecker Street, Apt. 10, New York, NY.*

Who was she? How bizarre for Father to have been carrying around a stack of letters from a woman whose name Ellie didn't recognize. An uneasy feeling came over her as she removed the letter from its envelope.

My dearest William,

How I miss you. I worry about you every day. Lucy misses you too. She yearns to know that you're safe. We love you so much. This is worse than all the times we waited for you to return to New York. During your absences, at least we knew you would be coming home. Now we don't know where you are . . .

Ellie dropped the letter as if it had caught fire. *How was this possible?* Her father was her hero, loyal, brave, strong, and honest—a man who always did the right thing. Her mother was a harridan at times, but that didn't mean her father would have an affair. *Would he?*

Ellie clutched the stack of letters, her breath coming in gulps. As a commercial pilot for United Airlines before the war, her father had flown a route that had taken him to New York. He was gone for days at a time. But he always called, and he always came home. Ellie knew he and her mother were legally wed—their wedding picture was framed on the mantelpiece. They received all official mail from the US Army, addressed to Mrs. Clara Morgan. Now one burning question pushed away all the others swimming around in Ellie's mind: Who was Lillian Dell?

Chapter Two

Ellie

Ellie turned on her heel and ran down the porch steps. Her hands were shaking so hard, she feared she'd drop the letters. She'd taken a moment to unlock the front door, depositing the cardboard box with her father's belongings safely inside her house, and then she'd slammed it shut again. Ellie ought to have left a note for her mother, but with Clara's daily dose of barbiturates, she wouldn't even notice Ellie hadn't returned home.

Ellie ran down Hyde Street toward the bay, then turned right on Lombard and took the pedestrian staircase as quickly as she could. Her eyes moved to the red-bordered flags that hung in her neighbors' windows, the blue and gold stars representing the brothers, fathers, and sons who were still fighting, and those who weren't coming home.

How could you?

Tears stung her eyes. She was furious with her father, and

yet she missed him so much. Ellie couldn't bear to be in her lonely, claustrophobic house with her mother right now.

She covered her trembling mouth, thinking of the booth she always shared with her father at Mayflower Donuts, a little place on the corner of Ellis and Stockton with the words "Maxwell House Coffee" on its white façade. They would eat glazed donuts and drink strong coffee while watching the Muni cars pass by down Stockton Street. Did her father have special traditions like that with Lillian in New York? Ellie felt a searing stab of jealousy.

Her first instinct was to telephone Tom, who had been her rock after they received the awful telegram. She'd met him six months ago, volunteering as a junior hostess at the Hospitality House. Tall, blond, and charismatic, Tom had caught Ellie off guard when he'd entered the Servicemen's Club on Larkin Street. With his striking blue eyes, he was by far the most handsome man in the room. At first, she couldn't find her voice, but then she managed a smile.

"Soldier, can I buy you a drink?"

Alcohol was forbidden at USO dances, but Ellie gestured toward the Coca-Cola vending machine. Tom's smile lit up his entire face.

"I'll match you for it."

He nodded at the Ping-Pong table. A heated game of Ping-Pong, which Ellie won, gave way to an exhilarating Saturday night. Ellie had danced and played cards with plenty of soldiers before, out of an obligation to "make the boys feel at home." Her mother had practically demanded that the hostess committee approve her, a "good and respectable girl," in the hopes Ellie would find a husband.

She hadn't planned to acquiesce to her mother's wishes, but Tom was a marvelous dancer and conversationalist. When he'd asked for her phone number, she'd explained she wasn't permitted to date service members she met at dances—a committee rule—but she agreed to say the numbers out loud and not write them down. By the time she got home, the phone was ringing.

Ellie smiled at the memory, but it soon slipped away. Tom came from a wealthy Catholic family with a strict moral code. He would be horrified to learn of her father's affair . . . she couldn't tell him just yet. She slowed her pace, reading the letters as she walked. *I love you . . . I miss you . . . Lucy admires you so much . . . When is your next flight to New York?* A picture began to form in Ellie's mind of another family, clearer now than before—Lillian complaining of New York traffic and her failed acting auditions, describing her daughter Lucy's love of playing piano, singing show tunes, and watching films. Lillian wasn't simply a fling—in her letters, she referenced the "wonderful times" she and William had shared in the past twenty years. This was a woman Father had loved for over two decades. Ellie covered her mouth.

She'd last seen her father in December of '41, right after the bombing of Pearl Harbor. Ellie had leaned into him as he'd hugged her goodbye, not wanting to let go. He'd kissed her on the forehead and his eyes crinkled at the corners when he smiled. *Don't you worry about me, El. I'll be fine. Take care of your mother. This old mule is too stubborn to die.* At forty-one, he was only four years shy of being declared IV-A, overage and unfit for active service. Despite his smile, Ellie had seen the apprehension in his eyes, mirroring her own fear and worry.

Now she wondered, how could he have left not one but two families behind? For her entire life, she'd been an only child. That was her identity—and now it was being thrown into question. The possibility of a sister brought up a multitude of emotions— shock, guilt, and anger, yes, but also something that felt like hope.

Ellie had longed for a sister throughout her childhood, someone she could confide in, giggle with, and learn from. She'd envied her friends who had older sisters, girls who'd taught them how to do their hair and makeup. *If Lucy were her sister, would she love her immediately? Would they have an inexplicable connection?*

Rubbing her temples, Ellie tried not to jump to any conclusions. Lucy could be completely unrelated to her, the product of another tryst . . . though Ellie had to admit the letters made it sound as if her father were the only one in Lillian's life.

Had her father said goodbye to Lillian in New York before he departed for Europe? Ellie thought of his trips home during training. She'd believed him when he said he was returning to Bruning Army Air Field in Nebraska, or to the navigation school in Selman Field, Louisiana. She'd devoured his letters, funny stories about the enlisted men—boys he related to by making jokes and playing cards, even though he was an officer and twice their age. *But what if he'd been secretly returning to Lillian every trip, cutting his time with them short?*

Ellie couldn't bear the thought of it. Her father's wartime letters to her hadn't revealed anything except his usual sense of humor, one of the reasons she loved him, but she thought of the last letter her father had sent regardless, trying to recognize clues of his affair.

Nov. 16, 1944

Dearest Clara and Ellie,

I am in fine health (as well as can be expected for an old fart like me) and I hope to hear the same from you. I think of you both always, even though I don't write as often as I should. I will miss you both dearly this Thanksgiving, but I hope we will all sit down together to a turkey dinner this time next year, as soon as this war is over. I will send you both a souvenir from Italy as soon as I get the chance. I sure miss that little restaurant below Iris's apartment (Clara, give your sister my love). The K rations here have my men complaining, though I don't think the little biscuits inside are so bad. But they sure don't compare to the Mayflower donuts! Save one for me, will you, El?

Love always,

Your William

Ellie never imagined he had been writing to anyone other than herself and her mother—except maybe to his brother, Uncle John, who lived on a farm in Idaho. Had Father written to Lillian more often? *How could he have been so duplicitous?*

Ellie wiped sweat from her brow as she reached the intersection of Lombard and Columbus, the letters in her pocket heavy with the secrets they carried. Though the walk had only taken fifteen minutes, she felt like she'd aged by fifteen years. Ellie crossed the cable car tracks on Columbus Avenue, reaching the clapboard building that housed Trattoria La Siciliana, where second-generation Italians cooked home-style meals. Her father loved their spaghetti carbonara. The maître d' called out to Ellie, but she pretended she couldn't hear him, stabbing the buzzer of number 724.

Aunt Iris's footsteps sounded heavily on the staircase overhead, and then her blue eyes widened as she opened the door. "My goodness, Ellie! Is everything all right?"

Ellie shook her head. Everything in her world was upside down.

Iris gripped her shoulder. "Come inside. I'll make you some tea."

Ellie took a deep breath as she climbed the steep, narrow stairs leading to Iris's flat. The door was ajar, and she breathed in the scent of lavender, which Iris always kept in a ceramic vase. Her aunt's cozy green velvet sofa sat beneath the bay windows.

"Here." Iris took Ellie's coat. "Sit down, dear. What's the matter?"

Iris's blue eyes shone with concern. The light hadn't gone out of them, despite the fact she'd lost her husband, Uncle Ed, to a heart attack two years ago. Iris hadn't let her grief consume her. Instead, she was often mistaken for Clara's younger sister, because she remained young at heart. She dyed her hair a rich chestnut brown and wore polka-dotted shirtwaist dresses and stylish snoods. Unlike Mother, Iris never imagined the worst. Though even her mother never could have predicted *this*.

"Aunt Iris, I found these letters, and I think—I think . . ."

Ellie couldn't bring herself to say the words. Hands shaking, she sat down on the sofa and gratefully accepted the blanket Iris wrapped around her shoulders. Ellie closed her eyes and shivered. When she opened them, Iris's brow creased with worry.

"You found letters? What do you mean? From who?"

Ellie nodded. "They're in my coat pocket. Let me get them." She returned with the stack of letters, her voice shuddering as she spoke. "I think my father was having an affair. The war office mailed his belongings and I found these."

Iris's mouth drew into a thin white line. As her aunt shuffled through the letters, something fell to the floor. Ellie reached over, picked it up, and looked at the photograph of a beautiful woman with painted lips and light eyes giving a sultry come-hither look.

Ellie's stomach wrenched. "My God, is this her?" She flipped the photo over to the back. In feminine handwriting it read: *To my William. Love, your Lillian.*

Something passed over Iris's face, but she quickly rearranged her features as she sat down on the couch and wrapped a comforting arm around Ellie's shoulders.

"Ellie, darling, you and your mother have been through so much. Perhaps it's best to tuck these letters away for now."

Heat rose under Ellie's skin. "Are you serious? I can't simply forget about them. These are love letters!"

Iris patted her knee. "Perhaps they are. If so, it's all in the past. You know how much your father loved you."

Loves me, Ellie thought.

"But this woman." Ellie jabbed at the photo with her index finger. "She meant something to him. Otherwise why would he have kept her letters and carried them around with him? And this girl, Lucy, why does she talk about her as if . . ."

The words tasted bitter on her tongue. Ellie couldn't complete the unbearable thought. *She* was her father's only child. Lillian looked like a tramp and she could have slept with any number of men. Ellie buried her face in her hands, while Iris rubbed her back, her voice calming. "There, there. It hurts, I know."

Ellie took a deep breath and let her words tumble out. "I've told you how I think he might still be alive. It's only been six weeks since we received the telegram. The wives of his crew members hope their husbands are alive too. Maybe he's wounded. Or maybe he's been captured by the Germans."

A pained expression crossed Iris's face.

"You don't believe me." Ellie's shoulders sagged. "You think I'm crazy."

"No." Iris patted her knee again. "You're grieving. It's natural to hope your father is alive, just like it's natural for those women to hope that their husbands are alive. I'm glad that you write to each other for comfort."

A look of concern remained on her aunt's face.

"What? You're frightening me."

"It's nothing."

Ellie couldn't bear for Aunt Iris to be like Mother, who never spoke of unpleasant things. "You've always been honest with me. Tell me."

Iris sighed. "I knew her."

"You knew who? *Lillian?*"

Iris rubbed her temples, looking as if she were making mental calculations. "I'm as shocked as you are. But yes . . . it's definitely her.

"I knew her when I lived in New York."

"You mean all those years ago? When you were a secretary?"

Iris gripped Ellie's hand, an apologetic look in her eyes. She let out a deep breath. "Well, you see, dear, there's more to this story than you know. The truth is, I wasn't really a secretary."

Chapter Three

Iris

Beautiful girls were summoned from all over the country, but the Great Ziegfeld chose to glorify only a few. We came from the East, the Deep South, and the far West; and a handful of us with the looks, charm, and grace to captivate audiences were pushed to the breathless peak of our profession. At twenty-five, I was the shining star of the Ziegfeld Follies, Broadway's most popular production.

I'd given my blood, sweat, and tears to the Follies over the past five years, climbing my way to the top, where I wanted to stay. Gossip columnists for the society pages wrote about me; and girls in the chorus—ambitious, beautiful young things— yearned for their turn in the spotlight. That warm autumn night in September, as I performed, the memory of John's lips on my skin sent a shiver down my spine. I could still feel his fingers trailing down my stomach, could still hear the echoes of him whispering my name.

"Spread your wings," I sang, winking at the crowd. "Fly to me and come get your honey." My sheer crepe silk dress hugged the curves of my naked body, gold sequins placed strategically to cover my nipples, while the plunging neckline reached my navel, exposing my pale skin.

I spread my arms, the stage lights illuminating silk bumblebee wings dotted with hundreds of tiny rhinestones, while the hem of my dress, embellished with black ostrich feathers, dragged across the floor. Having the most extravagant costume and a star's dressing room made me feel desired—men wanted me and girls wanted to be me—but no one adored me like John. He'd fallen for me hard and fast, telling me we were made for each other. I doubted he would ever leave his wife, but John Marshall had swept me off my feet quick as a riptide, and into his world of wealth and power.

I surveyed the crowd, their faces softly illuminated, captivated by my performance. John despised those men looking at me. But no other Broadway production had anything on the Ziegfeld Follies. I didn't only entertain for the money and the attention—though being a Follies girl provided both in spades—I truly admired Florenz Ziegfeld's ability to turn the stage into a unique work of art. Flo mixed the familiar with the fresh, dazzling both society dames and stevedores alike, and he knew how to set me off, a redhead in a sea of blondes. I wanted to soak up this feeling as long as I could.

Hilda and Louise appeared onstage beside me, bedecked in jewels and feathers like birds of paradise; and behind me, a wooden replica of the city of Paris sparkled, a wire Eiffel Tower glittering with globe lights. Hundreds of yellow long-stemmed roses bloomed onstage and stars made of glass hung from the ceiling. Flo always thought of his finales in terms of color—pink and white were his favorites, but tonight the chorus girls wore gold costumes, designed by Erté.

The band began to play "A Pretty Girl Is Like a Melody," my cue for the finale. Eddie Cantor, who'd been making the audience laugh all night, flitted around the stage as a clumsy bumblebee vying for my affection. But I thwarted his advances, because my onstage love interest was Roberto, a handsome gardener played by Bobby Green.

I didn't mind Bobby. He was kind, and he had a pleasant singing voice. Some of the gals wouldn't speak to Bobby offstage. They called him an Airedale, though I didn't think he was bad-looking. But Ziegfeld girls had a reputation for marrying millionaires, not stage actors. We collected jewelry like stamps and stirred up the stardust of Broadway like no one else could.

Hilda and Louise twirled offstage, their feathers aflutter, as Bobby dipped me low for a smooch. The chorus gals paraded down glass staircases, all sixty of them dazzling. Bobby took his cue to exit and Hilda and Louise reappeared beside me. In our sequins, we danced the most daring cancan outside of the Moulin Rouge. When I'd started out as a Follies girl, I'd learned the Ziegfeld Walk to balance my large and heavy headpieces, my arms stretched out horizontally, stepping toe-heel, toe-heel. Now, as a lead showgirl, dancing in costume felt as natural as breathing. If Ma and Clara could see me onstage they'd be absolutely scandalized.

Mother, an Irish immigrant, thought my mid-calf hemlines were immodest, while my gruff father hardly spoke to me, and my sister, Clara, read her Bible every night. As a child, my sister had let me doll her up with lipstick and rouge while we'd giggled uncontrollably, and I read to her from *The Tale of the Flopsy Bunnies*. Now Clara wasn't as much fun, but I missed her anyway. Unfortunately, traveling home wasn't an option. If I missed too many rehearsals, Flo would replace me.

Finally, the band piped down, and I caught my breath. Hilda squeezed my hand too tightly as we took our bow. Her star was on the rise, and she made it no secret that she'd gladly knock me out of the top spot. The crowd erupted into applause and I beamed at the audience. Hilda could try to take my place as principal dancer, but she wouldn't succeed. I'd worked too hard, moving from the second line of the chorus to the front line, and then becoming an understudy for Marilyn Miller. When I'd gotten my first solo, I'd danced my heart out under the lights, wearing a crown of stars. Ziegfeld created an environment of beauty and grace, and through his mission of "glorifying the American girl," he made me feel supernal.

Backstage, flowers and clutter lined the hallways while messengers with telegrams ran to and fro. Tempers flared—the reputations of writers, composers, and producers of Broadway's biggest musical at stake. Flo anxiously waited for the reviews to come in, and I hoped I'd made him proud tonight—after all, I'd sacrificed most of my personal life to get here. Three years ago, I'd missed my little sister's wedding because Flo had forbidden me from leaving the Follies mid-tour. I'd written my apologies, explaining that the law firm I worked for was too busy to allow me to take time off.

Back then, I hadn't realized how lying about my life was widening the divide between us. Mother with her strict morals and Victorian corsets, Father with his lined face and calloused hands, and Clara with her Bible—I thought they would shun me if they knew I was a Follies dancer. Other gals told me stories of being disowned by their mothers, their pointe shoes burned. I didn't want that to be my fate—even though I didn't always agree with my family, I still loved them.

While Clara diligently read Corinthians, I was learning the grizzly bear, the bunny hug, and the turkey trot. All over the country, these dances were deemed inappropriate, which only made them more appealing. I watched my father return home bone-tired from his factory job at Bethlehem Steel shipyard, and my mother, up to her elbows in other people's dirty laundry, and I knew I didn't want that life. I yearned to dance onstage in the center of a big city.

Back then San Francisco wasn't the destination it is today. Men with wheelbarrows and horses carved up the hillsides for new developments or worked at the flour mills, at the tanneries, and in the coal yards. They were rough and boorish—not the type of fellas I wanted to meet.

At nineteen, I'd gotten a job selling hats at the I. Magnin department store, earning twenty-five dollars a month. By twenty, I'd saved enough money to move to New York, pay for dancing lessons, and pursue my dream of becoming a professional dancer. It had been a struggle for my parents to allow me to leave, though

I was an adult by then and they had no idea why I was really drawn to the Great White Way. But Clara knew I loved to dance. Sometimes I wondered if I'd told her my secret, could we have held on to the closeness we'd shared as children?

"Did you hear Marion Davies is making millions in the pictures?" Hilda closed the curtain to our dressing room, snapping me back to the present. "She's not even *that* pretty."

"Baloney!" Louise fit her cloche over her dark bob. "She's a dish."

Hilda pursed her lips in the mirror. "Her lover is the only reason she's famous. Mr. Hearst spends his millions like pocket money."

Lou giggled. "Where can I find a man like that?"

Butterflies filled my stomach, thinking of John. Everyone knew about Marion Davies and William Randolph Hearst, but no one knew about John and me. The gossip columnists tried, but they always got it wrong. The *New York Globe* said I'd been stepping out with Eddie Cantor.

I looked at Hilda. She and I fought like cats and dogs, but we never had a dull moment. "Marion was one of the most talented Follies girls Flo ever had. From what I heard, she's a real doll. Her diamond cigarette case was held together with a rubber band. I bet she doesn't care about money."

"Bull," Hilda scoffed. "Everyone does."

Hilda was right. If I didn't give a hoot about diamonds and furs, I'd never have gotten involved with a married man old enough to be my father. But I had never been with someone so attentive, so romantic. As if on cue, a stagehand arrived with a bouquet of long-stemmed roses and a bottle of French champagne.

He looked at me. "Miss Stella Parsons?"

I smiled. "The one and only."

When Ziegfeld had chosen me for his famed revue, I'd been floating on air after hearing the good news. But there was another dancer named Iris in the Follies at the time, so I'd been asked to come up with a stage name. Stella Parsons sounded terribly glamorous, and before long I'd grown into my new persona.

The boy handed me the champagne bottle, which glinted with diamonds underneath the globe lights of my mirror. A necklace with a large sapphire pendant shaped like a pear was draped around the bottle's neck. I gasped at the size of it, and then I opened the card. *A little trinket for my pet. I'll be waiting for you.*

Briefly, a wave of guilt washed over me. Did John ever give his wife extravagant gifts like this? But he'd told me she was cold and loveless—a bitter woman who spurned his affections. They remained married in name only.

"Oh my Lord." Louise fingered the priceless necklace. "Who's your fella? He must have more dough than Mr. Hearst!"

Hilda smirked, fastening a string of diamonds and pearls around her neck, gifted to her by one of her many admirers. "Now, Lou, don't be jealous."

"Why not?" Lou sulked. "Y'all get gifts like that and I don't."

I winked at Lou. "You need to find the *right* kind of gentleman."

The first time John had seen me onstage, he'd sent me

diamonds wrapped around a champagne bottle, just like he had tonight. I'd been unable to resist him. That night he made love to me with confidence and skill. I didn't think an older man could satisfy me in that way. But oh how he did. He'd brought me into his glamorous and elegant social circle and told me I was unlike any woman he'd ever known.

"Oh, I look a sight." Lou fanned her flushed face. "Hilda, lend me your powder. Or better yet, give me a drink. I'm parched."

"Here." Hilda slipped her silver flask from her rolled stocking top and handed it over. "But don't go jumping in fountains like Zelda Fitzgerald; you don't have half her charm." Flo didn't like us drinking, or making any kind of public scene. We were a reflection of him, always wearing our hats, heels, and gloves in public. He paid us a hundred dollars at the end of the summer if we didn't get suntanned.

"Well, look at you three." Lillian pushed aside the velvet curtain and stepped into our dressing room. "Clucky as hens." She blew out a plume of smoke from her cigarette. Then her eyes fixed on the diamond and sapphire necklace wrapped around the bottle of champagne. "How elegant. A real orchid, I'll say."

"Yes." Every time I saw Lillian, her sharp angles and green eyes unnerved me. She was a chorus girl—not traditionally pretty like some of the blondes—but her dark, feline features were striking.

"Aren't you going to put it on?" Lillian raised her eyebrows.

As I draped the necklace around my collarbone, its heaviness surprised me. The sapphire glinted in the light, the precious stone cold against my sweaty skin.

"Oh, it's to die for." Lillian's lips formed a moue of envy. Then she turned to Hilda. "What's the scoop?"

Hilda swigged her gin. "We're headed to the Silver Slipper tonight. So let's make like the wind and blow."

"I can't." I thought of Clara's letter, which had arrived last week, telling me how much it would mean to her if I met William. "I'm meeting my sister's husband at the Algonquin. He's in town for the evening. And I can't be wearing *this*."

I unclasped the diamond and sapphire necklace. Holding it in my hands, I felt the thrill of something dangerous. I didn't know much about John Marshall—we'd only been dating for a month—but I wanted to know more, to discover the secrets behind his blue eyes.

Would John be upset that I hadn't told him about my plans to meet my brother-in-law? He had a tendency to get jealous, which I found cute, because it showed how much he cared. And he was waiting for me at the Waldorf-Astoria. But I'd already let Clara down so many times, she would be devastated if I didn't meet William tonight.

Lillian raised an eyebrow.

"He thinks I'm a secretary." I laughed. "I have to keep up the charade. And secretaries don't wear diamonds."

Chapter Four

Ellie

Ellie tried to concentrate during her last hour at work, but all she could think about was her father, and the lies he'd told, and the fact that, as furious as she was, she still missed him more than anything. She hadn't fit the mold of the perfectly domesticated child pictured in magazine advertisements, but her father had never seemed to care about that. He'd made her feel accepted and loved.

Once, when she was nine, she and her father had shared a soda pop while she passed him nails so he could fix the porch railing. "You try," he'd said, handing her the hammer. Ellie was terrified she'd smash her thumb, but her father had shown her how to hold the heavy tool with one hand and the nail with the other, and he'd beamed with pride when she'd whacked the nail right on the head. "You see? You're a natural."

Meanwhile, her mother had nothing but critical things to

say when Ellie attempted to help around the house. "Don't be such a dolt!" Clara spat, eyes narrowed as she shook out the wet laundry in their backyard. "You nearly let this clean sheet drag in the dirt. Can't you do anything right?"

Ellie blinked back tears. Now her father was gone, and she and her mother would never share the bond of those cartoon mothers and daughters. Their grief had driven them even farther apart, instead of bringing them closer together. Ellie had longed for a sibling to have someone to comfort her. After her fights with her mother, she imagined a sister's soothing arms wrapped around her. But perhaps love between siblings only occurred when they had grown up sharing the same memories . . . and perhaps Lucy wasn't her sister after all.

To make matters worse, Ellie was still struggling with her aunt's confession. Besides Tom and her father, Iris was the one person she thought she could always rely on, but it turned out Iris had known Lillian—and while she was a Ziegfeld girl, no less! Ellie couldn't imagine Iris, or rather "Stella Parsons," dancing semi-nude for strangers, or being in a relationship with an older *married* man. *Had Uncle Ed known about any of this?* Both revelations were deeply troubling and made Ellie feel as if she didn't know the two people she thought she knew best. In fact, she'd left before Iris could continue her story further, unable to bear any more secrets coming to light that evening.

Ellie had nearly fainted this morning when she'd seen someone who looked like her father on her commute to the *San Francisco Chronicle* offices. He was tall, walking down 5th Street with the same confident gait, his dark hair graying at the temples. Of course it wasn't him, but the moment when she thought it might've been had made her heart seize. Had Father become grayer in the years since he'd deployed? Had the men in his crew teased him for it? She missed the humor she shared with him—her mother rarely laughed about anything.

At her desk, Ellie blinked back tears as she found her notes on the Victory gardens that had sprung up in every vacant lot and backyard—vegetables grown by citizens to aid the war effort. Rick Johnson, the reporter who'd caused her to trip over his briefcase the previous day, had an article due on the Victory gardens tomorrow morning, but he'd passed his assignment along to Ellie. It wasn't the first time he'd done this—as a former war correspondent, he didn't deign to write about anything he deemed "too feminine." She did the research and wrote up a draft, yet Rick's name would be the byline.

Ellie didn't mind writing about the Victory gardens. She herself traded homegrown tomatoes and lettuce with her neighbor Mrs. Cook for weak black-market coffee. It didn't compare to the strong coffee at the Mayflower, but Ellie couldn't bring herself to go for glazed donuts and coffee without her father.

The phone rang, and she took in a deep breath before she picked up the receiver. "*San Francisco Chronicle*. How may I help you?"

"Well, good evening, Ellie! How are you today?"

Ellie dropped her chipper veneer. "As well as can be expected. You?"

Around Jack Miller, Ellie didn't have to pretend to be someone she wasn't. Though she'd never met the newspaper legman who scoured the streets for stories, she and Jack had become pals during the past year, laughing over the telephone when he called in with information at the scene of an event. Like her, Jack also had to run errands for Frank, and he wasn't treated with much respect. He'd been declared 4-F, unfit for military service, due to tuberculosis that had scarred his lungs as a child. But Jack insisted he was perfectly healthy and remained determined to enlist, convinced the army had made a mistake.

"Shivering my socks off. It's cold today, ain't it?"

"Sure is. What have you got for Frank?"

"We busted a guy with a trunk full of nylons. I know some gals will pay through the nose for a decent pair."

Ellie missed the way real nylon made her legs look and feel, but the material was being used for parachutes. She pushed back the painful thought of wondering if her father had crashed his plane into the Adriatic Sea before he could open his own. "Some gals *need* a decent pair. Have you ever tried drawing a seam down the back of your leg with eyeliner? Trust me, it doesn't look right."

Jack laughed. "I can't say that I have."

Ellie grabbed a pen. "Do you think they're real?"

"No, probably fakes. But it'll make a good story."

"Oh, I'll say. Even the good fakes will cost you. Give me the details and I'll send your notes along to the rewrite men."

"The suspect drove a blue Chrysler Windsor and it was parked on the corner of Sixteenth and Mission. You ought to write the article yourself and save them the trouble. You get my stories firsthand, don't you?"

Ellie smiled ruefully, making sure Frank was out of earshot. "I'm no reporter, I'm Frank's secretary. And secretaries don't get promotions."

"And I don't have my own bylines. Hell, half the office thinks I'm illiterate. The rest think I'm a coward. But I don't let it get to me. I think you'd make a fine reporter."

"Thanks, Jack, but you know recipes and society events don't interest me. And those are the only stories that get assigned to women."

Ellie declined to mention the sting of her rejection letters. She didn't want to count how many stories she'd sent to literary magazines. With every rejection she heard her mother's voice in her head. *Oh, Eleanor, you'll never become a writer. The best you can do is to find yourself a husband.*

"Wait, you're a woman? You don't say."

Ellie rolled her eyes. "Unfortunately. Do you know how uncomfortable it is to wear a girdle? I feel like I'm a sausage inside a sausage casing."

Jack chuckled. "Wait until Frank hears you talking about your unmentionables at work. He might give you the sack."

Ellie giggled, her eyes darting to Frank's office door. Too old to be drafted, Frank barked his orders at his employees instead of soldiers. She smiled. "You're right. I ought to go. Thanks for the tip. Take care, now."

When she hung up the phone, it was nearly six o'clock. The whole building hummed and vibrated as the printing presses rolled in the pressroom. The nightshift crew had arrived—copyboys that'd formed a tight bond working together each evening until midnight. Ellie envied their camaraderie and the fact that they got to accompany the photographers on assignment. Meanwhile, she was practically chained to Frank's desk. Sometimes she ventured outside to fetch him a sandwich, or downstairs to the composing room, where the Linotype operators worked, and makeup men inspected Linotype slugs. But she never went anywhere in pursuit of a story.

Ellie slipped to the ladies' room, touching up her makeup in the mirror. Though she preferred not to wear so much, her job required that she always look her best. Also, Tom had gotten a leave pass from the army base tonight, and he liked her with a bit of lipstick on. In anticipation, she'd worn her favorite blue cardigan and gray skirt, and pin curled her shoulder-length auburn hair. Tom always said he loved her long hair, and he would toy with her curls, telling her never to cut it short.

Right at six o'clock, Tom strolled into the lobby of the Chronicle Building, handsome in his military uniform—an olive wool coat with shiny brass buttons, a brown leather belt tight around his waist. His face lit up when he saw her.

"Well, aren't you a sight for sore eyes."

He swept her into his embrace, kissing her softly. Ellie breathed in the spicy scent of his cologne, enjoying his height, his strong arms, his blue eyes, and his hands on her waist. There was no denying the chemistry between them. Ever since they'd met at the USO dance six months ago, she'd been captivated by his presence. He possessed charisma like no one she'd ever met. Everyone seemed drawn to him, and strangers tipped their hats, respecting his authority in uniform.

She smiled. "You're not so bad yourself."

Tom stroked her cheek. "Mama sends her regards. She's on my case about our wedding. I'm afraid she's fixin' to invite the whole of Atlanta society. But I've warned her we might need to have it here, in the chapel on base."

Ellie's mouth went dry. Tom came from one of Atlanta's most prominent families, his grandfather having been an oil tycoon, whereas her grandparents had been blue-collar immigrants. She wanted her future in-laws' approval, but her stomach knotted at the thought of a large crowd. She preferred to marry in a simple ceremony at Fort Scott instead of before an entire congregation of strangers in Tom's hometown, at the end of Sunday Mass. Ellie felt more at home wearing a suit-dress than she would in a big lacy creation with a veil and train, and marrying on base made sense given the circumstances.

"Well, perhaps your mother and father can travel here?"

Ellie looked down at her ring, a nearly three-carat brilliant round-cut diamond, with two diamond baguettes on either side. It felt ostentatious to wear when the world was at war. She had wanted a plain gold band, but when Tom had gotten down on one knee in front of the Union Square Christmas tree, a dormant feeling of nervous excitement had awakened inside of her. The ring was absolutely stunning, and it had been so long since she'd had anything to look forward to. When she'd shown the ring to Clara, her mother had been so *happy*—an emotion Ellie hadn't seen cross her mother's face in years.

Tom squeezed her arm. "I'll ask my commanding officer what he thinks is best. It depends on how much furlough he'll grant me. But let's get married as soon as possible."

Ellie forced a laugh even though she was thinking of the book she'd thumbed through at the library, *Marriage Is a Serious Business*, written by the Rev. Dr. Randolph Ray, rector of New York's Little Church Around the Corner, where thousands of wartime weddings were performed. He wrote: *The hasty marriage, caused by glamour and excitement, rather than genuine affection, is one of the evil products of war.* Of course, Tom was a catch. And at her age, she was no spring chicken. But Tom had only proposed last month, after a short courtship. She loved him, but were they rushing things?

"Tom." Ellie licked her dry lips. "I know you'd love to get married soon, but it feels wrong to do it without Father."

His eyes held pity. "Sweetheart . . ."

Ellie blinked back tears. "I know you think I'm foolish for believing he's still alive, but I do. And I don't want to walk down the aisle without him."

Tom sighed. "I'd love your father to walk you down the aisle too, doll. But what if he isn't coming back?"

Ellie felt as though she'd been punched in the gut. Tom was only stating the obvious, but that didn't ease the pain of his words. He'd lost so many friends in the war and she knew his stoicism belied his anger, pain, and grief. Still, she wished he could share a little bit of hope with her. She swallowed, her mother's voice telling her that she was being difficult. "Can we please wait just a little while?"

Tom became stern. "Ellie, do you know how many soldiers were stationed at the seventeen batteries along the San Francisco coast right after Pearl Harbor was bombed?"

Ellie crossed her arms, tensing at the condescension in Tom's voice. "Why don't you tell me?"

"Over two thousand men. We had one hundred and twenty-five men stationed at each battery. Fort Cronkhite, Fort Barry, Fort Baker, Fort Point, Fort Funston, all filled. Do you know how many men we have now?"

Ellie hated it when he began to lecture her like this. "No, I don't."

"Fifty. Some batteries are completely empty." Tom ran his hands through his hair as he continued. "It's obvious to the army commanders that an invasion of San Francisco isn't going to happen at this point. Our soldiers are needed on battlefronts elsewhere. The Harbor Defenses is phasing out its operations. It's only a matter of time before I'm sent overseas, probably to the Pacific Theater."

The awful icy feeling Ellie had when she opened the telegram started to creep up her spine again. She drew in a sharp breath. "Tom, please don't say that."

"But it's true." He grabbed her hands. "I'll only be given ten days' notice. None of us are guaranteed tomorrow. Which is why I want to marry you now. We don't have time to wait."

Ellie pressed her head against his chest. Tom made her feel beautiful, loved, and safe. He told her she was unlike anyone he'd ever met. She needed him here where she could hold him, not overseas in the Philippines or Japan.

But still, Ellie couldn't imagine reciting her wedding vows without her father's blessing. Having her future in-laws by her side wouldn't be the same. Ellie had never met them, but she'd spoken to them by telephone on a few occasions. Despite their impeccable Southern manners, their conversation had lacked warmth. Grief swelled in her chest, but Ellie didn't want to be difficult. Tom had been patient with her, and now his patience was wearing thin. Perhaps he was right, and they ought to be married as soon as possible.

"All right." The tightness in her gut felt like a rock, but it was important for her to make Tom happy. Their relationship had progressed quickly, but so far, he'd proven himself to be a good man. He deserved a loving wife. "Ask your commanding officer when he'll grant you leave."

Tom smiled. "Maybe we'll get lucky, and we can marry as soon as next week. Depending on how much time I get, we could also travel home to Atlanta."

She bit her tongue, her mind drifting to her father at the word *home*, as it always did now, ever since she learned of his visits to Lillian in New York. She would give anything to know where he was. *If her father were a prisoner of war, would he be treated well?* He could have been captured by the Germans and been moved anywhere by now, to a remote farm in the north of Italy or a labor camp somewhere else.

She'd read about mail limits imposed on prisoners of war in an international law book she'd checked out from the San Francisco Library. Under the Geneva Convention of 1929, article 36 stated: *Not later than one week after his arrival in camp, and similarly in case of sickness, each prisoner shall be enabled to send a postcard to his family informing them of his capture and the state of his health.* What if her father could only write *one* postcard, and he'd chosen to write to Lillian?

Tom smiled the brilliant smile that had charmed her the moment she first laid eyes on him. "What's troubling you, doll? You're too pretty to frown."

Ellie kissed his smooth cheek, hiding the depth of her concern. *Certainly her father would contact her and her mother first if he were in trouble?*

"Only the thought of you leaving."

Tom hugged her close. "I'm here now, El."

Walking arm in arm with Tom down 5th Street, past theater marquees and neon advertisements, Ellie couldn't force the knot in her chest to loosen. *Be grateful,* she told herself. *Tom truly cares about you. He wants to spend the rest of his life with you.* It hurt knowing Tom didn't believe her father was still alive, but Ellie had to continue looking for him, even if she knew she was supposed to grieve and move on. The army wasn't trying hard enough to find him and his crew. This was her quest, and hers alone.

"Mother?" Ellie walked down the hallway to her mother's bedroom and then rapped her knuckles on the wooden door. "Are you awake?"

She twisted the brass knob and found her mother sitting up in bed. Ellie released the breath she didn't realize she was holding. "Tom and I went to dinner before the picture, and I brought home some fried chicken. Would you like some?"

Clara stared off into the distance, her hair a bird's nest where it had once been a tidy upsweep of curls. Her face, usually perfectly made up with Max Factor, was bare, and she looked older than her forty-five years. "No, Eleanor. I'm not hungry."

"Are you sure? You really ought to eat."

Clara's eyes flashed. "Don't tell me what I ought to do."

Ellie gritted her teeth. Her mother could get under her skin anytime she liked.

"Fine. I'll leave the chicken on the kitchen counter in case you change your mind."

Clara studied Ellie, her mouth a frown. "You're lucky that fiancé of yours keeps you around. You've always been difficult."

Ellie felt a familiar surge of anger, clenching her fists at her sides. She slammed the door, leaving her mother alone with her bottle of pills.

Ellie had been miserable as a child whenever her father was gone on his cross-country flights, his absence amplified by her mother's cutting remarks. Ellie was *lazy, obstinate, messy, ungrateful, and daft.* To combat her loneliness, Ellie found solace in books, their characters making her feel seen and understood. She longed to be like Laura in *Little House in the Big Woods,* surrounded by siblings, her hard work rewarded by Ma's hugs. Instead, her mother punished her for every small infraction, and she had no brothers or sisters to play with.

By the time she'd moved on to *The Hobbit,* Ellie dreamed of escaping the only house she'd ever known and going on a grand adventure like Bilbo Baggins. The idea that children around the world were also reading Tolkien's story made Ellie feel a warm sense of connection. It wasn't long before she started writing stories of her own and filling them with characters she longed to be friends with. She sighed. In twenty-four years, she'd never stood up to her mother. She set down the paper bag, stained with chicken grease, on the kitchen counter, knowing Clara might eat the food later if she got hungry. The house was dark and lonely, its silence oppressive. Her father's hugs and smiles, his praise and rewards, made up for every cruel word Ellie endured while he was gone. But now he wasn't coming back. *How would she survive without him?*

Ellie wanted to call the widows, but it was too late now—and the long-distance charges were too much. Was Diane managing all right alone with two little ones at home? Had Diane or Wilma found out any more information about the downed plane? Father's planes rotated, Ellie knew that much. Sometimes he had flown a shiny silver B-24 Liberator fresh off the factory line; other times he'd flown a tattered old warhorse, bomb icons painted on the cockpit to indicate successful bombing missions.

Father's outgoing mail was opened and read by censors—a pair of scissors used to snip out any explicit references to his unit, his location, his missions, or the enemy. But Ellie picked up enough to know he was in constant danger. She pictured the day of his final mission: Father firing up his engines, the radioman at his console, the gunners clipped in, and the navigator poring over a mountain of maps. Ellie imagined her father steering his plane down the taxiway, then streaking up the runway into the sky. Her throat tightened. *Had he been frightened when his engines failed? Had he tried to make it back to a landing strip? Had he gotten out of the cockpit safely?*

If her father had gone missing before the war, she could have called hospitals and prisons, or run a "missing persons" advertisement in the newspaper. Now she felt so helpless.

The Signal Corps Photographic Center was located in Queens, New York, where training films were made and U.S. Army photographs of combat missions were stored. At the *San Francisco Chronicle*, Ellie had heard that over ten thousand combat photographs arrived at the Signal Corps library each month—invaluable information. But as a civilian, Ellie couldn't very well demand to see classified footage of her father's mission. *What could she do?*

Ellie felt tears pricking her eyes and a sob escaped her mouth. She hadn't truly cried since the telegram. She had been too numb. But now that the tears were coming, she couldn't stop them. Ellie thought of Bob Hope's voice on the radio: *The only thing that saves boys out here from flipping the lid is the mail from home.* But this just made the pain in her chest worse. Her father had received plenty, apparently.

Ellie opened her closet, reaching deep into the shoebox where she'd stashed Lillian's letters. She'd read every single one, and yet Father's secret life with Lillian remained a puzzle.

A puzzle.

Suddenly, Ellie was struck by a thought. Her father loved completing the Sunday crossword in the newspaper—he never skipped it. When she was a little girl, he read to her from *Alice's Adventures in Wonderland*, but he also told her about Lewis Carroll's lesser-known book *Symbolic Logic*.

She could still hear his voice: "If these three sentences are true, what can you conclude? 'No experienced person is incompetent. Jenkins is always blundering. No competent person is always blundering.'"

Her mother had rolled her eyes. Clara never held an interest in logic puzzles. Ellie had furrowed her brow. "Papa, I don't understand."

He'd smiled. "Here's how you can solve the riddle. If Jenkins is always blundering, then by the third sentence he is incompetent, and if he is incompetent, then in the first sentence, he cannot be experienced. So, we can conclude that Jenkins is inexperienced."

Though Ellie hated to admit it, Lillian appeared to be both articulate and witty in her letters. She seemed like the type of woman who would love puzzles. Rubbing her temples, Ellie remembered the coded messages in her father's letters home. She could always tell when it was the night before combat. He would write things like *busy day ahead* or *I need to wake up early.*

What if he'd written Lillian cryptic messages in a cipher, disclosing his exact location or his plans to escape from a POW camp? Lillian wasn't his spouse, so she wouldn't have received a telegram from the army. But if her father loved Lillian—which he clearly did—he would want Lillian to know where he was, and if he was alive.

Ellie told herself not to be stupid. Her father would contact her mother first if he had been captured. So she would stay here. Her life at the moment was fine—she was employed; she exchanged pleasantries with the neighbors while hanging laundry on the line outside to dry; and besides, she had Tom. She would move in with his parents once they were married, and she would quit her job at the newspaper. It was what he wanted—what most men expected—and though Ellie worried she'd feel terribly alone in Atlanta, soon they would begin their life together. She and Tom always had such a swell time, whether they were playing a board game or sharing peach cobbler, his favorite dessert.

But then Ellie remembered something her father used to say, his voice coming through as if he were standing right beside her. *You can do anything you set your mind to, El. Don't let anybody tell you any different.* Her arms prickled with goose bumps. When had she stopped believing in those words? In that place inside her where fear had grown, a door opened, shining a beam of light.

She had set her mind to finding him. No matter what anyone said, Ellie couldn't bring herself to believe her father was dead. Then she had a horrible thought—*What if he was alive, but he didn't want to be found?* If both she and her mother believed he was dead, then he was free to start a new life . . . with Lillian.

Ellie took in a deep breath, her heart pounding with a mixture of determination and fear. She didn't want to believe the worst about her father—that he would fake his own death—but she was desperate for the truth. *What if Lillian knew where he was? What if he'd written to her after his plane crash?*

Staring at Lillian's letters, Ellie fretted over what Tom would think. He was protective, and he wouldn't want her traveling across the country alone. Also, Frank needed her in the office, and her mother needed her at home.

A mother who belittled and criticized her . . .

Straightening her spine, Ellie felt a surge of inner strength. For the first time, she would make a decision based on what she wanted to do. Not her mother, not Tom, not Frank. If she didn't act now, she never would. Lillian's address was written right there before her eyes: *48 Bleecker Street, Apt. 10, New York, NY.*

Tomorrow, she would go in search of answers. She was going to New York.

Chapter Five

Ellie

Ellie rubbed her eyes. "What time is it?"

Iris sat across from her in their Pullman sleeper car. "Two in the afternoon. We're nearly there."

Ellie couldn't believe she'd actually gone through with her plan. She wasn't an impulsive person, and yet here she was on a train to New York.

"Wonderful." Ellie pressed her gloved fingertips to the window, her emotions a roller coaster: giddy, hopeful, confused, and guilty all at once.

Convincing her aunt to accompany her on the trip hadn't been easy—Iris had been reluctant, and Ellie had resorted to begging, insisting that Tom would never allow her to travel across the country alone. Luckily, she'd saved enough money by working at the *San Francisco Chronicle* and living at home to make this trip possible, since she only intended to stay in New York three or four nights.

Finally, Iris relented, and Ellie concocted a story for Tom: her aunt had booked a special vacation for the two of them months ago, and she'd simply forgotten. *As if she'd forget about a vacation to New York!* But Ellie couldn't very well tell him she was going in search of her father's mistress, no matter how bad lying to him felt. She couldn't imagine what her future in-laws would think if they found out.

With the train barreling through a tunnel, Ellie saw nothing but black. After forty-five hours traveling through the dusty expanse of Las Vegas, Arizona and New Mexico, Kansas and Missouri—she and Iris had reached Chicago. There, rumpled and exhausted, they'd changed over to the 20th Century Limited at LaSalle Station, and spent another sixteen hours on the train.

Ellie rubbed the back of her neck. *What was she thinking, running off to New York with nothing but an address and a name?* Maybe she truly was an idiot, sending herself and Iris on a wild-goose chase.

"Ladies and gentlemen, we're approaching Grand Central Terminal," the conductor announced. "Please gather your things."

Clara had remained silent when Ellie told her that she was going to New York. In her mother's haze of pills, nothing seemed to matter. Yet even as a grown woman, Ellie still yearned for her mother's approval. *What did she have to do to get it?* Marry Tom and raise well-mannered children? Her heart clenched, thinking of her own childhood. With every A on her report cards and every letter written in perfect cursive, Ellie had been saying, *Please love me.* But her mother had only given a brief nod of approval before returning to her housework. Even then, Clara had been more concerned with Ellie getting an "MRS degree" than an education—not that she'd gotten any nicer now that Ellie was engaged. Clara's joy and excitement had all but vanished after they'd received the telegram.

At least her aunt showed her love in ways her mother couldn't seem to. Iris smoothed her blue suit-dress. She looked out the window with an expression Ellie couldn't read. *Wistfulness? Regret?* Now, seeing her aunt's troubled face, Ellie wondered if there was a reason why Iris had been so reluctant about coming to New York. *Was she hiding something other than her long-ago affair?*

Frank had also been tough to convince. Ellie reminded him she'd never taken any sick days, and for the past year she'd been a model secretary. When she found a girl to fill in for her, Frank relented. Her skin heated at how she was treated compared to the male reporters. They came in to the *Chronicle* hungover or late every day, and yet when Ellie had asked for her first vacation ever, Frank blew a fuse. No wonder she was afraid to show him samples of her writing.

"Did you sleep?" Iris placed her knit turban on her head.

Ellie nodded, removing her compact from her handbag. "I did, thanks."

She frowned at her reflection in the little mirror. She'd been so edgy during this trip that she couldn't stop licking her lips. Now they were terribly chapped.

Iris smiled sympathetically. "Train travel has never been good for the complexion. I used to travel all over the country when I toured with Ziegfeld. It was the reason I couldn't return home for your mother's wedding or for your birth."

Ellie swiped on a coat of berry-colored lipstick, feeling a twinge of sadness. "You never wanted to tell Mother the truth about your life as a dancer?"

"I was afraid to. Ziegfeld girls had a reputation back then. *Flapper* was a dirty word. And the Ziegfeld girls were the most infamous flappers of all—well, next to Zelda Fitzgerald, I suppose. I thought my parents would disown me, and Clara too. I love her dearly, in spite of our differences."

Ellie's stomach tightened, remembering her mother's vacant-eyed stare and her white knuckles around the bottle of barbiturates. "Do you think she'll be all right?"

Iris nodded. "Your mother is stronger than she seems. And we left enough food in the Frigidaire to last a month. We'll call and check in soon."

Ellie put on her red wool beret, appeased by the answer. She reached beneath her seat to retrieve her smaller suitcase. As the train pulled into Grand Central Terminal, she stood up and followed Iris to the baggage car, where they had checked the rest of their luggage. After retrieving her other suitcase, Ellie was swept along with the crowd. *Who else among this group of people were the sons and daughters or mothers and fathers of men who had gone missing?* Theirs was a special kind of grief—a pain that no one else understood. There were no rituals. No burials. No memorials and no closure.

Bringing herself back to the present, Ellie looked up at the Oyster Bar Restaurant, its arched ceiling awash in neon light, and its white-tiled walls like something from another century.

Men shucked oysters with impressive speed. How had her life been completely transformed in only a few days, leading her to the other side of the country?

Emerging onto the cavernous main concourse of Grand Central, Ellie took in the sights and sounds. Beneath a tarnished four-sided clock, round as a bowling ball, voices reverberated. Ringed chandeliers with lights sparkling like diamond brooches hung from the ceiling and sunlight streamed in through the half-moon windows. Ellie looked up at the mildewed ceiling. It must have been breathtaking once, but the painted blue sky had faded to khaki and the gold stars in the constellations had flaked away. The majesty of the terminal was overshadowed by a photomural plastered on the wall, a soldier promoting the sale of defense bonds. Reminders of war were inescapable.

Iris walked with purpose, as if she'd traveled all her life. Ellie caught up to her, and Iris smiled, though her eyes held sadness. "I've missed this place."

Outside on 42nd Street, they waited for a cab. Ellie breathed in the smells of the city: oil, snow, and fried food from a nearby diner. It smelled different from San Francisco. It was colder too—far colder. She buried her chin in the fur collar of her coat, staring at the Beaux Arts façade of Grand Central, which featured a winged sculpture of Minerva, Hercules, and Mercury framing a huge gilded clock made of Tiffany glass. A gold sun burst against a blue background, and the clock's white numbers were contained within crimson circles.

Good thing she'd come to New York before her courage had deserted her—though she wished this trip had been made under different circumstances. Iris raised her arm, flagging down a yellow cab. The driver pulled over and loaded their suitcases into his trunk.

The cabbie looked at them. "Where can I take ya?"

"The Algonquin Hotel," Iris replied.

"Yous from outta town?"

"Yes. From California." Saying it aloud, Ellie felt incredibly far from home.

"Welcome to New York."

Ellie smiled at his accent. *New Yawk.* She felt overwhelmed by emotions: excited to be in a new city, guilty for leaving Tom and her mother—and even Frank—behind, and fearful at what she might find. But she also felt a thrilling sense of anticipation— of being able to spend her days in New York how she pleased. *When was the last time she'd done something for herself alone?* She had never abandoned her obligations at home like this before. Until recently, it had never occurred to her that she could.

Ellie looked out the window at passing buildings. She heard a chorus of engines, horns, and shouted chatter, and watched as men and women in business suits all hurried to be somewhere. Outside, sunlight glinted off skyscraper windows, green double-decker busses rumbled past with sightseers sitting atop, and yellow cabs honked at pedestrians. Ellie looked at the street signs: 42nd Street, 5th Avenue, and then 44th Street. Within a few blocks, they had arrived at their destination.

"Algonquin Hotel."

Ellie stepped out of the cab onto 44th Street while the cabbie unloaded their luggage. She looked up at the impressive red-brick and limestone façade of the Algonquin, still in shock that she'd followed through with coming here. She felt a shiver of excitement, the kind she used to get before beginning a story. *Who had stayed in these rooms, and what had their lives been like?* She used to write for pleasure, before the sting of her rejection letters paralyzed her. Could she recapture that joy? Iris stood beside Ellie, wearing the same odd look she'd had on the train. But in a moment it was gone.

Iris nodded. "Shall we freshen up?"

"Yes, please, and then let's eat. I'm starving."

They walked beneath the green awning into the lobby, an elegant room of dark, carved wood with a plush green carpet, potted ferns, and red velvet furniture. A tabby cat curled up on one of the chairs and Ellie reached down to pet it. She leaned closer to hear its throaty purr. "Hello, sweetheart! What a pleasant surprise to find you here."

Iris smiled. "The cat is hotel tradition. The first cat was named Hamlet. Every male cat after him has been named Hamlet. The females are named Matilda."

Matilda, or Hamlet, stretched out its paws and then purred as Ellie scratched behind its ears. She would have loved to have a cat growing up, but her mother never wanted one. She'd ask Tom for a pet cat when they married.

After Iris checked them in at the front desk, a bellhop took their luggage and they rode the elevator to the tenth floor. Ellie tipped him and then shut the door. She flopped down on the hotel bed, sinking into the comfortable mattress. After the cramped train compartment, it felt like heaven. "I'm beat. How about you?"

Iris stared out the window, lost in thought.

"Is everything all right?" Ellie unfastened her heels.

Iris shook her head. "Memories. Writers from the Round

Table used to meet here. They called themselves 'The Vicious Circle.' One of them, Dorothy Parker, panned a musical revue starring Billie Burke, Ziegfeld's wife. Flo was so angry about it that he had her fired. We all stayed out of his way that day."

Ellie rubbed her feet. "Did you choose this hotel because of its storied history?"

They were in Midtown Manhattan, which bustled with restaurants and shops. Though she'd come in search of Lillian, Ellie couldn't help but feel the pulse of the city drawing her closer—a place her aunt had once called home. On the train, Ellie had hoped Iris would continue her story about being a Ziegfeld Follies girl, and her relationship with Lillian, but Iris hadn't broached the subject, and Ellie hadn't the nerve to pry. Perhaps Iris was worried about other passengers eavesdropping, or she wasn't ready to open up.

"Actually." Iris's blue eyes grew serious. "It's where I met your father for the first time."

Chapter Six

Iris

Standing outside the New Amsterdam on 42nd Street, I was struck by the brilliance of the Great White Way. What was relatively busy by day became divinely mad at night. Every wall, every cornice, every nook and cranny, danced with electric signs—a kitten played with a spool of thread advertising Corticelli Silk, a girl whose skirt appeared to flap in the wind glowed for Heatherbloom Petticoats, and the bulbs advertising Fatima cigarettes burned brightest of all.

Other cities tried to imitate New York, but none of them could capture the effect of jazz interpreted in light, a mile of streetlamps illuminating the car-choked streets around Broadway. The effect was dazzling—just as magical as the day I had first arrived. Once I'd made it as a New Yorker, I'd vowed to never move back home.

"You're truly going to miss the fun at the Silver Slipper?" Hilda asked, lighting up another Chesterfield.

Tucked away on 45th between 6th and Broadway, the Silver Slipper was a tiny room located at the top of a narrow staircase behind a door with a peephole, our favorite after-hours haunt. My eyes darted to the street, crowded with theatergoers and revelers. "We can ankle over together since I'm walking that same way, but I can't be seen with you gals. My brother-in-law can't know I'm a Follies girl."

If I told Clara the truth about my life as a dancer, would she shun me? I didn't need my little sister's approval, but I wanted it—and Clara could be so terribly judgmental.

Falling into step with Hilda, I breathed in the scent of dry leaves and automobile exhaust. "Besides, that Silver Slipper hostess, Tex, is a real bearcat."

Lou laughed. "I'll say. But that's what I like about her. She's a Texan, like me, and we're spitfires."

Tex wore diamonds and pearls, her large bosoms spilling out of tight dresses. She was a character—a loudmouth who claimed she was a cowgirl, but I suspected she was a washed-up vaudeville actress, and not even a real Texan.

"You're no spitfire," Hilda scoffed. "You're a piano-playing debutante with wealthy parents and a fancy education."

Lillian chuckled. "Your poor daddy has no idea what a degenerate you've become, or he'd stop sending checks. Isn't that right, Lou?"

"Girls!" I shot them both a reprimanding look.

Lou began to sulk. Hilda was beautiful with her bedroom

eyes, upturned nose, and perfect bow lips—but she'd grown up in hardscrabble Baltimore, where she'd lived in an orphanage. I didn't know much about Lillian's background, but she didn't come from money. Meanwhile, Lou had led a privileged childhood in Walnut Springs, Texas, a young Southern belle. I wondered if John liked my working-class background because of all the things he was able to teach me. I thought about his note, sent with the diamond and sapphire necklace.

A little trinket for my pet. I'll be waiting for you.

I regretted forgetting to tell him I was meeting William after my performance. But certainly John wouldn't mind if I arrived at his hotel a bit later?

I felt a flutter of nerves, knowing how overprotective John could be. But my brother-in-law was hardly a threat. My anxiety dissipated and I turned to Lou. "How old do you think Tex is?"

"Lord knows." Lou laughed. "Hard to tell, ain't it?"

Lillian took a drag of her cigarette. "Thirty-five."

"Forty." Hilda smiled at us. "That old face stretcher. But with bubs like hers, no one is looking at her face."

We all giggled. The night air had finally cooled, and leaves crunched beneath our kid leather heels. Would William think I was one of the furious-drinking, fast-driving, flirtatious women caricatured in magazines? Bobbed hair was the sign of youth gone wild, and nice girls didn't meet men at eleven at night.

I swallowed. My likeness could be found on posters around New York, and my stage name, Stella Parsons, was mentioned in playbills and papers. I prayed William wouldn't put two and two together. If he asked, I'd laugh it off and thank him for the

compliment, reminding him I was merely Clara's sister, the secretary.

"I detest the smell of frankfurters." Hilda wrinkled her nose
as we passed a hot dog stand. Thanks to the Volstead Act, the
great old restaurants of Broadway had all but disappeared.
Fine dining wasn't the same without fine wine. Gone were the
lobster palaces and in their place were soda fountains, cafeterias,
and speakeasies in brownstones. A sliding door, a whispered
password—the same places would be repainted by morning, so
fellas who'd been robbed the night before couldn't recognize
them.

"Here's where I leave you." I slowed my pace as we passed the
Knickerbocker Hotel and approached 6th Avenue.

"I'll join you." Lillian's eyes, ringed with black kohl, fixed on
mine.

"And miss hoofing it with Tex? Why?"

Lillian lit a cigarette and took a drag, then exhaled a plume
of smoke. "Maybe a writer from the Vicious Circle will take a
shine to me."

Hilda pursed her lips. "Writers don't make any dough. They
make a few clams a story. You might as well shack up with a
longshoreman."

I pressed my lips together, annoyed at the unexpected turn
of events. But Lillian could lend credibility to my charade about
being a secretary. "All right, but you must pretend we work in the
same office uptown. And for God's sake, whatever you do, don't
call me Stella. We're *secretaries*, understand? We work for the law
firm White and Jones. Do you know anything about law?"

"She knows how to break it." Lou giggled.

"I'm an actress." Lillian narrowed her cat eyes. "I'm sure I can convince the fella I know my way around a typewriter."

As we stepped into the dining room of the Algonquin, I looked around for a man matching William's description. Clara had written that he was tall, had reddish-brown hair, and was quite handsome—but my kid sister's definition of good-looking might be different than my own. I noticed a young man sitting alone at a table in the corner, checking his watch. When he looked up, his eyes met mine and he smiled.

"I think that's him," I whispered to Lillian.

"He's a dish."

I elbowed her, then walked over to the man's table. He stood up, easily six feet tall, early twenties, handsome in his gray suit. He had warm brown eyes and a pleasing face. Though it was my first time meeting him, I already felt he was someone I could trust. I smiled. "William? Is that you?"

"Iris!" He grasped my hand in his warm palm. "It's such a pleasure to finally meet you, dear sister-in-law. Clara has told me so much about you."

"And she's told me lovely things about you."

"Ahem." Lillian nudged me.

"And this is my friend Lillian. We work together at White and Jones."

"Pleasure to meet you too." William shook her hand. "Do they always make you gals work so late?"

"Only tonight." Lillian gave me a knowing look. "Our boss

is working on a big case. We had pages of notes to transcribe. My fingers are sore from typing."

Perhaps letting Lillian tag along hadn't been a mistake after all.

I smiled at William. "And then we met some friends for dinner after work. Thank you for agreeing to meet so late. Once again, I apologize."

"It's no trouble." William pulled out a chair. "Please, allow me to take your coat."

Upon closer inspection, his eyes were a golden, amber color. There was a hint of stubble along his jawline. His wool suit and matching vest, though a few years old, fit his tall frame nicely. Clara had done quite well, snagging herself such a handsome husband.

Before I could protest, he'd removed my sumptuous mink coat from my shoulders and placed it on the back of my chair. His eyes widened as he fingered the fine fur. I cringed—it was one of two expensive fur coats John had bought for me, and I realized how outrageous it must appear compared to Clara's wardrobe.

My neck flushed with heat. "It's on credit."

William helped Lillian out of her coat and she smiled at him, tucking her hair behind her ear. "We charge everything these days. Why wait? As the papers say, we've gone installment mad."

William laughed. "Indeed we have. Oh my, there's a cat over there."

An orange tabby strolled through the restaurant like he was right at home. A waiter chased him down. "Shoo! Hamlet. Go back to the lobby."

I liked William's deep voice and calming manner. He was a good match for nervous Clara, and he seemed like he would be capable in a crisis.

"Clara tells me you deliver mail by aeroplane. However did you find such an interesting profession?"

"Before I moved to San Francisco, I ran a family farm in Idaho. My father died when I was young and I cared for my mother and younger siblings. Farmers were needed to send produce to feed the troops during the Great War, so I wasn't sent overseas. After the war ended, a barnstormer came to town."

"What's a barnstormer?" Lillian leaned closer to him, exposing her décolletage.

William laughed. "A fighter pilot. After the war, loads of these fellas came to small towns all over America to show off their skills. You could pay to take a flight with one of the men. I was nineteen when I went up in a plane for the first time. The adrenaline was like nothing I'd ever experienced. I knew right then I was meant to fly."

"What happened to the farm?" Lillian widened her eyes.

"My brother took it over."

"And now you fly a plane all the way from San Francisco to New York?"

"That's right, a Curtiss Jenny. I carry bags of mail."

"I think it's brilliant." Lillian's eyes twinkled and her lush crimson lips parted. "We get mail so quickly now."

Was she flirting with him? I dismissed the thought. She knew he was married. William was an intelligent, yet unpretentious gentleman, and Lillian was simply enjoying his company.

William leaned forward, his smile wide. "Our planes can

carry up to twelve passengers. In Europe, airlines are already flying the wealthy to and from France, Britain, and the Netherlands. I think commercial plane travel could happen here too. Just think—flying people across the country could become profitable one day."

"I would love to fly in an aeroplane." Lillian moved her arm closer to his. "It would beat train travel any day. To think of the countless hours we've spent on trains."

"We?" William looked at me, eyebrows raised.

Lillian had forgotten our cover story and was referring to our grueling tour schedule with Ziegfeld. But she recovered without missing a beat. "My mother and I. We traveled frequently when I was a little girl."

A waiter appeared and took our orders. With a whispered password, I could have gotten an orange blossom or a mint julep but I ordered an Earl Grey tea and hoped Lillian would follow suit. In our Lanvin dresses, we were far too glamorous for secretaries, but William seemed ignorant to the fact we were wearing French couture. Thankfully, no one in the restaurant appeared to recognize me—or if they did, they didn't approach. It's not as if I was a film star like Lillian Gish.

As my tea arrived, I turned to William. "So tell me, how is my dear niece, Eleanor? I'm terribly sorry I haven't met her yet. I must change that."

His eyes twinkled. "She's a lovely little girl. Rosy, chubby cheeks, and she can speak! She says 'Dada, watch me,' and she can be quite demanding."

My throat tightened with guilt for having missed so many milestones in my sister's life. Maybe I could visit my family at

Christmastime if I managed to convince Flo I deserved some time off.

"How old is she?" Lillian asked.

"She's two. Do you have any children?"

"No." Lillian lowered her lashes. "I'm not yet married."

I didn't know Lillian well enough to know if marriage was something she wanted. She had her fun just like the rest of us, but she wasn't too wild.

"And how is Clara?" I sipped my tea.

"Your sister is well." He smiled, studying my face. "You resemble each other, you know that?"

"You think so? But she's much fairer than I am."

"True, she's blond and you're a redhead, but she's cut her hair short like yours, and you both have the same beautiful blue eyes."

"*Clara* has bobbed her hair?"

He laughed. "Yes. It suits her. She said little Ellie was always tugging on her hair when it was long."

"Excuse me, miss?" Our waiter reappeared.

"Yes?" I set down my teacup.

"There's a telegram for you at the front desk."

Flo was absolutely mad about telegrams. Sometimes he sent twenty a day, usually to Eddie Cantor or to our costume designer, Charlotte—but it was rare for him to send one to his dancers. And if he did, he would have sent it to my flat, not here. A disquieting feeling came over me.

I forced a smile, scooting my chair away from the table. "Please excuse me for a moment."

Lillian's laughter rang out behind me as I walked away. I couldn't hear what she said to William. The dark walls felt like they were closing in, tighter and tighter. I took a deep breath, but I couldn't slow my beating heart. *What if someone has died?*

But if there had been an emergency, the telegram would have been sent to my flat. No one other than Hilda and Lou knew I was here tonight.

I approached the front desk, my palms sweating. The concierge looked up. "Miss Iris Eaton?"

"Yes." My voice was small.

"A telegram for you."

I took the piece of paper, then read it with shaking fingers.

WHO IS THAT MAN YOU'RE DINING WITH? I DON'T LIKE YOU STAYING OUT LATE MY PET AND YOUR DRESS IS TOO REVEALING I'M AT THE WALDORF- ASTORIA WAITING FOR YOU DON'T KEEP ME WAITING ANY LONGER

I pressed my lips together, fighting the queasiness in my stomach. *Did John have me followed?*

I looked down at my dress, an ivory silk and gold beaded sheath with a scooped neckline. It was hardy risqué—I'd chosen it to *avoid* looking like a flapper. Yet John had managed to make me feel both guilty and ashamed. I looked toward the dining room, the clink of silverware punctuating the hum of conversation. I needed to get back to John, to explain there was nothing for him to worry about. I would tell William I was overcome with fatigue. He would understand.

Now I found myself standing before Lillian and William with sweat beading on my brow, worrying I looked as flustered as I felt. In contrast, Lillian was lovely in her sequined lilac sheath, which exposed her bare shoulders.

"Is everything all right?" William's eyes shone with concern.

"Fine." I clasped my hands in front of me to stop them from trembling. "The telegram wasn't for me. Someone made a mistake."

"Would you like another tea?"

I gathered my coat. "No, thank you. I'm so very sorry, but it's late, and I'm quite tired. It's been lovely to meet you. Lillian, shall we?"

A sultry smile played at the corner of Lillian's lips. "I haven't yet finished my tea. You go on. I'll follow along in a few minutes."

Too shaken to argue, I put on my coat, waved goodbye, and walked through the hotel lobby and out onto the street. John told me what to order at restaurants, how he liked my hair, and what composers to listen to. He despised it when other men tried to flirt with me. But up until now, his actions had seemed refined and charming. He knew the best dishes in Manhattan, what styles suited me best, and more about classical music than I did. I'd found his jealousy harmless—*but what if it wasn't?*

In the September chill as I waited for a cab, I caught my ghostly reflection in the hotel glass. My face was pale, and my eyes were frightened. Even as I assured myself everything would be fine, my gut told me something wasn't right.

Chapter Seven

Ellie

NEW YORK, 1945

Ellie was dumbstruck. There were too many pieces of information to process at once—too many emotions to juggle. She felt concern for Iris, followed by a flash of anger and a stab of hurt. Finally she found her voice. "You left my father alone with Lillian. *You* introduced them to each other."

Iris put a hand on Ellie's knee. "I'm so sorry, sweetheart. I didn't see her as a threat. I never knew that she would . . ."

"Have an affair with him?" Ellie laughed bitterly. It came out harsh and wrong, like a dog's bark. "And you truly didn't know about the two of them? For heaven's sakes, they carried on together for over twenty years!"

Iris flinched. "After that night, Lillian never mentioned your father again. I honestly had no idea they kept in touch. And that's the truth."

Once again, Ellie felt jealous to have shared her father with

Lillian, a woman whom she didn't even know. "What did he see in her?"

Iris sighed. "She was smart. Unlike some of the chorus girls, Lillian was well-read. And she had an effect on men."

"Apparently." Ellie stood abruptly. Her aunt's hand fell away.

"I hate that I played a part in this." Iris lowered her eyes. "And I'm very sorry."

Ellie took a deep breath. Iris would never intentionally hurt her, but Ellie couldn't stop the awful feeling of betrayal. All of her anger that had been simmering under the surface was bubbling into rage. She had to get out of this room. She slipped on her brown leather heels and fastened the ankle straps. "I'm going out."

Iris's brows knit together. "May I join you? Where are you going?"

Ellie didn't know, but she needed to be alone. She gathered her coat and her address book. "Just out. I'll be fine on my own. You stay here and rest."

The door clicked shut behind her a touch too hard, and Ellie felt infused with restless energy. Suddenly, she knew where to direct her anger: Lillian. It was time to get her hands on her father's letters, to see what secrets he'd written to his mistress. Ellie's inner voice sent a warning. *Are you sure you're ready for what you might find?*

Ellie dismissed the voice, even though she was tired from a long day of travel. She had planned to visit Lillian's apartment tomorrow, after a full night's rest, prepared with a well-thought-out speech. But right now, a confrontation couldn't wait. She had already come this far, and she could do this on her own.

Ellie rode the elevator down to the lobby, then walked through the revolving doors and out onto the street, where the air smelled like snow. Tugging on her gloves, Ellie shivered in the winter cold. Everything was gray—even grayer than San Francisco, save for the neon lights and flashing advertisements. She looked for a passing cab and soon spotted one, waving her hand at the driver.

The cabbie stopped and called out his window. "Need a ride?"

"Yes." Ellie opened the door and slipped inside. "Greenwich Village, please."

THE MEANDERING STREETS of Greenwich Village would have seemed charming under different circumstances. The cabbie pulled up in front of a weathered redbrick building on a narrow, winding block. "We're here. Forty-eight Bleecker."

Ellie opened her wallet and handed him his money. "Keep the change."

She stepped onto the unfamiliar sidewalk, gazing up at Lillian's building. A hard lump lodged in her throat. *Was this Father's second home?*

The neighborhood was shabbier than she'd expected. Old redbrick buildings nestled together like crowded teeth. Grayish white sheets, shirts, and undergarments hung from the fire escapes, and pigeons cooed in the trees overhead, bare winter branches scraping the gritty windows. The nearby businesses included a pawnshop, a dingy Chinese restaurant, and a Laundromat with a tattered awning.

Ellie's heart thudded as she opened her notebook to check the address she'd copied from Lillian's letters. The tarnished brass number on the nineteenth-century row house in front of her read 48. She was in the right place.

She swallowed and walked up the eight stone steps of the apartment stoop. She cupped her hands around her face and peered through the door, her breath fogging the glass. *How uncouth*, her mother's voice said. But this was New York—Ellie could be as uncouth as she liked. The lobby had a black-and-white checkered floor, its tiles cracked and worn, while a dim bulb hung overhead.

With a shaking finger, Ellie pressed the button for number ten. It buzzed loudly, causing her to flinch. She held her breath as she heard heavy footsteps coming down the stairs. Lillian had broken her family and shattered the most important relationship Ellie had in her life—the one with her father. Did Lillian know the damage she'd caused? Ellie's heart began to pound.

What if her mother had always known about the affair, and Ellie had borne the brunt of her mother's anger? Ellie grimaced. She was furious, filled with a desire to confront the woman who'd tainted her childhood memories, but also hungry for information—for the pieces of her father Lillian had kept all to herself.

"Who's there?"

"Eleanor Morgan." Ellie prepared herself to look into those light eyes with a glint of mischief, that beautiful face her aunt had described—the face of the woman who had stolen her father from her. She had a mind to slap it.

An elderly Black woman appeared on the other side of the glass, hands placed on her hips, gray hair pulled back. Ellie's shoulders sagged with a mixture of disappointment and relief. She cleared her throat. "I'm here to see Lillian Dell."

"Lillian? I don't know anybody by that name."

Ellie's shoulders tightened. She had to know for herself that Lillian wasn't hiding inside. Perhaps Lillian had spotted Ellie from an upstairs window and sent her neighbor down, instead. Maybe she'd even asked her to lie.

"Please. I've come all the way from California."

"Well, she's not here." The woman narrowed her eyes.

Heat crept up Ellie's neck. It would be intrusive of her to ask to see this woman's apartment, but she needed to know that Lillian wasn't there, hiding upstairs like a coward. This address had been written on every letter sent to her father.

"Lillian is a friend of my father's." Ellie's tongue tripped over the word *friend*, which tasted as bitter as vinegar.

"Like I said, she isn't here." The woman shifted her weight to her other foot. "We moved in six months ago."

"I'm so sorry to trouble you, but do you know of anyone in your building who might have an idea where Lillian has moved?"

She sighed. "Mrs. Walker might. She's been living here a long time. She'll be over in a moment to mind my grandchildren." The woman opened the door and looked Ellie up and down. "Who did you say you were?"

"Eleanor Morgan." Ellie extended her hand, which had become clammy with nerves. "If you could introduce me to Mrs. Walker, I'd truly appreciate it."

The woman shook Ellie's hand, her palm dry and warm. "Alice Davis. Look, I've got to be at work in an hour, so you can't stay long. Understand?"

Ellie nodded. "I understand."

Alice gestured to the stairs. "Come on, then."

Ellie followed Alice as she climbed up one flight, muttering to herself. Opening the door to number ten, Alice pursed her lips. "This here's my place, and these are my grandkids."

Two small children playing on the floor looked up at Ellie with wide eyes. She smiled tentatively. "Hello."

"Who are you?" the little girl asked, her hair worn in twisted pigtails fastened with barrettes. She held a doll in a pink dress.

Ellie smiled at her. "I'm Ellie."

"I thought Mrs. Walker was gonna babysit us?"

"She is." Alice gave Ellie a side-eye, reminding her she was short on time. Ellie smiled at the children. "Your grandmother was kind enough to let me inside, so I can meet your neighbor."

She looked around the small apartment. It was simply furnished with a faded couch and some worn armchairs, and it had a large window overlooking the street below. Ellie tried to imagine her father spending nights with Lillian in this place. Meanwhile, she waited for Mrs. Walker to arrive, fidgeting with her coat buttons. Ellie smiled at Alice. "You have a lovely apartment."

When another woman appeared, older and thinner than Alice, her dark eyes appraised Ellie over half-moon glasses. Alice lifted her chin. "Edna, this young lady has some questions for you."

Ellie bit her bottom lip, hoping Mrs. Walker had answers.

"Good afternoon. I'm looking for the tenant who used to live here. Miss Lillian Dell?"

Mrs. Walker harrumphed. "We weren't friendly."

Ellie's heart beat faster. "Can you tell me who lived here with her?"

"Like I said, we didn't speak much. She lived here with her daughter. Men came around sometimes too."

"*Men?* More than one?"

"Yes. I never saw a ring on her finger either. And yet she acted like she was better than us. She played her records so loud, everyone in the building had to listen to that Artie Shaw whether they wanted to or not. Couldn't bother with a hello."

"Do you know where she moved?"

"I sure don't." Mrs. Walker folded her arms across her chest, giving Ellie the distinct impression their conversation was over.

Of course she didn't. Why would she?

"Thank you both for your time and I apologize for the intrusion." Ellie smiled at Alice and then waved at the children, who sat quietly on the rug. "Bye, now."

She held back tears of frustration as she walked down the stairs. She'd come to New York assuming Lillian would still be living right here. And now she'd found herself at a dead end. *What had she been thinking?* She should have known answers wouldn't come easily. And yet she'd traveled all this way.

ELLIE STEPPED OUTSIDE the building and then looked around. It was best to keep moving, lest the unfamiliar neighborhood become unsafe after dark. Some of the dingy shops were already closing their gates. Her heels clicked against the pavement as she followed the curve of Bleecker Street. A telephone directory— that was what she needed.

A diner on the corner up ahead cast a warm glow onto the sidewalk, advertising hot coffee and an egg for twenty cents. Ellie stepped inside, taking a seat at the greasy countertop. "What can I get ya?" A waitress with a raspy voice approached her.

"A coffee please." Ellie took off her coat, placing it on the stool.

The waitress set a mug of coffee down in front of Ellie.

"Thanks. Could I trouble you for some milk and sugar? And do you have a telephone directory by any chance?"

"We don't have any milk and sugar. Ration coupons are all used up."

"Then just the phone book, please."

The waitress returned with the heavy telephone book, plunking it on the countertop. Ellie flipped through the directory to the residential listings, but she couldn't find a Lillian Dell. She chewed her bottom lip. Her search was becoming more complicated than she'd hoped. Ellie pulled out her address book, tracing her finger along the page until she found her contacts at the *San Francisco Chronicle.* Then she walked over to the diner's pay phone, where she put a coin in the slot and dialed the operator.

"How may I connect your call?"

"Delta Hotel, San Francisco, please."

If there was anyone who could help, it was Jack. Ellie inserted another dime for the long-distance charge.

"Delta Hotel." The voice on the line sounded like someone who'd swallowed a fistful of rocks—gruff and bothered by the intrusion.

Ellie paused. "Oh. Can you place my call to a Jack Miller, please?"

"Room number?"

"I'm afraid I don't know it."

The man on the line grunted. Then Ellie heard a muffled sound, and then voices in the background as the receiver was set down. A few minutes later, someone picked it up.

"Jack Miller. Who's calling?"

Ellie breathed a sigh of relief. "Jack! It's Ellie from the *Chronicle*. I'm sorry to call you unexpectedly like this, but I was hoping you could help me with something."

"Sure, I'm your guy. Hey, Frank said you were in New York. Is that true?"

Ellie smiled. "It is."

"I can't believe the bastard let you go! Did he give you an earful?"

Ellie laughed. "He sure did. But I convinced him I deserved time off."

"Good for you, kid. Are you after a story?"

Ellie wished she could tell him about her father, but she hardly knew him aside from their work banter. "You could say that."

"That's swell, Ellie. I'm proud of you."

She could hear the smile in his voice. Ellie hesitated and then gave a partial truth.

"I'm looking for an old acquaintance of my aunt's, Lillian Dell. She used to live in Greenwich Village, but she's moved. She's not in the telephone directory and I need to find her."

"No dice, huh? Is Dell her married name?"

"Maiden, I believe."

"Hey, pipe down over there, will you?" Jack spoke over shouting men and swing music. "Sorry, it's the other boarders. The phone here is in the lobby. Someday I'll have a place of my own, but until then, this joint will have to do."

Ellie thought of her mother, always prying. "At least you have your privacy."

Jack chuckled. "Not exactly. The Delta is right in the center of all the skid row action, home of the winos. There's always some kind of racket going on. I share a bathroom down the hall with the other fellas, but I have my own room, my own desk, and my own sink, and the rent is cheap."

Ellie laughed. "Sounds like a nice place. Say, you're right by the *Chronicle*. It's a wonder we haven't run into each other yet."

She envied Jack's independence, even if he lived in a sleazy single-room occupancy hotel. Anything was better than the dreary silence she shared with her mother.

Jack cleared his throat. "First, I'd try the other Dells in the directory. Maybe they're of some relation. Does this Lillian have a job?"

"She was a dancer, a Ziegfeld Follies girl. Mind you, this was twenty years ago."

"A Follies girl?" Jack let out a low whistle.

"And a tramp." The words left Ellie's mouth before she could stop them, and she blushed.

Jack let out a loud guffaw. "You're talking like a New Yorker already!"

Ellie laughed. She could only imagine what would happen if she spoke that way in front of Tom—or, God forbid, his mother. "So can you help me find her?"

"There's a club on Park Avenue, the Ziegfeld Club. The *Chronicle* ran a piece about it a while back. I don't have the address, but you might be able to find it."

Ellie pulled a pen from her purse. "The Ziegfeld Club?"

"That's right. Ziegfeld's widow, Billie Burke, runs the joint. They keep info on all the former dancers. And you might be able to find this—"

Ellie smiled. "Don't say it!"

"How do you know what I was going to say?"

"Because I *know* you."

"Oh, do you, now?"

Ellie didn't, but she thought suddenly that she might like to. Her whole body grew hot with shame. She was marrying Tom and she loved him, after all. *What was she thinking?* Jack was a pal and nothing more. She didn't even know what he looked like.

Jack's voice was playful. "Miss 'rhymes with stamp' might be there."

"Thank you. I'll give it a try."

"Hey, call me anytime. And if some other schmuck is keeping the line busy, you call back, all right?"

"I will. Thanks again."

Ellie returned to the counter, requesting another look at the telephone book. She found the listing for the Ziegfeld Club, 593 Park Avenue, and wrote it down in her notebook. Then she walked into the cold winter evening and stretched out her arm to hail a cab back to the hotel, where Iris was waiting for her. In a flash, she had a moment of cognizance as Jack's words sounded in her head. *Are you after a story?*

What if she was? What if this trip could give her more than answers—what if this was what she needed to find the perfect story idea? Could she work up the courage to ask Frank for her own newspaper column if she had a compelling story to show him?

You're a secretary, soon to be a wife, her inner critic reminded her in a voice that sounded eerily like her mother's. But Ellie had come all the way to New York, without anyone's permission. And now she began to wonder if maybe she could be something more.

Chapter Eight

Ellie

Back at the Algonquin, Iris sat in a cozy leather wingback chair, looking at Ellie over her reading glasses.

"Oh, Ellie, thank goodness you've returned. I was terribly worried."

Ellie's shoulders sagged. "I'm so sorry. I shouldn't have left like that."

Iris set down her book. "Where have you been?"

Ellie hung her coat in the closet and then sat down on the bed, next to Iris's chair. "I went to Greenwich Village to find Lillian."

Her aunt's eyes widened. "Oh, darling, what happened?"

Ellie shook her head, the exhaustion of the day hitting her all at once. "She doesn't live there anymore."

Iris pressed her lips together. "I'm so sorry."

Had she imagined it, or did Iris look relieved?

Ellie smiled. "The search isn't off. I called a reporter friend, and he gave me a tip. There's a club, the Ziegfeld Club, with information on former Follies girls. I say we go there tomorrow."

Iris seemed nervous, clearing her throat. But she forced a smile, which didn't reach her eyes. "That's a swell plan."

Ellie took off her shoes, rubbing her sore feet, and dismissed her aunt's strange behavior. Maybe Iris was just tired and hungry like she was. "I'm famished. Have you eaten?"

"I was waiting for you. Shall we order room service? It looks awfully cold outside, and I think we deserve a treat."

Ellie could have hugged her. When she was a little girl, her mother often denied her dessert as punishment for her offenses—although what they were, Ellie couldn't recall. But whenever Iris was around, she snuck Ellie the butterscotch candies they both loved. Now Ellie was old enough to buy her own candy, but being given permission to treat herself to a nice meal felt really wonderful.

"I'm going to have the Southern fried chicken with cream gravy." Iris perused the hotel menu. "And chocolate mousse."

"Make that two orders."

ELLIE WAITED FOR the long-distance telephone operator to connect her to Tom. Last night she'd been so tired, she'd fallen asleep right after dinner. Now it was a gloomy Tuesday morning in New York, and she was anxious to leave for the Ziegfeld Club, but she had already put off her phone call to Tom long enough.

"Well, it's about time," Tom said as the line connected. "Why didn't you phone earlier? I've been worried sick about you."

Ellie pressed the receiver to her ear. "I'm sorry. Yesterday we were so tired after a long day of travel and—"

"You should have called."

"I know. I should have."

His tone softened. "So where are you and Iris headed today?"

"The Metropolitan Museum of Art." The lie came easily. In fact, Ellie would have loved to see the Met, but finding Lillian was more pressing. She wondered how many pieces of airmail paper her father had used in his letters to Lillian. His letters to her and her mother were never more than a page. Her heart clenched like a fist.

Tom sighed. "I ought to be there with you, keeping you safe. I hope you don't think I'm being sappy, but I miss you, dollface. I hate the idea of you walking those dangerous big-city streets alone."

Ellie smiled. "I miss you too. But I'm not alone, I'm with Aunt Iris."

He sighed. "Every day you're gone is a day pushing our wedding further away."

Ellie rubbed the back of her neck, her stomach knotting. "I know. I'm sorry."

"It's all right, I suppose. You forgot about your trip. But you ought to get our invitations engraved while you're there. Mama wants them sent by mail, not telegram."

Ellie felt guilty for not wanting to devote her time in New York to planning her nuptials, and she swallowed at the thought of the expensive stationery.

"But we won't know our wedding date until you're granted leave."

"We can write in the date later. I've told Mama we'll marry at Fort Scott, so it's decided. If there's time, we'll travel home to Atlanta for our honeymoon."

Ellie twisted the phone cord around her finger until her fingertip turned red.

"Yes, I suppose I can do that."

"Good. And hurry home, please? I miss my beautiful fiancée."

Ellie smiled. No man had called her beautiful before Tom. In high school, she'd wanted to stay home reading *Pride and Prejudice* instead of getting dolled up for the prom. But Betsy and Mabel had convinced her to go to the dance with them, and once she'd seen herself in her hand-sewn dress, with a flower tucked in her hair, Ellie *had* felt beautiful. But at the prom, she'd avoided the roaming hands of an older boy with foul breath while they swayed to "We'll Meet Again." When she refused to kiss him, he told her she wasn't anyone special and to stop being so stuck-up.

In secretarial school, Ellie had gone to the pictures with some gals and a group of fellas they knew, but the boy seated next to her had groped her through her sweater, the awful experience putting her off dating entirely.

She'd nearly given up on men when she'd met Tom. But he was different: kind, respectful, honest. Their first kiss, so unlike the sloppy firsts she'd shared with others, had been absolutely perfect. Tom had waited until their third date, and she'd leaned in toward him, intoxicated by his cologne. He loved his family and simple pleasures, like slowly savoring a home-cooked meal or holding her hand while they walked. Once he'd made his mind up about something, he was certain of it.

"I will. I promise."

"I miss you, El."

Ellie warmed at her nickname. "I miss you too."

She hung up the phone and pulled on her fur-trimmed traveling gloves that matched her gray wool gabardine suit. She tried to imagine her wedding invitations on thick cream paper with an embossed border:

Mr. and Mrs. William P. Morgan announce the marriage of their daughter, Eleanor Jane, to Thomas Henry Davenport, Sergeant, Army of the United States.

But how could she include her father's name if he wasn't there to give her away? She couldn't bear for the calligrapher to write *the late William P. Morgan*. Once again, the uncertainty of what had happened to her father was worse than anything. The widows of his crew members were always on her mind. Wilma had sent another letter, which arrived the day Ellie departed for New York.

I am thankful for our thread of hope. Do you still believe our men might be alive?

Iris put a hand on Ellie's shoulder. "Is everything all right?"

Ellie startled, brought back to the present moment. "Tom's mother wants me to buy engraved wedding invitations. But I don't know how to word them because of Father . . ."

Iris furrowed her brow. "Are you sure you aren't rushing into this?"

Ellie felt her whole body tense. "Tom only wants what's best. And, no, we aren't rushing. Most girls my age are married already."

"You aren't most girls, though, are you?"

Iris meant it as a compliment, but Ellie wasn't in the mood. Most girls knew how to make meat loaf with rationed supplies and had bought linen napkins to match their place mats. They sewed curtains for their first apartment as newlyweds, and had vases, crystal, and candlesticks. Meanwhile Ellie lived with her mother in a dark, old Victorian house where sadness permeated the walls.

What was Iris suggesting—that she shouldn't marry Tom? "I love Tom." Ellie looked at Iris pointedly.

Iris frowned. "But will being his wife be enough for you? I haven't forgotten all the notebooks full of stories you used to share with me."

Neither had Ellie. In fact, she couldn't stop thinking about working up the courage to ask Frank for her own newspaper column. But she wanted it so badly, she was afraid to admit her desire aloud. Instead, Ellie put on a tight smile. "Writing isn't a practical career. Tom is a pragmatist, what's wrong with that?"

Iris spoke carefully. "If Tom truly loves you, he will accept you and your ambitions. His opinion isn't the only one that matters."

Ellie's cheeks heated. "I value his opinion very much." She clenched her fists, feeling flustered that Iris had managed to get under her skin. "Let's be on our way. I'd like to get there when the club opens."

ON THE CAB ride uptown, the numbered streets felt unfamiliar: East 57th, East 59th. In San Francisco, the numbered avenues stretched toward the ocean in the Sunset District, a sleepy neighborhood made up of identical stucco homes and sand dunes. Here in New York, the aging brownstones turned to tall and narrow redbrick row houses. The cab pulled up in front of a neo-Gothic cathedral.

"Five ninety-three Park Avenue."

Ellie and Iris stepped out into the January chill, the air smelling like a mixture of car exhaust and snow. The church's weathered gray sandstone façade was like a Parisian cathedral Ellie had seen in a book once, its spires pointing toward the moody winter sky, where pigeons circled overhead.

"A church?" Ellie smiled. "Well, I suppose it's a fitting place for a woman who has plenty of sins to atone for."

But Iris didn't laugh at the joke. Ellie felt a hot rush of shame as she realized she'd possibly offended her aunt. Iris had danced right alongside Lillian, after all, and she wasn't a bad person— instead, she was one of the warmest, most generous and admirable people Ellie knew. Clara had poisoned Ellie's mind with the belief that women should be submissive and that displays of female sexuality were immoral. But Ellie wanted to be more open-minded than her mother.

They walked to the side entrance on East 64th Street, and Ellie rapped her gloved knuckles on the door and waited. She turned around and saw Iris lagging behind. The door swung open and an elevator operator stood before her, wearing a double-breasted coat and a hat with a shiny bill. "Can I help you, miss?"

Ellie beckoned to Iris, annoyed at her aunt for standing there, as if she was second-guessing her decision to enter.

"We're here to visit the Ziegfeld Club."

He ushered them both inside the church and into a mahogany-paneled elevator and shut the door. "The Ziegfeld Club is on the fifth floor, miss."

The operator pushed the control handle to the left, and with a jolt, the elevator began to lurch upward. Ellie stared at the ropes and pulleys through the elevator's birdcage ceiling, listening to the hum of the motor, the creak of turning wheels, and the click of the passing floors. She tried to temper her expectations but remained hopeful about what she would find inside the club.

The elevator stopped on the fifth floor, and the operator opened its gate. Ellie stepped into a compact office, where a blond girl about Ellie's age sat behind a desk. She stood to attention, smoothed her suit-dress, and smiled.

"Welcome to the Ziegfeld Club. My name is Irene. How can I assist you?"

Portraits of starlets in alluring poses lined the walls. In this tiny, secluded space, memories of the flamboyant past came alive. It was one thing for Iris to have told Ellie about her days as a Ziegfeld Follies girl, but quite another for Ellie to see the photographs up close, the women clothed in nothing but feathers and beads.

"Pleased to meet you." Ellie shook Irene's soft hand. "I'm Eleanor Morgan and this is my aunt—"

"Mrs. Thompson," Iris interjected, giving her married name and shooting Ellie a sharp look.

Ellie bit her tongue. She understood why Iris had never told Clara about her past as a Follies girl, but why wouldn't she want to tell Irene she was once Stella Parsons, one of Ziegfeld's biggest stars? Didn't being here sweep her back into the glamour of those days? Ellie frowned in confusion, but for now, she was focused on the task at hand. "We're looking for a dancer who was in the Ziegfeld Follies of 1922."

"My." Irene clasped her hands together. "What a welcome surprise. Mrs. Thompson, you aren't a former Follies girl, are you?"

Iris smiled tightly. "I'm afraid not."

"Forgive me." Irene's cheeks flushed. "It's just that you remind me of someone, and I can't put my finger on it."

Iris looked like she'd rather be anywhere else.

"Can you tell us a bit about the club?" Ellie looked expectantly at Irene, eager to take the focus off her aunt.

Irene nodded. "Miss Billie Burke started this club in honor of her late husband, to help former Ziegfeld girls who have fallen on hard times. Unfortunately, many of the girls died penniless or died young. Sadly, many met tragic endings."

Ellie began to worry about what had become of Lillian.

"Tragic how?"

She knew Billie Burke from her role as Glinda the Good Witch in *The Wizard of Oz*. With the actress living in Los Angeles and making films, she'd assumed the other former Follies girls would have found similar success.

"Well." Irene frowned. "Olive Thomas died in Paris in 1920 after drinking mercury. She was only twenty-five. The papers wouldn't stop talking about her. Some girls died by suicide, others died in childbirth or from disease, and some were murdered." She smiled ruefully. "I'm painting a grim picture, aren't I?"

"Murder and mercury poisoning . . . how awful." Ellie winced.

Irene opened a drawer that overflowed with folders. "You wouldn't believe how many letters we get. And of those former Follies girls who are still alive, well . . . a lot ended up in pretty bad shape. Here, take this."

Ellie accepted the manila folder, stuffed with letters written on slips of powder blue paper, some so old, they felt as though they might disintegrate into dust. She took one from the top of the stack. *I'm living in desperation and the Ziegfeld Club is the only place I can turn. I'm in Hell's Kitchen in a cold-water flat. I have nothing. I have no one. Please help me.* Ellie sucked in her breath. To go from a life of such promise to a life of poverty must have been so difficult for these women.

Another woman needed money for aspirin, rent, and cat food. Ellie looked at the framed photograph on the wall beside her. Three lovely young women sat naked on a crescent moon, their hair cascading over their breasts, their lips dark and their bright eyes full of mischief. The date read August 1913. *Had one of those girls written one of these letters?*

Ellie frowned. "Why are there so many?"

Irene braided her fingers. "Follies girls started young on the stage and had no job training or savings. Ziegfeld cared about the well-being of the girls. But after they left his employ, well . . ."

Ellie glanced over at Iris. *Was she remembering these girls? Remembering Ziegfeld?* Iris had found work as a secretary in a San Francisco real estate office, despite her lack of training. It was where she had met Uncle Ed. Ellie suddenly felt guilty for never probing Iris about her life before marriage. Her aunt had been a young woman with big dreams who had succeeded in becoming a star. *What caused her to leave New York?*

"I apologize." Irene brought a gloved hand to her chest. "I haven't asked you whom you're looking for."

Ellie waited for Iris to say something, but her aunt remained oddly silent. Ellie spoke instead. "We're looking for a woman by the name of Lillian Dell. She was a Follies girl in the year 1922."

Irene smiled. "Let me get our registry." She reached into a desk drawer and returned with a three-ring binder. Flipping through the yellowed pages, Irene arrived at a tab with "1922" written in cursive handwriting. Women's photographs were glued to the pages, with addresses and phone numbers written underneath.

Irene turned to the back of the section, trailing her finger down the page. She scrunched her nose. "I'm sorry, but we don't have anyone by that name. Can you tell me more about Lillian? Or perhaps she performed a different year?"

"No, it was 1922." Ellie looked to Iris for confirmation. "May I?"

Irene nodded, and Ellie gingerly removed a group photograph from its sleeve, faded from age, and a bit blurred. The women wore sequin shifts and feathered headdresses. Ellie nearly gasped, seeing a young Iris standing in the front row, looking powerful and confident. She handed the photograph to her aunt, who squinted and then placed her fingertip on a dark-haired woman in the corner.

"There. That's her. She was a chorus girl."

Irene leaned closer. "Wonderful!" She took out a pencil and

made a mark above Lillian's head. Then she wrote, "Lillian Dell" in the book.

"She was a friend of Hilda Ferguson," Iris offered, appearing lost in thought.

Irene sucked in her breath, her eyes wide. "Why, Hilda Ferguson was also a friend of Dorothy King!" She clucked her tongue. "Such a tragedy."

The tension in the air grew thick. Ellie frowned. "What happened?"

Irene leaned in closer. "Dot King was the victim of one of New York's most notorious unsolved murders. Hilda was her chum, and she gave interviews to the newspapers, which dubbed Dot King 'the Broadway Butterfly.' She was a model whose murder captivated the nation. Here, I'll show you—"

Iris rubbed the back of her neck, her face pale. Ellie frowned at her aunt. *Why was she acting so strangely?*

Irene opened a drawer and pulled out a blue binder. Flipping through the pages, she found the page she was looking for, handing it to Ellie.

Ellie read the newspaper headline:

WHO KILLED THE BROADWAY BUTTERFLY?

Beneath it was a picture of a beautiful blonde with a wavy bob, resting her chin on a bejeweled wrist, staring intently at the camera. Her lips twisted into a smirk and her pale eyes held power. The article, clipped from *The Philadelphia Inquirer*, was recent. Apparently, the newspapers were still fascinated by this woman. Ellie turned to the text.

You always are seeing her where the lights are bright. . . .
Not the first Broadway Butterfly. Those wings are long
since dust. . . . Many recall her dancing feet . . . her hair
like copper. Even today's playgirls know her story. What
happened to Dot King can happen to anyone who lives
by the lights.

A shiver went down Ellie's spine. The warning, though not
meant for her, made her feel a sense of foreboding.

"She was an infamous It girl," Irene volunteered. "A wild
flapper with ties to gangsters and powerful businessmen."

Ellie continued reading. Dot's body was found in a stylish
apartment on West 57th Street, in the month of March 1923, on
the top floor of a five-story brownstone a few doors east of Carnegie Hall. She was wearing only a loose-fitting yellow silk chemise. To the maid, she looked as if she were sleeping: her head
half-buried under the pillow, one arm dangling over the edge,
her feet exposed, the other arm wrenched behind her back. Her
mouth was burned by chloroform.

Fifteen thousand dollars' worth of jewelry had been stolen,
and the police found a pair of men's yellow silk pajamas tucked
beneath the sofa. Ultimately, it was decided that robbers had
committed the crime.

Ellie pushed the binder back to Irene. With a story so lurid,
it was no wonder papers around the country were still writing
about Dot King. An uncomfortable feeling came over her. *Had
Iris also known Dot? Was that part of the reason she'd never shared
her past—the memories were too painful?* Ellie felt hurt that her
aunt had never confided in her. But then she remembered the

offhand judgmental remark she'd made, and she felt a fresh wave of shame. "May we leave our information with you, should you find anything on Lillian?"

"Of course." Irene grabbed a pen. "Here you are."

Ellie's shoulders sank with disappointment as she wrote down their names and their room number at the Algonquin. She also included her San Francisco address and telephone number, in case finding Lillian's information took longer than expected. Her search for her father's mistress was turning into a dead end. She handed Irene the slip of paper. "Please phone the hotel if you find anything."

Iris blinked as if suddenly remembering where she was. Ellie bit her lip, feeling worried for her aunt. There was something off about her.

She smiled at Irene. "Thank you for your time."

"Thank *you* for visiting." Irene waved. "Bye, now. Have a wonderful day."

The hum of the elevator motor punctuated the silence as Ellie and Iris returned to the building lobby. Ellie spoke first. "You were awfully quiet in there. Why didn't you tell Irene you were one of Ziegfeld's biggest stars?"

Iris lowered her voice. "Let's talk outside."

They found a bench in front of the church, and Ellie sat beside her aunt in the wan sunlight. Iris wrung her hands, her face crumpling. Ellie felt a rush of dread. Iris never lost her composure—she was always calm, even in challenging situations.

"Eleanor, I have to tell you something."

Ellie's heart beat faster. "What?"

"Tom has been pressuring you to marry him. And I don't

like it. With romantic relationships, you never really know what you're getting into."

Ellie stiffened, her concern quickly turning to anger. She was used to doubting her decisions, thanks to a lifetime of criticism from her mother. She didn't need judgment from Iris too. "Aunt Iris, I assure you that Tom is a gentleman and he—"

"Listen to me." Iris's voice became stern. "I didn't tell Irene I was the star of the Ziegfeld Follies because there are parts of my past I'm not proud of." Iris blinked away a tear.

"I thought I was in love once. I thought I knew John well. But I was wrong."

Chapter Nine

Iris

I wasn't always frightened of John. At one point, I thought I loved him, before I knew that monsters could disguise themselves in fine suits. That September night after meeting William, I went back to John's hotel, though my gut warned me something was wrong. John fumed at me for leaving him waiting, and then he told me to never make plans without informing him first. But after we made love, he relaxed.

Perhaps I had overreacted. *So what if John had me followed?* He was worried about me walking around Manhattan after dark. As I drifted off to sleep in John's arms, I thought about how quickly our relationship had progressed and of the night he'd introduced himself to me backstage at the New Amsterdam Theatre.

I had just returned to my dressing room after my performance, and I gasped when I saw an arrangement of long-stemmed roses and a sparkling diamond necklace wrapped around a bottle of French champagne sitting atop my dressing table. I'd received gifts backstage before, but never anything so valuable.

I fingered the diamonds, wondering if they were real, when a stagehand arrived and told me the gift had been sent from an admirer who wanted to meet me. At first, John sent someone else to my dressing room in his place, a man I came to know as Mr. Wilson. Tall, thin, ferret-like, and beady eyed, Mr. Wilson told me he was Mr. John Marshall's secretary and that his boss, a wealthy businessman, required the utmost discretion.

I shooed Hilda and Louise out of my dressing room. They wanted to meet the big cheese, but I managed to get them out of my hair. Meanwhile, Mr. Wilson stood guard outside, ensuring there were no prying eyes in the hallway. It seemed like an awful lot of hullabaloo for just one man. John Marshall entered, elegant and broad shouldered, with a strong jaw and nose, striking eyes, and silver hair.

When he spoke, his voice was deep and warm. "Stella Parsons, you are a scarlet rose in a sea of silver blondes." He smiled, his eyes sparkling. "They pale in comparison to you. I've never been so captivated by beauty onstage."

I felt myself blushing—something I didn't often do, as once I'd become accustomed to dancing in the buff, it took a lot to embarrass me. John's eyes were a piercing shade of blue, like an alpine glacier.

I returned his smile. "Flo likes to play up each dancer's best asset. I suppose mine is my red hair."

His gaze lingered on my legs, then my breasts, and then my face.

"I beg to differ."

The spark between us was instant. John asked me to dinner and Mr. Wilson drove us to an upscale restaurant where we were served champagne in a private booth. The joint was nicer than any place I had ever been.

"Try the caviar." John's eyes sparkled. "It's Russian; you'll like it."

I looked at the beady, black fish eggs, not sure what to expect.

"Here." With a mother-of-pearl spoon John smeared a dollop of crème fraîche onto a small piece of toast. "Start with a small bite so you can experience the flavor."

I took a bite and surprised myself at how I enjoyed the salty taste of the caviar against the sweetness of the cream. "It's very good."

He laughed. "Then you have good taste. Do you like Tchaikovsky? He's Russian too, like this caviar, and one of my favorite composers."

I admitted that I wasn't familiar with Tchaikovsky, preferring jazz to classical music. John surprised me after dinner by taking me to Chumley's, a notorious speakeasy on Bedford Street, so I could dance to the ragtime music that I loved. Over the course of one night, he swept me into his world of wealth beyond measure. Wearing the diamond necklace he'd gifted me, and dining on oysters and caviar, I felt as if *this* was the life I had been missing out on all along.

For two years, I had been living in a cold-water flat on Ludlow Street. My tiny room had a folding bed, a gas stove, and a shared sink and toilet down the hall. The brownstone was filled with Russians and Jews, shoemakers, tailors, and prostitutes. Night and day, folks yammered and fought, their conversations carrying through the thin walls. In the summer when it got too hot, families slept on the roof. Downstairs, a little shop sold egg creams. Bookmakers would come and place their bets on horses, then buy an egg cream soda. Now, as winter neared, my flat would be bitter cold. But I was so busy that by the end of the day, just thinking about moving apartments exhausted me. It was simply easier to stay put.

When John told me he was a Boston businessman, I asked if he was in business with Mr. Rockefeller. John smiled at my joke in a funny way, as though maybe he could've been. What his business was, I had no idea. He admitted he was married but quickly explained that he and his wife were no longer intimate. His eyes glistened with tears as he described how much her callous behavior hurt him.

My heart went out to him in that moment, so much that I reached for his hand. Our fingers intertwined, and a jolt of electricity shot through me. I knew getting involved with a married man was wrong, but John was vulnerable and in need of a woman's comfort. Within minutes, we were kissing, and John was stroking my face and telling me I was the most beautiful woman he'd ever met.

Over the next week, we traveled in his chauffeured car, ate only at the finest restaurants, and swilled the best champagne. It tasted better than anything I'd had before—no bathtub gin for Mr. Marshall. We stayed on the Upper East Side, dining at every hot spot in Midtown Manhattan. Until I met John, I had never tried escargot. I didn't like it, but I knew I had to develop a taste for it if we were to continue keeping company.

We spent nights together at the Waldorf-Astoria, John's favorite hotel. Mr. Wilson would accompany me wherever we went, like a chaperone. I was never seen alone with John. Mr. Wilson would take me upstairs and then travel back downstairs again to tell John when the coast was clear. Wilson would tip the elevator boy handsomely, and then he'd wait in the car until John and I were finished.

I'd brushed elbows with upstage people before at Flo's theater, but no fella had ever taken a shine to me like John had. For weeks, my dressing room at the New Amsterdam was filled with flowers: roses, rare violets, tulips, orchids, and freesias—irises too, for he knew my real name by then—until eventually the smell became cloying. John also began to buy me new clothes, which arrived in designer boxes tied with silk ribbons. As I sat in my robe, toying with the diamond necklace John had given me, I turned to Hilda. "He's coming on awfully strong, don't you think?"

Hilda waved her red-varnished fingernails at me. "With baubles like that, why complain?"

She was right, of course. What woman would make a fuss?

I'd thanked John for the stunning necklace. But he didn't realize that as precious as his gifts were, I would rather have hot water. He'd asked to stay at my flat before, but I told him it wasn't suitable. Nights spent in hotels were far more comfortable.

And now here we were again, in John's suite at the Waldorf. I shivered, even though the down duvet and the weight of John's arm draped over me kept me warm. *Did I have cause to worry, or was I being ungrateful?* I thought of the sapphire necklace in my dressing room, and how heavy it had felt on—almost like a restraint.

SEPTEMBER ROLLED INTO October, and I grew accustomed to wearing Lanvin, Poiret, and Chanel. My closet was filled with furs, hats, dresses, and shoes, all gifts from John. Hilda was beside herself with envy, often borrowing anything I happened to leave in my dressing room and then forgetting to return it. I couldn't fault her—my new clothes were exquisite, and John gave me so many, I feared I'd begun taking them for granted. Wearing my new designer dresses with their daring hemlines, I felt feminine, strong, and proud of my body. Dancing on Ziegfeld's stage empowered me, and knowing I could be vulnerable and exposed in front of a crowd made me feel as though I could do anything.

I wished I could show Clara my favorite haunts around New York, and everything I had made of my life, but her role as a young mother was so different from mine as a Broadway star. But she'd chosen it, hadn't she? Clara didn't need to be a homemaker—it was what she wanted. And I had worked so hard to create a name for myself. Nothing compared to seeing "Stella Parsons" in print, and I assuaged my guilt about how lavish my tastes were compared to her modest ones by sending money home whenever I could.

Even though Clara couldn't stay with me in Manhattan, I had managed to save up for an ocean liner ticket to visit her in San Francisco, and I smiled thinking of how good it would feel to wrap my sister and my niece in a hug, and how surprised my family would be to see me. I would take them all out to dinner at a fine restaurant because they too deserved to experience what luxury felt like. With John, extravagance was a way of life—and I was getting accustomed to it.

He would be gone for a week, and then he'd return to me for the weekend. We attended parties sparkling with New York's leading financial, social, and theatrical celebrities. The women gleamed like night boats on the Hudson and the men wore gold cuff links studded with tiny diamonds. They spent their winters in Palm Beach and their summers in Rome and Paris. I'd never been to Florida, but it was mentioned so often in the papers, it seemed like a sixth borough.

John owned a home in Palm Beach too, where he often went, a mansion on the peninsula. I knew he vacationed there with his wife. Sometimes I would feel a stab of guilt, but then I'd think, who wasn't having an affair these days?

One evening, while John laughed with his colleagues at the Ritz-Carlton, I spent the duration of the party sipping gin fizz with Mr. Wilson. I grew glummer by the minute, feeling cast aside and ignored. Later, at our hotel, I asked John why he brought me out when we couldn't be seen together. He looked at me with hungry eyes and licked his lips. "I like watching you and knowing that you're mine."

"ARE YOU STILL seeing the big cheese?" Lou asked me one evening after rehearsal. By then, John and I had been keeping company for over two months, and I'd all but forgotten about the night of the telegram. Now I asked John's permission before going anywhere, and though his constant monitoring tired me, it felt harmless.

"I am." I smiled coyly.

"What's a gal gotta do to meet this fella? Does he have any rich pals?"

I laughed. "Sorry, doll. He's my secret."

Though I would've loved to spend a night on the town with Hilda, Lou, and John, he preferred to be alone with me. He had to socialize in Boston with his wife's circle, and it exhausted him. He told me he wanted me all to himself, and I understood. Still, I wished I could introduce him to my friends.

When John was at home in Boston, I enjoyed having time to myself. I would spend hours reading novels in cafés, and then I'd walk around town, visiting museums while wearing the furs and jewels he'd gifted me. Then I'd wear them out dancing, enjoying the envious looks of every gal in the room. Walking home on sore feet after a night of gaiety with Lou and Hilda—sometimes Lillian too—I didn't have a care in the world.

Then my father fell ill a few days after Thanksgiving. Though Father and I had never been close—he was a devout and strict man—Clara's letter concerned me. I'd left home in part because I didn't want a job—or a husband with a job—like his, unglamorous and physically taxing. I'd always felt I was destined for more than San Francisco had to offer. But now my father was getting older, and lifting heavy steel plates to build ships had taken a toll on his body. I felt a surge of discomfort knowing I was so far away and unable to help in this time of need.

With Father unable to work, Mother and Clara had taken on odd jobs mending clothes and washing laundry to keep food in the icebox. William didn't earn much with his mail route as a pilot, and what he did earn went to feed and clothe their baby girl. They struggled to put food on the table for a nice Thanksgiving meal of meat pies, persimmon pudding, and turkey stuffing, and here I was, parading around Broadway in jewels fit for a queen. I felt awful for frittering away my money on frivolous things.

The next week, when John met me at the Waldorf-Astoria, I mentioned I was worried about Ma and Clara making ends meet without Father's job.

"I'll have Mr. Wilson write them a check." John stroked my cheek. "Should four hundred dollars be enough?"

I shook my head. It was too extravagant. "I can't ask that of you."

"I absolutely won't take no for an answer."

I realized it was a small sum of money to him. But I couldn't allow him to do such a thing. Instead, I resolved to use the money I had set aside for my ocean liner ticket. It would be enough to last Clara and Mother until Father recovered. Perhaps with the extra money, Clara and William might find an apartment for themselves, so they wouldn't have to live with my parents.

"It's all right." My shoulders sagged, thinking of my postponed visit. "I've been saving up for a ticket aboard the S.S. *California* to San Francisco, but Mother and Clara could use the cash more than my company right now."

His eyes flashed briefly, and I wondered what I had seen. But then they locked on mine, full of understanding. "Iris, I told you I would take care of you. Allow me to help your family in this time of need."

I hesitated, but only for a moment.

"Thank you. You don't know what this means to me."

He drew me in for a kiss. At first, it was tender and sweet, until his tongue became hot and insistent. He threw me on the bed—expensive sheets rumpling beneath us as our bodies tangled. John gripped my wrists hard, asserting control in a way I found both desirable and frightening. "You're mine," he whispered. "All mine."

Afterward, he slept like a baby.

AT THE START of December, John and I were riding in the back of his Bentley TT. He'd been gone for ten days, presumably at home with his wife in Boston, but I didn't ask. While away, he had mailed me a letter.

> *My pet. I miss you, O so much. I want to kiss your pretty pink lips.*

The return address was from Philadelphia. I found that a bit odd, since he was supposed to be in Boston, but brushed it aside. As Mr. Wilson drove us through midtown, my mind turned to John. Sex had become rougher of late, his hands tangled in my hair, his breath hot on my cheek, and his body always in control.

The car swerved, Mr. Wilson honked, and I gasped, gripping John's hand. Perhaps my sister, Clara, was right to call automobiles death mobiles. The paper ran a monthly toll of people killed by autos. I could feel my pulse throbbing in my wrist, and when I looked down, I noticed fingerprint-shaped bruises on my skin.

I frowned, realizing where they had come from. Last night, after my performance at the New Amsterdam, I had been chatting with one of the stagehands behind the curtain. Joe was twenty or so, a good-looking fella, hotsy-totsy by some gals' standards. I could tell he'd taken a shine to me. My mermaid costume had a long beaded train and as I tried to take a step forward, my heel snagged the delicate mesh fabric. I fell straight into Joe's arms. He hoisted me back onto my feet, but someone grabbed my wrist.

"It's all right, I've got her." John's eyes blazed with anger.

I looked at him in shock. *Holy Moses!* He'd appeared out of nowhere. And what was he doing backstage? I hadn't even known John would be in New York. A chill came over me as I realized he must have arrived through the secret passageway. The theater had a discreet doorway on 41st Street, which led to a warren of tunnels winding through the bowels of the New Amsterdam's basement. Flo provided this service for his most esteemed clients, so they could leave the show undetected.

Joe's eyes narrowed. "Iris, do you know this fella?"

"Yes," I stammered. "I do. I'm fine. Thank you."

But John's fingers had dug into my skin, his hand encircling my wrist so tightly it became painful. He pulled me toward him.

"There, pet. I've got you now."

Darkness clouded his face, and for a moment, I worried he'd pull back his manicured hand and punch Joe in the nose. Joe, perhaps sensing the tension, skulked off like a gorilla that'd been threatened by an alpha male.

John's ice-blue eyes narrowed. "Do you greet all your male colleagues with such enthusiasm?"

I laughed, but John wasn't smiling.

"I tripped. Joe caught me. There's nothing more to it."

"*I* could have caught you." John took me by the shoulders.

"John." My voice was soft. "I didn't even know you were here. Why didn't you tell me you were coming tonight?"

"I wanted to surprise you. Whether you see me or not, I'm always watching."

An uneasy feeling came over me. John had pulled us into a dark corner, away from prying eyes. Suddenly, I felt short of breath. I looked around, hoping to find a gaggle of chorus gals gawking at us. I heard them giggling somewhere in the distance, but their voices grew fainter as they moved farther away.

"I ought to go change." I glanced down at my costume, my mouth dry. "Flo is going to cast a kitten when he finds out I've torn my dress."

"I'll be waiting in the car outside. Don't be long."

The remainder of our evening together felt as precarious as a tightrope act. I tried to be pleasant, but despite my efforts to please John, it seemed as though nothing was good enough. He was insufferably rude to the waiters and anyone who came near him. In the lobby of the Waldorf-Astoria, a bellhop approached John, addressing him as Mr. Mitchell, before handing him a telegram.

My stomach knotted. "Why did he call you that?"

John glared at me. "Call me what?"

"Mr. Mitchell."

John frowned. "He didn't. The boy clearly said Mr. Marshall."

He read the telegram without a word and then folded it into his pocket. *Was John intentionally trying to make me appear crazy?* I knew what I'd heard. In our hotel room, John scowled at me for choosing the wrong glass for his scotch. Then he accused me of setting a napkin in the wrong place. I was fed up with his attitude. Was he angry because of Joe? The boy was harmless. Perhaps John felt threatened by Joe's youth.

"Darling." I stroked John's arm as he sipped his amber liquor. "If you're worried about other fellas, you needn't be. The only man I have eyes for is you."

His jaw set into a hard line. "Is that so? Because tonight you kissed another man."

I laughed, but John didn't crack a smile.

"You mean my bit with Bobby? That's part of my stage act. He's just a pal."

John leaned closer, his breath hot on my face.

"Don't ever take me for a fool. Because, Iris, I will know if you're lying."

"I'm not." Goose bumps prickled my arms.

"Good." John set down his scotch with a thump. "Because you won't be kissing anyone else ever again."

He began undressing me carelessly, ripping the buttons on my silk Poiret gown. When he pinned me on the bed and his knee spread apart my legs, I wasn't ready. But I thought about how much he needed me, and so I tried to become aroused, breathing in the scent of his cologne. When he rolled off of me, panting, he looked deeply into my eyes.

"You belong to me. And there are advantages to being mine."

I hadn't forgotten what John had done for my family. Father had recovered from his bout of illness and had gone back to work at the shipyard. Mother and Clara had been so grateful for the money. Because I still had my savings, I planned to visit them soon, once I could get the dates cleared with Ziegfeld.

Mr. Wilson sped along 7th Avenue, and I rubbed the goose bumps on my arms. My bruises from last night would fade, but the memory of John grabbing me like he owned me wouldn't. Lately, his mood would change from charming to critical at lightning speed. What if I *had* been canoodling with someone else?

Flo would be furious if I told him I could no longer kiss Bobby Green as part of our skit, and he had plenty of other gals to choose from. I looked out the window, trying to shake the uneasy feeling in my gut. An inner voice warned me that I had felt this way before—something wasn't right. Midtown passed by in a blur, a place of unimaginable wealth and stark poverty. Hell's Kitchen to the west had its Irish gangs, tenements, fishmongers, and rumrunners, while mansions lined Millionaires Row across town on 5th Avenue. That was New York—everyone trying to get a piece of the pie.

As Mr. Wilson drove through the Theater District, the lanes of the Forties became crowded with taxicabs parked five deep. Laughter carried on the breeze from partygoers, causing me a pang of envy. I loved jazz—anything that I could dance the Charleston to—but John had taken to educating me in the ways of classical music.

He revered Beethoven and Tchaikovsky, forcing me to listen to concertos again and again on the Victrola. He would watch me intently, asking me what I thought. To be honest, I couldn't stand Beethoven's Moonlight Sonata. It was intense and dark, much like John's moods. As we passed West 56th Street and approached Carnegie Hall, I wondered if John might've purchased tickets to a classical concert.

"Darling, please tell me where we're going."

I was wearing a Chanel coat, a brimless hat, a fox stole, an ivory crepe day dress, and snakeskin shoes—all gifts from John—but hardly attire appropriate for the most prestigious concert venue in the world. He smiled, a glint in his eyes. "It's a surprise, my pet. Wilson will show you. And then I'll join you shortly."

I shifted my weight in the back seat. Though I'd become accustomed to Wilson's constant companionship, I didn't like the man. He followed me around like a shadow, and I had the feeling if John ordered him to strangle me, he would.

Suddenly, Mr. Wilson pulled the car to a stop.

"We've arrived." John smiled with satisfaction.

Wilson turned off the engine, got out, and then came around to the back door and opened it for me. I stepped outside, blinking in the late afternoon light. We stood on West 57th Street, only a few doors east of Carnegie Hall.

"This way." Wilson pointed.

I followed him, taking in the stylish neighborhood, the windows dressed with Christmas wreaths and garlands. We stopped in front of a five-story brownstone. A tearoom on the bottom floor bore the name the Yellow Aster, and it was filled with fashionable ladies chatting over pots of Earl Grey and scones. Wilson walked through the doorway to the building, marked number 144.

We passed through a small lobby. Mr. Wilson asked the elevator boy to take us up to the fifth floor. As the elevator rattled, Wilson spoke to the boy in a low tone.

"A distinguished, gray-haired gentleman will enter the lobby.

You will ensure that no one sees him. Do you understand? My client requires the utmost discretion."

And with that, he pressed a crisp bill into the boy's palm.

"Yes, sir," he answered.

The elevator jolted to a halt. The boy pushed the gate open, and we stepped out. Mr. Wilson produced a silver key from his coat pocket and stuck it in the lock to apartment number five. The door creaked open and our footsteps echoed in the empty space as we walked inside. *My God, it was gorgeous!*

The apartment was small but stylish, furnished with an elegant blue velvet sofa and chairs in the living room and a large mahogany four-poster bed in the bedchamber. And next to the bedchamber, a private toilet and bath! I ran my hands over one of the blue velvet chairs. The wood floors shone in the abundant sunlight.

"Mr. Marshall shall be here shortly." Wilson nodded at me. Then he disappeared, shutting the door behind him.

I stood alone in the empty apartment. Then I crossed the living room and peered out the south-facing windows at the backyard below. Snow covered the ground, and a tree with barren branches pointed toward the sky. It probably had beautiful blooms come spring. I noticed a cushioned bench by the window, a lovely place to sit in the sun and to read a book. When I turned around, John was standing in the doorway.

I gasped. "You frightened me!"

He smiled, stepping toward me. "Do you like it?"

"It's beautiful. Whose is it?"

"It's yours."

I brought a hand to my lips. "You can't be serious."

"Oh, I'm very serious."

I swallowed. "You bought this? For me?"

He grinned like a cat that'd caught a canary. "You said you wanted a nicer flat. A place where I can visit as often as I like."

Had I told him that? I couldn't recall.

It would be wrong to accept this apartment. I was capable of paying rent on my own. Yet John would be offended if I said no. And looking around the beautiful sun-drenched room on the fifth floor of this stylish brownstone, I couldn't imagine going back to my dank basement apartment on the Lower East Side.

I thought of the shared toilet at the end of the dimly lit corridor, the families arguing upstairs, the battered furniture that belonged to my landlord, and the walls stained like tobacco juice. In the summer, it was so hot I was constantly drenched in sweat. My only window led to an airshaft, and in the winter, snow danced about inside it like popcorn. I'd been meaning to find a nicer apartment, but I couldn't afford anything as nice as *this*. Here, I could let in a breeze while looking out over the city below, like a woman on top of the world.

"Oh, John," I whispered. "It's marvelous."

"You'll have your own maid."

I laughed. "My own *maid*?"

At home in San Francisco, my life had been modest. Clara and I did the mending and washing and tended to our chickens and vegetables in the back garden. On Sundays, we would pop over to Gibson's grocery for a nice cut of beef for dinner after attending church services. But mostly we'd made do with giblets or Mother's Irish coddle. Even with my fine clothes and fame, I still hadn't forgotten my working-class roots. Many Follies girls had started off like me: as waitresses, farmer's daughters, and office workers, dreaming of being "glorified."

"I can't even imagine." I looked at the gleaming surfaces of the furniture, wondering if this mystery maid had freshly polished them.

John's lips curved into a smile. "I've thought of everything."

I looked around the living room, noticing the details. The Victrola had phonograph records stacked in alphabetical order: Bach, Beethoven, Brahms, Chopin, Debussy. I would have to sneak King Oliver's Creole Jazz Band in there.

John led me into the kitchen, where the cupboards were filled with fine china and crystal. The wall had a little white door. I opened it and discovered a dumbwaiter, presumably for the maid to bring up groceries so that she needn't carry them. The Frigidaire was a more modern model than the old icebox I'd grown up with. I opened the door and looked inside.

"Vegetables and orange juice. Oh, John, how very thoughtful of you. But have you forgotten the milk and the eggs?"

He looked at me, unblinking. "Now that you won't be dancing as often, you'll need to keep your figure."

I bristled. "What do you mean?"

"You dance five nights a week. Those are five nights you could be with me."

"But I want to perform." My muscles tensed. I'd worked hard to become a principal dancer in the Ziegfeld Follies. I loved the stage, adored the spotlight. So few of us had the height, the talent, and the stamina to make it. I thought back on reading my very first review in the newspaper as Stella Parsons—it was everything I dreamed of and more, right there in black and white. If I stepped down, Hilda would take my place in a heartbeat. She was already gunning for it.

I kept my voice low and steady. "I'm not going to stop."

"You will quit the Ziegfeld Follies." John rubbed his palms together matter-of-factly. "You don't need to dance anymore. Everything that's mine is yours."

"But it isn't." My voice rose in anger. "You have a *wife*, and your home in Boston. Do you expect me to sit around this apartment waiting for you while you're away, with nothing to keep me occupied?"

John glared at me. "You ungrateful bitch. Don't you realize everything I've done for you?"

An icy feeling came over me. John had never spoken to me like that before. I nodded, dumbstruck.

John leaned closer, his fists clenched at his sides. He looked like a volcano ready to erupt—inches away from losing control. But then his features relaxed and he caressed my cheek. "We are not equals, my pet. Do you understand?"

He straightened his tie. "I leave tomorrow morning. You will tell Ziegfeld you are no longer in his employ. When I return, I will find you here."

My body continued to tremble.

"Do we have an understanding?"

"Yes," I whispered.

"Good." John's eyes were cold. "Because, Iris, I'm watching."

And with that, he left the apartment. The door clicked shut behind him. I sank to the floor and began to sob, hugging my knees to my chest. *Was I overreacting?* It wasn't as though John had struck me. Then I remembered my savings, and I wiped away my tears. Perhaps I needed some time away to think. Tomorrow, I would purchase my ticket to California aboard the Panama Pacific line.

I'd remind Flo that I hadn't taken a vacation in five years. If I left immediately, maybe I would make the boat journey home in time for Christmas, and I would be able to surprise my family. John's overprotectiveness, which I'd once found charming, was changing into something more frightening.

But in San Francisco, he couldn't control whom I saw, what I ate, or what I wore. And by the time I returned to New York, he'd either apologize to me or have moved on to another pretty young thing.

At least that's what I told myself as I picked myself up off the floor.

Chapter Ten

Ellie

"Iris." Ellie reached for her aunt's hand, wrapping it in hers. Iris's fingers were as cold as ice. "I had no idea. I'm so sorry."

Iris wiped a tear from her eye. She took a deep breath and let it out in a shudder. "This has been harder for me to talk about than I expected."

Ellie squeezed her hand. "Would you like to go back to the hotel?"

"Yes, dear. It's freezing and I'm tired. I'll finish my story later."

Ellie nodded. Iris's story was terrifying, and she understood why her aunt was so shaken. However, she felt her hackles rise at the implication that Tom was anything like that monster John Marshall. He would never speak to her in such a vulgar and hurtful manner.

Ellie hailed a cab and they rode back to the Algonquin, where they ate a light lunch of shrimp salad and soup. After they'd finished their meals, Iris decided to take a nap, and Ellie remained in the hotel lobby to enjoy a cup of tea. She sat there for about an hour, reading the newspaper and thinking about Frank yelling his demands at the copyboys back at the *Chronicle*. Though it was a relief to have a reprieve from his hurled insults, Ellie missed the sense of purpose she felt at the paper. What would she do all day when she became a homemaker?

This New York trip had ignited a spark inside her. For twenty-four years, she'd been longing for an adventure, living vicariously through books. Her mother and magazine advertisements had taught her she was expected to stay home, make babies, and take to her domestic role without complaint. But what if she wanted more? Women around the country were taking on men's jobs to aid the war effort and proving just how capable they were. Now that she was making decisions for herself, the world seemed full of opportunities.

Being here in New York was exhilarating—she was captivated by Iris's memories of the Ziegfeld Follies, and by Greenwich Village's meandering streets—but Ellie hadn't forgotten the real reason she'd come here: to find out what had happened to her father. There was still hope for his rescue or at least a known status. She hated that she'd allowed herself to believe he would fake his own death in order to begin a new life with Lillian. Perhaps he'd been captured and he'd written to Lillian first, but another letter to her and her mother would soon follow. After all, he'd spent decades writing to them both.

Ellie took a deep breath in and let it out. She needed to process her thoughts through writing—journaling had always helped her make sense of the world. But she wanted to do more than journal; she wanted to write articles that conveyed truth and beauty alongside sadness and hope, to touch people in the same way the books she'd loved had touched her.

How would Tom react if she told him she wanted to write a column for the newspaper? Perhaps that's why Iris had shared her story—she feared Tom wouldn't allow her niece to pursue a career. Ellie chewed her bottom lip. Even if Tom weren't amenable to the idea at first, she was sure he would come around.

The tabby cat ambled into the lobby and rubbed against Ellie's legs, pulling her back to the present. Ellie smiled at a passing bellhop while stroking the cat's soft fur. "Is this Matilda or Hamlet?"

"Matilda," he said. "She's sweet, isn't she?"

"She sure is." Ellie scratched underneath Matilda's chin. Matilda jumped into her lap, and Ellie set down her cup of Earl Grey. "Well, hello. Aren't you precious?"

As she stroked the cat's fur, a disturbing thought came to mind. The article she'd read about Dot King stated Dot had been murdered in her apartment on West 57th Street. Hadn't Iris said the apartment John Marshall had gifted her was also on West 57th Street? Ellie shook her head. It couldn't be the same apartment, could it? And if it was, how did Dorothy King end up living there?

The elevator doors opened, startling Ellie from her thoughts. Iris emerged, dressed in a knee-length red coat and matching hat, the color restored to her cheeks. She waved a gloved hand at Ellie. "I feel much better after my nap."

Matilda jumped off Ellie's lap, and Ellie stood up, smoothing her skirt. "I'm glad to hear it." She pressed her lips together, contemplating whether she should ask Iris about the apartment; but before she had the chance, the bellhop returned, holding a very large bouquet of red roses and a cream-colored envelope. "Miss Eleanor Morgan?"

Heat warmed Ellie's cheeks. "Yes?"

He presented her with the bouquet. "These arrived for you."

Ellie took the flowers, overwhelmed by their sweet scent and feeling slightly embarrassed by the extravagance. "Oh my." She read the card tucked into the bouquet. *Dollface. Come home. I miss you. Love, Tom.*

A chill came over her. Tom's note and flowers were eerily reminiscent of the gifts Iris had received from John. Ellie shuddered. *But that was ridiculous! Tom was nothing like John.*

Iris pursed her lips. "They're not quite your style, are they?"

Ellie bristled. Iris was right—she would have preferred a simple bouquet of handpicked wildflowers to these long-stemmed red roses. But it was the thought that counted, and Tom was always thoughtful.

The bellhop cleared his throat, and then he handed Ellie the cream-colored envelope. "A letter has arrived for you."

Ellie shifted the large bouquet to her left arm to accept the envelope. "Thank you."

The bellhop smiled, eyeing the roses. "I'll bring you a vase for those."

Ellie tore open the envelope, the loopy cursive on the back written in blue ink: *Mrs. Arthur Davenport, 15 Peachtree Lane, Atlanta, Georgia.*

Iris wrinkled her nose at the intense floral scent. "Is that letter from your future mother-in-law?"

Ellie ran her finger along the thick paper inside, embossed with the name *Davenport.* She swallowed. "It is."

Her wedding invitations were going to cost a pretty penny if this stationery was any indication. Ellie studied the names of the relatives Tom's mother wanted to invite to her wedding, and she wondered what they would think of her. She was no Southern belle, that much was certain.

Ellie turned to Iris. "I don't suppose you'd like to come with me to the stationer?"

"No, dear." Iris's blue eyes filled with purpose. "What I'd like is to see the New Amsterdam again."

"The theater where you performed with the Ziegfeld Follies?"

"That's right." Iris looked into the distance. "It was the most beautiful theater you've ever seen. I've kept my past a secret for so long, but it's time to revisit it."

Ellie nodded. "Then let's go. That theater was a big part of your life."

Iris's eyes glinted with pride. "I performed there, every night, for five years, and most of the time, I was nearly nude."

Ellie laughed, struggling to imagine her aunt barely dressed, even though she'd seen pictures of the girls at the Ziegfeld Club. "I can't believe it."

"I was! Flo insisted we were better than the girls in George

White's *Scandals*. Those girls wore nothing but original sin. But we didn't wear much more." Iris's eyes narrowed. "John was drawn to me at first when I performed onstage, but then he forbade me to dance for anyone else but him."

The bellhop returned with a vase half-full of water, took the bouquet from Ellie, and placed it inside. "Would you like me to take these up to your room?"

"Yes, please." Ellie reached into her coin purse for a tip, pressing it into his palm. "Thank you for your help."

Then she turned to Iris. "I'm sorry you had to give up a career you loved."

Iris gave Ellie a tender look. "In spite of the way things ended, I'm glad I came home to you and your mother. Watching you grow from a toddler into the beautiful woman you are today has been one of my greatest joys."

Ellie grabbed her aunt's hand. "I don't know what I'd do without you."

Iris squeezed it. "The same goes for me, sweetheart. Don't ever dim your shine for anyone. Now, what do you say we walk over to the New Amsterdam?"

ELLIE AND IRIS passed dive bars and late-night cafeterias, pinball arcades and gimmick shops, while vagrants dug in garbage bins looking for discarded food. Some of the great old theaters had been turned into grind houses showing cheap action movies late at night, and a number of others had shuttered their doors. Iris's face fell as they walked down West 42nd Street toward 7th Avenue. She pursed her lips. "This is not the glamorous theater district of my day."

Iris sighed, waving her hand at the surroundings. "Back then this was called the Great White Way. Actresses, flappers, celebrities, and gangsters all rubbed shoulders here. It was a place like no other, just magical."

They stopped before the New Amsterdam Theatre, and Ellie looked up at a tall, narrow slice of brick wedged in between two shorter buildings, like it had popped out of the toaster. Its white limestone façade had faded to a dull gray, and its brick siding, painted with faded advertisements, had seen better days.

Iris frowned at the grimy marquee displaying showtimes for a horror film called *House of Frankenstein*. "Oh my."

Ellie took in her aunt's disappointed expression. "I take it it's not how you remember it?"

"Not at all. For one, it's a movie theater now, if what's playing inside can even be called film." She shook her head. "And the lovely façade has been stripped away and replaced with this awful neon sign."

"What did it used to look like?"

"It had a stone arch carved with flowers, scrolls, and garlands, and yellow marble columns." Iris gestured toward the ticket agent. "The vestibule used to jut out onto the street, with *Ziegfeld Follies* in globe lights."

"Shall we go inside?" Ellie nodded at the bored ticket clerk behind the glass. The next showing of *House of Frankenstein* wasn't until 3 p.m.

Iris rubbed her gloved hands together. "I suppose so, if only to get out of the cold for a while."

Ellie rapped her knuckles on the glass and the ticket agent

looked up. He narrowed his eyes. "Movie don't start for another hour."

Ellie put on her brightest smile. "I was hoping we might take a look around inside the theater. Is that all right?"

He shrugged. "Fine by me. Just don't sneak into the picture without paying."

"As if we would," Iris muttered.

Ellie suppressed her chuckle and then followed Iris into the narrow lobby.

Inside, Iris's eyes widened as if she had crossed a threshold into another time. Ellie watched her aunt take in the faded grandeur of what once must have been breathtaking. Chipped floral motifs on terra-cotta pilasters framed murals of nude women, their colors muted. Sconces of female faces carved from dark wood embellished the walls, light bulbs adorning their flower crowns, while chandeliers hung from the ceiling, each one like a Fabergé egg, surrounded by sculpted vines and flowers. Ellie's arms prickled with goose bumps. Now, *this* was a place she could write about. It was like a lost portal into the past.

"This brings back memories." Iris blinked away tears. "But the gold leaf has all worn off. This room used to sparkle like a treasure chest."

Ellie followed Iris into the next room, marveling at its stained glass dome, marble fireplace, and two marble fountains with mosaics that she couldn't make out, due to the missing tiles. Marble stairs with intricately carved balustrades curved up toward the balconies and down toward whatever rooms lay below.

"It's beautiful," Ellie whispered.

"If only you could have seen it before. The New Amsterdam was intended to dazzle even the most blasé theatergoer."

Ellie pointed. "What do those stairways lead down to?"

"The men's smoking lounge and the ladies' lounge. The lounges were unbelievably lavish, places to socialize before and after the show."

Iris pushed through the double doors leading to the auditorium. Ellie gasped as she stepped inside, looking at the domed ceiling, three stories above her. The cavernous space, though faded from its glory, was like an enchanted garden. Curved walls held trees laden with roses, blooming in between the box seats, ornamented with vines and fruits. Plaster peacocks and flowers had remnants of green and pastel hues, but they had chipped and dulled to drab beige.

Ellie covered her mouth. "It's like walking into a dream."

Iris smiled sadly. "The first play that was ever performed here was *A Midsummer Night's Dream*. When the theater opened in 1903, it was called 'the House Beautiful.'"

The box seats, like teacups, appeared as if they were floating in air, each sculpted with apples as large as baseballs and bunches of grapes. But a few boxes had been ripped from the walls, their absence like gaping wounds in the plaster. Their faded outlines had been spray painted a dark brown, giving the impression the new owners intended to paint the entire theater in that awful color. *Oh, but how could they?*

Iris brought a trembling hand to her mouth. "Poppy, Tulip, and Peony."

Ellie looked around, confused. "Who?"

"The box seats. Each one was named after a flower. Oh, what have they done?"

Ellie rubbed her aunt's back. *How could anyone want to destroy this beautiful space?* "Perhaps the box seats cast a shadow onto the movie screen?"

Iris wiped a tear from her eyes. "I can't bear to see it like this."

Ellie remembered when her parents had waited in breadlines and could no longer afford the luxury of a night out. Even though she'd been only a child during the Great Depression, she'd felt its effects like everyone else. Many theaters had suffered. But to let a place of such grandeur fall into disrepair—it was heartbreaking. Hadn't anyone tried to drum up support to save it?

"Do you want to sit down?" Ellie gestured to the velvet seats.

"Yes." Iris wiped her eyes. "I should have known it wouldn't look how I remembered it. Oh, but it was spectacular."

Ellie took a seat next to her aunt. "Tell me."

"There was a roof garden beneath a glass dome where I performed in the Midnight Frolic—a racier version of the Follies. A glass ramp led to a glass parapet, so the audience could view our undergarments . . . or lack thereof."

"Aunt Iris!" Ellie covered her smile.

"It's true. My favorite act was sitting on a crescent moon, wearing nothing but balloons and letting men pop them one by one with their lit cigars."

"You did not."

"I did." Iris looked at the empty stage. "But Flo always insisted his Follies Revue was not lowbrow. That's why he started using the French word *revue*. He wanted to draw in the upper class. He would let society dames backstage after the show; he cared ever so much about their opinions."

"Did anyone famous come to see the Follies?"

"Oh, absolutely. On opening night, the lobby of the New Amsterdam glittered with aristocracy—the Huttons and the Astors, the Whitneys and the Stotesburys. I remember their silk hats and ermine wraps, their diamonds and their talk of summering in Europe and wintering in Palm Beach."

"It sounds magnificent." Ellie imagined the rooms downstairs, filled with attractive men and women in Parisian couture, sipping champagne.

Iris's mouth tugged downward. "The Stotesburys . . . that's how I found out who John Marshall really was."

Ellie sat still. "He wasn't a businessman from Boston?"

Iris shook her head. "No, he was even more powerful than I imagined. And he had a reputation to protect." Iris closed her eyes and shuddered, as if a chill had passed through her. When she opened them, she stood up. "Let's go."

Ellie wanted to know more about John, but Iris was already walking in the direction they had come, as if the ghosts from her past were haunting her.

A FEW BLOCKS later, and they had returned to the Algonquin Hotel. Ellie had so many unanswered questions, but on the walk back from the theater, Iris had seemed distracted and rattled, keeping her thoughts to herself.

Iris turned around. "I must ask the front desk for an extra blanket. I was a bit chilly last night. Were you?"

"No, I was fine." Ellie fell into step beside Iris. "But I'll make the request; the room is in my name." When they approached the front desk, a young woman dressed in a red uniform stood at the counter. She smiled.

"May I help you?"

Ellie read the woman's name tag. "Yes, please, Rosie. I'd like an extra blanket for room ten fourteen. Our booking is under my name, Eleanor Morgan."

Rosie nodded. "I'll make sure housekeeping brings you another blanket. Oh—and you received a telephone call while you were out."

Ellie frowned. "From whom?"

Rosie tapped her red fingernail on a piece of paper and pushed it toward Ellie. "Someone named Betty who works at the Ziegfeld Club. She asked you to return her call as soon as possible. She says she has some information for you."

Ellie's heart beat faster. "May we use your hotel phone?"

"Of course. I can dial the number for you if you'd like."

Ellie nodded. "If you would, please."

Rosie dialed and then spoke into the telephone receiver. "This is Rosie calling from the Algonquin Hotel. The guests you asked after have just returned. Yes, I have Miss Morgan here. One moment."

Ellie gripped the receiver. "This is Ellie speaking."

"Hello, Ellie. My name is Betty. I work the shift after Irene, but I read her note about Lillian Dell. I heard you were looking for her?"

"Yes." Ellie held her breath, hoping for news.

"I met Lillian several months ago. She came into the club to see if we could assist her with her job search—acting auditions, mostly. Unfortunately, she didn't leave her address or contact information."

Ellie's heart sank. "Did she mention anything else?"

"Well . . ." Betty paused. "There was one thing. I complimented her on her bracelet—a lovely antique made of diamonds and pearls. Lillian said she was going to pawn it. A shame it had come to that, but she wouldn't be the first former Follies girl to pawn her jewels."

"Thank you, Betty." Ellie felt a renewed sense of hope. "You have been very helpful. Please call again if you think of anything else."

"Will do. Have a nice day, now."

Ellie hung up the telephone and returned it to Rosie.

Iris looked at Ellie, her mouth in a frown. "What did she say?"

Ellie pressed her hands together. "Lillian came into the club a few months ago, looking for a job. She didn't leave her information, but she said she was going to pawn her bracelet."

Iris's brow furrowed. "How does that help us?"

Ellie smiled. "I think I know where she might've gone."

Chapter Eleven

Ellie

NEW YORK, 1945

"Is this the place?" Iris asked, tilting her head toward the run-down pawnshop on the corner of Bleecker and MacDougal. Metal bars covered the windows and a neon sign blinked, with only a few remaining letters illuminated. Ellie was able to make out the the words *We buy gold.*

Ellie nodded, looking up at the tattered green awning. She remembered seeing this shop on her first visit to Greenwich Village.

Iris frowned. "And you think Lillian pawned her bracelet here? Knowing her, I think she would have chosen a more up-scale establishment."

Ellie squared her shoulders. "Lillian lived in this neighbor-hood a long time. What if she chose someplace familiar? It's worth a try."

Swallowing her apprehension, Ellie took a step closer. An

array of guitars hung in the barred window, framing a display of gold and silver watches, bracelets, necklaces, and rings. Ellie pushed open the door, Iris following her.

The shop was warm and smelled like pipe tobacco, the front room filled with a hodgepodge of antique furniture, fur coats, grandfather clocks, and cameras. Ellie approached the counter, eyeing the middle-aged, paunchy pawnbroker standing behind the glass countertop. He grinned, flashing a gold tooth. "Now, what's a gal like you doin' in a place like this?"

Ellie flinched as his eyes traveled the length of her body. But she kept her voice steady. "I've come here to inquire after a diamond and pearl bracelet."

The pawnbroker rubbed his balding head. "And who's paying? I don't see your father or your husband nowhere. That is, if you got a husband."

"I'm paying," Ellie replied curtly, ignoring his lecherous gaze. Her cheeks flamed. *Couldn't a grown woman spend her own money without a man's permission?*

The pawnbroker grinned, his gold tooth shining. "You've got sass. I like that. So, diamonds and pearls, eh? You rich or something?"

Ellie and her aunt were the only two customers in the pawnshop, and yet this sleazy man wasn't taking them seriously. Ellie removed her gloves, revealing her engagement ring, its breathtaking diamonds sparkling in the light.

The pawnbroker's eyes widened, and Ellie pictured him calculating how much he intended to overcharge her. She sighed. "Sir, we don't have all day. If you had a diamond and pearl bracelet, I'd be very interested in seeing it."

"All right." He surveyed the shop. "Wait here."

Ellie's heart thumped as he disappeared into the back room. She half expected him to return with a security guard to escort her and Iris outside. *But what law were they breaking exactly? Shopping without a husband?* Ellie took a deep breath, reminding herself she was capable.

The pawnbroker returned with a black velvet tray covered in dust motes. He lifted a single strand of pearls, holding them up to the light. "Now, these would look nice on you, don't ya think? They're natural pearls."

Iris leaned over his hairy arm to inspect them and frowned. "Cultured is more like it. Their size is too uniform. These aren't natural, and they aren't what we asked for."

The pawnbroker furrowed his brow. Ellie smiled at Iris, who she now realized had owned enough fine jewels in her day to show this fella she wouldn't be taken for a fool. Ellie was more familiar with riding the city bus than traveling in a private car, but he didn't need to know that. She wrinkled her nose. "I asked to see a *diamond* and pearl bracelet. If you don't have one, I'll take my money elsewhere."

The pawnbroker puckered his mouth. It was entirely possible the bracelet wasn't here. *But what if it was? Could she walk away from the shop?* Ellie gathered her gloves from the glass countertop, willing to take the risk. She touched Iris's arm. "We're wasting our time here. Let's go."

Ellie took one step and then another toward the door. The pawnbroker's voice rang out behind her. "Wait just a minute, now."

She exhaled. He disappeared again into the back room. This time, he took longer, and Ellie heard the creaking of a metal door, a key unlocking a safe. He returned and approached the counter, his shiny forehead beading with sweat, which he wiped with a handkerchief. Then his eyes moved to the shop windows. Without a word, he strode to the front door, flipped the sign over to read Closed, and lowered the window blinds.

The pawnbroker returned behind the counter and pulled a velvet drawstring pouch from his jacket pocket. Slowly, he opened it and tipped a bracelet into his palm. Iris gasped. The pearls were luscious, milky and round, while the antique diamonds glinted under the shop lights. Iris stepped closer, picked up the bracelet, and rubbed a pearl between her fingers. Her face drained of color.

"It can't be . . ."

Ellie sensed a charge in the air, like an electric current before a thunderstorm. The hairs on the back of her arms stood up. "What is it?"

Iris turned to Ellie, teary-eyed. "I know you said Lillian had pawned a diamond and pearl bracelet, but I didn't think it would be *this* bracelet." Iris clutched the bracelet in her fist, shaking it at the man before them. "Who brought you this?"

The pawnbroker gave her a condescending sneer. "That's none of your business."

Iris's voice was harsh as gravel. "Tell me who pawned this bracelet, and I won't tell the police you've acquired it illegally."

He laughed. "And what makes you think that?"

Iris gestured toward the windows. "Do you always shut your blinds and close your store when showing jewelry to customers?" She gently turned the clasp of the bracelet over, her hands shaking. The smooth platinum on the other side held a faint inscription. Iris covered her mouth and then dropped the bracelet onto the counter as if it had burned her.

"Hey, careful, lady!" The pawnbroker scooped it up in his meaty palm. "Do you have any idea how much this cost me?"

Iris's eyes shone with tears. "How did she . . ."

The pawnbroker squinted at the clasp to read the writing. "Huh, I didn't see that before. He leaned in close, so Ellie could smell his mixture of sweat, aftershave, and cheap cologne. His tobacco breath warmed her face as he pointed. "Look here."

Ellie read the cursive inscription on the clasp. *My pet.*

A shiver ran through her. Her eyes turned to Iris, and then to the heavyset man in front of her. "Who pawned this bracelet?"

He shook his head. "Sorry, beautiful. Like I said, I can't tell you. We keep things confidential around here."

Iris put a firm hand on Ellie's shoulder, her voice low and menacing. "This bracelet was stolen. I know, because the last time I saw it, it was on the arm of a dead woman."

Ellie felt a shiver run all the way down her spine. *What was Iris talking about?*

The pawnbroker looked as if he'd seen a ghost.

Iris lifted her chin, stretching to her full height. She was a tall woman, dressed smartly in her red suit and feathered hat, and her stance was intimidating. "You have no papers for this item. No provenance. But I do: newspaper photographs that can establish this bracelet belonged to the murdered Broadway Butterfly in 1923."

Ellie felt clammy with sweat. *Iris had kept newspaper articles about Dorothy King? Why?* Ellie thought back to the picture she had seen at the Ziegfeld Club. Dot King *had* posed with her hand on her chin, wearing a diamond and pearl bracelet strikingly similar to this one. But how could Iris be so sure that this was the same bracelet?

Iris drew herself up to her full height, her eyes full of fire. "Lillian Dell came here to pawn this bracelet. But how did she get it in the first place?"

The pawnbroker tucked a finger beneath his collar and tugged at it. "What I do off the books is my business."

Ellie's heart beat faster. He had information on Lillian. She slammed her palm on the countertop, shocking them both.

"If you don't want us to report you to the police, then tell us everything you know about Lillian Dell, including where she is."

The pawnbroker's lips formed a snarl. "I don't have to tell you nothing."

Iris removed a bundle of bills from her wallet and slapped them on the countertop. "Perhaps this will change your mind?"

Ellie's mouth fell open. It was far too much money. But she could finally see how Iris had once been one of Ziegfeld's greatest stars, how she had commanded attention in a room full of men, and how empowering that must have been. Iris didn't ask for permission—she had a boldness Ellie only dreamed of. Though dancing onstage was something Ellie would never do, Iris's unconventional career choice was just as valid as Ellie's desire to be a writer. Both paths offered independence, creative self-expression, and freedom.

The pawnbroker's round belly pushed against the countertop as he thumbed through the bills. Then he nodded, stuffing them in his pocket. His eyes darted from right to left, and then he lowered his voice to a whisper. "You didn't hear this from me, understand? Miss Lillian was a neighborhood regular. I helped her out here and there when she needed a buck. Then six months ago, she comes in with this bracelet. I didn't ask questions. She wanted cash—and lots of it."

Ellie licked her dry lips. "Why?"

He rubbed a hand across his shiny head. "Said she didn't want to live in this neighborhood no more. Told me she was moving to some hoity-toity place on the Upper West Side, near some museum, with a fresh paint job done on the front door, 'robin's-egg blue,' she called it."

Ellie felt a spark of hope. It wasn't an address, but it was a new location.

"Now, tell me, where did she—"

The pawnbroker grinned at her as if she were a piece of meat, cutting her off mid-sentence. "You know, you look like Lillian's daughter, Lucy. You don't see too many pretty redheads like yous. The two of you could be sisters."

Ellie doubled over at the waist, grabbing the counter for support. Her legs turned to jelly beneath her. *It couldn't be.* But hadn't part of her wanted it to be true? Without saying a word, she turned on her heel, pushed open the shop door, and ran outside, the winter air hitting her face like a slap.

"Ellie, wait!" Iris cried.

But Ellie's heels were already pounding the pavement. Tears streamed down her cheeks. Pedestrians gave her wary glances, but no one tried to slow her down. Instead, they provided a wide berth as her legs pumped harder, the twists and turns of Greenwich Village like a fun house maze.

The pawnbroker's words rang in her ears.

The two of you could be sisters . . .

A few blocks later, Ellie slowed to a stop and rested with her hands on her knees, her breath coming in ragged gulps. The brick buildings surrounding her all looked alike, and tears stung her windswept cheeks. Newspaper boys sat in front of bodegas, calling out at passersby. Across the street, Ellie spotted a large stretch of brown grass and an elegant stone arch rising into the sky.

She walked toward the park, her feet sore and blistered, her chest aching. She sank onto a bench, hugging her sides, rocking back and forth while gray storm clouds gathered overhead. *This trip had gone too far.* Tears kept silently streaming down her cheeks. A few young people—likely New York University students—leaned against the fence, their textbooks held to their chests.

Ellie wept for the father she thought was hers alone, and for the sister she never knew she had. She wanted to scream at the sky. The shock of the pawnbroker's words had shaken Ellie to her core. She felt angry, sad, and betrayed. Then she took a shuddering breath and wiped her nose with her coat sleeve. *How much weight should she give his words?* She wasn't sure she wanted the truth anymore, especially if the answers would only hurt her.

How foolish she had been to come all this way when Tom was at home waiting. She wanted to return to the familiar grid of San Francisco's streets where she could wander without getting lost, and where her life made sense. What was she doing delaying wedding planning and running around New York?

But a chill came over her as she thought about the parallels between Tom's actions and John Marshall's behavior at the beginning of his courtship with Iris. Tom was overprotective, just like John had been. He discouraged Ellie from telephoning her childhood friends Betsy and Mabel, reminding her that they had moved on with their lives and that she should too. Any time her colleagues at the *Chronicle* invited her for drinks after work, she demurred. Ellie told herself it was because she was tired, but it was because Tom would be unreasonably jealous if she went.

Ellie shook her head, incredulous. *What was she thinking?* Tom had a right to be worried about her—he cared about her. Yes, their relationship had progressed quickly, and his grand romantic gestures could be excessive, but that didn't mean he was anything like John Marshall. Tom would *never* swear at her or demean her.

This trip with Iris was playing tricks on her mind.

Ellie's stomach rumbled, reminding her she hadn't eaten anything since lunch, but she ignored it. She needed to find a pay phone. It was time to tell Tom why she was really here, so he could comfort her. Something about the assured way he said things made Ellie believe his decisions were the right ones. And she was fairly certain he would tell her to come home. Her life was complicated enough as it was, and learning of her father's long-term affair had only made everything worse.

She didn't know where he was, or if he was still alive. But Tom loved her, and he was at home in San Francisco. What was she doing away from him when it was possible he would get deployed? She needed to return home before Tom got tired of waiting for her, and before Frank decided to fire her. Ellie's heart clenched thinking of her mother, whom she'd left all alone. *Was she eating? Was she all right?*

Ellie scanned the park, her eyes landing on a delicatessen across the street with a striped awning. There was a pay phone out front. Breathing a sigh of relief, she gathered her purse, wincing as her shoes rubbed against her blisters. She crossed the street, then ducked inside the phone booth and dialed the operator.

"Long distance. How may I connect your call?"

"San Francisco, California. Fort Winfield Scott, Harbor Defenses."

"One moment. Please remember the recommended time of five minutes."

Ellie waited, semi-delirious with hunger and exhaustion. She knew Tom had to wait in line at the bank of public telephone booths installed at the military base. Evening phone volume got so heavy that civilians were discouraged from making long-distance calls between the hours of seven and ten. But it was afternoon in San Francisco. Hopefully someone would pick up, and go get him.

"Jim speaking. Mother, is that you?"

"No." Ellie drew in a deep breath, yearning for Tom's steady voice. "This is Eleanor Morgan. Can you please get Sergeant Thomas Davenport?"

Ellie leaned against the dirty booth, light-headed and dizzy. She heard some muffled sounds and waited.

"Sorry, miss. I couldn't find him."

"Tell him his fiancée, Ellie Morgan, called from New York. Tell him to call me back as soon as he can. It's important."

Ellie hung the phone in its cradle. She hoped Tom would get the message, because right now she needed a hot bath, a meal, and a nap. Once she'd done those things, she would book the first available train ticket back home.

Stepping out of the telephone booth, Ellie spotted Iris beneath the arch in the park, standing next to the New York University students. She nodded as they pointed in Ellie's direction, shielding her eyes against the glare. Ellie broke into a run toward her, causing a cab to honk as she crossed through traffic.

A fresh set of tears pressed against her eyelids as she ran into her aunt's open arms. "Oh, Iris, I'm so sorry. How did you find me?"

Iris hugged her tightly. "I ran after you down Bleecker Street, and then when I lost you, I asked everyone I passed if they'd seen you running. It didn't take long for me to follow you here to Washington Square Park. I may not be as fast as I once was, but I still know my way around this city."

Ellie wiped away her tears. "I want to go home."

Iris tucked a strand of Ellie's hair behind her ear. "Don't worry, dear, we'll catch a cab back to the hotel."

Ellie shook her head. "No, I mean I want to return to San Francisco. Coming here was a mistake."

Iris held Ellie by her shoulders, studying her face. "Are you sure?"

Ellie felt so confused. She wanted to be the kind of woman who wasn't afraid to search for the truth, a woman who stood up for herself and spoke her mind. But now she wasn't sure she could become that person. And the familiar comfort of home was beckoning her. "I don't know. I'm so tired."

Iris offered a reassuring smile. "Let's return to the hotel."

Ellie nodded, feeling relieved but also unsettled. Her aunt, who normally challenged Ellie to think about her decisions, hadn't even tried to change her mind. They could leave New York tomorrow morning and that would be that.

Ellie chewed her bottom lip, remembering a detail that had been nagging at her. She wondered if it had anything to do with Iris's strange behavior.

"Back at the pawnshop, when we saw that bracelet, how did you know it belonged to Dorothy King?"

Iris's eyes filled with pain. She let out a deep breath. "Because that bracelet once belonged to me."

Chapter Twelve

Iris

The day after John called me an ungrateful bitch, I went straight to the New Amsterdam Theatre just before morning rehearsal, when I knew Flo would be in. Though I'd promised John I would quit the Follies, I had other plans. My looks wouldn't last me forever, and I had a few good years left to star in Broadway's biggest show. I wasn't going to waste them because John Marshall wanted me all for himself. I hoped he would apologize for his abhorrent behavior, but I also felt deeply unnerved. I couldn't stop thinking about the name the bellhop had called him—Mr. Mitchell.

When I stepped inside the theater, I kept my head down, making my way through the warren of hallways beyond the stage, and up the stairs toward Flo's office. Midway there, I heard a door open and then slam shut. Suddenly, a diminutive blonde began descending the staircase, mad as a bat out of hell.

I stepped aside as she flung her fur stole over a perfectly creamy bare shoulder, her hips swaying as she walked, exaggerating her hourglass shape. Her deep blue gaze locked on mine, and her lips formed a luscious pink pout. A sprinkling of freckles dusted her nose and cheeks, giving her a youthful sweetness, though something about the girl made me think she was older than she looked.

Then she sneered at me, her pink lips curling around her teeth. "I know who you are, and you ain't nothin' special, honey."

I stood there speechless, surprised at the strong New York accent that had come from her lovely mouth and the venom in her words. "Excuse me?"

Her eyes narrowed, then moved as if calculating the total worth of the diamonds in my ears, on my wrist, and around my neck. "I told Ziegfeld you're ruining his show, you no-talent hack. Mark my words, I could do better."

Hilda and Louise appeared on the landing beside me, gawking at the blonde as she stormed away. I was so dumbstruck, I momentarily forgot about John. *Who was this woman, and what had I ever done to her?*

Hilda raised her eyebrows. "Looks like *her* audition didn't go well."

I caught the lingering scent of the woman's perfume, a heady mixture of roses, jasmine, musk, and patchouli. "Who is she?"

Hilda pursed her lips. "Dorothy King. She's in the room next to mine at the Great Northern Hotel. She's a hostess at a nightclub called the Cat's Meow, and I've never met a gal more desperate for wealth and fame."

Lou nodded. "She's also a dress model. But nothing she wears compares to our costumes. I bet you she's jealous."

That explained her hostile behavior toward me. Still, Dorothy King's comment about me being a no-talent hack stung like a slap.

I frowned. "Why didn't Flo sign her? She's gorgeous."

Hilda turned to me, whispering conspiratorially. "Because she has no class. She flits from one after-hours cabaret and speakeasy to another, and most nights she doesn't come home. Behind that sweet face, she's a tough Irish broad from Harlem who never finished high school. Her mother runs a laundry, her brother is a cabbie, and her father disowned her. Oh, and she's a twenty-eight-year-old divorcée."

My mouth fell open. "*Twenty-eight?* Well, I suppose she'll have trouble starting in show business at that age, but with a body like hers, I'm surprised Flo didn't select her for the Follies anyway."

Hilda shook her head. "Dot's been around the block a few times too many."

Lou giggled. "Now, Hilda, you've been around the block more times than any of us and that didn't stop Ziegfeld from picking *you.*"

"Very funny." Hilda shot Lou an annoyed look and then turned to me.

"Dot King is an honest-to-goodness vamp who sleeps with fellas she meets at these clubs for money. Gangsters, businessmen, it doesn't matter. Oh, and get this. Dot King isn't even her real name."

I frowned, thinking of John. *Mr. Mitchell.* "It isn't?"

Hilda smirked. "She was born Anna Marie Keenan. But she's reinvented herself as Dorothy King because she's looking for some heavy sugar."

Before I could remind Hilda that I had reinvented myself as Stella Parsons, Lou giggled. She turned to me.

"I heard she dropped that first husband of hers like a hot potato—only used him to get out of Harlem."

Hilda nodded. "It's true. Dot told me it was a *small-time* marriage, he was only a chauffeur, and that she can do better. The poor man is still pining over her, living alone in Jersey. But she wants a fella with some *very* deep pockets."

"And she had her perfume custom made to snare a man!" Lou snickered. "Or so I've heard. God, I can still smell it, can you?"

I could. The alluring scent was earthy, musky, and bold—quite different than the Chanel No. 5 that I and every other gal wore.

As awful as Dot King had been to me, I couldn't stand around gossiping with Hilda and Lou all day. I wanted to ask Flo for time off so I could get away from John. *How dare he tell me I wasn't allowed to perform?*

I smiled. "Forgive me, gals, but I've got to run."

I felt them watching me as I continued up the stairs toward Flo's office. His voice carried down the corridor as I approached. "Don't tell me it can't be done! It shall be done. And why haven't I been named as a judge in Atlantic City? It is an affront, I tell you. No one knows beauty like I do."

Flo had forgotten he'd publicly stated the Miss America contests were fixed, and the Atlantic City judges still resented him for it. I knocked on his door as he slammed his telephone back in its cradle. He looked up and smiled at me.

"Stella! To what do I owe this pleasure?"

Flo was a handsome man, in his mid-fifties with slick gray hair parted neatly in the middle and a trim black mustache. He beckoned me to his desk, covered with clipped pictures from magazines, his inspiration for settings and costumes. He would see a photograph of a girl's legs in the paper and demand she be brought to him straightaway. In spite of all Hilda and Lou had said, I wondered again why he hadn't chosen Dorothy King—she had a face you didn't forget.

"I want to show you something." Flo picked up a lovely silver sequined gown and then turned it inside out, exposing the lining. "Touch this."

I ran my fingers along the smooth pink silk. "It's marvelous."

"The finest. Imported from China. Cost me a fortune."

"Did Charlotte reproach you for such extravagance?"

He winked. "Of course. But she designs the costumes. She doesn't *dance* in them. And it is the quality of the lining that allows a woman to act and feel more feminine. My dresses enhance your movements, do they not?"

I swallowed my nerves. "They do. We are fortunate you take such good care of us." I took a deep breath. "Flo, I need to ask you a favor. As you know, I've wanted to visit my family for quite some time, and I need a few weeks off."

"A few weeks!" Flo scoffed, shuffling his stack of papers. "And who would you have fill in for you while you're away?"

"I was hoping Fanny Brice might. Everyone loves her act."

Fanny was Flo's favorite star, a comedienne rather than a

beauty. She'd performed a parody of our act at a rival theater; a burlesque show titled "Follies Girls." Ziegfeld had found it so funny, he'd asked her to work for him instead.

Flo shook his head. "Fanny does not entertain in the same way you do, my dear. But perhaps Hilda would like her turn to shine."

Yes, she would. And perhaps I would not have my starring role to return to. *Had Dot King put that thought in Flo's mind— that I ought to be replaced?* But it was a chance I had to take. "So, is that a yes?"

Flo's dark eyes locked on mine. "Do you know why I telephone and telegraph so much?"

"Because you're the hardest-working man in show business?"

He wagged his finger at me. "I not only have to find new girls, but I have to guard the old ones. Don't let me find you onstage in London or Paris."

"You won't." I breathed a sigh of relief. "And, Flo, if anyone comes looking for me, don't tell them where I am. Tell them I quit."

Flo leaned forward on his elbows. "Have you gotten yourself into some kind of trouble?"

Ziegfeld had a soft spot for his girls. He had a hundred rules: *Don't get fat. Don't stay out late. Don't go too wild at parties.* And yet sometimes leading dancers would be absent for a few weeks at a time with no explanation. There would be hushed whispers that a "problem" had been taken care of. And then the girl would return to Flo's gruff *Where the hell have you been?* And he would let it go at that.

"Not that kind of trouble." I looked down, afraid he would notice how shaken I was from my fight with John. "But I need to go to San Francisco."

He shook his head, returning to his papers. "Do what you must. The sooner you leave, the sooner you can return."

As I turned to go, he shoved a copy of *The New York Times* at me. "But wait just a minute. I've been meaning to show this to you."

I groaned. "Not James Henry. He hates me."

Flo grinned, his eyes sparkling. "Read it."

I scanned the review from the notoriously prickly theater critic.

Any more dazzling stage pictures than the Follies, I have never beheld. They deserve every word that the advertisements say of them, and more besides. I never knew there were as many pretty girls in the world as gathered together on the New Amsterdam stage today, the most beautiful being flame-haired principal dancer, Stella Parsons.

"You see?" he cried enthusiastically. "I can't lose my biggest star."

I forced a smile. "You won't."

When I turned to leave, my eyes landed on the black social register on Ziegfeld's desk, a semiannual publication listing the most prominent families in the Northeast. I touched its gilded spine with my fingertips. "Do you mind if I borrow this?"

Flo laughed. "Not at all, my dear. Every single one of those patrician families has come to see my revue. The blue bloods of the Eastern Seaboard adore me!"

Leaving the New Amsterdam Theatre with Ziegfeld's social register tucked under my arm, I nearly bumped into a woman outside, smoking a cigarette.

"Watch it, will you?" She narrowed her eyes, exhaling a plume of smoke in my direction. I coughed, waving the tobacco cloud away.

It was *her* again, that awful little blonde, Dorothy King. Up close, she was even more beautiful—something about the way her mouth turned up at the corners made her look like she had a secret. Underneath the scent of her musky perfume, I smelled something else—gin. She looked at me glassy-eyed.

"Who gave you that necklace and those earrings?" She pressed her finger into my chest. "They aren't paste. Somebody's takin' *real* good care of you."

I glared at her, wondering if she planned to yank my diamonds from my neck and run. But then I realized—I didn't want to be wearing John's gifts anymore. I wanted him gone from my life entirely.

Unclasping my necklace, I placed it in Dot's palm. Her mouth fell open. Now it was my turn to smirk. *Kill her with kindness.*

"Here, you can have it."

Dot's eyes glittered as she wrapped her fingers around the diamonds. "Is there more where that came from?"

I laughed in disbelief. I'd never met someone so brash. Eager to get rid of her, I removed my diamond studs from my earlobes and dropped them into her hand.

"Courtesy of Mr. John Marshall. You can have *him* too."

As I turned to leave, I caught sight of Lillian lurking in the shadows of the theater, a look of shock on her face. I hadn't forgotten how she'd ogled the pear-shaped sapphire John had sent me backstage, but it was too late now to give all my jewelry away, so I pretended not to see her. I had a boat to catch.

ON THE BROADWAY Line to South Ferry, all of my savings tucked into my coat pocket, I cracked open the spine of the social register. It included eight cities in one volume, lending it heft. My mouth dry, I flipped to Boston, trailing my finger down the page in search of John Marshall. No John Marshall was listed.

A shiver ran down my spine. I moved my finger to "Mitchell." There were several Mitchells, but no one by the name of John. Then I touched my lip, remembering the postcard John had mailed me from Philadelphia. Flipping to the Philadelphia listings, my eyes scanned the members of the Philadelphia elite, their academic affiliations; clubs and societies; and notices of births, deaths, and marriages.

A page titled "Married Maidens" caught my eye: *The following maiden names taken from the present and previous numbers of the social register are arranged alphabetically for the purpose of convenient reference to the married name.*

I stood there frozen, my heart caught in my throat. There beneath *Stotesbury, Frances . . . Mitchell* was a photograph of John with his arm around a dark-haired woman, both of them standing in front of a massive colonial-style mansion.

I sucked in my breath as I read the caption.

Mrs. Frances Stotesbury Mitchell, daughter of E. T. Stotesbury, with her husband, J. Kearsley Mitchell, in front of her Palm Beach estate.

I brought my trembling fingers to my mouth, staring at the dignified woman with the dark bob and prominent nose. She and John were younger here, newly married in the 1910 photograph, and I felt a stab of guilt, followed by a moment of dread.

E. T. Stotesbury was the wealthiest man in America . . . and he was also John Marshall's father-in-law. John wasn't John Marshall at all. He was J. Kearsley Mitchell.

The media would go wild if they found out that he was involved with a Follies girl. The Stotesbury mansion in Pennsylvania had one hundred and forty-six rooms. I shivered, studying John's wife, the socialite. My palms began to sweat as I realized the lengths John might go to, to protect his identity, his legacy, and his reputation.

The bus pulled to a stop just north of Battery Park, with Castle Clinton in the distance, and I accidentally left the social register on the seat as I disembarked at 1 Broadway, making my way to the International Mercantile Marine Company Building. I was too shaken to worry about replacing it.

Walking through the double doors, I noticed a man in a fedora sitting outside, his hat obscuring his face. My heart beat faster as my heels clacked across the marble floor of the lobby while I approached the ticket agent. I told myself John couldn't have sent that man. He was already there when I arrived—probably just a vagrant.

With shaking fingers, I unfolded the advertisement tucked in my coat pocket and slid it across the counter: SEE THE

MARVELOUS PANAMA CANAL EN ROUTE TO CALI-
FORNIA. *Go via the wonderful Panama Canal, engineering marvel
of the world. See sparkling Havana, Caribbean metropolis en route.
Cool breezes all the way.*

The ticket agent was a young man.

"Hello." I fought the urge to tug down my cloche, wishing I
could conceal my face. Instead, I tapped the advertisement. "One
tourist-class ticket to San Francisco, please. I'd like to ask after
your special round trips."

The agent nodded. "That'll be two hundred and seventy-five
dollars. The route is one-way water, one-way rail. When would
you like to depart?"

I braided my fingers together. "As soon as possible."

"The next ship departs this Thursday at eight in the morning.
I suggest arriving thirty minutes early. You will return to New
York by train, which I can book now."

"Excellent, please do."

I reached into my coat pocket, withdrawing the stack of bills,
and slid them across the counter. It was every last cent of my
savings, but I was one step closer to putting an ocean between
John and myself. He was controlling everything: from what I
wore to whom I saw. But soon I would be safely back at home,
where I could be alone with my thoughts. I needed to forget about
him and move on.

After taking my information, the ticket agent handed me my
boat ticket, and I slipped it into my coat pocket. "Thank you. I'll
arrive early on Thursday."

To my relief, the man in the fedora outside had left. I

shuddered, thinking of the apartment at 144 West 57th Street, John's parting gift. I couldn't accept it, no matter how lovely it was. I had to assert my independence, not become more reliant on John. I caught a streetcar to the Lower East Side to return to my basement flat on Ludlow so I could begin packing.

Nearing my stop, I couldn't shake the feeling that someone was watching me. I turned around and spotted a man in a gray coat and a dark fedora—the same man I'd seen lingering outside the ticket office. My stomach lurched. I could see his face now; he had a broken nose and a nasty scar. My palms began to sweat.

The streetcar curved onto East Broadway and rattled through lower Manhattan, passing tenements, theaters, and tailor shops. My heart thudded in my chest. I had to lose him, and quickly. At the next stop, I pushed through the streetcar doorway, then jumped out and ran. Looking behind me, I saw the man following, his face like something out of a nightmare.

I ran past pushcarts and Jewish theaters, tailor shops and delicatessens, the sound of people yelling out their wares and the smell of baking rye bread and pickle juice filling the air. My feet hurt, my Louis heeled leather shoes pinched my toes. I was already dog-tired, but I pushed myself to go faster.

Old women wearing colorful headscarves spoke in Russian beneath laundry flapping overhead. I turned onto Orchard Street, my legs pumping harder. Ducking behind a street cart vendor, I paused to catch my breath. The man selling pickles said something to me in another language, his dark eyes full of concern. I looked for the thug in the fedora, but he was gone. Children played in the street in tattered winter coats.

By the time I reached my brick tenement on Ludlow Street,

the back of my dress had soaked through with sweat and my silk step-ins and brassiere clung to my skin. I reached into my coat pocket for my key, but before I could stick it in the lock, a hand gripped my elbow, spinning me around. I screamed.

The man in the fedora clapped a heavy hand over my mouth. Up close, he smelled of liquor and sweat. I fought to break free, but he was too strong. When he released my mouth, I gasped for air. "Let go of me!"

His eyes glinted and dark stubble peppered his square jaw. "I can't do that. *He* already paid me."

I looked in the direction where he'd lifted his chin. Mr. Wilson stepped out of John's black Bentley, the automobile parked in front of my building.

"Stop!" I yanked my elbow, trying to break free. Chills came over me as I realized John was perhaps more dangerous than I'd thought. I glared at Wilson. "I don't want anything to do with you or Mr. Marshall."

The thug in the fedora gripped me harder. "Get in the car."

My sweat had cooled, and goose bumps rose on my skin. "No!"

A couple of kids stopped and stared. They were scuffed and dirty and wore clothes that had probably belonged to several siblings before them. I wanted to scream for help, but what could they do? The Poles and the Russians, the few remaining Germans and the many Jews, stuck to themselves. They were wary of the gangsters and rumrunners who came through the Lower East Side neighborhood.

Mr. Wilson opened the back door to John's Bentley. Wrenching my arm painfully behind my back, the broken-nosed gangster shoved me into the back seat and then slammed the door behind me. I thought of my belongings—my clothing, my trunk, my jewelry, and everything that I had planned to take with me to San Francisco.

"This is kidnapping!" I yelled at Wilson as he started the car. "What have you done with my things?"

"They're waiting for you." He smirked as if he was enjoying himself. "At your new apartment."

"It was very kind of John to gift me that apartment." My voice trembled, and I decided it was best not to reveal I knew who John really was. The less he thought I knew the better. "But he can't force me to live there."

Wilson's eyes met mine in the rearview mirror, their glint telling me this was a game to him. "Mr. Marshall is a very powerful man."

I turned to ice, all the way to my core. If I had settled for a simple life with a simple man like Clara had, I never would have met J. Kearsley Mitchell. I had fallen prey to fame because of my desire to be seen, and I had prided myself on making more of my life than Clara had. But look where my vanity had gotten me.

I thought about opening the Bentley door and rolling out onto the street, but I'd likely get myself killed. Instead, I tried to reason with Wilson.

"Please. You can have the jewelry John gave me. It's worth a fortune. He never has to know you found me."

"I'm loyal to Mr. Marshall." Wilson smiled as if money didn't matter to him.

We arrived at 144 West 57th Street, and Mr. Wilson rode the elevator with me in silence. On the fifth floor, he turned his key in the lock and opened the door. I sucked in my breath. John stood in the middle of the room, holding me in his direct, un-blinking gaze. "Were you trying to leave me, my pet?"

Lie, I told myself. *Make him believe you love him.*

"John." I lowered my lashes and parted my lips. "I've told Flo I'm leaving the Follies, that's all. There was no reason for Wilson to have me followed."

His eyes grew hard. "Do you think I'm stupid?"

My voice came out in a whisper. "No."

John reached into my coat pocket and removed my ocean liner ticket. "You won't be needing this."

I watched in horror as he tore it into pieces.

"No!" My heart caved in on itself like a collapsed building. Clara and Mother, Father and little Eleanor . . .

"You're not going back to your worthless Irish mother and your bastard father who can't provide for his wife and children."

"But I can repay you." I swallowed hard, regretting accepting John's money.

"By dancing? I think not."

"Please." I took a step backward, wondering if I could make a run for it. "I'm so grateful for everything, but I need to see my family."

He clenched his fists. "You want to go back to your cold-water flat? To your garbage family? Look how I've elevated you."

His gravelly voice was sending a chill down my spine. John turned to his secretary. "Wilson. You may leave us."

Wilson nodded and left the room, shutting the door behind him. Fear coursed through me. I searched John's face for a trace of the person I'd fallen in love with. Perhaps that man was still inside and I could reason with him.

I took a deep breath, my eyes pleading. "I'm sorry. I needed some time to myself."

A smile played at the corner of John's mouth, but it held no warmth. "Is that so? My little whore is getting grandiose ideas."

Recoiling, I flinched at the word. Ziegfeld girls were respected, and no one had ever called me that before. Hearing it stung like a slap.

John walked over to the Victrola and wound the crank gently and slowly. He selected a record from its sleeve and set it down against the turntable, then slowly lowered the needle.

The haunting notes of a Chopin piano solo filled the room, the beauty of the instrument incongruent with the ugliness of what was taking place. "Etude Opus Ten, Number Three in E Major." John licked his lips. "Chopin believed this melody to be his best."

I took another step backward.

"Tell me." John's eyes glinted beneath the electric lights. "Who are the greatest pianists?"

I wanted to say his musical taste didn't make him superior to me. But now was no time to argue the merits of jazz.

"Rachmaninoff." My heart began to pound.

"And?"

I couldn't think quickly enough. My mouth was dry. Then I remembered. "Beethoven."

"You see all that I've taught you?" He turned up the volume on the Victrola, Chopin filling the room. "You're becoming too smart for your own good, giving yourself ideas that you can get on a boat to San Francisco." He brought his face inches from mine, so I could feel his breath on my cheek. "But you're worthless." The music reached a crescendo. "You're nothing without me, don't forget that."

I shut my eyes, praying I'd wake up somewhere else—anywhere else. When I opened them, John had left the room, but he returned with a blue velvet box. "Open this."

My fingers shook as I opened it. Inside, a diamond and pearl bracelet sparkled in a platinum setting. *What kind of sick game was he playing?*

His blue eyes glinted in the dark. "Put it on."

But I couldn't. My body was paralyzed by fear.

John smiled, taking my left wrist. "Shall I do it for you?"

He undid the platinum clasp and then turned the bracelet toward me so I could read the inscription inside. The words swam before my eyelids. *My pet.*

John fastened the bracelet around my wrist, its diamonds and pearls cold against my hot skin. "I can't trust you to make your own decisions, so I'll make them for you. You're mine, Iris. Never forget it."

Chapter Thirteen

Ellie

NEW YORK, 1945

Ellie clapped a hand over her mouth, her stomach wrenching. She couldn't shake the image of Iris as a young woman, cowering in fear. A shudder ran from her head down to her toes. She knew about Edward T. Stotesbury and his immense wealth from her history textbooks. Iris had been his son-in-law's mistress.

"Oh, Iris." Ellie's voice cracked. "I'm so sorry."

The hotel room materialized around her—the leather wingback chair, the striped green wallpaper, Tom's roses on the bedside table. Iris's story reminded Ellie of the terrible secrets people kept from one another, and her throat tightened, thinking of the pawnbroker in Greenwich Village and the words he'd uttered.

The two of you could be sisters.

Iris's eyes hardened. "Seeing that inscription on the bracelet again . . ." She shook her head, unable to finish her thought.

Ellie looked down at her aunt's clenched fists.

"Are you still afraid of him?"

Iris laughed, but it rang hollow. "No, he's an old man now. He'll die soon, with his loyal wife by his side."

"How could she stay with him?" Heat burned under Ellie's skin. "He's a monster."

"The mind is a powerful tool." Iris shrugged. "We see only what we want to see."

A pit formed in Ellie's stomach as she considered the parallels between Iris and Dorothy King—a shared bracelet, possibly a shared apartment. Her hands felt clammy. *Had her aunt given Dorothy King the bracelet inscribed with "My pet," just like she'd given her the diamond necklace and earrings?* The thought made Ellie uneasy—she wasn't sure if she wanted to know Iris's secrets.

Ellie pulled a Chesterfield from her purse and reached for a book of matches on the nightstand, courtesy of the Algonquin. She lit a cigarette and took a drag, the tobacco calming her nerves. Iris hadn't told her what had happened after John gifted her the bracelet. And Ellie's story—the truth about her father— also remained unfinished. But she didn't know if she wanted to remain in New York. The deeper she dug, the more she feared what she might discover about those she loved most.

THE HOTEL TELEPHONE startled Ellie awake. She groped around the nightstand, nearly knocking over the vase of Tom's roses. Their smell had become cloying, filling the room with a sticky, sweet scent. Ellie lifted the receiver and pressed it to her ear.

"Hello? Eleanor speaking."

"Ellie! Good heavens, I called as soon as I could."

Ellie sat up in bed, rubbing her eyes. *Tom.* She'd nearly forgotten she'd left him a message from the pay phone yesterday, when she could hardly think straight. Looking around, she didn't see Iris, who must have gone down to breakfast early. Rain slapped against the windowpane, and the room was dark, though it was half past eight in the morning. She'd slept in. Meanwhile, Tom was awake before dawn, as usual, his bunk in the barracks already tidied and inspected.

"Oh, Tom. It's so good to hear your voice."

Ellie gnawed her bottom lip. She could tell him everything was fine, and she was having a swell time taking in all the sights. But if she wanted a real connection with her future husband, then she needed to be honest.

Ellie took a deep breath. "Tom, I have to tell you something. I didn't come to New York on vacation."

She hurried on: the long-distance charges were exorbitant, and Tom never had much time to talk. "I came here because I found out my father was having an affair. Tom, I know you think I'm crazy, but his mistress might know something about where he is."

Tom was silent.

"Tom? Are you there?" Ellie rubbed the back of her neck.

Tom's deep voice, normally her safe harbor, grew loud. "I'm sorry, *what*? Your father was having an affair?"

Pinching the bridge of her nose, Ellie sighed. "It all started when the army mailed Father's belongings last week. His jacket had letters in it, written by a woman named Lillian Dell in Greenwich Village." Ellie exhaled. "She wasn't just a fling. Lillian and my father carried on together for over twenty years. And she has a daughter, Lucy."

Tom sucked his teeth. "My God. Does anyone else know about this?"

"I didn't show my mother the letters. They would break her heart. I took them straight to Iris and we decided to come here to see what we could discover."

Tom exhaled. "Good. Now, listen carefully. No one can know about your father's affair, especially not my parents. We don't want any kind of scandal associated with our family, especially not before the wedding."

His words stung. "But, Tom . . . these women, Lillian and Lucy. What if Lucy is my—"

"Don't even think it." Tom's voice was sharp as a razor. "We don't know who that girl is. Do you want to drag your father's good name through the mud? I never should have allowed you to go to New York."

Ellie bristled. *"Allowed* me? I'm searching for answers—for the truth about my father's life. Isn't that reason enough to be here?"

Tom groaned. "You ought to have told me about those letters, and some skeletons are better left buried. Your father was a good, honorable man who loved you and your mother. Let's remember him that way."

"But what if he isn't dead?" Ellie furiously blinked back tears.

Tom sighed. "El, you know that's not likely."

Speaking through clenched teeth, Ellie felt anger overcome her sadness. "I know what the odds are, but I choose hope over despair. I wish you would do the same."

Tom's voice grew aggravated. "I choose a future with you! If that's not hopeful, I don't know what is. Now, I think it's high time you come home."

Ellie heard commotion in the background, men's voices and clattering plates. With a crackle, the switchboard operator came on the line. "Sir, you'll need to insert another dime if you wish to continue speaking. And please remember the recommended five minutes."

Tom spoke like the sergeant he was. "Book your ticket home on the next available train. No good is going to come of this trip."

Ellie pressed her lips together. It was Wednesday, and she'd only spent two nights in New York. Before she could speak, the line went dead. She brought a trembling hand to her mouth. Tom usually made her feel loved and safe, but just now he had made her feel insignificant and small. Why couldn't her voice hold equal authority?

She took a shuddering breath. Her stomach growled and she needed a cup of coffee to think clearly. She washed her face, brushed her teeth, and slipped on her undergarments. Then she opened her toiletry case and began brushing powder across her nose and cheeks. But when she met her large amber eyes in the mirror, she paused. *Who was she doing this for?*

Slowly, she lowered her red lipstick, placing it inside its tube. Her mother had taught her never to eat breakfast without makeup. And Tom liked her all dolled up. But men weren't expected to make themselves up for anyone—they could do as they pleased. Besides, her mother and Tom weren't here.

Ellie gathered her hair into a ponytail and then looked for

her nylons. She found them folded neatly atop her suitcase, but when she tugged them on, she noticed a new run, long as a ladder. "Dammit!"

She'd managed to make this pair last through the war, but it was too cold and rainy outside for nylons anyway. Ellie remembered how she'd hated to wear dresses as a little girl, how she'd cried putting them on. *How much of what she'd learned growing up had been from women's magazines?* Women weren't supposed to have opinions, and yet her father encouraged her to think for herself.

At what point had she forgotten all he'd taught her and become overly concerned with fitting in? Ellie couldn't remember why she had decided to go to secretarial school, when becoming a secretary had never been her passion. It had seemed like the proper thing to do at the time, but perhaps it wasn't too late for her to become someone else. Feeling a newfound sense of independence, Ellie set the nylons down and stepped into a pair of gray flannel trousers. She pulled on a cream-colored cardigan and then paused.

Her fingers began dialing the long-distance operator before she could talk herself out of it. Ellie wanted the opinion of someone she trusted. When the line connected to the Delta Hotel, the gruff front-desk clerk answered and then begrudgingly agreed to fetch Jack. Ellie's stomach felt full of butterflies as she waited to speak with her friend. He ought to be awake by now.

"Jack Miller speaking."

She was comforted by the sound of his voice. "Jack, I'm so sorry to trouble you again, and so early in the morning. It's Ellie, from the *Chronicle*."

Jack chuckled. "Hey, kid, don't worry about it. You still in New York?"

"I am." She took a deep breath, suddenly nervous. "Say, do you remember the article Frank ran a few years back about the lost crew of the *Zebrina*? 'Vanished at Sea, *Zebrina* Mystery'?"

As much as Ellie wanted to tell Jack about her father, it felt too personal.

Jack whistled. "Who could forget? British schooner found derelict in the English Channel, undamaged in any way, with no souls on board, but all the tables prepared with a meal for the crew. And their fate remains unsolved."

Ellie smiled at Jack's near photographic memory of the text. Perhaps he'd been sent down to the morgue in the *Chronicle* basement, where clippings of every conceivable subject were filed for reference. Ellie remembered the article well too. The *Zebrina* was transporting coal from Falmouth to a French port south of Cherbourg during the Great War. The ship's voyage should have taken thirty hours, but she never reached her destination. When French authorities found the ship, it was in perfect condition, but every member of the crew was missing.

"Remember the details, like the galley fire still burning? And the lifeboat still on board, along with the men's belongings?" Ellie's heart began to thud.

"Uh-huh. And the *Zebrina*'s papers and logbook were on board too."

Furrowing her brow, Ellie spoke her thoughts. "If the missing men fell victim to a German U-boat, wouldn't the Germans have blown up the *Zebrina*, just like they did so many other ships transporting coal to France?"

Jack chuckled. "The U-boat theory, though popular, is a poor theory indeed."

Ellie's stomach clenched, thinking of her father. "What do you think happened?"

He paused. "Well, it doesn't matter what I think, does it? That was twenty-eight years ago. We're fighting a new war now."

"It matters to me." Ellie's cheeks warmed as she spoke. "I care about your opinion, because I value our friendship."

Jack's voice held a smile. "Wow, kid. That might be the nicest thing anyone's ever said to me. I value our friendship too."

His words sent a tingle down her spine, all the way to her toes.

Then Jack grew contemplative. "Honestly, I think the *Zebrina* was caught in a severe gale which swept through the English Channel. If the five-man crew was on deck, then they were blown overboard, and lost to the mists of eternity."

Ellie was surprised by Jack's poetic way with words. But she felt the pain of those five families in her bones, knowing they had never stopped wondering what happened to their loved ones. She looked up at the ceiling and blinked, to keep her tears at bay.

"Say, kid." Jack's voice was empathetic. "What brought up the *Zebrina* mystery?"

With her heart pounding, Ellie found herself on the precipice of something dangerous—she was about to reveal her deepest secret to a man who wasn't Tom. But she wanted to open up to Jack; he felt safe.

"Remember how I told you I was after a story?"

"I do."

Ellie sighed. "Well, it's personal. And it's complicated. My father is missing"—her voice cracked—"but I think he's still alive. Just like the men aboard the *Zebrina*, my father and his crew disappeared after his plane was shot down over the Adriatic Sea. One crew member parachuted out, but then he died. . . ."

"I'm so sorry about your father." Jack's voice was kind. "I didn't mean—"

"It's all right." Her throat tightened, realizing the awkward position she'd put him in. Without knowing she'd been referencing her father, Jack hypothesized that the crew of the *Zebrina* had perished. But Jack didn't know about Lillian.

Ellie pinched the bridge of her nose. "Remember how I told you I was looking for an old acquaintance of my aunt's? The Follies dancer?"

He chuckled. "Miss 'rhymes with stamp.' I remember."

She swallowed, her cheeks burning. "Well, let's just say she's connected to my father. I dug deeper than I meant to, and now I'm not sure if I want the answers."

Jack paused for a moment and then spoke. "A good journalist seeks truth and reports it. And you have the makings of a good journalist. But it's up to you to decide if you want to pursue this further. I know uncertainty is a killer—but I also know what it's like when the story is personal."

"Really?" Ellie wiped away a tear, feeling grateful he hadn't pushed to know more about her father's *connection* with Lillian.

Jack sighed. "My father walked out on my family when I was a kid. I spent years wondering if he was alive or dead."

Ellie twisted the phone cord around her finger, surprised Jack would reveal something so personal. "Did you ever find him?"

"I didn't." Jack paused. "There was a time when I felt desperate; and among my relatives, there were so many rumors going around. But I decided to make peace with the fact that my father didn't want to be part of my life."

Her heart ached for Jack. "That must've been difficult."

"It was. But I want you to remember something. First, I hope your father is nothing like mine. And second, a man is only missing if he is forgotten."

Ellie smiled through her tears. *How did Jack always know the right thing to say?* "Thank you. Your words mean a lot to me."

"Anytime." Jack paused. "Take care, all right? I'm here if you need me."

Hanging up the phone, Ellie felt a bit uncomfortable, realizing she'd had an intimate conversation with a near stranger. *What would Tom think if he found out?* Ellie shut the door to her hotel room behind her. Tom wouldn't find out. And, anyway, Jack was a colleague, nothing more. She needed breakfast and a cup of coffee to think with a clear head.

In the lobby, Ellie smiled as she spotted the tabby cat, Matilda. The hotel pet came running toward her and rubbed against Ellie's legs. Ellie bent down to stroke her soft fur and looked around for Iris.

Her aunt sat at a table in the corner, wearing a navy skirt suit with a peplum jacket. She'd dressed for train travel, right down to her pillbox hat and her favorite pair of gloves. Ellie swallowed before crossing the room and taking a seat across from Iris. Iris smiled, pushing a steaming mug of coffee toward her. "I figured you'd like some."

It smelled heavenly, less watered down than the coffee at the diner in Greenwich Village. "Mmm. Thank you."

Iris nodded at Ellie's flannel slacks. "You look different today."

Ellie smiled. "I like how I feel, like Katharine Hepburn."

Iris picked up her mug. "Yesterday you said coming here was a mistake." She took a sip. "Would you like to check train departure times?"

Ellie bit her cheek. She'd come to this city of brick tenements and sleek skyscrapers, of back alleys and grand theaters, jazz clubs and neon lights, to discover the truth about her father. Though only yesterday she'd wanted to turn back, today she felt stronger. She had summoned the courage to tell Tom about her father's affair, and despite how difficult that was for her, she'd stood her ground. Ellie felt different here—alive in a way she hadn't at home in San Francisco—not since before the telegram, anyway. *What if what she needed to find was here?*

Ellie pushed down the guilt in her stomach. Tom expected her to return home and to keep quiet about her father's affair. Frank expected her back at the office, so she could brew his coffee and open his mail. And her mother expected her to be a dutiful homemaker. Ellie's father was missing, and she couldn't ask him the tough questions burning inside her. But she was twenty-four years old—old enough to think for herself.

Ellie exhaled a deep breath, the clarity of her choice exhilarating and terrifying all at once. She looked at Iris.

"I want to stay in New York. I want to find Lillian."

Chapter Fourteen

Ellie

As Ellie walked down 42nd Street, theater marquees glowed neon under dark winter skies. She could scarcely get her umbrella up against the wind, but she was filled with strong coffee and an even stronger sense of purpose. Yellow taxis sped past in sprays of water, and shoppers stood beneath hotel awnings, seeking shelter.

Tom wanted her to remember her father as a good, honorable man. But her father was more complicated than that. And right now he could be lost, wounded, or captured. Ellie needed to know if he'd parachuted out of his plane and then sent word to Lillian. Whether he'd written her coded messages in his letters or sent her a postcard from a POW camp, Ellie felt certain that Lillian had answers. She prayed her father was nothing like Jack's, and that he would never intentionally abandon their family. The pain of that thought burned like acid.

She buried her chin in the fur collar of her coat as the rain came at her sideways. Sadness must have shown on her face, because Iris gave her a reassuring smile. "That pawnbroker, unsavory as he was, gave us a good tip."

Ellie looked at Iris. "You think so?"

Iris reached out to hail a taxi. "I do."

A cab pulled over, and they both gratefully slid into the warm interior.

Iris leaned toward the driver. "The American Museum of Natural History, please." He nodded and pulled away from the curb.

Iris settled into her seat and then turned to Ellie.

"He said Lillian moved near a museum on the Upper West Side, so I suggest we start with the most famous museum on Central Park West."

Ellie nodded. "Is it near any others?"

Iris smoothed her dress. "Yes, it is. We can't go wrong."

By THE TIME the taxi pulled up in front of the Museum of Natural History, the rain had stopped, but the clouds hadn't disappeared.

Ellie frowned at the mercurial sky. "Shall we walk?"

"Why not." Iris handed the cabbie a crisp bill.

They exited the taxi, the world appearing bright and new, a small ray of sun shining on the wet pavement. Ellie looked at the sandstone fortress before her, complete with a large turret. Then she gazed across the street at the boxy gray granite structure of the New-York Historical Society.

"Right. Where should we start?"

Iris pointed. "Let's walk south."

Ellie buttoned her coat against the wind. The sheer scale of New York felt daunting. Her diamond engagement ring snagged the inside of her wool glove, and she swallowed. Tom had likely called the Algonquin to ask if she'd booked a train home. He would be so disappointed when he found out she hadn't left yet.

Approaching West 77th Street, Ellie stopped. It was tree-lined and serene, with classic town homes from the turn of the century.

"Shall we walk down this one?"

Iris shrugged. "Why not?"

Ellie remembered the pawnbroker's words: . . . *with a fresh paint job done on the front door, "robin's-egg blue," she called it.*

In this neighborhood, she felt as if she had departed New York City altogether. The four-story brownstones were stately and inviting. Some were ash white while others were pinkish. Some had awnings and some did not. Ellie slowed to a stop in front of a door that may have been blue once, but it had faded, chipped paint exposing dark wood underneath.

Ellie shook her head. "Let's keep looking."

They walked for a few blocks, past doors mostly painted black. When Ellie reached Amsterdam Avenue, she tried a door—navy, almost black—but no one answered when she rang the bell. Ellie bit her lip, looking down Amsterdam Avenue. The street became more commercial at the far end, with a jeweler, a bar, an Automat, and a Woolworth's. Like the rapidly gathering clouds, Ellie's mood was turning bleaker by the moment.

Across the street, a diner on the southwest corner of Amsterdam and 77th Street advertised cube steak sandwiches. Ellie looked at the sign in the window: Do with less so they'll have enough. She blinked back tears of frustration. She *was* doing with less, living on ration coupons and tending to her Victory garden at home, all in the hopes that the war would come to an end. But sometimes it felt as though nothing she did made any difference.

Iris winced, bending over to rub her knee.

Ellie frowned. "Are you all right?"

Iris's mouth drew down at the corners. "It's my knee—it's acting up from the cold. Do you mind if we stop for a while?"

"Not at all. Let's eat."

They crossed Amsterdam Avenue and entered the diner, the bell jingling as the door opened.

A plump waitress smiled at them.

"Welcome! Please, follow me."

She led them to a booth in the corner with a red leather bench, worn with age. Ellie slid in, and the waitress handed them two menus.

"I'll give you gals a moment."

When the waitress returned, Ellie ordered an egg salad sandwich, and Iris ordered tuna on rye. Rain began to fall outside the window, and Ellie let her eyes wander down the street. Aging brownstones framed both sides, and bicycles leaned against iron fences. Ellie's eyes widened when she made out the marquee of a storefront through the rain: Beacon Paint & Hardware. They could have known someone who completed the paint job for Lillian's building.

She turned to Iris. "There's a hardware store across the street and up the block. I'm going to pop in to ask the clerk a few questions."

Before Iris could answer, Ellie put on her coat and stepped

outside, forgetting to grab her umbrella. Her loafers slapped the pavement as she ran, and she ducked beneath the awning of Beacon Paint & Hardware, smoothing her hair.

The large plate-glass windows bore *EST 1900* in neat cursive. If the business had been in the neighborhood that long, hopefully the owner would know something. Ellie stepped inside, eyeing cans of paint stacked against the walls beneath advertisements for radios and appliances. She approached the clerk, an older man, graying at the temples. Ellie's heart went out to him, imagining he'd said goodbye to whoever used to help him in the shop, perhaps his sons or nephews.

The clerk looked up, his eyes brightening. "Welcome to Beacon Paint and Hardware. How can I help you, miss?"

Ellie removed her gloves. "Good afternoon. Do you happen to carry a paint color by the name robin's-egg blue?"

His brow furrowed. "Are you looking to buy a can?"

She smiled. "I'm looking at colors for . . . a baby's room." As she said it, Ellie flushed with heat. She didn't look pregnant. *But what would she be doing here alone in a hardware store?* Then Ellie caught herself—that was the way her mother had conditioned her to think. But if women could build planes and work in factories, surely they could be just as handy around the house as men?

The older gentleman returned her smile, his eyes crinkling at the corners. "Congratulations to you and your fella. Now, Glidden, Moore, and Acme all have a nice range of blues. But none have robin's-egg in the name."

Ellie frowned. "Oh. Would another store carry that color?"

He chuckled. "We carry the best selection of house paint in New York. If you can't find it here, you won't find it anywhere."

Ellie's stomach began to sink. Lillian must have come up with the description of a robin's egg herself. She probably had a flair for the dramatic.

"Here." The clerk pulled three thick pieces of card stock off a hook.

He spread the paint samples across the counter, each card painted with dozens of thumb-sized streaks of color.

He pointed to a light blue with his thumb. "This here's called Stratford blue, and this here is powder blue."

Ellie shook her head. They were both too gray.

The store clerk pushed the card aside. "All right. Here's Acme's paint colors: cashmere blue, Wedgewood blue, and—"

"What's that one?" Ellie pointed to the card for Moore Paints. The color was delicate turquoise, just like a robin's egg.

"That's skyline blue. Are you expecting a little fella, then?"

Ellie managed a smile. "Um, that's what we're hoping for." The lie made her shoulders tense uncomfortably. Tom would want children soon. But pretending to be expecting didn't bring on a sense of excitement or joy. In fact, Ellie felt a twinge of dread when she considered the loss of freedom a child would bring. How could she write a newspaper column and care for a baby at the same time?

"Do you happen to know if anyone has purchased this color from you within the last year?"

The clerk rubbed his chin. "My pal Ed bought a gallon of skyline blue a while back. He runs Paterno's Painting."

Ellie felt a swell of hope. "Do you remember the job?"

His grizzled face looked perplexed. "Oh, say, it's been months now. I think it was for a town house on West Seventy-Sixth Street. The building owner wanted to spruce up the place."

"Thank you!" Ellie turned on her heel.

"Wait just a minute, now. Do you want his number?"

Ellie felt bad for leaving the hardware clerk with no explanation as the door slammed shut behind her. She hurried across the street and opened the door to the diner, the bell jingling in her wake. She slid into the booth across from Iris.

Iris set down her sandwich. "Any luck?"

"The store clerk told me he sold a gallon of light blue paint to someone who did a job on West Seventh-Sixth Street. Let's go."

"To be honest, I'm quite tired. Maybe we should leave it for a different day." But Iris didn't look tired—she looked nervous.

Ellie stiffened, remembering how Iris had dragged her feet throughout their search, staying silent at the Ziegfeld Club and seeming relieved when Lillian wasn't at her first address. And Iris's words when she first showed her the stack of letters Lillian had written—*you and your mother have been through so much. Perhaps it's best to tuck these letters away for now.*

"But this is why we've come! And besides, Seventy-Sixth isn't far."

Her aunt grimaced as she pressed a hand against her chest.

Ellie froze. "Are you having chest pains?"

Iris took a deep breath in, and then let it out. "No. It's only my nerves."

A prickle of unease crept up Ellie's spine. "What's making you nervous?"

Iris toyed with her teabag. "Now that we're getting so close . . . I'm not sure if I'm ready to see Lillian just yet."

Ellie's stomach knotted. "What aren't you telling me?"

Iris's blue eyes filled with remorse. "Remember when I told you I gave Dorothy King my diamond necklace and earrings?"

Ellie nodded.

"Lillian saw me do it. And the consequences of my actions were fatal."

Chapter Fifteen

Iris

The top-floor apartment at 144 West 57th Street became my prison. Days went by in a blur, and it became clear I had no way to escape. Like clockwork, John's black Bentley would arrive in the morning and park on the street below. Then Wilson would emerge smoking a cigarette, and he'd stand sentry outside the building, day and night, just in case I managed to unlock the door. Any time Wilson took a break from his post, John was with me. Every minute of every day, I was watched.

Cooped up inside, I paced from room to room, listening to the elevated train rattling down 6th Avenue and watching the trail of cars snaking along 57th Street like ants. I missed dining at restaurants, chatting with friends over coffee, and dancing up a sweat at the newest jazz joint. I missed being onstage and the satisfaction of nailing a new routine. But mostly, I missed my family.

John had planned everything perfectly—Ziegfeld thought I

was traveling to San Francisco, while my family didn't know I had intended to. Clara believed I was going about my day in New York, while my friends in the Follies thought I was aboard an ocean liner somewhere in the Caribbean. Blinking back tears, I looked through the glass at the street below.

Christmas wreaths hung in shop windows, and my heart ached seeing the cheerful decorations. I ought to have sent a Christmas card to Clara and William, and a present for Eleanor. I hadn't thought to, because I'd intended to surprise them with a visit instead. Now my family would think I had forgotten them, or worse—that I didn't care.

John threatened to harm them if I ever left him. Even though my family was in San Francisco, I didn't doubt his powerful reach. That Christmas Eve, I felt lonelier than I ever had in my life.

"I must return to Boston tonight." John adjusted his gold cuff links and then looked at me. "Wilson will keep an eye on you."

Philadelphia, not Boston.

But I wouldn't tell him I knew who he really was. Being the mistress of J. Kearsley Mitchell would only put me in more danger.

John's eyes glinted. "And remember, Iris. I'm watching."

I searched his face for any trace of the man who had swept me off my feet. My voice quavered. "If you truly loved me, you wouldn't force me to stay here, like a prisoner. I *truly* cared for you. Why are you doing this to me?"

He pulled me close, his mouth inches from mine. "I don't know what you're talking about. I treat you like a princess."

And with that, John slammed the door, off to spend the Christmas holiday with his wife and children. Even though he'd locked me inside the apartment, I wept with relief. I felt safer away from him, and cringed remembering how enamored I'd been when he talked about Russian literature, French wine, and Viennese art. I had thought him to be so refined, and he told me I was his muse.

How did it take me so long to see him for what he was? John understood how to act like a gentleman and how to blend in to polite society, but he had no empathy for others. He was nothing but a brilliant mimic.

I looked down at my wrist, the soft, pale skin chafed from the diamond and pearl bracelet encircling it like a manacle. I struggled to unbuckle the platinum clasp with my shaking fingers. The bracelet popped open, and I flung it across the room, where it landed with a satisfying clack on the hardwood floor.

There, I was no one's *pet* anymore.

I AWOKE TO the sound of footsteps and slipped on my silk robe, wrapping my arms around my waist. Pushing open the bedroom door, I let out a startled gasp.

The woman in the living room straightened her spine, her light eyes flinty beneath her white cap. "My name is Mary O'Connell, and I am in the employ of Mr. Marshall. He's given me strict orders that you aren't to leave the premises."

She sounded like a Dubliner, like my mother. Her body was wiry and small, practically swimming in her black dress and white pinafore. I couldn't tell if she was forty or fifty, but her face bore the markings of hardship.

I smiled, hoping she'd warm to me. "I'm Iris. It's a pleasure to meet you. Merry Christmas."

The maid sniffed in response. "Stay out of my way."

My heart went out to her. *Didn't she have her own family to spend the holiday with?* Perhaps she was indebted to John, and as loyal to him as Mr. Wilson. I walked into the kitchen, where the scent of chicken soup hit me, and hungrily poured a ladle of the homemade broth into a bowl.

After finishing my soup, I watched Mary mop the front room and cleared my throat. "Thank you. That was delicious."

She lifted her eyes but didn't reply. Would I be able to force my way past her? She was small, but likely stronger than she looked. And I felt so weak and tired. Instead, I retreated to the bedroom.

The hours passed by slowly. I read from John's copy of *War and Peace*, wishing he'd brought my Jane Austen and Emily Brontë novels. While I waited for Mary to finish her chores, the sun made its way across the sky. I moved on to *Crime and Punishment*. I could have finished cleaning this apartment in less than half the time. But Mary wasn't an ordinary maid—she was my warden.

Finally, when the clock struck six, she left. Setting down my book, I walked to the window overlooking the street, where Mary crossed below—a free woman. She was done watching me for the day, but Wilson hadn't yet appeared to stand guard for the night shift. I tried jimmying the lock with a kitchen knife and then threw it down in frustration. The churlish maid had been given the apartment key, and now it was her responsibility to lock me inside for the night, while Wilson made sure I never left the building, should I somehow succeed in picking the lock.

The days that followed were monotonous, and I feared I might lose my mind.

More than once, I tried to get Mary to talk. *Where in Ireland did she come from? Who was her favorite celebrity in* Photoplay *magazine? Did she have any children?* But she was like a locked vault. Thankfully, she brought the newspaper daily, and I read through it after she'd finished, hungry for information.

Mary only cooked low-calorie foods like cabbage soup, obeying John's orders to keep me slim. I'd followed strict diets before when I was performing in the Follies, but suddenly I felt ravenous. *Who could live off citrus fruits, salads, and hard-boiled eggs alone?* Even so, now that I was no longer dancing, my body began to soften, my thighs thickening and my stomach rounding.

My mouth watered as I dreamed of the Italian pasta at my favorite Lower East Side speakeasy, tucked in among the fishmongers and pushcarts on Houston Street.

The wife served spaghetti with meatballs on tables with checkered cloths, while her husband made wine in the basement. I craved their clams stuffed with buttered herb crumbs, veal cutlets cooked with Parmesan, and shrimp sautéed with wine and garlic. Sometimes, my hunger was enough to make me cry.

That night, I awoke to the sounds of raucous celebration— laughter, glass breaking, and cars honking. *What in the devil?* Then I realized—it was New Year's Eve. While all Manhattan feted the year 1923, I sat shivering in bed. The apartment had become bitter cold.

Shutting my eyes, I tossed and turned, trying to fall back asleep. Were Hilda and Lou dancing on tabletops in satin heels and beaded dresses, swilling champagne? They lived on this very block at the Great Northern Hotel, only a short walk away, yet the distance stretched like an eternity. The things I'd valued—fame and fortune—I didn't want them anymore. I only wanted my freedom from John.

A FEW DAYS later, he returned to the apartment smelling of scotch, standing before me in the doorway in his tailored black suit. His pale blue eyes traced my body, and he looked at me with disgust.

"You look a wreck."

I hadn't washed or styled my hair, bathed, sprayed myself with perfume, or applied any makeup. I didn't need to look at myself in the mirror to know I looked dreadful. I hoped I repulsed him as much as he repulsed me.

I glared. "So what if I do?"

He grabbed my arm and pinched the flesh so hard I yelped. "You stink. Is this any way to greet me? Get in the bath."

I tried to yank my arm away, but his grip was firm.

His eyes narrowed. "If you are good and obey, everything will be fine. Now, get in the bath."

He shoved me, and I stumbled to the bathroom. He followed me inside, sending a shiver down my spine. I crossed my arms. "Some privacy would be nice."

He sneered at me. "Take off your clothes, like you used to onstage."

I watched his eyes become hard. "John, please."

He traced his finger along my jawline, causing me to flinch. "I want you as soon as you are clean."

I made my mind go blank while slowly unbuttoning my dress and then letting it drop. I peeled down the straps of my silk brassiere, shimmying until the garment fell to the ground.

Then I slowly lowered myself into the bath, with John watching me.

He unbuttoned his cuff links and rolled up his sleeves. Taking a heavy bar of soap in his hands, he ran it up my leg from my ankle to my thigh, until he was brushing the spot that had once caused my body to betray me.

He smiled. "You like that, don't you?"

Never had I been so disgusted, but I didn't dare move. *Would he hurt me?* I took a deep breath, my heart pounding in fear. Instead, he unzipped his pants.

His voice was hoarse. "You don't deserve me. Do you know how many women would love to pleasure me? Now, don't act like it's a chore."

I squeezed my eyes shut and did as I was told. I had an odd sensation, like I was floating outside my body, watching myself from somewhere up high. This woman inside her beautiful apartment overlooking Carnegie Hall had countless furs, diamonds, and designer gowns. But there was nothing enviable about her life.

When John finished, I vomited over the side of the tub. He stood up, zipped his pants, and left me alone and weeping in the bath. I got out, toweled myself off, and found him waiting for me in the bedroom. A beautiful crepe georgette evening dress with a silver sash was laid across the bed.

He smiled. "I bought this for you. It's Chanel."

I nodded dumbly.

His eyes passed over my curves, and he sneered. "Aren't you going to thank me? I expect you to wear this dress tomorrow night. We're attending a party at the Brevoort."

"Thank you." My voice came out in a whisper.

I thought back on the times we'd spent together in the West Village, sipping champagne while John talked with the Brevoort's owner, Raymond. He was fond of the Frenchman and never missed one of his parties. Café Brevoort served up haute French cuisine to everyone who was anyone in New York City, and parties at the hotel were the place to see and be seen. Everyone from socialites to celebrities to visiting European royalty attended.

Mercifully, John fell into a deep slumber, uninterested in humiliating me again. I lay awake, too frightened to breathe, unable to make the queasy feeling in my stomach go away. Pleasuring John disgusted me, but I still felt physically sick. Finally, I fell into a fitful sleep, and dreamed of sinister things.

THE NEXT MORNING, I applied rouge and lipstick and wore a yellow dress—John's favorite. I'd lost my will to fight. I let him lecture me about Rachmaninoff and Rasputin as I served him scotch. When I vomited again after breakfast, I began to worry. John would be furious if I couldn't attend tonight's party. I washed my mouth with water and sprayed perfume in the bathroom, hiding the sour scent.

When darkness fell, my stomach roiled after a measly dinner of cabbage soup. Meanwhile, John dined on filet mignon and roasted potatoes. I ran to the toilet to vomit again. The soup came back up in a stream of burning green bile.

John stared at me with disgust. "Clean yourself up. We leave in ten minutes."

I'd managed to shimmy myself into the Chanel dress he'd bought me, though the hook and eye closure at the side barely fastened. Now I knelt on the cool tile of the bathroom floor, hugging the rim of the toilet.

"John. I'm sick. I can't go."

Had I caught a stomach bug? I didn't feel feverish at all, but I had a niggling feeling something wasn't right.

His nostrils flared. "I've spent the last five months grooming you to be a mistress worthy of me. And you look awful."

I couldn't stop the tears from coming. I wiped my eyes, knowing I'd smudged kohl and mascara all over my face, and vomited again. Shaking, I stood up, turned on the tap, and drank some water. I had to flatter him, and quickly.

"I'm so sorry. I know I look dreadful. You shouldn't be seen with me." I gently touched the lapels of his suit. "You ought to go to the party without me. Raymond is expecting you. And you two always have such a laugh."

He gripped my wrists hard, his ice-blue eyes boring into mine. "Next time you break plans with me, there will be consequences."

My heart thudded. "I understand. I will never do it again."

He released my wrists, and I held my breath. Then I picked up the gold pocket square he'd laid on the bed, gently folded it, and tucked it into his suit.

"There. You look so handsome."

I prayed my tone was the right mix of apologetic, flattering, and demure. John looked me up and down and then curled his lip. "You look like a sow in that dress. What have you been eating?"

"Only what you allow me to." That was the truth. I'd never been hungrier, and yet I was still bloated in my stomach and hips.

John straightened his lapel. "I'll return at midnight."

He left the apartment, slamming the door behind him. Hearing his key turn in the lock, I breathed a deep sigh, sinking to the floor. Then I reached beneath my armpit and unhooked the dress, gratefully slipping out of it. I went to bed wearing my loose silk pajamas, and prayed John wouldn't touch me when he came back.

At two o'clock in the morning, John entered the room, waking me. I squeezed my eyes shut and kept the rhythm of my breathing even. He was two hours late—he must have enjoyed himself. John settled next to me in bed, grunting as he turned over. I smelled scotch on his breath, but also something else: musk, roses, jasmine, and patchouli—the unmistakable scent of Dorothy King's perfume.

My body went rigid. *Had she been at that party?* Hilda and Lou had described Dot as an infamous social climber who would do anything for money and status. The Hotel Brevoort was certainly the right place to find a wealthy suitor. But Dot King hadn't gone there in search of just anyone . . .

I covered my mouth. This was my fault.

My words that day outside the New Amsterdam Theatre, after I'd given Dot my diamond necklace, came back to haunt me:

Courtesy of Mr. John Marshall. You can have him too.

Chapter Sixteen

Ellie

NEW YORK, 1945

The diner's greasy tabletops slowly came back into focus. Ellie felt the hairs on the backs of her arms stand up. She tried to swallow, but her mouth was dry. Her voice came out barely above a whisper.

"But when you said, 'You can have him too,' you didn't really mean it."

Iris's mouth twisted into a grimace. She blinked back tears, looking up at the ceiling. "It was never my intention for anyone to get hurt."

Ellie reached across the table. "Iris."

Iris wasn't to blame here. She was a victim of that horrid man. Did Iris think John Marshall had murdered Dorothy King? Is that what she meant by fatal consequences? Ellie shuddered, remembering the newspaper article she'd read at the Ziegfeld Club, which described how Dorothy King was found in her stylish apartment on 57th Street, on the top floor of a five-story brownstone a few doors east of Carnegie Hall.

Ellie rubbed her arms. She didn't want to think about *that* apartment and whether Iris had, however unintentionally, involved Dot King with a murderer.

She looked at Iris. "You're worried because Lillian saw you give Dorothy King your diamond necklace?"

Iris nodded. "And Lillian heard me say John's name. I'd never named him before—not even to Lou or Hilda. We always called him the *big cheese*. I don't know why I said his name to Dot—I wasn't thinking."

Frowning, Ellie looked down at her hands. She didn't think it was Iris's fault—her aunt had simply spoken in the heat of the moment.

"But that doesn't mean he murdered her. He was horrible to you, but do you really think he was capable of taking a human life?"

Iris blinked back tears, her lip trembling. Ellie swallowed, waiting for her aunt to answer. Iris had kept her past buried, until Ellie burst in to her apartment carrying a stack of letters and uttering a name Iris hadn't heard in years. Once again, Ellie felt sad that her aunt hadn't felt comfortable confiding in her, and then guilty for inadvertently releasing a flood of memories Iris didn't want to relive.

"Here's the check." The friendly, plump waitress set a receipt down on the table, startling them both.

"Thank you." Ellie opened her coin purse. Iris composed herself and smiled tightly at the waitress.

The afternoon sun wouldn't last much longer, and though

Ellie wanted to hear more about John Marshall, she could see from her aunt's body language that Iris was done talking for the day. Telling the story had upset her.

Ellie hadn't forgotten why they had come to this neighborhood in the first place. She'd been absorbed in Iris's story, but now, realizing how close they were to finding Lillian, Ellie pictured her father, with his soft curly hair and warm amber eyes that looked so much like her own—*How could he have done this to her?* The pain of his betrayal smarted like a broken bone.

During family meals in San Francisco, sometimes the telephone rang, and even as a child, Ellie could sense tension in the air. Dinners had always been formal. Her mother and father would have a cocktail alone in the living room. Then they'd sit down to a table laid with linen, silverware, and candles. Ellie's mother had taught her to be a lady, sitting ramrod straight with a napkin in her lap, like a proper Irish Catholic.

And Ellie had obeyed. She'd been tidy, punctual, and quiet. She made her bed every morning, and she tried to please her parents. But whenever the telephone rang, she got nervous, knowing her mother would become angry. Yet she'd done nothing wrong. Funny, how these memories were coming to her now.

By the time her parents had settled into middle age, Ellie doubted they still shared romantic love, but she thought they shared a commitment to modesty, honesty, and family. She thought in their way, they'd been happy. And she'd been wrong. *If what her parents had wasn't real, then what was?*

Ellie took a deep breath, looking Iris in the eye. "This is difficult for me too. But we can do this. We'll confront Lillian together."

And Lucy. Ellie's heart began to thud, thinking about meeting her potential half sister face-to-face. *Would she be funny and unpretentious like their father?* If they truly were sisters, once the initial shock wore off, Ellie hoped she and Lucy could get to know each other.

Iris nodded, her gaze determined. "Together."

Bracing themselves against the wind, they walked arm in arm down Amsterdam Avenue. A longshoreman in a wool overcoat and a derby cap sat outside an Automat, listening to his portable radio. Ellie caught fragments of news about the war. They walked past diners, jewelers, and barbershops. The neighborhood grew a bit rougher around the edges. *What would Tom do when he found out she hadn't left New York?*

Ellie gritted her teeth. She couldn't think about Tom now. But her entire faith in marriage—and in men—had been shaken. Anger rippled through her, feeling the immense pain Lillian had caused her family. Ellie had idolized her father; she'd thrown her arms around him every time he returned home, eager to touch his pilot's wings and hear his stories. Lillian had turned him from a hero into a flawed man.

William Morgan knew how to take complex scientific information and break it down simply so Ellie could understand. She could still hear his voice, explaining, *"You have two enemies, clear ice and rime ice."* He'd taught her about cold fronts, warm fronts, and occluded fronts, and how important it was to maintain flying speed.

Ellie blinked back tears. Her father meticulously studied every aircraft he flew, and he knew how to improvise in difficult moments. But the cockpit of his B-24 Liberator would not have been easy to escape. The B-24, with its four engines, flew faster and farther than a B-17, but it had its weaknesses.

Ellie had read about the B-24 Liberator in her father's copies of *Aeroplane* magazine. The corridor that ran down the plane was cramped and narrow, and it would be difficult for a man with a parachute strapped to his back to fit through. Yet one of Father's men—possibly more—had parachuted out. There was still hope that he was alive and that Lillian knew where he was right now.

When they reached West 76th Street, Ellie braced herself. The street was quiet, winter sunlight filtering between the tall, narrow buildings. A bicycle sat chained to a railing, and every old brownstone had a staircase bordered by regal iron bannisters. The double doors on the buildings looked heavy and formidable.

Brown, black, dull brown—then Ellie stopped, drawing in her breath. There, at number 152, the door was an unmistakable shade of robin's-egg blue.

"Iris." Ellie's feet rooted to the concrete. "Look."

Iris covered her mouth. "That's *very* blue."

Ellie looked up at the stately Romanesque revival row house. She forced one foot in front of the other until she was climbing the stairs, and she noticed that a window on the parlor floor had been left open, right next to the stoop. Though it was only cracked open a few inches, if the building owners weren't careful, the lower unit could get robbed. Four doorbells had metal placards nailed above them. And there, next to number 1A, was the name she'd been looking for:

Dell, Lillian.

Ellie was shaking. She practiced the words she'd repeated in her mind: *You hurt me. You hurt my mother. That's all I need to know about you. But if you know anything about my father's whereabouts, you must tell me.* She glanced behind her to make sure Iris was still there. Iris stood with her gloved hands clasped in front of her, looking as nervous and pale as Ellie felt. Storm clouds had begun to gather again. Ellie's heart pounded, but she forced herself to press the bell.

The ring echoed in the empty lobby. Minutes ticked past like hours. Then a figure was walking down the hallway, and Ellie steeled herself, her body holding as much fear as it held anger. A woman appeared on the other side of the glass, her green eyes striking, framed by crow's-feet, her eyebrows plucked into thin arches. Though she'd aged by decades, she still resembled the woman in the photograph.

Lillian.

The woman pulled the door open, then froze. Her green wool dress was perfectly tailored and nipped in at the waist. Her eyes widened, meeting Ellie's.

Blood rushed in Ellie's ears like the ocean. And then she spoke. "My name is Eleanor Morgan. Are you Lillian Dell?"

Lillian's mouth twitched. "I am. And I know who you are. I thought this day might come." She lifted her chin. "Come inside."

Ellie stepped over the threshold into the lobby, beneath a large brass chandelier. Iris followed her. The heavy door clicked shut behind them.

"Iris." Lillian's mouth formed a wry smile. "I didn't expect to see you again."

"Likewise." Iris's normally warm voice was dry as sand.

Lillian walked down the narrow hallway with the grace of a

woman who could still dance. Ellie gritted her teeth, observing everything from Lillian's shapely legs to her small waist and her shiny hair, a deep shade of brown. *So this was the woman her father had risked everything for?* She seethed with anger.

Lillian opened the door to her parlor-floor apartment and led them inside.

"Sit wherever you like."

A pink velvet love seat perched beneath the bay window overlooking the street, and camel leather club chairs framed either side of an antique coffee table. A vintage Persian rug felt soft beneath Ellie's feet as she walked toward the sofa, past bookshelves crowded with novels. Silver picture frames adorned the walls, filled with photographs and abstract art, and plants spilled their tendrils everywhere. Pillows of all prints and textures were strewn about, making Ellie feel like she'd entered some kind of bazaar. She moved a zebra-striped pillow aside to sit on the love seat.

Ellie's heart ached with unexpected loyalty toward her mother. The bohemian feel of Lillian's apartment stood in stark contrast to Clara's sparse and bare aesthetic, where a wooden crucifix hung in every room. Ellie's mother believed setting out her best linens and silver, keeping everything uncluttered and clean, meant she was creating the "right" kind of home.

Lillian's sofa was too firm, and Ellie shifted her weight against the tufted seat. Then she felt a breeze and realized Lillian hadn't shut her window properly. This was the same parlor-floor window she'd noticed earlier, from the stoop. Her heart continued to thud. Iris sat down beside her in a show of solidarity Ellie was grateful for.

Lillian walked over to a brass bar cart and removed the

stopper from a crystal decanter. "Drink? I believe this visit calls for vodka."

"No, thank you." Ellie spoke through clenched teeth.

Lillian pursed her lips. "Iris? For old times' sake?"

"Why not." Iris shared a look with Lillian. "Make it neat."

Ellie's hands trembled as she watched Lillian pour two vodkas. Lillian gave one to Iris and then took a seat in one of the leather club chairs.

Ellie wanted to shout the words she'd practiced. She was so, so angry. But instead, everything came out unrehearsed. "Why did you do it?"

Lillian paused, took a sip of her drink, and then let out a sigh. Ellie wanted to slap the lipstick off her perfectly made-up face.

"Because Billy and I were in love."

"*Billy?*" Ellie couldn't hide the disgust in her voice. No one had ever called her father by that nickname. Will perhaps, but never Billy.

Lillian lowered her eyes. "Eleanor, you're a grown woman now. You might as well know your father and I were two consenting adults."

Ellie clenched her fists, her nails digging into her palms. "With no regards for who you hurt. What about me? What about my mother? Didn't you think about us?"

Lillian looked chastened. "Of course."

"And yet you carried on anyway." Ellie's face grew hot, and she stared at Lillian's long crimson nails, painted in a stylish half-moon manicure. *Like the tramp that you are,* she wanted to add. But then she stopped herself. Her father was just as much to blame here as Lillian, though she hated to admit it.

Lillian's eyes narrowed, accentuating her feline look. "There's a lot you don't know about your father. I stayed with him because he asked me to. I gave him intimacy, both physical and emotional, that he wasn't getting at home."

"How dare you." Ellie's voice trembled. But the truth of Lillian's words pierced the air between them. Clara had never been affectionate.

Ellie's body felt tight as a coil. "Did you ever call my father at home?"

"Sometimes." Lillian sipped her vodka.

The burn of humiliation seared Ellie's skin. Her mother was deeply religious and the church was her solace. If her mother had known about the affair, it would have killed her. But maybe it hadn't, and instead had turned Clara into a bitter and hateful person who took her anger out on Ellie. Tears clogged Ellie's throat. It explained so much.

"You had no right to do that." Ellie's voice trembled. "Why couldn't you leave us alone?"

Lillian squared her shoulders. "Because I loved him! Your father promised me so many things. I wanted to be the pilot's wife. I wanted to live in the house overlooking the ocean. He's Lucy's father. Did you know *that?*"

Ellie recoiled. Pain gripped her chest like talons, and she heard buzzing in her ears.

It wasn't true. It couldn't be true. And yet, all along, she'd suspected that it was.

Ellie tried breathing in through her nose and exhaling through her mouth to slow her heartbeat. She felt Iris's palm rubbing circles on her back. But through her blurry vision she managed to breathe one question. "How?"

Lillian spoke slowly.

"I fell pregnant five years after the affair began. Billy visited New York as often as he could. When Lucy was born, he was overjoyed to be a father again. He bought her a silver toy plane, and he cheered her on as she took her first steps. Over the years, as she grew, he helped her with her schoolwork."

Lillian smiled, but her eyes held sadness. "Lucy would put on plays for us when she was little. We'd get Chinese takeout in my Greenwich Village flat and eat dinner together. Then afterward, we'd go for ice cream. Lucy called your father Papa. He always let her win at checkers. We were a family."

Ellie's heart broke with every detail. No matter what she wanted to tell herself, the reality was this: her father had loved this other family.

Lillian wiped away a tear. In her grief, she looked older.

"There were times when Billy told me he wished he could leave your mother. But he didn't believe in divorce, and I was desperate to be acknowledged, so I phoned him at home."

"That's enough." Iris put her arm protectively around Ellie's shoulders. "You don't need to listen to any more of this."

Ellie looked at Lillian's tear-streaked face. She wanted to hate this woman, but she recognized something—her father had manipulated Lillian too. Ellie rubbed her temples, her head spinning. The very foundation she had built her life upon was crumbling. Everything her father had taught her about love, about planes, about paddling a canoe—it all seemed suddenly false and corrupt.

"Where is Lucy?" Ellie had to see her with her own eyes.

Lillian lifted her chin. "I asked her to pick up my tap shoes from the repair shop after school." She laughed dryly, looking at Iris. "My daughter is a high school senior and I'm still a tap-dancing instructor. Theater work isn't easy to come by these days."

Iris's face was hard, but she nodded in agreement.

Ellie's hands shook as she spoke. In the midst of how frightened and confused she felt right now, she hadn't forgotten why she'd come.

"I don't know why my father strayed. But from the number of letters you sent him, he must have also written letters to you. I want to see them."

Lillian's mouth fell open. "You found my letters to your father? I don't understand."

Ellie drew in a sharp breath, the reality hitting her for the first time: Lillian wasn't family, so she hadn't received an official telegram. *But if her father had contacted Lillian since then, he would have mentioned his plane crash.* An icy-cold feeling came over her. She never imagined she would be the person to break this devastating news. *Lillian didn't know about the crash.* Ellie tried to keep her voice steady as she spoke, but she was beginning to panic.

"The army sent his belongings in a box. A jacket of his was in there, with your letters inside. We got a telegram. His plane was shot down over the Adriatic Sea."

The color drained from Lillian's face. She covered her mouth with a trembling hand. "*No,*" Lillian whispered. "Dear God, no."

"Please." Ellie's voice was desperate. "I haven't heard from him since November. Please tell me he's sent you another letter since then."

Lillian doubled over at the waist, a wail escaping her throat, and Ellie's stomach clenched as she prayed. *Please, please, tell me he's written something, anything.*

Lillian looked up, her green eyes rimmed with red.

"I haven't heard from Billy in months."

Chapter Seventeen

Ellie

Ellie sat there, horrified. Never in a million years did she expect to be united in her grief with Lillian. Panic welled up inside
her like a tidal wave.

"You haven't heard from him?" Ellie's voice rose in pitch.
"When did he send his last letter to you?"

Lillian wiped her eyes. "November fifth. He wrote that he
missed me, and he missed Lucy, and he hoped the war would end
soon. Oh, Billy."

Jealousy heated Ellie's skin like something insidious. Father
had written to Lillian *before* he'd written to her. *What if he'd loved
Lillian and Lucy more than he'd loved her?* Had he shared the
same sentiments with both of them? Ellie's father was the man
she trusted most in the world, and he was not entirely a good
person.

"Please." Ellie licked her dry lips. "May I see my father's letters? I have to know what he said to you. I *need* to know."

Lillian's mouth formed a thin line. "Those are private."

Ellie shifted her weight on the love seat, its buttons poking her thighs.

"What if he mentioned something, like the tail number of his plane? He could still be out there—captured by the Germans. I've been trying to track him down."

Lillian's eyes softened. "I want to believe he's alive too, Eleanor. And I'm grateful for your efforts. But he didn't share anything like that. You know his mail is censored."

A lump rose in Ellie's throat. She wanted to despise Lillian for everything. And yet Lillian was the only person to share her hope that her father was alive. Both of them needed him to come home—wherever his home was.

The building door slammed, startling them into silence. Ellie locked eyes with Iris as footsteps sounded in the hallway.

Lillian wiped her eyes, quickly composing herself.

"If you say anything to hurt Lucy, I'll never forgive you. It's bad enough that you're here without warning."

The knob turned, and the door to Lillian's apartment opened. A teenage girl entered the living room, carrying a paper bag marked Saul's Shoe Repair. She looked up, and her hazel eyes met Ellie's. Everything moved in slow motion, and Ellie heard her heartbeat thudding in her ears. The planes of Lucy's face, her straight nose, her high cheekbones, the shape of her eyes—Ellie recognized them as her own.

"Mom?" Lucy dropped the bag to the ground. "Who are they?"

Lillian put an arm protectively around Lucy's shoulders. "That's your half sister, Eleanor, and that's her aunt, Iris."

Ellie stared at Lucy, who stared back with eyes of liquid fire. Lucy's voice was at once familiar and new. Her auburn hair was pulled back at the sides, and she wore a camel-colored, double-breasted wool trench coat with a tie belt. She was beautiful, in that awkward teenage way where she didn't yet know it. But she also possessed an air of confidence. Ellie felt paralyzed, simultaneously wanting to wrap her sister in a hug and to close her eyes and make her go away.

"What are they doing here?" Lucy's eyes widened, like a frightened animal, and then narrowed. She stared at Ellie as if she were ready to fight.

Ellie's voice cracked. "I wanted to meet your mother. I wanted to see for myself if you were really my sister."

But Ellie already knew. She could feel it in her soul. She felt like she was going to cry, not from sadness but from the sense she had returned to a familiar place after being gone a long time.

Lucy scoffed. "Because you didn't know about me, right? But I always knew about *you*. Papa kept my existence secret for your sake! I couldn't even tell anyone he was my father."

Ellie's heart plummeted. Lucy was only seventeen or eighteen, not equipped to deal with any of this. Being a young woman was hard enough. While Ellie held bragging rights to the best father in the world, Lucy had grown up without that. What did she tell children at school? *Was she teased for being fatherless? Or had Lillian lied and pretended she was married, in order to protect Lucy?*

Lucy's lip quivered and her eyes filled with tears. "I only got to see him in bits and pieces. And I had to share him with you!"

Lucy covered her face with her hands and ran out of the room, slamming the door behind her. Lillian set down her glass on the coffee table, shot Ellie a look that could wither flowers, and followed. Lucy's sobs filled the apartment, and Ellie heard Lillian murmuring something in a voice too low to make out.

Guilt crept through Ellie like poison in her veins. As painful as this was for her, Lucy had every right to be angry. Ellie had her father's last name. She had gone to Sunday matinees with him, gone on camping trips to Lake Tahoe and on special visits to the San Francisco Airport to sit in the cockpit of his plane.

Ellie was the pilot's daughter.

Meanwhile, who was Lucy? *A bastard?* Tears pressed against Ellie's eyelids. Her father's affair had hurt so many people.

Ellie wanted to knock on the bedroom door and to wrap her arms around Lucy. But Lucy didn't want her touch or her pity. How cruel that all these years Ellie had spent her time lonely and lost in books, pining for a sibling. Ellie swallowed the lump in her throat. *Did her mother know about Lucy?*

Lillian returned and crossed her arms over her chest. "Lucy's had a terrible shock and now she's miserable. Are you happy?"

The fire had gone from Ellie's voice. "No. Not at all."

Grief, anger, and sadness flooded her. She'd been robbed of a relationship with her sister, someone she desperately wanted to know. Ellie wanted to discover if they had idiosyncrasies, like the same smile, or the same laugh, a shared sense of humor. She thought back to Lillian's letters, describing Lucy's love of performing and watching films. What parts of Lucy were like their father? What traits did Ellie and Lucy share?

Lillian turned to Ellie, her eyes defiant. "I want to show you something." She retreated to a bedroom and then returned holding a photograph.

"You see? We were a family too."

Ellie's throat tightened. In the picture, her father wore his army uniform, and he had his arms around both Lillian and Lucy. It had been taken perhaps five years ago, at the start of the war. The three of them stood smiling, in the middle of a park. Looking at the photograph, Ellie felt an uncomfortable mixture of resentment and shame. Her father had kept his families on separate coasts, leaving both yearning for more of him.

"How could you do this?" Iris's voice rose in anger. "You knew William was married to my sister when you met him."

Lillian scoffed. "You're one to talk."

Ellie placed a hand on Iris's arm. She didn't need her aunt to fight her battles for her. "How did the affair begin?"

Lillian looked wistful. "The night I met your father, I stayed at the hotel into the early hours of the morning. He was unlike anyone I'd ever met. Broadway was full of charlatans and swindlers. Billy was something else—smart, genuine, and funny."

Ellie clenched her teeth. "What did you do to make him cheat?"

Lillian glared. "I didn't *do* anything. We enjoyed each other's company so much, I told him to contact me the next time he was in New York."

Ellie blinked back tears. "And he did?"

Lillian looked down at her nails. "He did. We had so much

in common. We both enjoyed crossword puzzles, playing chess, and discussing politics. There was an undeniable spark between us, and we both could feel it. He had a lot of stress at home, with a small child, and your mother—"

"Don't talk about my mother." Ellie's voice came out loud and angry. No matter Clara's faults, Ellie would defend her.

Lillian smiled sadly. "We tried to fight our attraction to each other. But the pull was too strong. I gave your father what your mother couldn't—love, intellectual conversation, spontaneity, and fun."

Ellie quickly came to her mother's defense. "Because *you* weren't the one home alone raising a small child!"

Clara was cold, a nag, and so many other things, but she had done the best she could. Christian women were taught to be pious, to fear sex, to bear children, and to keep a clean and modest home. But had Clara been beautiful once? Fun? Kind?

Ellie's mother had given so much, volunteering for every church activity and potluck, making sure dinner was on the table, and clothes were washed and folded. She showed love in the only way she knew how.

Ellie blinked back tears, feeling a rush of empathy for her mother. Clara was stern because she believed in heaven and hell, and she wanted to be a "good" wife. But that had pushed William away, and he was drawn to Lillian with her intellectual curiosity and her bohemian ideals. Her father wanted to feel free, just as Iris had.

"Unbelievable." Iris pursed her lips. "I let you come along with me that night because I thought you could be decent."

Lillian laughed. "Decent? Take a look at yourself. You danced on that stage right alongside me."

Ellie frowned at Lillian. "Did my father know you were a dancer?"

Lillian nodded. "I told him everything. We shared a deep intimacy. And he knew Iris was a dancer too."

Iris's mouth fell open. "But he never mentioned it to Clara."

Lillian smirked. "He was waiting for *you* to do that. And you never did, because you're ashamed. You're not so different from your sister after all."

Ellie gritted her teeth. "Enough!"

Her mind was reeling. *Had Father really known Iris was a Follies dancer?* Her aunt's secret was safe with him because his affair with Lillian was private. Perhaps New York represented another life for both of them—a place they kept quiet about.

Iris glared. "I thought telling my sister I was a dancer would upset her. How was I to know you were having an affair with her husband?"

Lillian's eyes became hard. "As if you've never had one! Don't think I don't know about John Marshall. From what I heard, he was dangerous."

Iris sucked in her breath.

The air in the room changed, like the crackle of lightning before a thunderstorm.

Iris lowered her eyes. "I'm not proud of what I've done." Her knuckles were white as she gripped the love seat, like she was holding on for dear life.

Goose bumps prickled Ellie's arms. She turned to Iris,

feeling sick. "But you never intended for Dorothy King to seek John out. You didn't know what he was capable of. He had a temper, but—"

Iris covered her face with her hands. Then she wiped a tear from her cheek.

"I discovered what he was capable of. And it's time you knew the truth."

Chapter Eighteen

Iris

As I lay there in bed next to John, who still smelled of Dorothy King's musky perfume, I shut my eyes, feeling sick to my stomach, realizing the danger I had put her in. She had no idea what a monster John was. I hadn't known either when I'd given Dot my diamond necklace. At that point, John Marshall had simply been controlling—and I'd decided to leave him. But now I needed to find Dot and warn her, before it was too late.

When John awoke, I did everything I could to pretend as though nothing unusual had happened. Mary cooked us breakfast, and I asked John if he'd enjoyed last night's party at the Brevoort. He muttered something into his coffee and then pushed away from the table, saying he had work to get done.

After John left the apartment, my pulse was racing. I had no proof that he'd been with Dot King—except that I recognized the unique scent of her perfume on his clothing. Perhaps nothing had happened between them yet, but I'd named him, and flaunted those diamonds, showing Dot the kind of life he could give her.

I knew Dot King lived next to Hilda at the Great Northern Hotel, which was only a few steps away. If I could somehow sneak out of the apartment, I could deliver my warning in person.

THE NEXT MORNING, sitting at the kitchen table, I opened the newspaper. John hadn't returned from the Waldorf-Astoria yet, where he'd stayed the night, presumably to finish his work. Though I was grateful to have him out of the apartment, it didn't escape me that the Waldorf was the very hotel where we'd shared our early trysts. *What if he was there with Dorothy?*

I returned to the newspaper, skimming the national headlines and local news. Next, I turned to the society pages, where a headline stopped me cold.

HILDA FERGUSON SHINES LIKE A DIAMOND

Blond beauty Hilda Ferguson has replaced Stella Parsons in the Ziegfeld Follies, and all of New York is bedazzled! The seductive siren is sure to be a star. I predict we shall see her on the cover of "Theatre Magazine" in no time. With her lithe figure, shimmering gold hair, and alluring blue eyes, Miss Ferguson sets pulses racing with her daring dance numbers. Perhaps this leggy lady has outshone Stella Parsons all along.

I couldn't read any further. Had Ziegfeld waited for me to return before offering Hilda the part? Had either of them worried about me when I didn't come back? I swallowed the hard lump in my throat. At the end of the day, the success of Ziegfeld's revue was all that mattered to him, and Hilda was merely a fair-weather friend. No one was coming to save me. I went back to reading the article—written by James Henry, the same critic who'd once sung my praises. But then the gossip item below caught my eye, and my mouth fell open.

DASHING DOT SNARES A NEW BEAU

Girl-about-town, model Dorothy King, was spotted with a gray-haired gentleman at the Brevoort Hotel on Saturday night, a wealthy businessman whom sources were unable to name. Shapely and beautiful Miss King, known as the Broadway Butterfly, flits from one suitor to the next, with rumored lovers from fiery Albert Guimares, "the man in the fur coat," to Draper Daugherty, son of the United States attorney general. Will the silver-haired "sugar daddy" wearing a gold pocket square win Dashing Dot's heart? Only time will tell.

My blood ran cold. I had tucked a gold pocket square into John's suit before he left for the party at the Brevoort. I stood up and paced around the apartment. Would Dot have the smarts to outwit John? I'd heard that Albert Guimares was a con man—perhaps the two of them were after John's money.

Mary hummed to herself, dusting the living room. I wondered if she kept the apartment key in the pocket of her pinafore.

Perhaps now was the time to overpower her, grab it, and then run down the stairs leading to the street?

If I made it outside, there was a chance I could blend in with the crowd. Plenty of people strolled past Carnegie Hall and gawked at the Vanderbilt Mansion on 5th Avenue, which took up an entire city block. Once I reached the Great Northern Hotel, I'd be safe.

I pictured its lobby, where large palm fronds burst from ceramic vases beneath a gilded ceiling. I'd wandered the hotel's halls before, after nights out drinking and dancing with Hilda and Lou. Those carefree times felt like ages ago.

"What are you lookin' at?"

Mary's voice startled me, and I realized I was standing before the door, staring off into the distance.

She straightened her spine and jutted out her chin. "Don't be getting any ideas, miss." But then she gave me a sympathetic look and disappeared into the kitchen. When she returned, she unfolded a piece of wax paper, revealing a thick loaf of soda bread. "For you, miss."

My eyes met hers as I gratefully accepted the bread.

"Thank you."

She shrugged and then returned to her cleaning. I stuffed a bite of the warm Irish soda bread into my mouth and closed my eyes, savoring the sweet raisins and the tangy buttermilk. It was even better than my mother's. Wrestling the apartment key from Mary wasn't a good plan. She would ring the cops—or John—as soon as I set foot outside. And besides, she had just shown me kindness. I would have to find another way.

. . .

JOHN HAD IT bad for Dorothy King. Within days, his demeanor improved. Instead of spending nights with me at the apartment, he insisted work kept him busy and that he had to stay overnight again at the Waldorf-Astoria.

Dot's musky perfume lingered on John's clothing. One night, after he'd taken off his jacket, I discovered a smear of red lipstick on the collar of his white shirt. I closed my eyes and hoped I could send Dot a warning. I'd found stationery and a pen inside a drawer in the dining room.

The next Friday, to test my theory that John was still with Dot, I asked him if I could join him at the Waldorf-Astoria. I had been on my best behavior, making myself look beautiful and attending to his every need. But John demurred, insisting he had too much work to get done. Knowing he wouldn't come home that night, I relished my time alone, even though the guilt over what I had done was still weighing heavy on my mind. Without Mary's watchful eyes on me, I removed John's gold fountain pen from its case. Pressing the nib into the stationery, I let my words flow as quickly as the ink would allow.

Dear Dot,

You may not remember me, but you know me as Stella Parsons. I was principal dancer in the Ziegfeld Follies, and I met you outside the New Amsterdam Theatre, where I gave you my diamond necklace and earrings. I told you they were courtesy of a Mr. John Marshall. This may seem forward, but please, I must warn you, he is dangerous. No

amount of furs or jewelry is worth getting involved with
him. I know. John Marshall is not who he says he is. His
name is J. Kearsley Mitchell, and he is the son-in-law of
E .T. Stotesbury. But most importantly, he will hurt you.

Though I couldn't leave the apartment, and I hadn't found stamps, perhaps if I threw the letter in an envelope out the window, someone would pick it up and deliver it? I could only hope for a Good Samaritan—they were few and far between.

A wave of nausea gripped me, interrupting my train of thought, followed by a sobering moment of clarity. *How long had it been since I last had my monthly?* I looked down at my swollen breasts and my rounded stomach. Sometimes, in the Follies, when I rehearsed for twelve hours a day and didn't eat enough, I would miss my period. But this wasn't that. I hadn't been dancing at all.

I knew to insert my sponge before intercourse—Follies girls knew how to protect themselves better than most. But sometimes John was so eager, I didn't have time to slip it in. I brought a trembling hand to my mouth.

I was pregnant with John's child. And J. Kearsley Mitchell would never risk the scandal of the press discovering he'd gotten a Follies dancer pregnant. I had to get away from him, and quickly, before he put my baby in harm's way.

IN SPITE OF my fears, I felt full of life and hope. Now it was more important than ever to formulate an escape plan. I began observing Mary's daily routine and noticing when Wilson stepped away from his post to relieve himself in the alley. While John spent time with Dorothy King, I caressed my stomach, humming to my baby. With my love, this innocent child would never turn out to be anything like him.

I wore long and heavy clothing, grateful for the chill in the air, and I avoided John's touch. I'd hidden my letter to Dot in back of a desk drawer in the bedroom, and I hoped I could bribe Mary to deliver it. Though she was rough around the edges, I believed that deep down, she had a good heart. She continued to bring me bread, and once even a hunk of cheese—a true gift, because I was ravenous.

Sometimes, late at night, I heard John talking on the telephone in the lobby downstairs, outside the tearoom. Though he didn't know it, sound carried through the dumbwaiter. I would open the cupboard and put my ear to the open shaft. Perhaps Dot had given him an ultimatum—choose her or lose her—and John would finally let me go. The more my pregnancy began to show, the more desperate I felt. Time was running out.

The next day, John returned to the apartment, smelling of scotch, his eyes filled with a look I recognized—lust. I'd done everything I could to repel him, wearing long clothes to increase my sweating, and speaking to him with food lodged between my teeth.

But he came up behind me, grabbed my shoulders, and spun me around. His face was inches from mine. Even now, I smelled Dorothy King's perfume on him. *If he'd already had her, why did he want me too?*

My pulse began to race. He pinched my bottom and made a face. "You're getting fat. Take off these clothes and let me measure you."

My heart thudded. "John, I don't think—"

Before I could come up with an excuse, he lunged at me and began ripping the buttons on my dress and pulling the garment up over my head. I struggled, but I couldn't stop him. My silk camisole and step-ins fell to the floor. I stood there naked, my hands placed protectively over my belly. His eyes widened, and his jaw fell open.

"You're pregnant."

I stepped backward. "John. I'll never tell a soul. I swear on my life."

His eyes glinted menacingly. "Is it mine?"

Anger coursed through me. "Of course it's yours! I haven't left this apartment in months! You've made sure of that."

He sucked in his breath. "Do you know what the papers would do if they found out about this? I already have two children. I can't have a bastard."

I knelt on the ground, interlocking my fingers in prayer as I looked up at him, like a street beggar. "I won't ask for anything. Not for your money, not for your name. *Please.* I'll raise this child on my own. No one has to know."

John pushed me aside. "I'll have this taken care of."

An icy feeling rushed through me. "What do you mean?"

John glared at me. "Now that I can see *why* you've been gaining weight, I'll fix this. Soon, you'll be good as new. I'll call Dr. Morton now."

The hairs on the back of my neck stood up. Girls I'd danced with had been in trouble before and they had disappeared to the sound of hushed whispers and then returned to the stage pale and subdued. Ziegfeld ran a tight ship, but when it came to women's matters, he didn't ask questions.

But I didn't want to make that choice. Not this time. I was nearly twenty-six years old, and a voice inside me told me I would make a good mother. I already loved my baby, and I couldn't wait to tell Clara. We could raise our children together. I'd tell her the baby's father had died in an automobile accident and she'd believe me.

John slammed the door behind him, and I knew he was going down to the corridor outside the Yellow Aster Tearoom to use the telephone. I hurried into the kitchen and opened the door to the dumbwaiter, listening at the empty shaft. I wished I were small enough to fit inside it. If I could curl up in there, I could use the pulley to lower myself to safety. But I was five foot ten, and pregnant—too heavy and tall for a space meant for groceries.

John's voice rose in anger as it carried from the foyer up the shaft into the apartment. "What do you mean it can't be done tonight?"

I ran to the front door and tried the knob. Locked, of course. My heart began to pound. If John drove me to a back-alley doctor, I would open the door of his Bentley and roll out onto the street. I'd rather die making my own choice than have a man make one for me. My heart thudded, fear pumping through my veins. I could hear the elevator cables rattling—John was on his way back upstairs.

The apartment door opened, and John stood there, staring at me with his direct, unblinking gaze. He shut the door behind him. Then he walked toward me, a terrifying look in his eyes.

"You asked for this. This is your fault."

"John, what are you—"

And with that, he delivered a swift punch to my stomach, so hard that I doubled over in pain. I fell to the ground and curled up into a ball, stars bursting behind my eyelids, but he kicked me, again and again, until everything went black.

Chapter Nineteen

Ellie

NEW YORK, 1945

Ellie touched her face, and her fingertips came away wet with tears. Iris was crying softly too. A cold feeling settled over Lillian's living room like frost. Iris had been pregnant. But Iris and Uncle Ed didn't have any children. Ellie assumed her aunt didn't want them or couldn't have them. As a child, Ellie had basked in Iris's attention. Never had she imagined the horrors Iris had endured.

Lillian's mouth formed a hard line, but her expression held pain. *Was it her imagination, or did Lillian look both frightened and guilty?* Ellie's mind spun, and fear gripped her chest—Iris, Lillian, Father, John Marshall, Dorothy King—it was all too much. They were tangled together in a spider's web.

"That monster." Ellie's voice came out in a whisper.

"It's my fault John killed her." Iris buried her face in her hands, and her shoulders shook. "I'll never forget how quickly he turned violent."

Ellie's mouth went dry, remembering what she'd asked Iris at the diner: *He was horrible to you, but do you really think he was capable of taking a human life?* She blinked back tears, the answer to her question now clear.

Iris sobbed quietly, and Ellie wished Lillian wasn't there to witness her aunt's pain. She placed a hand on Iris's shoulder and then turned her gaze to Lillian. "We should go."

Ellie took Iris by the hand and gently pulled her to her feet. "Deep breaths. Come now, let's go back to the hotel."

Iris moved like she was in a trance. Ellie collected their purses, coats, and umbrellas and looked at the closed door of Lucy's room. Her heart ached. She'd come here expecting answers about her father and also closure, revenge, or vindication— but all she felt was empty and raw. She couldn't even hug her sister goodbye.

Lillian's eyes were weary. She held the apartment door, opening her mouth like she had more to say. But then she closed it.

Ellie felt overcome by fatigue herself. "Tell Lucy I'm sorry. For everything."

Lillian's tense posture eased. "Where are you staying?"

"The Algonquin Hotel." Ellie laughed at the absurdity of it—the spot where Lillian and her father began their affair. "I guess this is goodbye."

Lillian spoke softly. "Will you tell me if you hear anything?" With a sheepish look, she handed Ellie a slip of paper. "Here's my telephone number."

An hour ago, Ellie would have told Lillian to shove her

concern where the sun doesn't shine. But her anger had transformed into something else. They both cared about her father. Ellie gave her a small smile as she accepted the paper, folded it, and tucked it into her purse. "Yes, I will."

Ellie held Iris steady, and they walked outside onto the stoop, down the stairs, and toward Amsterdam Avenue. In the winter sunlight, the tree-lined avenues appeared the same, and yet Ellie's world had irrevocably changed.

IRIS WAS SILENT on the cab ride back to the Algonquin. Ellie didn't pressure her to talk. Her heart broke for Iris and all of the unspeakable things she had endured. When they arrived at the hotel, Iris walked toward the elevator, but a blond girl at the front desk spotted Ellie and waved to catch her attention. "Miss Morgan!"

Ellie nodded at Iris. "Go on ahead. I'll be right up."

The desk clerk was bright-eyed and chipper, oblivious to Ellie's pain and confusion.

"Miss Morgan, there you are. You received quite a few calls while you were out." She looked down at her notepad, filled with neat, looping cursive.

Ellie frowned. "I did?"

The desk clerk nodded. "Firstly, your fiancé rang . . . more than once." Her mouth formed a moue. "He was very insistent you ought to have checked out." She raised her eyebrows. "I hope you'll forgive me, but I told him you had not."

Ellie's stomach knotted. *Tom.* She had practically forgotten about him in the midst of everything going on. But if she didn't phone him with an explanation right away, he would become even more worried and upset.

"Thank you." Ellie turned to go.

The girl's eyes widened. "Wait! You received another message, from Frank Hardcastle with the *San Francisco Chronicle*. It's urgent."

Ellie stopped in her tracks. "Oh Christ. What does he want?"

The desk clerk's mouth opened, perhaps surprised at Ellie's language. She looked at her notes. "Well, let's see. He said the new girl had quit? I'm sorry—he was very angry, I couldn't get it all down on paper."

Ellie rubbed her temples. She wanted a hot shower, a stiff drink, and to fall into a deep and dreamless sleep. But her life at home in San Francisco hadn't ceased to exist in her absence, even if she felt like it had.

Ellie sighed. "Is there a pay phone here I can use?"

The concierge nodded. "To your left. There, in the lobby."

Ellie thanked her, made her way to the vestibule, and slipped two nickels into the coin slot. She dialed the long-distance operator.

"Long distance. How may I direct your call?"

Ellie pinched the bridge of her nose, dreading having to talk to Frank. "The *San Francisco Chronicle* offices, please."

"Please deposit another dime."

Ellie did as she was told and then held her breath. Perhaps Frank wouldn't pick up.

"Frank Hardcastle speaking."

Ellie winced. "It's Ellie Morgan, sir."

Frank's voice was hoarse, like he'd smoked too many packs of Camels. "Well, look who deigned to call me back!"

Ellie held the receiver away from her ear. He continued to yell.

"Do you know what a pickle you've put me in? That girl you had fill in for you, Lotta, Lena . . ."

"Letty." Ellie leaned against the side of the phone booth. Her former classmate had always been a reliable person, *until now.*

"She up and left! Which means *I* don't have a secretary. So get your keister on the next train to San Francisco, or you're out of a job."

Ellie rubbed her forehead. Even if she caught the next train home, she wouldn't arrive for a few days. "I'll see what I can do."

"Don't see what you can do. Do it already! Or I'll find someone else."

The disconnect tone sounded. Ellie rested her head in her hands. *What was she going to do?* She needed to call Tom.

Ellie took a deep breath in and let it out. Whether it was the physical distance between them, or something else, she felt disconnected from him. And she didn't like it. A pit formed in her stomach while she waited for the operator to dial the bank of public telephones installed at Fort Scott.

Tom didn't waste any time with pleasantries.

"What in the hell? I've been waiting all day for your call. I told you to get on the next train! Are you still in New York?"

Ellie rubbed the back of her neck. "I met Lillian today. My father's mistress."

Sarcasm dripped from Tom's words. "Jesus. That's just brilliant."

Ellie pressed her lips together. She hated when Tom got like this.

"I know you're angry. But I'm capable of making my own decisions." Her throat tightened, and tears pushed against her eyelids. "I met my sister today too. Her name is Lucy. She's a senior in high school."

Tom sucked air against his teeth.

Ellie blinked back tears. "Aren't you going to say anything?"

"What do you want me to say? I told you to let sleeping dogs lie. You know that my family can never find out about this."

"Don't worry, they *won't.*" There was no complacency in her voice, only angry defiance. "Lucy doesn't want anything to do with me."

Tom sighed. "I hate to say it, but what did you think would happen?"

Ellie clenched her eyes shut and then opened them again. Why couldn't Tom see that it had taken bravery to meet them? It was like he didn't want her to have her own thoughts and opinions—he only wanted her to share his.

Ellie's voice became sharp. "I thought maybe Lucy would want to meet me. That maybe we could get to know each other."

Tom's voice softened. "Maybe she just wasn't ready."

Ellie felt her body relax. Tom was beginning to sound more like the man she'd fallen in love with. She sighed. "Also, Frank told me I'm out of a job if I don't return immediately. The girl I had fill in for me quit."

"It's all right, El. Don't worry about that. Let Frank find a new girl. When we're married, you won't need to work. Now will you please come home?"

Hot tears pressed against her eyelids. "I will, soon."

Tom's voice held a smile. "Everything will be right as rain. You'll see. Just get back here in one piece, all right? I love you, dollface."

"I love you too." Ellie set the receiver back in its cradle. But in spite of what she'd said, she didn't feel warm and fuzzy inside.

Iris was asleep by the time Ellie went upstairs to check on her. The soft hotel bed with its fluffy pillows looked tempting, but Ellie's stomach was growling. She slipped on a clean cardigan and took the elevator downstairs to the lobby.

In the hotel restaurant, Ellie sat by herself at a table in the corner. Matilda came up and rubbed against her ankles, and Ellie stroked the cat's fur. Then she ordered French onion soup and a grilled cheese sandwich.

She observed the other hotel patrons as she waited for her food to arrive. A few elderly couples dined together, and Ellie's heart clenched. She wanted to grow old with someone. *But was Tom the right person?* During their courtship, they'd kept things light and fun, but Tom seemed to view marriage as serious business. Could she still best him in a game of Ping-Pong as his wife, or would she be expected to stay home while he went out? Would he allow her to assert her independence and pursue her career as a journalist? Fear wasn't telling her she would be lonely and incapable by herself anymore. It had been replaced by a quiet confidence, an inner knowing that she would be okay.

Ellie rubbed her temples. She'd been in New York for less than a week, and already Tom was hurt and Frank was livid. It felt as though there was no one she hadn't disappointed.

Her soup arrived, and she ate in silence, relishing the flavor of caramelized onions, beef broth, red wine, and Gruyère cheese. Then a thought came to her: she hadn't disappointed herself. Ellie had remained true to her internal compass, following through with her commitment to find Lillian, even though it was uncomfortable. She felt a swell of pride knowing she could do hard things.

And she didn't want to lose her job at the paper, not before she had the chance to pitch Frank on the idea of writing her own column. Blotting her lips with a napkin, she straightened her spine. She would not give up on her career.

Ellie returned to the pay phone. She inserted her coins and asked the operator to dial the Delta Hotel. Waiting to connect, she pictured Jack's modest hotel room—a desk, a sink, a bed, and a typewriter. He'd said that his place was a dump. But the more Ellie thought about the freedom of living alone, the more it sounded lovely.

Ellie cleared her throat. "Is Jack Miller available, please?"

Hopefully he wasn't out on his news beat. After some grumbling from the desk clerk, Jack's voice came on the line.

"Hello? Jack speaking."

"Jack! It's Ellie."

"Hey, kid. Good to hear from you. I've been thinking about you."

His voice sent a shiver down her spine. She'd been thinking about him too. Jack's advice about a good journalist seeking the truth had motivated her to follow through with her search for Lillian. And she felt connected to him now, especially after he'd opened up about his absent father. Jack had managed to make peace with the unknown.

There was an awkward moment of silence. Jack spoke first.

"So, did you get your answers?"

Ellie sighed. "Some. And to be honest, I'm not sure how I feel about them." Her voice cracked, and she covered her mouth, mortified. "I'm sorry."

"Don't be. It sounds like what you did took bravery."

"Thank you." Ellie smiled, wiping a tear from her cheek. "It did."

She appreciated that Jack didn't press her to tell him more. Perhaps she would in time, when she was ready. It felt like they shared a certain level of intimacy now, even though they'd never met face-to-face.

Ellie smiled. "Listen, I'm still in New York. Can I ask you for a favor?"

His playful tone returned, lightening the mood. "Sure. Anything for a pal."

Ellie toyed with the phone cord. "The girl I had fill in for me, she quit. Frank blew his lid. Do you know any secretaries looking for work?"

"Yeah, I know a few."

Ellie blushed. "Dare I ask *how* you know them?"

He laughed. "It's not like that. Actually, my little sister just finished secretarial school. She's looking for work."

Ellie relaxed. "Really? Would you mind asking her if she could fill in for me until I get back? It would mean the world."

His voice held a smile. "Of course. Anytime, kid. I've got you covered."

Ellie breathed a sigh of relief. "Thank you. For everything. I owe you one."

"No, you don't. You went to New York on your own, didn't you? That took guts. And you went after the truth, like a journalist. You ought to tell Frank you want to write your own column. He's a tough old bastard but I think he has a soft spot for you. How could he not?"

Ellie blushed. Was Jack saying *he* had a soft spot for her?

"I really appreciate your vote of confidence." She took a deep breath. "I'm going to do it. When I get back."

"That's great, kid. I'm rooting for you."

Hanging up the phone, Ellie felt warm inside. It sounded like Jack's sister would be a good fit, and because Jack already worked for the paper, he'd be a trusted referral. Frank would survive. And in the meantime, Ellie would write an article to impress him.

She stepped out of the phone booth, a weight lifted from her shoulders. Ellie returned to the restaurant, where she ordered a cup of tea. As she sat sipping it, she thought of all the places she'd been in the past few days. The New Amsterdam Theatre and Grand Central Terminal were architectural marvels falling into disrepair, but both had evoked such strong feelings in her. Learning about the theater's storied history had brought it to life in her mind.

She thought of Lillian and Lucy, and how even as a little girl, Ellie had intuited something was wrong at home. She had perceived her emotions as a setback—something feminine and unruly she needed to overcome. But what if her sensitivity was her power, allowing her to empathize with others and to imagine a different world that wasn't filled with hate and bloodshed?

Already, she could picture San Francisco's forgotten gems— old theaters, the Cliff House and Sutro Baths, and the grand

Victorian mansions that had been chopped up into boarding-houses. What if she were to interview the people who had seen these places in their glory days, and to tell their forgotten history? The *San Francisco Chronicle* didn't have any columns like that.

The women's section had "fashion faux pas" and tips on how to become the perfect homemaker. But there had to be readers, both men and women, who yearned for something other than war and crime and casserole recipes. Ellie had an idea of what that something could be—a love letter to San Francisco, in all its imperfect glory.

She set down her empty teacup, thinking of how this trip had changed her. She wasn't frightened to be on her own anymore. She wasn't afraid to write something unique, and to show it to Frank. When she asked Frank for the opportunity to write a column for the *Chronicle*, she wouldn't say, *sorry to trouble you but* . . . she would be direct, like a man. After all, she had already confronted her greatest fear—that her father had a second family—and she had survived after learning the truth.

Ellie's throat tightened. Her father wasn't who she thought he was. And Lillian didn't know any more than she did. Lillian hadn't even known that his plane had been shot down before Christmas over the Adriatic Sea. Ellie wanted to cry. *What had been the point of this trip if she was still no closer to finding him?*

Though Ellie had come to New York seeking answers, on this journey, Iris had been forced to confront her past. And right now, Iris was in pain, remembering the child she lost and feeling responsible for Dorothy King's murder. Ellie remembered her aunt's words: *Lillian saw me do it. And the consequences of my actions were fatal.*

She couldn't allow Iris to leave New York thinking she was responsible in any way for Dorothy King's murder. Not when Lillian was hiding something: Ellie hadn't imagined Lillian's look of guilt and fear back at the apartment, after Iris finished telling her story about John. Ellie bit her bottom lip, her heart racing as she had a crazy idea. *Could she truly go through with it?* She had never broken the law before. But she felt certain there was more to Lillian's story than she was letting on.

There was a reason Lillian had come into possession of Dorothy King's bracelet, and Ellie would find out why. Iris couldn't be involved—not this time. The risk Ellie was willing to take was hers alone.

Chapter Twenty

Ellie

Ellie awoke on Thursday morning with butterflies in her stomach. She joined Iris downstairs for breakfast but simply sipped her tea, too nervous to eat. The sun had barely risen in the sky, but she was determined to help her aunt. Iris had already done so much for her, and now the onus was on Ellie to take action.

Iris's heartbreaking story of her pregnancy—and miscarriage—sat like an elephant in the room. She believed John Marshall had taken Dorothy King's life because he had taken the life of her child. Ellie shuddered. She didn't want her aunt to shoulder that burden in addition to the pain of her loss.

Ellie took a deep breath. "If it's all right with you, I'd like to spend the day alone."

Iris looked up from her coffee, eyebrows raised. "Oh?"

Ellie's stomach fluttered with nerves. The best way to make

a lie believable was to blend in a little bit of truth. "I'm feeling really mixed up right now about my father, and I just need some time alone to think."

Iris nodded, compassion in her eyes. "I understand. Where will you go?"

Keeping her expression neutral, Ellie tried to act nonchalant. "Oh, to a café somewhere nearby. I'd like to do a bit of writing."

"That's wonderful."

Iris's smile was so genuine that Ellie felt a stab of guilt. But she remembered her purpose and asked the question that had been nagging at her.

"Iris, you said the diamond and pearl bracelet that Lillian pawned belonged to Dorothy King." She shivered, thinking of the inscription, *My pet*, and all of the horror that it entailed. "Did you give it to her?"

Iris scrunched her brow. "To who? Dot? No, I didn't give her that bracelet."

The wheels in Ellie's brain were spinning. "Do you think John Marshall gave Dorothy King the bracelet after it belonged to you? Did she become his new *pet*?"

Blinking back tears, Iris nodded. "That's exactly what I think."

A chill ran through her at the disturbing thought.

"And you saw photographs of Dorothy King wearing that bracelet? You're sure it was the same one?"

"I'm sure." Iris clenched her jaw.

Ellie felt renewed determination to solve the mystery she

was trying to untangle. "Then I don't understand how Lillian got the bracelet."

Iris rubbed her temples. "Neither do I."

Speaking about Lillian, Ellie's heart began to thud. She stood up from the table, carrying the steno notebook she'd brought along as a guise for spending the day at a café. Iris confirmed what Ellie already thought. Lillian was hiding something. *How did she come into possession of the bracelet of a murdered woman?*

"Maybe we'll never know. Anyhow, I ought to get going."

"What time will you be back?" Iris's blue eyes held concern.

"In the afternoon." Ellie swallowed, hard. *If she wasn't arrested first.*

"Will you be all right?"

Ellie smiled tightly. "I'll be just fine. Don't worry about me."

STEPPING OUT OF a cab on Amsterdam Avenue, Ellie thanked the driver and then ducked her head as she walked. She'd purposefully worn dark slacks, a dark coat, and a dark beret, with her auburn hair tucked underneath.

She checked her watch, hoping she had arrived early enough. It was almost eight o'clock in the morning. Keeping her head down, Ellie turned onto West 76th Street and moved quickly until she was standing across the street from Lillian's apartment. Her heart began to pound. *This was a foolish idea. What was she thinking?*

But remembering Iris's pain, Ellie swallowed down her fear. There had to be clues inside Lillian's house pertaining to the bracelet.

Lillian had wanted to rid herself of that bracelet, even at a loss, and Ellie wanted to find out why. Historical record of ownership could add value to a piece of jewelry, particularly if it was owned or worn by a person of note. But the "person of note" it had belonged to was murdered, and Lillian had chosen a pawnbroker who didn't work by the books.

Ellie stood, partially hidden behind a tree, and waited. A few mothers pushing prams and holding the hands of schoolchildren walked past, not paying her any mind. Finally, at 8:15, the door to Lillian's apartment building opened, and Lillian and Lucy stepped outside. Lillian wore a blue wraparound coat and carried a pair of tap shoes, while Lucy was dressed in the same camel-colored trench coat she'd worn yesterday. *Good*—they were off to work and school for the day, just as she had anticipated.

Holding her breath, Ellie didn't move, making sure the tree trunk concealed her from view. She watched the two women walking side by side and waited until they had disappeared around the corner. When the street had emptied, sheer willpower propelled her forward. Walking up the tall stoop to the parlor floor, Ellie stood below Lillian's window.

With her heart thudding, she prayed the street would remain empty long enough to jimmy the window open wider. Ellie set down her purse and steno notebook, her hands shaking as she looked to her right and to her left. An older gentleman walking a dog stood at the end of the block, but he was moving slowly. Ellie leaned over the ironwork railing, gripped the window frame, and shoved.

The window refused to budge. Giving the street another cursory glance, Ellie pushed down her nerves and tried again, this time swinging one leg over the bannister. With a squeak, the window gave way, its old wooden frame protesting as it opened.

"Hey! What's going on there?"

Ellie froze. This was it—she'd been caught breaking into Lillian's apartment. Slowly, she turned around, her hair spilling from where it had been pinned beneath her beret.

The old man with his terrier stood on the sidewalk before her, squinting behind his glasses. "Oh, it's *you.* Heavens, did you forget your key?"

Unable to find her voice, all Ellie could do was nod. This man, likely a neighbor, thought she was Lucy. His dog tugged on its leash, pulling him away. He nodded at her. "Be careful, dear. And don't forget your schoolbook."

Ellie looked down at her steno pad on the stoop. Her voice was so quiet it was nearly inaudible. "Thank you. I won't."

She climbed over the stoop railing and scrambled through the window as quickly as she could, and then fell to the floor next to Lillian's love seat. Pulling the window shut behind her, Ellie breathed heavily, sweating hard. *Already, this was terrifying.*

But her breathing slowed, and she wiped perspiration from her brow. Even though she'd seen Lillian and Lucy leave, she still feared one of them would pop out from behind a door. Slowly rising to her feet, she breathed a sigh of relief. The living room looked exactly as it had yesterday, with its picture frames and decorative pillows. Ellie walked through the kitchen and down the hall, where she tried the first door on the left.

A twin bed sat in the middle of the narrow room, next to an

oak bookcase filled with novels. The walls were covered in movie posters. Ellie's throat tightened, noticing the teddy bear that sat atop the bed, looking worn and loved. This was Lucy's room. *Had her father given Lucy the bear?*

Ellie shut the door behind her and then panicked, not remembering whether it had been open a crack when she entered. Taking a deep breath in and letting it out, she continued down the hall until she found Lillian's bedroom. Like the living room, it was rich and sumptuous. Her vintage bed frame was upholstered in pale pink silk with a rose pattern and looked French and expensive.

Bottles of perfume cluttered the vanity, and framed photographs of Lillian wearing her Follies costumes adorned the walls. Ellie felt her stomach clench. Lillian truly had been stunning—and she knew it. *Where would she keep her pawn ticket pertaining to the sale of the bracelet?* Ellie started with Lillian's ornate secretary desk, opening up the drawers.

Lillian chose to pawn the bracelet, knowing she would lose money—likely 40 percent of the bracelet's value. There were other methods of selling jewels besides pawning them, methods that could offer far better returns. But that required jewelry to be legal—not stolen—which Ellie suspected the bracelet was.

Then she came upon a drawer that was locked. Ellie licked her dry lips, making her way over to the vanity. She rummaged among the bottles of perfume and tubes of lipstick until she found a ceramic box shaped like a heart. Opening it, she let out her breath. Inside was a key.

Ellie stuck the key in the drawer lock, turned it, and smiled when the drawer opened. Inside was a vintage tin box with an

Art Nouveau illustration of vines and flowers, rusted at the corners and faded with age. Ellie lifted the lid, hoping to find a collection of receipts. Instead, she drew in a sharp gasp, seeing the familiar red and blue checked airmail paper. *Her father's letters.*

Blinking back tears, Ellie removed one and began to read.

November 5, 1944

My dearest Lillian,

How are you, my love? I am in good health, and thinking of you always. How is Lucy? Does she still dislike her math teacher? Though our girl loves her drama classes and watching motion pictures, she will need a head for numbers too. I wish I were there to help her with her homework.

It's getting colder here in Italy, and the men are grumbling about their K rations. But I heard and saw a swell concert last Sunday put on by some of the boys here, so we're keeping our spirits up. But my thoughts often drift to our life together in New York, and when I close my eyes, I picture myself with you. Do you remember the Chinese place we used to visit on Pell Street, downtown? I still think about the dumplings. With any luck, this war will come to an end, and I will see you as soon as I am able. Don't work too hard now, Lil. Your dancing feet are getting older (don't hate me for reminding you!). I miss you both so very much.

Love always,
Your William

Ellie wiped tears from her cheeks, the burn of her father's betrayal searing her skin. This letter was similar to the one he'd sent to her and her mother, except for a few significant differences. He'd addressed Lillian as an individual and called her by a nickname. He'd teased her affectionately. And the worst part, he'd said he pictured himself with her when he closed his eyes, and he would see her *as soon as he was able*. Did that mean upon returning to the United States, he intended to see Lillian and Lucy first?

Setting the letter aside, Ellie tried to compartmentalize her emotions as she read his other letters sent during wartime. Though she'd come here looking for traces of Lillian's connection to Dorothy King, she couldn't help herself. She looked for words with double meanings, for words hidden inside a string of other words, for anagrams—anything that could be interpreted as a coded message or a clue to his whereabouts. But all she saw was the love her father had for Lillian and Lucy.

She wouldn't have time to read all of the correspondence between her father and Lillian, but morbid curiosity propelled her to read a few letters from the beginning of their courtship. The letters before Lucy was born showed a young man completely enamored with Lillian. He mentioned his guilt—thoughts of leaving Clara, but how he couldn't, because of his Catholic faith and his love for his daughter. Ellie wiped hot tears from her eyes. This other side of her father was perhaps something she wasn't meant to see. *Had Lillian been trying to save her the heartbreak?*

Ellie picked up a letter from the very bottom of the stack, and her brow furrowed.

March 24, 1923

Dearest Lil,

    Your last letter concerned me greatly. What do you mean you've done something awful? If you're in danger, which it sounds like you are, please tell me. I want to help you. Have you done something illegal? Who are these "shady characters" you've gotten involved with? I can tell you're suffering a great deal, and it upsets me to see you in such pain. I wish you would tell me what's going on, because I think you ought to go to the police, and I don't understand why you can't.

    Your Billy

Ellie reread the letter, confused. *Why would Lillian get involved with shady characters, and then tell William about it?* Just then, the door to the building slammed, startling Ellie from her thoughts. She sat there frozen, surrounded by a pile of her father's letters. Suddenly, a key turned in the lock, Lillian's apartment door creaked open, and footsteps sounded inside.

Blood rushed in Ellie's ears. Panicked and still clutching her father's letter, she looked toward the bedroom window. *Could she climb out?* First, she needed to clean up this mess and lock the desk drawer. Scrambling to her feet, Ellie accidentally knocked into Lillian's desk with her knee, spilling a ceramic mug full of pens. She yelped in pain and then covered her mouth.

"Mother? Are you home?"

Her knee smarted, and Ellie wished she could spontaneously combust, right there in the middle of Lillian's bedroom. Lucy's footsteps sounded down the hall, and Ellie stuffed her father's letter into the pocket of her trousers. As she stood there, frozen with fear and embarrassment, Lucy opened the door to the bedroom.

Her eyes locked on Ellie's and she slammed a hand over her heart, drawing in a sharp gasp. "What are *you* doing here?"

Holding up her hands, Ellie burned with shame. "I'm so sorry. I—I—"

But there was no excuse. She had broken into Lucy's apartment, a crime punishable by law. Yet in her panic, she turned the question around.

"Why aren't *you* in school?"

Lucy jutted out her chin defiantly and then looked at the letters scattered across the floor. "Are those my papa's letters?" Her lip began to tremble. To Ellie's utter shock, Lucy burst into tears, covering her face with her hands.

"I'm not in school because his plane was shot down! How am I supposed to study when my father is *dead*? I don't give a damn about anything anymore!"

Seeing Lucy's anguished face, with features so similar to her own, Ellie felt overcome with emotion. Lucy had only just learned about the crash, because Ellie had imparted the information to Lillian. She didn't hesitate, or overthink her decision— she walked across the room and wrapped her sister in a hug.

Lucy stiffened in her embrace but then relaxed. Ellie hugged Lucy tight as her body was racked with sobs. Tears spilled down Ellie's cheeks as she felt in her heart how real this all was. The skepticism she'd had about Lucy being a family member disappeared. Hugging her sister felt like coming home.

After what felt like a long time, they both pulled back, and Ellie realized she was trembling as she looked into Lucy's hazel eyes. The resemblance in their features was stunning—Ellie didn't know if she'd ever get used to it.

She wiped away a tear. "I am *so* sorry. About Father, about yesterday, about all of it. I wish I could change things . . . I don't know where to start."

Lucy gave her a small smile.

"How about starting with what you're doing here?"

Ellie's cheeks burned. She was here because she thought Lucy's mother was somehow involved in Dorothy King's murder, and she'd broken in looking for evidence. Instead, Ellie improvised.

"Yesterday, your mother wouldn't show me any of my—I mean our—father's letters. So, I climbed in through your window to read them." Her stomach knotted. "Are you going to call the police?"

Lucy furrowed her brow. "Were you planning to *take* anything?"

Ellie shook her head, her father's letter burning a hole in her pocket. She couldn't remove it *now*, though—especially if it might upset Lucy.

"No. I only wanted to see with my own eyes what he'd written."

Brushing an auburn strand of hair away from her face, Lucy looked at Ellie like she was trying to decide whether or not she could trust her. "If you don't tell my mother I skipped class today, I won't tell her you broke into our apartment."

Ellie felt a rush of warmth and affection toward Lucy. "It'll be our secret."

Lucy bent down and picked up one of the letters. She nodded

at the desk. "Mother never let me go inside this drawer. It's always been locked."

A lump rose in Ellie's throat. "Reading these, it's clear how much Father loves you. I believe he may be out there somewhere, still. It's not hopeless."

Lucy's lip trembled. "You really think so?"

Ellie fought back the wave of grief that threatened to consume her. Deciding to give up on her quest to find her father and his men felt like a betrayal—like giving up on him, on them. She hadn't forgotten about the twelve families who had received a telegram identical to hers, or their heartbreak.

"I want to believe so badly, I'm afraid I've become desperate." Ellie began carefully refolding the letters. "I was hoping Father included a clue about his mission or his location, a coded message for your mother."

Lucy smiled. "He does love puzzles."

Feeling a strange combination of jealousy and recognition, Ellie smiled. "Yes, he does. Especially the Sunday crossword." She reached into Lillian's desk drawer for the empty tin. "I ought to put these letters back."

Then she paused, realizing Lucy might want to read them. But not all of the letters were suitable for her to see.

Lucy nodded. "I'll help. My mother will be very upset if she finds out."

Ellie smiled, removing the vintage tin from the drawer, touched by her sister's act of loyalty. She felt a surge of happiness. "Thank you."

A stack of newspaper clippings atop a mess of papers in

Lillian's drawer caught Ellie's eye. She lifted the newspaper clippings out, their pages yellowed and curled with age. A shiver ran through her as she read the headlines.

THE BROADWAY BUTTERFLY ROBBERY
ENDS IN MURDER

BOBE HOLDUP LINKED WITH KING MURDER

KING MURDER CLUE

Ellie licked her lips and turned to Lucy, feeling uncomfortable. "Why do you think your mother kept these?"

Lucy looked confused. "I don't know. Like I said, she never let me go in that drawer. They're just old newspaper clippings."

Ellie picked up one of the articles and read.

Police believe the holdup and robbery of Robert L. Hague, superintendent of the marine department of the Standard Oil Company of New Jersey, and Edith Bobe, a modiste, in Miss Bobe's home at 158 East 63rd Street, late Monday night, have been committed by the same group of professional criminals who murdered Dorothy King in her apartment.

Lucy pressed her lips together. "I saw my mother open the drawer a few times when she didn't know I was watching. She would take out a diamond and pearl bracelet and cry."

Ellie shivered at Lucy's mention of the bracelet—*Dorothy King's bracelet.* Lillian was definitely hiding something, and more evidence could very well be in the bottom of this drawer. But now that Lucy was here, Ellie couldn't continue searching. Though she wanted to vindicate Iris, she also didn't want to hurt her little sister.

A look of guilt passed across Lucy's face. "I don't know why I told you that. I guess . . . it made me feel strange, and I wanted to tell someone."

"It's all right." Ellie looked at Lucy sadly. "As I've learned, parents keep secrets."

Lucy's face clouded. And then Ellie remembered her sister's words: *Papa kept my existence secret for your sake! I couldn't even tell anyone he was my father.*

Ellie reached for Lucy's hand, wishing she could make up for every missed moment. She smiled. "I know my coming here has been a shock for you, but discovering I have a sister has been the best thing that's ever happened to me."

Lucy blinked back tears. "I'm sorry I was awful to you yesterday."

Ellie shook her head. "No, you weren't. I apologize for coming into your home without any warning."

"And now you've done it again, like a cat burglar."

Seeing Lucy's wry smile, Ellie burst into laughter. Lucy began to laugh too, and Ellie delighted in hearing how similar their laughs sounded.

Lucy looked down, and then up at Ellie. "I'm really glad to have a sister too. You're different from who I thought you'd be."

Ellie frowned. "How did you think I would be?"

Lucy shrugged. "Stuck-up. Snobby. Mean."

Guilt passed through Ellie. There was so much they still needed to learn about each other. She smiled, hoping they could develop a relationship, gradually grow closer, and make up for lost time.

"I suppose I'm a quiet person. I like to read and write. People have mistaken me for being stuck-up before."

Lucy smiled. "What's your favorite book?"

Ellie thought for a moment. "It's so hard to choose just one. When I was your age, I loved *The Hobbit.*"

Lucy's face lit up. "*The Hobbit* is my favorite too!"

"Really?" Ellie couldn't stop a smile spreading across her face.

Working together cleaning up the papers on the floor, they shared their favorite foods and films. Lucy preferred comedies and romances, while Ellie preferred mysteries, but they both loved *The Wizard of Oz,* and they both thought beets were disgusting. Talking with Lucy felt so natural, like slipping on a favorite sweater. After they returned their father's letters to the tin, and the newspaper articles to the drawer, Ellie locked it and then put the key back inside the ceramic heart box on Lillian's vanity.

"So that's where she keeps it." Lucy shook her head. "Such an obvious place, and yet I was frightened to look."

Ellie's heart sank, seeing the time on her watch. She didn't know how long Lillian taught her tap lessons, and she didn't want to overstay her welcome.

"Lucy, I ought to go. Thank you for not calling the police, and for not telling your mother I was here. But mostly, thank you for giving me a chance."

Lucy's eyes widened. "Will I see you again?"

Ellie smiled. "I hope so. Can I write to you from San Francisco?"

"Well, you know my address, so I suppose you can." Lucy winked.

Blinking back tears, Ellie pulled Lucy into a tight hug. This time, Lucy didn't stiffen, she hugged her back, and it was the most marvelous feeling in the world.

"Did you get a lot of writing done?" Iris looked up from her book, smiling as Ellie entered their hotel room.

Ellie felt like she had been infused with new life. Though a war still raged on overseas, though her father was still missing, she had a *sister*—and years of catching up to do. Her stomach tightened as she met Iris's gaze.

"Actually, I lied to you this morning. I didn't go to a café."

Iris set her book down. "*What?* Where did you go?"

Ellie sighed. "I went back to Lillian's apartment. I think there's something important she's not telling us." She bit her lip. "I climbed in through a window, hoping to find clues about Dorothy King's bracelet. But instead I found my father's letters, and I had to read them."

Slapping her forehead, Iris took a deep breath. "You *broke* inside? What were you thinking?"

"Technically, I didn't break in. The window was open."

Iris glared, clearly not finding the statement funny.

Ellie shrugged. "Then Lucy came home from school early. We got to know each other better. She's—she's really lovely."

Her aunt's eyes softened. "Oh, Ellie, I'm so happy to hear that."

Ellie chewed her bottom lip. "But I did find something about Dorothy King."

Iris looked alarmed. "What did you find?"

"Lillian kept old newspaper clippings related to the Dot King case in a drawer." Ellie frowned. "I read about a couple who were robbed in front of their home on East Sixty-Third Street. Police believe the crime was committed by the same group of professional criminals who murdered Dorothy King."

Iris nodded. "Yes. There were a string of robberies back then."

"But you don't think robbers murdered Dorothy King?"

Iris's mouth became a hard line. "No. John Marshall murdered Dot King. He used the robbery as a cover-up. He was acquitted of the crime because of his wealth, power, and connections. But he was a prime suspect in her murder case. I'm not the only person who still believes he's guilty."

Looking at Iris's pained expression, Ellie could see her aunt held strong in her convictions. "But why are you so certain?"

Iris wiped away a tear. "This is the hardest part of my story to tell. But I can tell you this. I'm certain he killed her, because of what he did to me."

Chapter Twenty-One

Iris

I woke in pain. My vision blurred, then refocused, and I found myself staring at the ceiling. Trying to sit up, I gasped, blinded by a sharp twinge in my midsection. Then I looked down. My legs were caked with blood. I put a hand to my throbbing belly, which was tender and still rounded. *No. God no.*

Panic swelled inside me. "Where is my baby?"

Tears spilled from my eyes, and my heart tore into pieces remembering John's punch and his swift kicks to my stomach— my baby was gone, my body bruised. Beneath the foggy haze of pain and confusion, my emotions rushed to the surface— betrayal, fury, and heartache.

I sat up slowly, wincing as I moved. *My baby.* John had caused me to lose my child—he'd taken everything from me. My ribs ached as I tried to take a breath. I looked around, fearing I'd see John standing over me. Somehow I'd moved from the living room floor to my bed. A key turned in the lock to the apartment, and grimacing, I quickly lay back down. Closing my eyes, I waited with bated breath, my heart pounding, dreading John's return. If I willed my soul to leave my body, perhaps I would die here. Afraid to breathe or move, I pictured myself as a statue, cold and lifeless. The door creaked open, and heavy footsteps crossed the room.

"Good God."

The voice that spoke wasn't John's . . . it was Wilson's. I gritted my teeth as I felt a strong cramp, worse than my monthly, and fought the urge to scream. Here I was mourning the child I wouldn't hold, and John's horrible henchman had been sent for me. What was he doing here?

Wilson exhaled and then muttered under his breath.

"It's done."

His footsteps slowly backed away, and then the door closed behind him.

I remained motionless until after I'd heard the key turn in the lock to the apartment. Opening my eyes, I looked down and saw the blood that had soaked through the white sheet covering my legs. Horrified, I held my face in my hands. Cramps continued to seize me, and I cried for the child who wouldn't greet me with coos and smiles, who wouldn't suckle at my breast, and who wouldn't wrap its tiny fingers around mine. I wept for the sweet scent of the baby I wouldn't smell, and the soft touch of skin I wouldn't feel against my own.

Hours passed, and still I wept for the little girl or boy I had lost. The depth of my sorrow was bottomless—an abyss I wanted to die in. Guilt over what had happened consumed me.

I should have known John would turn violent.

I cried until thickness fell over me, and my eyelids became weighted. And then I allowed my exhausted body to drag me into a dreamless sleep.

MY RIBS ACHED when I awoke, but the painful cramps had passed. The door to the room opened, and Mary entered. Seeing me, she gasped and made the sign of the cross over her chest.

"Jesus, Mary, and Joseph."

"Mary." My voice cracked.

She approached me and gently laid a hand on my sweaty forehead. Then she grimaced, looking down at the bloody sheets.

"We must call a doctor."

I reached out, weakly grabbing her wrist. "No, don't."

Mary's dark eyes were full of concern. "I'll get some rags."

She went to the lavatory and returned with some towels. Gingerly, she peeled the soiled sheet from my legs, revealing a blue silk dress caked with blood, which clung to me like a second skin. John must have dressed me at some point.

"Let's get that off." Mary was calm as she lifted up the hem. Then her eyes fell to my throbbing midsection, and she drew in a sharp breath.

"Did he do this to you?"

I looked down at my stomach, covered in dark, purple bruises. Tears stung my eyes. "Yes."

She made the sign of the cross again, her face full of pain.

"You weren't hysteric, were you?"

I chuckled bitterly. "Is that what he told you?"

Mary nodded. "He said I wasn't to let you leave. For your own good."

The Irish lilt of her voice soothed me. I closed my eyes and hot tears slid down my cheeks. Already, my short conversation with Mary had exhausted me. I wasn't dead, and yet I felt dead inside. So many thoughts fought for space in my mind. John had taken my baby from me. He'd taken away my career as Stella Parsons, darling of Ziegfeld's stage; and when he returned, I would never see my mother, my sister Clara, or anyone else, ever again.

I felt Mary place a damp cloth on my forehead, and a towel beneath me. She muttered under her breath as she moved about. I could hear her in the bathroom, running the tap. When she returned, she gently washed my legs with warm water. Then she carefully pulled the towel out from beneath me, and I winced. When I opened my eyes, Mary took my hand. "Let's pray for the wee soul."

I nodded, touched by the gesture.

"Our Father, who art in heaven, hallowed be thy name; thy kingdom come, thy will be done, on earth as it is in heaven."

Feeling Mary's warm, rough hand in mine, I felt more grounded in reality.

"Please, Mary, I'm not safe here. Where is John?"

Mary squeezed my hand. "In Atlantic City. I heard him say he'd be gone ten days. There was a woman in his car with him, a blonde."

John had taken Dorothy King on a trip out of town? He wanted to be far away from me and the "problem" he had taken care of.

Heaviness settled over me, and I longed to drift back to sleep—to feel nothing at all. But instead I felt a mix of heartache, guilt, and fear. Dot King would not be safe with him, no matter her hardscrabble Harlem upbringing. And now it was too late to warn her.

I sat up in bed. "I can't stay here."

Mary frowned at me. "Miss, you ought to rest."

But I swung my legs over the side of the bed, and Mary steadied me by the elbow as I walked to the lavatory. She left me alone while I ran a bath and slowly lowered myself into the hot water. Tears trickled down my cheeks as I said my own prayer to my baby, even though I didn't consider myself a Catholic anymore.

"My dear sweet soul, you were loved and you were wanted. I am so sorry. May God protect you until we meet again. Amen."

I washed myself, my muscles tensing as I remembered John and all of his abuse. He'd plucked me from the stage at the height of my fame, when my star burned the brightest, and turned me into a shell of myself. But I was not going to let one monstrous man ruin me.

Rising from the tub, I dared to look down. My stomach still rounded above my pelvis, and my lip trembled. I would never, *ever* forget. After toweling myself off and returning to the bedroom, I slipped on a pair of embroidered silk tap pants and folded a napkin inside. Reaching into my closet, I pulled a simple day dress from the hanger, one of the few not given to me by John, and laid it on the bed.

Once I'd finished getting my clothing on, I looked at myself in the mirror. Wearing my old polka-dot rayon dress, my hair dull and unstyled, and my face pale and full of grief, I looked ordinary—like a simple working-class girl.

I walked into the living room. "Mary?"

Her eyes held compassion. "Yes, dear?"

But I paused, a white envelope on the mahogany credenza catching my eye. I picked it up and then recoiled, seeing John's handwriting. *Wilson* was written across the back, and *for your trouble.* My memory flooded with images of postcards John sent from Philadelphia and Palm Beach, love notes telling me he wanted to kiss my pretty pink lips. I shuddered, but then felt something in the envelope—padded and thick.

Opening it up, I gasped. Bills, a whole stack of them, were tucked inside. I thought back to Wilson entering the bedroom while I lay there bleeding through the sheets, and the words he'd muttered: *It's done.* A chill ran all the way from the crown of my head down to my toes. I turned to Mary, and the fear on her face mirrored my own. I swallowed. "John left this for Wilson."

We both knew what Wilson had been paid to do.

Her face went white as a sheet. Then she brought a trembling hand to her mouth. My voice was pleading.

"Wilson will come back for this money. Please, Mary, he thinks nature has taken its course. Perhaps he was counting on you to telephone the police when you found me. *Please.* I can't stay here."

Removing half the cash from the envelope, I pressed it into her palm.

"I know you have a good heart. You can start a new life."

Mary drew in a sharp breath. Then she closed her fist around the money, met my eyes, and nodded. "Quickly."

With my heart pounding, I grabbed the remaining bills and ran into the bedroom. My mind was razor focused—I would take no jewelry, no handbags, no dresses, and no furs. John could keep everything he'd ever given me.

I slipped on a long wool coat and a cloche. When I returned to the foyer, Mary held the apartment door open. Her dark eyes met mine. "Go now."

I hesitated for a moment—I had so much I wanted to say, but in the end I only managed two words.

"Thank you."

She urged me forward. "*Go.* I'll find my own way."

I CAUGHT THE El to Grand Central Terminal. Though my legs felt stronger, I didn't dare get caught when I was so close to freedom. Every man in a suit, and every uniformed officer, caused my heart to skip a beat. John was in Atlantic City, but Wilson would return soon, to check on me.

I walked from 42nd Street Station until I passed the towering Pershing Square Building, which was still under construction. Then I continued through the foyer of Grand Central with its acorn-shaped lanterns. Hurrying down the ramp to the main concourse, I felt eased by the crowd. Light spilled from the towering windows in hopeful rays, the room as beautiful as a cathedral. My shoes clacked against the tiles as I made my way to the four-sided brass clock, shining like a beacon from atop the information desk. I approached a ticket clerk at one of the windows. He smiled. "How can I help you today?"

I removed the cash from my coat pocket. "I need to get to

San Francisco. I'll take any train, whichever departs immediately."

He raised his eyebrows and then opened a drawer to consult a pamphlet.

"Second class?"

I shoved the bills at him. "Yes. I don't need a sleeper car."

Sensing my distress, his eyes held kindness. "All right, then. You'll have a few connections, but I'll write them down."

I nodded, terrified of being followed.

"There's a train to Chicago departing in ten minutes." He smiled at me. "At LaSalle, you'll transfer to the Southwest Limited, and then transfer again in Missouri and Colorado before reaching California. Would you like me to book that?"

I nodded, drumming my fingers. "Please."

"All right." He took my bills, counted them, and then handed me back two dollars. I smiled, relieved. It was enough to buy food over the four-day journey, and to have a little extra when I reached San Francisco.

"You'll go from here to the upper tracks, where you'll find track thirty. Departure times are written on the chalkboard."

The clerk handed me my ticket, his eyes lingering on my absence of luggage for a cross-country trip. "I wish you the best of luck on your journey."

"Thank you." My throat tightened with emotion.

I walked toward track 30 with my head down, holding on to my ticket for dear life. Was it only a few months ago that John had torn apart my ticket to board the ocean liner? But I was no longer John's pet. Nor was I a star of the Ziegfeld Follies.

I boarded the train and found a seat by the window. When it rumbled to life, I felt a rush of exhilaration followed by a sharp pang of sadness. This was the last time I would see New York— a place of beauty and memory, of Central Park and speakeasies and tenements and jazz music, and oysters at the Oyster Bar, and unparalleled architecture, and nights dancing on the roof in Ziegfeld's Midnight Frolic—a city like no other.

But I was someone else now—a new woman. And in spite of all the pain I had endured, I would rise from the ashes and begin again.

Chapter Twenty-Two

Ellie

Ellie wiped tears from her cheeks. Though Iris had told her what she already suspected, hearing the story directly from her aunt's mouth was heartbreaking. *Had Iris and Uncle Ed tried for children but been unable to have them?* Ellie didn't know, and she didn't want to ask. She was beginning to understand why Iris felt convinced John Marshall had murdered Dorothy King—not only had he caused Iris to miscarry, but he'd left Wilson an envelope full of money.

Ellie swallowed, turning to Iris. "When John wrote, *for your trouble,* do you think he meant . . ."

Iris clenched her jaw. "I believe he intended to have me killed."

A shiver worked its way down Ellie's spine. From everything Iris had told her, John Marshall sounded terrifying. Though she desperately wanted to believe there was another explanation for the money and John's words, Ellie couldn't think of one. And Mary—she'd risked her job, and possibly her own life, to save Iris. That had taken courage. Ellie gnawed on her bottom lip.

"Did you ever hear from Mary again? Did she continue to work for John, after what happened?"

Iris looked sad. "No. A different maid was mentioned in the papers, when she discovered Dorothy King dead. Her name was Billy Bradford."

Hopefully, Mary had escaped John's reach and found work elsewhere. But hearing about the discovery of Dorothy King's body reminded Ellie of the mystery at hand—*How had Lillian gotten Dorothy King's diamond and pearl bracelet?*

The bracelet would have gone into police evidence if it were on Dorothy King's body when she was found. Which meant that either Dot had given the bracelet away before she was murdered, *or* the bracelet was included in the haul of stolen jewels that the police never recovered. Remembering how Iris had once worn Dot King's bracelet inscribed with the words *My pet*, Ellie shivered.

"Iris." She reached for her aunt's hand. "You've been through so much. And I don't want you to leave New York feeling responsible for Dorothy King's murder."

Iris managed a sad smile. "Dear, that's very kind of you. But I do feel responsible, and it's my burden to bear."

Ellie squared her shoulders.

"When I was at Lillian's, I discovered a few things that led me to believe she knows something about Dot's murder."

"What things?" Iris's eyes widened.

"Well, in addition to the newspaper clippings related to the murder investigation, I found a letter from my father."

Ellie retrieved her father's letter from her pocket and passed it to Iris. The gossamer-thin paper covered in blue ink revealed both her father as a young man, and his betrayal. It was painful to share. But she wanted her aunt to read it. Ellie's voice dropped, even though they were alone in their hotel room.

"I took this letter from Lillian's apartment. My father sent it to her. Look at the date it was written."

Iris squinted, her forehead creasing as she read. She frowned at Ellie.

"I'll admit . . . it is a bit suspect."

"I think so too." Ellie licked her lips. "Dorothy King's body was discovered on March fifteenth, 1923. This letter is dated March twenty-fourth."

Iris sighed. "That doesn't necessarily mean Lillian knew anything about Dot's murder. The timing of this letter could be coincidental."

Ellie considered her aunt's perspective, and then she shook her head.

"Whatever Lillian did, it was serious enough that my father felt she ought to go to the police. He was concerned for her safety."

Iris shrugged. "Lillian tended toward dramatics. Maybe she merely wanted your father's attention."

Ellie swallowed. Purchasing a bracelet stolen from a murdered woman, even unknowingly, would be a legitimate reason for Lillian to be scared and to reach out to her lover for comfort.

But then Ellie thought of her father's words: *What do you mean you've done something awful?* Ellie had a gut feeling Lillian knew she was at fault for more than just an innocent mistake.

Ellie bit her bottom lip. "It's possible Lillian knew something about the crime itself. Was she an acquaintance of Dorothy King's?"

Iris frowned. "I'm not sure. I heard Hilda and Dot threw wild parties together at the apartment on West Fifty-Seventh Street." Rubbing her arms, Iris took a shuddering breath. "Lillian may have gone to one of those parties."

Ellie felt for her aunt. She feared Iris was reliving painful memories from her past, as a woman held captive in that apartment. *Had Dot and Lillian been close?* That would explain why Lillian had cried while looking at Dot's bracelet. Dot could have given it to her, and maybe Lillian simply missed her murdered friend. But then what "awful" thing had she done?

Ellie cracked her knuckles. "I want to confront Lillian, but I think first we need more information about the Dorothy King case." She turned to Iris. "And I know where to go."

ELLIE STOOD IN front of the New York Public Library, taking in the imposing Beaux Arts façade of the columned building that towered above her. She noticed the magnificent marble lions that flanked its steps.

Iris nodded at the sculptures. "Patience and Fortitude."

"Beg pardon?" Ellie scrunched her brow.

"The lions. Patience is on the south side. Fortitude is on the north."

Ellie smiled as she passed between them, as if their names were a personal message of encouragement: *patience and fortitude*.

She climbed the steps, shook the water from her umbrella, and then walked inside the welcoming warmth of the library. She admired the classical details of its interior—the arched doorways, the cornices and lamps. She and Iris passed through the marble lobby to a cage elevator, which they rode up several floors. When they stepped out, Iris whispered, "The main reading room is this way. Follow me."

Inside, it was silent as a church, save for clacking typewriters and chairs scuffing against the tile. Tiered chandeliers held empty rows of electric bulbs, making it difficult for Ellie's eyes to adjust to the dim light. But then she gasped. The breathtaking space was majestic, the chandeliers softly illuminating a ceiling painted with celestial skies and billowing clouds in faded pinks and blues.

The ceiling was as high as a cathedral nave, and the room twice as long. Fifteen large windows brought a sense of Old World elegance, but they had been painted black, adhering to the restrictions of war. *How wonderful this room must have looked with light spilling in.* And what if the plaster rosettes on the ceiling were restored? They'd dulled and chipped but must have once been painted gold or bronze. Ellie was reminded of the New Amsterdam Theatre, another great beauty slowly falling into decay.

Iris's face fell. Perhaps she was remembering the reading room as it once had been. Reference books lined the walls, some spines illuminated, others ensconced in darkness where bulbs in the bookcases had gone out.

"I'll ask the librarian where we can find the microfilm reader," Ellie whispered, making her way toward the librarian's desk.

A wartime poster hung overhead, catching Ellie's eye. Bold text overlaid an image of a book being burned by Nazis.

Books cannot be killed by fire. People die, but books never die. No man and no force can put thought in a concentration camp forever. No man and no force can take from the world the books that embody man's eternal fight against tyranny. In this war, we know, books are weapons. —Franklin D. Roosevelt

Ellie swelled with pride. The Nazis could burn books, but they would not win this war. America would keep fighting. Books were magic, and reading was freedom.

"Pardon me." Ellie smiled at the librarian. "Does this library have a microfilm reader?"

The librarian, a girl around Ellie's own age who wore stylish glasses, smiled. "You're in luck. Take the elevator down to the first floor, and you'll find the microfilm machine in room one nineteen."

Ellie thanked her, watching as she scribbled a book request on a slip of paper and then put the folded slip into a pneumatic tube, where it was whisked away, down to the stacks below. Ellie wondered what it would be like to spend all day in the bowels of the old building, surrounded by books.

She wouldn't mind that sort of job—to be unseen, sending books up by dumbwaiter to those who had requested them. But she also enjoyed speaking with people, making her neither introvert nor extrovert, but a mixture of both. Then Ellie remembered Tom didn't want her working *at all*, and a sour feeling filled her stomach. Here in New York, doubts about him had materialized.

Ellie clutched her steno notebook to her chest as she made her way toward the elevator. She had taken notes with Lillian as her subject. So far she had written:

> *Cried while looking at Dot's diamond bracelet— indication of guilt?*
>
> *Wrote letter in March of 1923 (a few days after Dot's murder) expressing fear over "shady characters."*
>
> *Chose to pawn bracelet rather than sell to reputable jeweler.*
>
> *Kept newspaper clippings regarding 1923 robberies and murders.*
>
> *Knew Dorothy King personally?*

Iris touched Ellie's shoulder, pulling her back to the present moment. "What exactly are you looking for?"

"Newspaper articles about the Dorothy King case."

A pained expression crossed Iris's face, and Ellie felt guilty for dragging her aunt back into a past she longed to forget. *Was she crazy to think Lillian was involved in these crimes?* She and Iris rode the elevator together in silence. Though Ellie could have purchased their train tickets home today, she didn't want to leave

New York without trying to solve the mystery of the Broadway Butterfly. Iris deserved to know the truth. The elevator stopped with a jolt on the first floor. Ellie took a deep breath and then walked down the hall with purpose.

Approaching the desk attendant in room 119, Ellie smiled politely. She cleared her throat.

"Excuse me, miss? I'd like to use your microfilm reader. I'm looking for newspaper articles from March of 1923, pertaining to the murder of Dorothy King."

The librarian nodded, adjusting her tortoiseshell glasses. "Allow me to check our microfilm collection. One moment, please."

The girl left her post and then returned a few minutes later, handing Ellie a film reel with tiny photographic images. "These are articles in the *Daily News*, March 1923, the month Dorothy King was murdered." She frowned. "Are you familiar with how to use the microfilm apparatus?"

Ellie nodded. "Yes, I've used one before at the San Francisco Public Library, thank you. I'll come to you if I have any trouble."

Carrying the film reel over to the large microfilm machine in the corner, Ellie felt a thrum of anticipation. Perhaps there were details in these articles that would help her determine what Lillian knew.

"How does it work?" Iris frowned at the hulking machine.

Gently pulling the carriage assembly toward her, Ellie waited for the little glass plate to pop open.

"You place the microfilm reel here, on the left-hand spindle." Ellie set the film reel where it belonged. "Then you feed the tail of the microfilm through the rollers here, between the glass plates and around the core of the uptake reel."

She gave the reel a turn, to make sure it was taking up the film. Then she looked to the right side of the reader for a hand crank. Pushing the carriage assembly back into place, Ellie heard it click shut.

She smiled at Iris. "It's amazing, isn't it? Microfilm has a shelf life of five hundred years. Libraries have been filming newspapers, music scores, books, and pamphlets for the past decade, so they can keep these materials forever, long after the originals have disintegrated."

Ellie wound the crank, and newspaper text filled the screen. Using the lever to adjust the image, she positioned the first page just right. Picking up a magnifying glass, she read the headline: *Four Dead in Rum War at Sea.*

The rumrunners' bodies had washed ashore on March 10. Ellie continued to crank, while the microfilm whirred by. There were articles about "hooch raids" in cafés and mob arrests, but nothing yet about Dorothy King.

Several pages in, her hand stilled.

MODEL LIVED LIFE OF EXCESS BEFORE DEATH

NEW YORK, MARCH 17, 1923

Enamored by the sparkle of wine, Dorothy King had a predilection for kicking the glass out of taxicab doors when the flames of alcohol stole away her senses. She was not averse to "smoking hop" and often she could be found at the apartments of her lovers.

Gentlemen and con men alike showered her with

gifts—furs, jewels, and savings bonds in the amount of one thousand dollars each. The Broadway Butterfly sparkled as bright as the lights of the Great White Way. One must only look at what she was wearing the night before she died to see she owned an assortment of jewels, fit for a queen.

Dorothy King's maid, Ella "Billy" Bradford, recalls dressing Miss King the evening of March 14. Miss Bradford has a photographic memory of Miss King's jewels: a magnificent diamond and pearl bracelet with a platinum clasp sparkled on one wrist, and about her neck on her bosom hung a lavaliere built around a two-and-a-half-carat pear-shaped sapphire. A solitaire diamond of almost three carats glowed on one finger and a great black pearl shone on her other hand, which also gleamed with lesser jewels. But on the cold morning of March 15, when Miss Bradford found Dorothy King dead, every single one of those glimmering jewels was gone.

Ellie sucked in her breath. "Iris. You must read this."

She handed her aunt the magnifying glass and waited for Iris to peruse the article. Iris's eyes narrowed and then widened. She frowned, gently setting the magnifying lens down.

"The media never portrayed Dot kindly in death."

Ellie felt bad for the murdered woman, her life choices picked apart by people who never knew her. But she needed Iris to see what she had seen.

"The bracelet mentioned in the article, it sounds an awful lot like yours, doesn't it?"

Iris rubbed her chin. "Yes, I suppose it does."

Ellie's arms prickled with gooseflesh. "Iris, you told me you believed John gave Dot King your bracelet when she became his new *pet*." She took a deep breath. "I believe Dorothy King was wearing that bracelet when she died."

A shudder ran from the crown of her head down to the soles of her feet. Ellie now felt certain of one thing: Dot had *not* given Lillian her diamond and pearl bracelet—a murderer had unclasped it from her lifeless wrist. And if Lillian truly had done something awful, then Ellie would find out what it was.

STANDING BENEATH THE green awning of Caffè Reggio, Ellie drew in a deep breath. She didn't want Lucy to know anything about Lillian's potential involvement in a crime—she'd asked Lillian to come to Greenwich Village alone.

"I'm hoping that being back in her old neighborhood will disarm her," Ellie had said to Iris as they'd used the library's pay phone. "She'll be swept up in reminders of the past, and more likely to tell us what happened."

Ellie didn't know what had transpired in the time between Dorothy King's murder and Lillian's acquiring her bracelet, but she suspected it wasn't good. On the phone, Lillian had agreed to meet them, though she'd seemed perturbed; and now they were here. Ellie's stomach knotted. She looked at the café's plate-glass window holding plaster busts and statues, and she glanced at her wristwatch.

"Shall we?"

Iris nodded, a look of apprehension on her face.

Ellie entered the dimly lit café and surveyed the room, painted a deep brown and filled with a hodgepodge of Renaissance art, oil paintings, and yellowed Italian newspaper clippings. Vintage wrought-iron chairs clustered around marble-topped tables, and Ellie spotted Lillian sitting in the corner. People read and talked while sipping their cappuccinos, café patrons with a bit of artistic flair.

Squeezing past a large, nickel-plated espresso machine, Ellie felt the tension in her body mounting. Her heart thudded and her palms were sweating, but in order to coerce Lillian into revealing her secrets, Ellie had to maintain a cool façade.

Lillian wore a tight-fitting cloche, her lips painted a bold red. Ellie marveled at her ability to take a vintage hat and make it look chic. Steam from the espresso machine whistled, a shriek so loud nothing could be heard above the din. Ellie took a seat across from Lillian, and Iris sat down beside her. They smiled tightly at one another as they removed their gloves.

Lillian pursed her lips. "So, what's this all about?"

A mustachioed waiter appeared and grinned at the three women. "Welcome in! What will you be having today?"

Ellie felt the knot in her stomach harden, but she smiled at the friendly waiter. "One cappuccino, please."

Iris and Lillian ordered cappuccinos as well, and their server departed. Ellie took a deep breath, uncertain of how to proceed. She felt a sharp pang, remembering the donuts and coffees she had shared with her father at Mayflower Donuts. *How many more memories could they have had together, if he hadn't spent so much of his time with Lillian?* Tapping into her jealousy, Ellie summoned the strength she needed. She fixed her hazel eyes on Lillian's green ones. "I invited you here because I don't think you've been honest with me."

Lillian's thin, arched eyebrows rose in amusement. "Oh really?"

"You're not listed in the phone book. Why is that?"

Lifting her chin, Lillian smirked. "I value my privacy. Not being listed in the telephone book isn't a crime, is it?"

Ellie's heart beat faster. "No. But that doesn't mean you didn't commit one."

The color drained from Lillian's face. She took a beat too long to answer. "I have no idea what you're talking about."

The waiter returned with their cappuccinos, and Ellie willed him to make himself scarce. When he left, she hardened her gaze.

"Do you know how I found you?"

Lillian sipped her cappuccino. "Why don't you tell me?" She seemed to have recovered her equilibrium.

"The Ziegfeld Club gave me a tip about the diamond and pearl bracelet you pawned."

Lillian's face remained impassive, but Ellie thought she saw the corner of her mouth twitch. She stared at Lillian. "I found the bracelet at a pawnshop here in Greenwich Village."

Lillian shrugged. "So what? I pawned a bracelet. It was my grandmother's."

Iris came to life then, fixing her cold blue gaze on Lillian.

"That bracelet belonged to Dorothy King. I saw the engraving on the clasp."

Beads of sweat began to form on Lillian's forehead.

"*My pet.*" Iris spat the words. "It's what John used to call me. That bracelet was mine, part of a past I long to forget. I suppose John gave it to Dot when she became his new pet. But I don't understand how *you* got it."

Ellie watched Lillian's body language. Her father's mistress sat still as a statue. Whatever was going on in Lillian's mind was too taxing for her to move. Lillian spoke slowly. "I didn't know Dorothy King." She licked her lips nervously. "I've received plenty of jewelry over the years. The bracelet must have been a gift from an admirer. I never noticed the engraving before."

Taking a deep breath, Ellie refused to fall for Lillian's lie.

"Oh really? When you were involved with my father, you still accepted gifts from other men? I thought you loved him."

Lillian's nostrils flared. She blinked rapidly. "I did—I do."

"But you accepted a diamond and pearl bracelet from someone else?"

Lillian shook her head. "I must have received that bracelet as a gift before I met your father."

Ellie leaned forward on her elbow. "How odd. You see, I read an article today in the *Daily News*. It described Dot King wearing this *very* bracelet on the night before she died. You couldn't have received this bracelet as a gift from a gentleman caller, because it was *stolen* on March fifteenth, from Dot King's wrist."

Lillian rubbed the nape of her neck. "I had no idea this bracelet once belonged to Dorothy King, or that it was stolen." She crossed her arms.

Ellie reached into her bag and retrieved her father's letter. She unfolded it and slid it across the table toward Lillian.

Lillian's mouth fell open. "Why, how did you—?"

Leaning forward on her elbows, Ellie spoke slowly. "My father wrote this on March twenty-fourth, 1923. Not only had you already met him by the time you purportedly received Dorothy King's bracelet as a gift, but you confessed to him that you'd done something awful—and possibly illegal."

Lillian began to tremble. She shook her head.

Ellie's heart was pounding. "I think you feel guilty about this bracelet. That's why you cried every time you took it out of your drawer."

A sharp gasp escaped Lillian's mouth. "How could you *possibly* know that?"

Ellie continued. "You kept this bracelet hidden for twenty years. But you must have needed money, or wanted to finally be rid of it. You went to a pawnshop that didn't do business by the books. Because you *already knew* this bracelet belonged to Dorothy King."

Lillian's breath grew rapid and shallow. "I didn't know her. I swear I never met her."

Iris spoke then, her eyes hard. "You never went to one of Dot's parties? You didn't envy her jewels like you envied mine?"

Lillian snarled at Iris. "You thought you were so high-and-mighty. I saw you give away your diamonds like they were nothing! And then you lost *everything*, including your fancy midtown apartment with its little dumbwaiter."

The air seemed to vanish from the room. Suddenly, Lillian slapped a hand over her mouth.

Iris spoke slowly. "You saw me give my jewels to Dorothy King outside the New Amsterdam Theatre. And I *never* had guests at that apartment. But you've been inside." She narrowed her eyes. "Why is that?"

Dropping her spoon with a clatter, Lillian looked up, her eyes wet with tears.

"Because I was booted from the Ziegfeld Follies like a piece of garbage, all right? I never got another stage role in spite of my talent." Her face twisted into a grimace, looking at Iris. "I was so envious of you back then. I coveted everything you had, including your role as principal dancer."

Lillian clenched her fists. "Seeing you give away your diamond necklace . . . and then later watching Dot King's neck and wrists sparkle while I struggled to find work, it was too much." Lillian exhaled with a shudder. "That's when Mickey O'Malley hired me as a spotter."

Iris grew pale. "The mob boss? That—gangster?"

Lillian nodded. "Like you, I've done things I'm not proud of." Her lip trembled. "Why be beautiful if you can't get what you want? I wasn't going to get a speaking role in a film, or become a serial bride, and so I agreed to help Mickey. I ran in the right circles, I knew women with money. They trusted me."

Iris's mouth fell open. "But they were your *friends*. How could you?"

Lillian wiped away a tear. "I felt I had no friends."

Ellie didn't understand. She turned to Lillian. "What's a spotter?"

Lillian's shoulders drooped. "A spotter is a person who spots targets to rob. Mickey wanted a girl like me who knew the right people—women like Dot with so many diamonds and furs, they wouldn't know which ones went missing."

Ellie grimaced. She couldn't believe her father had been involved with a criminal—protective of her, even—especially when Lillian had done something so awful. She glared. "So you told this gangster about Dorothy King?"

Lillian covered her mouth with a trembling hand, nodding. "I told Mickey about the dumbwaiter in Dot's apartment. That's how he got the boy inside."

A shiver ran through Ellie. "But wasn't the dumbwaiter too small?" She remembered Iris had wanted to use it to escape.

Lillian's voice dropped to a whisper. "He was a skinny kid. Short. Only sixteen or seventeen." She looked around the café. The espresso machine shrieked, and everyone appeared lost in conversation. Lillian wiped away another tear.

"It was a botched job. I don't think that boy meant to kill her. The bracelet Mickey gave me felt like blood money. I regretted what I had done immediately."

Ellie's heart was pounding. "So the police had it right?"

Blinking back tears, Lillian nodded. "Yes."

Ellie swallowed, hard. "Did you do other jobs for Mickey?"

Lillian placed her palms flat against the table. "*No.* I got out as soon as I could."

Iris sat still as a statue, a stunned look on her face. Then she turned to Lillian, as if seeing her for the first time.

"But I read the papers. The police found yellow silk men's pajamas, which belonged to John. The stolen furs and jewels were just a ruse to cover his tracks—"

Lillian's voice was firm.

"Mickey O'Malley planned the robbery. The boy chloroformed Dot, all right? He gave her too much accidentally. Not John. That's what happened."

Finally, Lillian had given them the closure they needed. Ellie placed a hand on top of her aunt's, while Iris sat there wide-eyed. How many decades had she suffered in silence for a horrible act she had no control over? Ellie watched as her aunt began to tremble, her arms shaking, as if she was recovering from shock. Iris placed a hand over her open mouth, her relief palpable.

Lillian, meanwhile, looked ashamed. Ellie wondered what dark things lived inside Lillian's head—*Did she hear whispers of a guilty conscience at night?*

Iris rubbed her temples. "But I never should have gotten Dot involved with John. Even if she hadn't been robbed, he would have . . ."

Lillian nodded, blinking back tears. "Every single day, I wish I could take back what I did to her."

Iris swallowed. "So do I."

Their secrets laid bare on the table, the two women sat in silence. Then Lillian broke the tension by holding William's letter between her manicured fingers.

"*How* did you get this?"

Ellie felt her neck flush. "I broke into your apartment."

Lillian drew in a sharp breath. "The nerve! How dare you!"

Ellie held Lillian's gaze. "I did what I had to. Iris felt responsible for Dorothy King's murder. I needed to find the truth."

Lillian looked venomous as a viper, ready to strike. "If you *ever* tell Lucy about any of this, I swear I'll—"

Ellie shook her head. "You're Lucy's mother. I would never

do that." She smiled tentatively. "Lucy is really lovely. You've raised a wonderful, bright girl. And I intend to write to her—to be the sister she deserves."

Lillian's features softened, and she offered a small smile in return. "I think she would like that."

Something inside of Ellie began to unfurl. Slowly, she and Lucy were learning to trust each other—they had come so much further than where they had started, and Ellie wanted her little sister to feel safe around her. As much as she despised Lillian, she only wanted what was best for Lucy. But looking at the woman before her, Ellie came to a funny realization: she didn't hate Lillian anymore. They were now on a shared mission, to understand and make peace with the past.

Ellie turned to Iris, noticing how her aunt held herself taller. Though Iris still appeared to be in a state of shock, she looked lighter and freer than she had in years.

The waiter reappeared then. "Can I bring you ladies anything else?"

Iris fixed her clear, blue gaze on him, her chin lifted.

"No, thank you. We're finished here."

Chapter Twenty-Three

Ellie

The Southern Pacific ferryboat passed beneath the Bay Bridge, rocked by the choppy gray water, and Ellie wrapped her arms around herself, the February wind cold against her cheeks. She was exhausted from the two-day train journey that had taken her from Chicago to Oakland, and with her eyes fixed on San Francisco's familiar skyline, Ellie thought about the city she'd left behind.

In Manhattan, both she and Iris had changed, and with that growth came some discomfort. Nothing felt simple anymore, but perhaps it never had been. Now, as the ferry entered the Port of San Francisco, Ellie rubbed her arms, remembering Tom's words: *We don't want any kind of scandal associated with our family, especially not right before the wedding.*

Ellie bit her lip, a hard knot forming in her stomach. Lucy was family, and Tom was wrong about secrets. The more they festered, the more they hurt the people who kept them. Ellie refused to pretend her father's other daughter didn't exist. As painful as the discovery had been, it was her truth. And if Tom couldn't accept Lucy, well . . . then she couldn't accept him.

Taking one last look at the waterfront, Ellie went inside to gather her luggage. Iris sat on a bench, her suitcases placed on the tiled floor at her feet. Her eyes were tired, but she smiled.

"We've made it home in one piece."

One piece. They had traveled to New York so Ellie could put together the missing pieces of her father's life and so Iris could make peace with her past. In spite of the fact that Ellie hadn't gotten enough sleep on the train, she felt more clarity than she had in years.

They disembarked, moving along with the crowd, greeted by the cries of seagulls and the smell of baking sourdough. Ellie smiled, breathing in the salty sea air. Though New York had breathtaking architecture, charming neighborhoods, and lovely parks, San Francisco was where she belonged.

Iris raised her arm to hail a taxi. The cabbie pulled over and loaded their luggage into the trunk. The interior smelled of cigarette smoke and something musty, but Ellie gratefully sank into the seat all the same. While the driver navigated through traffic, honking and swearing under his breath, Ellie drifted off, the street noise fading into the background.

"Hyde Street, Russian Hill."

Ellie opened her eyes. The cab idled outside her home, its curtains drawn. She wrapped her arms around her aunt, hugging Iris tight.

"Thank you for everything."

Iris patted her back. "Thank *you*. I didn't realize I needed this trip."

They smiled at each other, a shared understanding passing between them.

She shut the cab door behind her, retrieved her suitcases, and climbed the creaking porch steps. Turning her key in the lock, Ellie opened the door. The house was quiet as usual, but she felt like she was seeing it with new eyes—the dark wood, the austere rooms, the wooden crucifix nailed to the wall. This place was neither warm nor inviting—it wasn't somewhere she wanted to stay.

Setting down her suitcase, Ellie called out. "Mother?"

The dishes in the sink had been washed, and laundry hung on the line outside—a good sign. She approached her mother's bedroom, her childhood fears flaring up as she walked down the hall. Ellie had never felt as though she belonged in this house.

Taking a deep breath, Ellie rapped her knuckles on the bedroom door and then opened it. Clara stood inside, wearing a cotton housedress with her hair in curlers. Ellie smiled with relief to see her mother awake and dressed.

"Hi, Mother. I'm so glad to see you're feeling better." Her arms hung limply at her sides. *Would her mother accept a hug if she offered it?*

Clara pursed her lips. "Mrs. Cook checked on me while you were away, which is more than I can say about *you* and my sister."

Ellie clenched her jaw. "I'm sorry I didn't telephone from New York. Did you eat the food I left you?" She felt the familiar sense of being small, and in trouble.

Clara sniffed. "The chicken was too dry and the soup was too salty." Her eyes swept critically over her daughter. "You look a fright. Why haven't you made up your face? Never allow your fiancé to see you like that."

Ellie stiffened. "And so what if he does?"

Narrowing her eyes, Clara took a step forward. "A man like Tom doesn't come around every day. Be careful, Eleanor, or you will lose him."

Ellie flinched, waiting for another insult that would cut to the bone. But then she paused. *This wasn't about her.* These were her mother's own fears about Lillian—the woman she had lost her husband to. No amount of carefully applied makeup had been enough to keep him.

Ellie took a deep breath in, steeling herself. "I'm sorry, Mother, that Father wasn't there for you in the way you needed him to be."

Clara's eyes flashed. "Watch your tongue!"

But the quiver of her mother's lips betrayed the grief buried beneath her anger. She was no longer in a numbed daze. Ellie looked around for the bottle of barbiturates the doctor had prescribed, and then she saw them on the bedside table.

"Are you still taking those?"

Clara shook her head. "They made me feel foggy."

Sadness welled inside Ellie as she mourned the relationship with her mother she would never have—a relationship in which they could talk about anything, and laugh, a relationship with a mother who didn't constantly criticize her. No matter how much she longed for a mother who baked cookies and imparted wisdom, that wasn't what she had. Her throat tightened, but she didn't cry.

"Good. I think you're better off without them."

Ellie turned and left the room. She would never have her mother's approval, no matter what she did, but she didn't need it anymore. In New York, she had made her own decisions. More and more, she was beginning to trust her intuition. And right now, it was telling her that she wasn't obligated to live in this house, under her mother's thumb.

Opening the door to her bedroom, Ellie took in the sight of her bed with its crisp white sheets and hand-sewn coverlet. She flopped down on top of the blankets, fully clothed, too tired to remove her shoes. Closing her eyes, she sank into the mattress, knowing she ought to unpack, but for once not giving a damn.

When Ellie opened her eyes, it was still dark. For a moment, she thought she was back in New York, but then her childhood bedroom materialized around her. The alarm clock on the bedside table read 5 a.m.—which meant it was eight in the morning, New York time. Birds chirped in the trees outside.

Flicking on the light, Ellie went in the kitchen and set the kettle on to boil. With a cup of tea brewing, she retrieved her 1945 edition of the *Writer's Yearbook* from her desk drawer and opened it to an earmarked page, "From the Slush Deliver Me! How to Write and Sell Articles" by Darrell Huff.

Ellie read the paragraphs she'd underlined. All her previous rejection letters from literary magazines had felt so personal. Yet now she could see her setbacks hadn't meant failure: they had been a learning opportunity. She cracked her knuckles at her desk. In order to impress Frank, she would need to stand out, especially with a column that didn't fit into any existing department.

Ellie loaded paper into her Corona typewriter and began to type. As the sun rose in the sky, she stepped away from her desk, satisfied with what she'd written. Returning to the kitchen, Ellie lit the stove to make another pot of tea. She would pitch Frank . . . today. There was no sense in waiting any longer.

THE DIN OF clacking typewriters and the scent of cigarette smoke welcomed Ellie back to the *San Francisco Chronicle*. She smiled, having forgotten how much she loved this place. She had telephoned Tom this morning, before coming in to the office, and they had arranged to meet at the army base later today. But Ellie pushed Tom from her mind as butterflies filled her stomach.

With her article neatly typed and tucked in a folder under her arm, she held her head high and strode across the room. A few male reporters raised their eyebrows as she passed. Ellie smiled, loving how comfortable she felt in her wool trousers. There was no law against wearing them—it simply wasn't the norm. Rapping her knuckles on the glass door to Frank's office, Ellie waited.

"Come in!" A lovely girl with dark hair and piercing green eyes pulled the door open. Ellie paused, blinking at Frank's empty chair.

"I'm here to see Frank. Is he in?"

The girl nodded. "He stepped out momentarily, but he'll be back soon. May I bring you anything? Coffee? Tea?"

A realization dawned on Ellie. "Wait a minute—are you Jack's sister?"

The girl smiled, her cheeks dimpling. "I am. Anna Miller."

Ellie shook her hand, which was soft and warm. "Ellie

Morgan. It's a pleasure to meet you. Jack was such a pal to have you fill in for me." She dropped her voice to a whisper. "I hope Frank hasn't been too hard on you."

Anna laughed. "Not at all! You ought to hear Jack and our brother Carl when they get riled up. They have mouths like sailors."

Ellie chuckled. "Are you enjoying the job?"

Anna nodded, organizing the papers on Frank's desk. "Oh, absolutely!" But then her face fell into a frown. "I hope Frank will give me a decent reference, even though I was only here for a short while."

"Hold that thought." Ellie winked at Anna as Frank entered the office, his tie askew and his bald spot flushed and shiny.

His eyes widened. "Miss Morgan. You came back."

Ellie straightened her spine. "Sir. May I have a word in private, please?"

Anna smiled. "I'll step out for a moment."

Frank's eyes met Ellie's when Anna shut the door. "The new gal's been doing a great job. I'm hesitant to let you back after that stunt you pulled."

Ellie took a deep breath in. "About that, I'm sorry. I'd like to make a proposition. It's regarding a potential new column for the paper."

Frank's caterpillar-like brows drew together. "Go on."

Ellie retrieved her article from her folder and handed it to Frank. Her heart was pounding, but she kept her voice steady. "It's a colorful profile of life, people, and places in modern San Francisco."

Frank's eyes narrowed as he took the paper from her. Ellie had poured her heart onto the page, and she held her breath as he read what she'd written.

Tales from the City

San Francisco has always been an oxymoron: some call it a beautiful disaster. Others call it Frisco, or simply, the City by the Bay. San Francisco's arms are outstretched to tourists, transients, and talented artists alike, and to our brave American soldiers, headed overseas from the port of embarkation.

Here, a wisp of fog can stir a memory, and the sound of the waves can feel like a song. San Francisco has vigor in every breath of its trade winds, the whisper of its bawdy past carried upon them like gold dust. On skid row, vagabonds beg for change, while across Market Street in Hayes Valley, aging mansions stand proud like grande dames. San Francisco is a place of terrible beauty and sweet sorrow, of honest thieves and seriously funny people.

From the streets of Chinatown to Little Italy to the Hunter's Point Naval Shipyard, multiple languages are spoken aloud by every color and creed of person. Artists and poets gather at North Beach cafés, while on the waterfront, longshoremen load cargo onto freighters. One doesn't need to read Kafka to be welcomed here.

Paupers and princes alike are privy to stunning views of the Golden Gate Bridge, an engineering marvel like no other. Admire its 80,000 miles of steel cable from the docks, where proud generations of fishermen sell Dungeness crab, or view its magnificent silhouette from the famed Fairmont Hotel, where delegates from 50 nations are designated to meet this June.

Politicians, businessmen, sailors, and immigrants: we San Franciscans are a hardy and scrappy lot. Our city emerged from the ashes of fire—and in these trying times of war, we are once again a symbol of the promise of resurrection. While some may call us beautiful, and others may call us a disaster, I call us survivors. San Francisco's resilience and character are sufficient to withstand any storm. And I, for one, am proud to call this place home.

Ellie cleared her throat. "It's something new—a reminder of where we came from as a city, and where we're going."

Frank rubbed his jaw. "Who's the writer? I'd like to meet this fella."

A smile tugged at Ellie's lips. "I'm the writer, sir."

His eyes widened. "*You?*"

Ellie heard her mother's voice, reminding her she wasn't a writer, and that she was destined to be a homemaker, but she dismissed it.

"Yes, sir. And while I don't have a traditional journalism

background, I have a vision for this column. I'll interview everyone from opera singers to longshoremen—I'll remind readers of our city's forgotten gems. Also, I've written quite a few articles for Rick Johnson that were published under his byline."

Frank scoffed. "You're kidding me."

Ellie shook her head. "Go on, ask him."

Taken aback by her direct approach, Frank popped his head outside the office, his voice booming. "Johnson! I need you in here. Now!"

Rick Johnson loped into the room. He stood a head taller than Ellie and glanced at her dismissively before turning to Frank. "Sir?"

"Is it true that Miss Morgan has written under your byline?"

Rick flushed from his neck upward. "I—well, no, not exactly."

"'The Victory Gardens.'" Ellie glared at Rick. "I wrote that piece. I've written everything in the past year that you haven't cared to do—admit it."

Tugging at his collar, Rick shrugged. "They were puff pieces, things I thought were better suited for a female—"

Frank waved his hand. "That's enough. Get outta here."

Rick ducked his head, leaving the office with an ashamed look on his face.

Ellie watched as Frank sat down and drummed his fingers on his desk. He heaved a sigh. "I suppose I might be able to squeeze something in."

Barely able to contain her smile, Ellie met Frank's eyes. "You'll run it?"

He nodded. "You've got moxie. I like it."

Happiness warmed her. "Thank you, sir. I won't let you down."

Frank shrugged. "Make sure you complete your secretarial duties first, and we have a deal."

Ellie smiled. "Actually, I think Miss Miller is doing a far better job than I ever did. So if it's all right with you, I believe she should keep the position."

Frank frowned. "Fine with me. Keep the column to five hundred words, max. We don't have a lot of space anymore."

"Understood." Ellie grinned. It would be a challenge to make do on a writer's salary—which she still needed to discuss with Frank—but she'd find out from Jack how much the male writers were making first. Then she'd work her hardest to earn the same. Suddenly, she remembered Tom and her bubble of happiness began to deflate. He'd made it clear in New York that he didn't want a working wife. Ellie twisted the diamond ring on her finger, which felt heavy with the weight of its expectations. She swallowed, knowing what she had to do next, no matter how painful it would be.

Fog blanketed Fort Scott in the headlands of the Presidio, and Ellie pulled her wool coat around her. Waiting for Tom in the designated visitors' area, she blew on her gloved hands. The damp air smelled like the ocean.

Tom approached the gate, looking sharp in his uniform, and Ellie's stomach knotted with nerves. He smiled broadly at her, and she smiled back. Opening the gate, Tom rushed toward her and swept her into a tight embrace.

"Dollface! I've missed you so much."

He looked as handsome as ever—his blond hair slicked back,

his blue eyes sparkling. Breathing in the spicy scent of his cologne, Ellie felt his cold lips press against hers, and she shut her eyes. But she didn't feel sparks like she had at the beginning of their courtship, confirming what she already knew.

She smiled through her discomfort.

"I've missed you too. And I have good news."

He raised an eyebrow. "You do?"

Ellie clutched his large hands in her gloved ones, her heart beating faster. A smile spread across her face. "I pitched my column to Frank, and he accepted it! Tom, I'm going to be a columnist at the *San Francisco Chronicle*."

Tom's brow furrowed. "A writer? But you're a secretary."

Ellie's heart sank, seeing the confused look on his face. Any hope she'd clung to that he could change had been dashed, and yet she carried on. "A new girl is taking over my secretarial position. My column is about rediscovering local gems, profiling different people and places. I'll interview folks from all walks of life—longshoremen, bakers, tailors, soldiers."

Chuckling, Tom ran a hand through his hair. "That's swell, doll. But we agreed you wouldn't work after marriage. Besides, San Francisco won't be your city for much longer. We're moving to Atlanta after the war, remember?"

A hard lump formed in Ellie's gut. It was something they'd discussed, and she had blindly accepted the possibility without much thought. At the time, she'd fooled herself into believing she could be happy anywhere with Tom. Now she realized she had been unfair to both of them.

Ellie licked her dry lips. "I know you miss Atlanta, but I'm meant to be here in San Francisco. It's my home."

Tom's eyes hardened. "You're meant to be where I am, and I don't want to stay in San Francisco."

Ellie swallowed. *Had she been so swept up in their romance because it offered an escape from her father's absence and from the oppressive loneliness of her mother's house?* Ellie couldn't continue to live there—that much was certain—but marrying Tom for security, and to create a family, wasn't what her heart wanted. It had been whispering, *What if there is something more?*

Tom's mouth turned down at the corners. "You've been acting funny since New York. Listen, I know it must've been difficult meeting your sister." He winced like the word tasted sour on his tongue. "But you don't have to worry. In Atlanta, we'll start over and she'll be nothing but a distant memory."

The space between them filled with an unbearable silence.

Ellie glared at Tom. "I intend to have a relationship with my sister. She will be much more than just a memory. And she has a name. It's *Lucy.*"

His jaw clenched. "Ellie, I don't think that's wise."

Ellie bristled. "Just like you don't think it's wise for me to write a column for the newspaper?"

Tom sighed, dropping her hands. "I can't have my wife running around the city, talking to longshoremen and God knows what other sorts of unsuitable characters. It's not safe. It's not *proper.*"

Ellie blinked back tears. She couldn't go on pretending. She removed her glove and tugged her three-carat diamond ring from her left finger. She held it out to Tom, feeling the finality of her decision.

"I'm sorry, Tom. I truly am."

The color drained from his face. Ellie could picture him as a towheaded little boy—she wanted to comfort him, this dashing, successful man who was willing to give her so much. But as his face contorted with rage, he began to resemble something more frightening.

Tom snatched the ring and stuffed it in his coat pocket. Spit flew from his mouth as he spoke. "Do you realize what a mistake you're making?"

Ellie's throat tightened. "I'm sorry. You deserve someone else, someone who's ready to be your wife."

His eyes glistened. "Mark my words, you *will* regret this."

Brushing off her coat, Ellie felt sad, but also relieved. She didn't regret her choice, not one bit.

"Goodbye, Tom."

And with that, she turned on her heel and left the military base, her pulse hammering. The future Tom envisioned for her had never been what she wanted. And now the future was hers to claim.

Iris pulled open her door, a look of surprise on her face.

"Ellie. Is everything all right?"

Blinking back tears, Ellie shook her head. "No. But it will be."

"Come in." Iris ushered Ellie into her apartment, where the familiar smell of lavender brought a sense of comfort.

Ellie took a seat on her aunt's velvet sofa, beneath the bay windows. Iris sat down too, her blue eyes filled with concern. "Tell me."

"I broke off my engagement with Tom." Ellie wiped away a tear and then sighed. "Don't look too relieved."

Iris held up her hands in surrender, but the corners of her mouth twitched. "How did he take it?"

"Not well." Ellie frowned, her stomach knotting with guilt. "But a man like Tom will have no trouble finding someone new."

"And how are *you*?" Iris patted Ellie's knee.

Ellie smiled. "I pitched my newspaper column to Frank, and he said he would run it. Iris, I'm going to be a writer at the *Chronicle*!"

Iris clapped her hands together, her eyes sparkling. "Wonderful! Oh, we must celebrate. I have a bottle of wine somewhere."

Iris disappeared into the kitchen, and Ellie heard a corkscrew turning. She relaxed her shoulders, knowing she could always count on her aunt to share her joys and sorrows. Iris returned holding two glasses of red wine. She handed one to Ellie and beamed. "To new beginnings. And to you, my brilliant niece."

Ellie clinked her glass against Iris's. "To new beginnings."

As she sipped the dark and fruity wine, a lovely pinot noir, Ellie's heart ached, thinking of her father. She wanted to tell him about her new job as a writer—he would be so proud. Ellie's search for him hadn't ended—she would keep going, no matter how long it took. Her father and his men would never be forgotten.

She had gone all the way to Manhattan in the hopes that Lillian would have answers—and instead, Ellie had been the one to tell Lillian about her father's plane crash. It had been an emotional and difficult trip, for both Ellie and Iris, and yet it had been a necessary one. Ellie looked at her aunt, seeing her in a new light.

Growing up, Ellie had always known Iris as one half of a married couple: Aunt Iris and Uncle Ed. She'd never thought to ask her aunt about her life before marriage, as if that was when a woman's life began. Now she knew better.

"Iris." Ellie sipped her wine. "Will you tell me what happened after you escaped New York? What was life like for you back then?"

Iris looked off into the distance.

"It was difficult at first." Then her face broke into a smile. "And also wonderful. After all, I finally met you."

Chapter Twenty-Four

Iris

The foghorn sounded long and low, and I shivered, looking out over the bay. Seeing the Ferry Building clock tower, rising ghost-like from the mist, I felt as if I were dreaming. But the scent of the ocean and the seagulls cawing were so visceral, I blinked back tears. After five long years in New York, I had made it home.

Days spent on trains had passed by in a blur of landscapes, brown and green, flat and mountainous. I'd slept sitting up in my seat, my body exhausted. At every station my heart pounded, and I expected to see John or Wilson in the crowd. But neither man appeared. Every state I passed through took me farther from New York.

"Port of San Francisco! Ferry Building."

The captain's voice boomed as the boat docked, the choppy waves rocking the vessel from side to side. Feeling unsteady on my feet, I looked around for my luggage and then remembered I hadn't brought anything with me. All I had to my name were the clothes on my back, and a few dollars.

I disembarked, marveling at the buildings that had sprung up during my absence. San Francisco reached toward the sky, with newly constructed hotels flashing neon advertisements and bustling shops filled with people. The streetcars along the Embarcadero flung open their doors, and groups of well-dressed commuters disembarked, hurrying toward the Ferry Building.

Walking up Market Street, I took in the city I had left behind—cosmopolitan, thriving, prosperous, and lively. Women were dressed to the nines, laughing behind gloved hands and wearing stylish cloche hats. I heard snippets of French and Italian spoken by businessmen in dark suits.

Though the spectacle of San Francisco's main thoroughfare wasn't as arresting as that of the Great White Way, my senses felt overstimulated. An automobile engine firing caused me to flinch, and I wondered if I would startle every time I heard a loud noise, like the men returned from the Great War, broken and afraid.

At the Powell Street turnaround, I hopped aboard a cable car, easily gripping the rail from muscle memory. As the trolley rumbled uphill, toward the gate of Chinatown, children played in the street, while immigrants hawked their wares. No one aboard the trolley had given me a second glance, or asked if I was Stella Parsons from the Ziegfeld Follies. Here in San Francisco, I was invisible. For the first time in a long time, I didn't mind. I wanted to blend in.

The trolley car made a sharp right and then charged up Hyde Street. At the crest of the hill, the San Francisco Bay stretched before me in its great blue glory, the finest view in all of San Francisco. Modest wooden houses dotted the hillside, laundry flapping in the breeze. I hopped off the trolley before Lombard. I had heard the unmanageable old street, paved with cobblestones, had been remade as a serpentine roadway, so autos could drive up the steep grade.

Looking up at the familiar clapboard façade of my childhood home, I could hear my mother's chickens clucking in the backyard, just as they'd always done. My throat tightened. When I left home at age twenty with stars in my eyes, I never expected to return. And yet here I was. I'd escaped John. I was safe.

With my heart in my throat, I climbed the creaky porch steps and rapped my knuckles on the heavy wooden door. My sister pulled it open, her blue eyes widening when they met mine, her face breaking into a smile.

"Iris! My goodness, what are you doing here?"

Pulling Clara into a hug, I blinked back tears. She smelled like soap, and she'd grown from a skinny teenager into a beautiful young woman, her wavy bob skimming her jawline. We held each other at arm's length and laughed. It felt as though we were children again, and that no time had passed at all.

I smiled. "I missed you, and I decided to come home."

"William!" Clara called down the hallway. "Come quickly—you won't believe who's come to join us for supper."

Suddenly, a small child tore down the hallway and flung herself at her mother's skirt. She wrapped her chubby arms around Clara's legs.

"Mama, Mama!"

Clara stroked the little girl's ginger curls, and the child looked at me with her large hazel eyes. "Who dat, Mama?"

"That's your aunt Iris." Clara smiled at her little girl. "Say hello to your auntie, Eleanor."

I bent down, eye level with my niece. "Hello, sweetie. It's so nice to finally meet you. My, aren't you a big girl."

A hard lump formed in my throat. I'd missed the birth of my only niece, her first steps, her first words . . . but I was here now. Eleanor giggled, and my heart broke, thinking of the baby who was no longer inside me—who would never grow up to meet her cousin. Still, I was delighted to meet Eleanor in person. She bashfully turned away, her curls swinging, and buried her face in Clara's skirt.

Clara's voice grew sharp. "Don't be shy, now. Say hello!"

I was taken aback by my sister's harshness. After all, Eleanor was only two. She was allowed to be shy.

"That's all right." I stood up. "She doesn't know who I am."

William appeared in the doorway, filling it with his tall, lanky frame. His eyes brightened when they saw me, crinkling at the corners when he smiled.

"Well, this is a pleasant surprise! Hello, Iris."

"Dada!" Eleanor let go of Clara's skirt and ran toward her father. William swooped her up in his arms and cuddled his little girl. I smiled at how naturally he'd taken to fatherhood and how much they adored one another.

Clasping my hands in front of me, I smiled politely. "I apologize for not writing first to tell you I was coming."

"Nonsense." Clara ushered me into the foyer. "You're always welcome here."

William frowned. "Where are your bags?"

Heat crept up my neck. "They were stolen . . . on the train."

"How awful!" Clara placed a hand on my shoulder. "I can lend you a few dresses. Come with me, Mother and Father will be so surprised."

I stepped inside, following my sister down the narrow, dark hallway of the railroad-style house, which had always made me feel claustrophobic, as if the walls were closing in on me. There were my parents, sitting at the kitchen table, looking older than I remembered. But I smiled, feeling a rush of affection for the people who raised me.

"Hello, Ma. Hello, Pa."

Mother looked up, her gray hair pulled back in a tight bun. She resembled a woman from the last century in her heavy, dark dress, buttoned up to her neck, and a woolen shawl draped around her shoulders.

"Oh, Iris! You've come home. Henry, look!"

Mother stood from the table, and I wrapped her in a hug, my eyes pricking with tears. Though I could never tell her the awful things I had been through in New York, I relished the comfort of her embrace. She patted me on the back and then held me at arm's length, her eyes appraising me.

"My, you've grown up, haven't you?"

My father remained in his chair, the dark circles beneath his eyes even more pronounced, his body stiff from days working at the shipyard. He had never been an affectionate man, but he nodded at me.

"It's good to see you, daughter."

Eleanor gleefully darted beneath our feet as we sat around the kitchen table. Soup boiled on the stove, and chicken fried in the pan. Clara quickly tended to both, stirring the pot and lowering the flame. "I wish I'd known you were coming, Iris. I would have prepared more food. I'll set another place at the table."

My poor sister looked more frazzled than I'd ever seen her. "Thank you. Please don't trouble yourself, Clara. I don't need much."

Perhaps I could stay here for the night, but after that I would need to find a room of my own. My family's resources were stretched thin. Clara, William, and Eleanor had taken one bedroom of the small house, while my parents had the other. I didn't want to crowd everyone even more.

William smiled at me. "There's plenty of food to go around, and we're happy to have you join us, Iris."

I returned his smile, wondering if he noted the absence of my sumptuous fur coat and French couture. If he did, he hid his reaction well. Taking my place at the table, I managed to avoid speaking about New York, deferring questions by playing up my exhaustion from the train ride.

Eleanor warmed to me, and when she sat in my lap, I snuggled her close, feeling the weight of her sturdy little body. She tugged at my hair, making me laugh. But her actions frustrated Clara, who nagged Eleanor to practice her table manners.

After dinner, as Clara and I washed up, I looked at my sister. "You know, I would be happy to mind Eleanor anytime. She's a lovely child."

Clara pushed a sweaty strand of hair back from her forehead. "Would you? Between caring for Mother and Father and keeping up this place, I find Eleanor to be such a handful. She's always underfoot, making mischief."

"As children are wont to do."

I laughed, but Clara didn't smile, and I worried perhaps she wasn't getting enough rest. She had always preferred things neat, quiet, and orderly—mothering a small child would come as a challenge for her.

That night, as I lay on the old sofa in the living room, listening to the sound of the foghorn, I slept well for the first time in months. Though John could still find me here, he couldn't do it with the same ease he had in New York. I prayed he would stop looking. Stella Parsons the stage starlet was gone. And in her place, someone else was emerging—a woman I had yet to become.

IN THE DAYS following, I found a respectable boardinghouse "for occupancy by unmarried women." I also found work as a secretary. The irony was not lost on me—but another boarder, a girl named Ruthie, had been hired as a stenographer, and she kindly offered me her former position at a real estate firm downtown.

"Can you type? Are you quick on your feet?"

Ruthie had no clue how quick on my feet I had been. Admittedly, I didn't have much experience typing, but I assured her I would be fine, and she gave me the address of an office on Kearny Street. I put on lipstick and styled my hair in a finger wave, knowing it wouldn't hurt my chances to be easy on the eyes.

In my interview, I reminded myself I was capable of learning to type—it couldn't be that difficult. Though I made a few errors in the beginning, and worked slowly, my new boss, Mr. Richards, did not check my references. Thank goodness, as I had never actually worked for White & Jones Law Firm in New York.

And so I fell into a new routine: answering the telephone, transcribing notes, and learning about a new neighborhood of stucco bungalows being developed out by the ocean, where previously there had been only sand dunes. My typing improved, and I made a few friends at the boardinghouse. To the new gals, I was simply Iris, doting aunt and secretary. But at night, I woke up with my heart pounding, a scream scraping up my throat, remembering John.

Ruthie, Helen, and Millie knew I suffered from nightmares. Our walls were thin, and everything from coughs to conversation could be heard. I told my friends I had a fear of heights, and that I dreamed of falling off a building. Sometimes the gals would come into my room, dolled up for nights out on the town, having snuck flasks of whiskey past our landlady, Mrs. O'Connell.

I enjoyed their laughter and conversation. San Francisco was wetter than it had ever been—there was no bathtub gin here, only real whiskey, rum, and vodka smuggled in by boats from Canada. Neighborhood bars masqueraded as soda shops, and speakeasies were everywhere, from the basements of little Italian restaurants to high-end offices in the Financial District.

But I eschewed boozy nights out, preferring to rest so I could get up early. I loved spending my weekends with Ellie, walking hand in hand with my niece along the massive expanse of the Great Highway, an open road running alongside the Pacific Ocean. Ellie would squeal with delight every time she saw the roller coasters at Chutes-at-the-Beach, our favorite seaside amusement park.

Seeing Ellie delight in simple pleasures allowed me to do the same. I didn't need liquor, nightlife, or the thrill of the stage to feel alive anymore—I felt perfectly happy sitting in the grass beneath the Dutch windmill, picking daisies. We spent sunny days together, riding the carousel and the Ferris wheel, and watching the slightly frightening automaton, Laffing Sal, whose cackle echoed through the park.

Sometimes, while we walked together sharing a cotton candy, a heavy cloud would settle over me, and I'd think of the child I'd lost. But then Ellie would grip my hand in hers and point out a bird, a flower, or a butterfly. She had a magical ability to pull me from the quicksand of my sadness and back into the present.

At night, in my room at the boardinghouse, I shut my eyes tight and willed physical exhaustion to bring on dreamless sleep. But John was always in the back of my mind, an ever-present threat. *How had he reacted when he found out I wasn't dead—and that both Mary and I had left him? Had he sent Wilson to search for us?* I wished I had the courage to contact the police, but his position in society was too powerful. John's word would be believed over mine, and influential lawmen were likely in his pocket.

I took deep breaths, reminding myself no one in New York knew where I lived, not Hilda, Lou, or Lillian. San Francisco was not a large city like Manhattan, but it was not small either. I was safe here—just another secretary, a face that could blend in with the crowd. Some nights, I dreamed I was onstage at the New Amsterdam, dancing beneath the globe lights in sequins and feathers.

When I awoke, I felt pangs of nostalgia, but that wasn't the life I wanted anymore. Seeing my sister, Clara, together with William and Ellie made me realize I wanted to be married someday, to try again for a child of my own. I didn't know if that was a future I could have, or one I deserved, but still, I hoped.

. . .

ONE FOGGY MORNING in the middle of March, my carefully constructed life came crashing down like a house of cards. I'd gone to buy the newspaper, and the front-page headline stopped me cold:

PRETTY ARTISTS' MODEL
FOUND DEAD IN HER APARTMENT

NEW YORK, MARCH 16, 1923

Lying in bed in a cramped, unnatural position, Dorothy King, a pretty artists' model, was found dead about noon yesterday in her apartment at 144 West 57th Street, on the top floor of a five-story building. A maid who found her mistress lifeless notified a policeman. The policeman called an ambulance. A surgeon made the fact of death official. The police have ruled the girl's death a murder.

I gasped, my legs buckling beneath me on the busy street. My heart began to pound, and dread filled my veins. That had been *my* apartment—the apartment where John had kept me prisoner. And Dorothy King had been murdered there.

Clutching the newspaper to my chest, I stumbled back to the boardinghouse on Jackson Street, opened the unmarked door, and climbed the narrow interior stairway leading to my room on the second floor. Sitting in bed, I spread the paper out before me on the coverlet and read:

Born Anna Marie Keenan in Harlem to poor Irish immigrants, she charmed her way out of Harlem's slattern streets, flashing her lovely blue eyes and finding herself in more sumptuous surroundings. She flitted from one club to another, and modeled the latest fashions. But with her hopes for a career in theater dashed, Dorothy King turned to entertaining gentlemen callers, who filled her bank account and showered her with diamonds.

Two men, a Mr. Marshall and a Mr. Wilson, whom an elevator attendant at Miss King's apartment said were seen with Miss King the night before her body was found, are being sought for questioning. It is believed that Mr. Marshall, a gentleman friend, is the last person to have seen her alive.

My stomach lurched and I feared I would vomit, but I forced myself to continue reading.

Assistant District Attorney Ferdinand Pecora is seeking the owner of a pair of large yellow silk men's pajamas, found stashed beneath the couch. An empty bottle of chloroform has also been found on the floor. The substance burned the model's mouth, and it has been ruled she was chloroformed to death.

Jewelry valued at fifteen thousand dollars and several expensive fur coats have been taken from the apartment. The possibility of robbery has not been

ruled out, though it is believed Dorothy King may
have known her murderer. Several other men, also
known to Miss King, are being sought for questioning by the police.

Clutching my sides, I rocked back and forth, my whole body
shaking. John had murdered Dorothy King with chloroform, and
it was my fault. I walked over to the sink in my room, turned on
the tap, and splashed water on my face. *Would the police arrest
John? Would they discover who he really was?*

I sat on my bed, paralyzed by dread. I had caused a woman's
murder. I could never, *ever* forgive myself for what had happened
to Dorothy King. I considered telephoning in sick to work, but
then decided typing notes would be a better way to spend the day
than being home alone with my guilty conscience.

When I arrived at the real estate office, my colleagues were
already talking about the case. "Did you hear about the murdered girl?"

"Terrible tragedy. What a beauty."

"Do you think that rich fella killed her?"

My fingers fumbled over the typewriter keys, and my boss
chided me for my sloppy work. In the lavatory, I burst into tears.
I wanted to hide beneath my desk in shame. No one knew what
I had done, but I would have to live with this guilt for the rest of
my life. I swallowed hard, considering whether I should contact
the police in New York. If I told them what I knew about John,
would they arrest him?

As the details in Dorothy King's case emerged, newspapers

ran daily updates. Dot became known as "the Broadway But-terfly" and "Dashing Dot," more famous in death than she ever had been alive. The public was fascinated by how she lived, "high on the bubbles of life," and how she died.

My stomach wrenched, imagining if it had been my name in the newspapers, how my family would have reacted and how the public would have perceived me. They did not look on Dot favor-ably. The fact that she was a dancer, a flapper, a girl with far too many boyfriends—somehow this made her murder her own fault, as if she'd brought this violence upon herself.

On a Saturday morning, before I was meant to go to the zoo with Ellie, Ruthie came into my room, her face animated. The murder case had captured the attention of all the gals in the boardinghouse. I loathed hearing them talk about it, but gossip was difficult to avoid.

Ruthie clutched the morning's paper and waved it at me. "There's been a break in the Dot King case. The police dis-covered a letter in her purse, sent from an admirer in Palm Beach. Read it!"

I held the paper with trembling hands, reading John's pri-vate words, printed for all to see: *Darling Dottie, only two more days and I will be in your arms. I want to see you O so much, and to kiss your pretty toes.*

The words swam before my eyes. He'd written me nearly identical sentiments from his mansion in Palm Beach. I thought I might faint.

"Iris? Are you all right?" Ruthie's voice sounded far away. "You're white as a sheet."

I shoved the newspaper back at her. "It's just so awful."

Was it my duty to tell the police about John's postcards? I didn't have them anymore, but I could call the authorities and give them an anonymous tip, revealing John's true identity. Yes, no matter how painful it would be, I had to tell the police the truth, even if I was arrested in connection with Dot's murder. I couldn't allow John to walk free after what he had done. But as I grappled with what to say, my eyes welling with tears as I thought about being taken away from Ellie, the truth John had fought so hard to hide was suddenly splashed all over the papers.

POLICE WILL QUESTION MILLIONAIRE PATRON OF GIRL

NEW YORK, MARCH 20, 1923

Officials who are investigating the murder will summon John Kearsley Mitchell, the Philadelphia millionaire who has admitted he was the patron of Dorothy King, to New York Friday. The authorities say they have learned of another wealthy man friend of the girl and he will probably be questioned too. This man's name has not been mentioned in connection with the case before.

Every day, I raced to the newsstand, praying the district attorney would get it right and arrest John for Dot's murder. She had other beaus, but I knew in my heart it was John who killed her. I shuddered, remembering the look in his icy blue eyes as he'd punched me in the stomach. Now that the authorities had his name, they only needed proof he had chloroformed Dot and killed her in a fit of rage. Within a week, John was brought in for questioning.

POLICE SEEK EVIDENCE IN DEATH PROBE

NEW YORK, MARCH 27, 1923

The first meeting of Assistant District Attorney Pecora and Mrs. and Mr. J. K. Mitchell was secured in the private car of E. T. Stotesbury, Philadelphia millionaire, at Union Station today. When Mitchell boarded the train, preparations were immediately made for transferring the car to another train bound for Philadelphia. The purpose of the meeting was said to afford Mitchell a chance to give an explanation of his relations with the murdered model. Assistant District Attorney Pecora will also summon Draper M. Daugherty, son of the attorney general, to his office for a conference in connection with the murder of Dorothy King.

The public knew John was the notorious "Mr. Marshall" who had written Dot King love letters, put her up in the apartment at 57th Street, and gifted her with furs and jewels. Seeing his photograph splashed across the tabloids was jarring. Though he could no longer hurt me, the sight of him made me sick. I hated that his wife had been allowed to join him for questioning—her being by his side would lend him credibility and sympathy, even though he was nothing but a monster. Would she eventually turn on him and leave him?

MITCHELLS HAVE NO STATEMENT TO MAKE

PHILADELPHIA, MARCH 28, 1923

Today in the magnificent mansion of John Kearsley Mitchell, tears flowed. He has explained his one-thousand-dollar visits to the apartment of Dorothy King, a New York beauty slain with chloroform, to his wife. Whether he has been taken back into her affections and those of his millionaire father-in-law, E. T. Stotesbury, has not been revealed. Reporters who surrounded the house today were able to learn nothing of what was transpiring inside. One report said that Mitchell's wife had decided to "stick" for the sake of the children. Another said he had been placed on probation, while another said the Mitchells would go abroad to escape unwanted attention. Mr. and Mrs. Mitchell remained in seclusion all day. They issued a one-line statement via the butler: "We have no statement to make and will not talk for publications."

That night, I couldn't sleep. I lay awake, awaiting developments in the case, listening to someone coughing through the thin boardinghouse walls. John was wealthy, polished, and the son-in-law of the richest man in America. He had his wife by his side, a respected socialite. I knew the robbery was merely a ruse to cover John's tracks.

The next morning, I read the paper at the breakfast table with my stomach in knots, too nervous to eat anything.

MITCHELL IS EXONERATED

NEW YORK, MARCH 29, 1923

John Kearsley Mitchell has been absolved of any connection with the death of Dorothy King, the Broadway gold digger, it was announced by Assistant District Attorney Pecora tonight. After questioning John Kearsley Mitchell, wealthy Philadelphia clubman, and his personal attorney, John H. Jackson, for five and a half hours tonight, Assistant District Attorney Ferdinand Pecora announced he had completed his investigation into the murder of Dorothy King.

I couldn't read any more. Tears pricked my eyes as I balled up the newspaper and threw it down in frustration. I'd ascertained that John's lawyer friend, John H. Jackson, was Mr. Wilson—and I hated them both with all of my being. A murderer had walked free. John and his wife boarded a boat to Europe to escape the attention surrounding them and that was reason enough for me to call in sick to work.

I spent the day in bed crying, sick to my stomach with the knowledge that John would continue to abuse his wealth and power—and likely women as well. I felt helpless and alone, and overcome with rage. A piece of me shriveled up inside, knowing a rapist and murderer remained a free man.

. . .

BY APRIL, THE newspapers speculated that Dot and her con artist beau, Albert Guimares, had been involved in a plot to blackmail John. He had been reframed as a victim, a wealthy older gentleman conned by a gold digger and her Portuguese lover—though some people still believed John to be guilty.

Many nights I struggled with whether I ought to tell the authorities about John's violent streak. But seeing the media tear apart Dorothy King, and the spectacle surrounding every individual mentioned in her murder case, I was loath to subject myself to scrutiny. *Why would the police believe me?* John had already been exonerated, and I too was a dancer who had frequented nightclubs.

The police would question what I wore, what I drank, and whom I spent time with. Bleary with anger, I realized being a woman was a crime. Women could not be promiscuous, drink alcohol, or break the law. The paragon of womanhood was the virtuous mother, and I was neither. A man like John could cause a miscarriage and still be deemed a Christian. But if a woman did such a thing out of necessity, she would be arrested as a murderer. The only thing that gave me solace was the knowledge that John was in Europe, with an entire ocean between us, and under so much public scrutiny, he would likely leave me alone.

I spent my days buried in work, trying to force everything about the Dorothy King case from my mind. I had become proficient at typing, and I relished my new skill, which would long outlast my looks. If I couldn't have justice, then at the very least I wanted a life of peace and solitude, and weekends with my beloved niece. Looking at brochures of neat stucco bungalows, I imagined happy families moving in, and my throat tightened. I didn't want to live in the boardinghouse forever, but I'd resigned myself to a lonely life as penance for what I had done.

BUT ON A warm spring morning in May, I woke up and realized I wasn't afraid anymore. Like the buds that sprang forth from the cold ground and from the barren trees, my heart was slowly unfurling. As the dust of my past settled, I became comfortable in the routine of my new life. I laughed more freely, playing cards with Ruthie, Helen, and Millie, and I didn't startle so easily anymore.

Though men made passes at me in cafés, or while I walked to work, I felt no guilt in telling them no. Slowly, I had emerged from the dazed fog I'd been living in, and my nightmares about John became less frequent. My friends at the boardinghouse didn't push me to explain why I wasn't interested in dating. They simply accepted me as I was. And I had learned to accept myself too. I deserved happiness, and I knew I was worthy of love.

It would take courage for me to become physically intimate again, and for now, it was better for me to keep my past locked away. My story was mine alone, and I could choose whom—if anyone—I would tell it to. But for the first time in months, I forgot about the Dorothy King case, about John, and about Ziegfeld's stage and all that I'd left behind. Instead, I embraced life as it was—my new job, my city, my love for Eleanor—and I focused on the possibility of a bright future.

And yet it still came as a surprise when on a beautiful day in June, a gentleman strode into the real estate office, with a tanned face and a wide, friendly smile, awakening long-dormant feelings in me. He was tall and rugged, muscular like he was no stranger to manual labor. He removed his fedora and held it to his chest, running a hand through his wavy dark hair. He was perhaps a bit older than me—twenty-eight or so—and good-looking.

"Hello there." His deep brown eyes made my stomach flutter. "Perhaps you can help me, miss."

My boss, Mr. Richards, had stepped out for lunch. At present, I was the only person in the office.

I smiled. "I'll certainly try."

The man looked around sheepishly. "I'm interested in any affordable properties you have for sale, here in San Francisco."

I didn't see a ring on his finger, but he seemed like a family man. Perhaps in whatever his line of work was, a wedding ring would only get in the way. I gestured to a photograph of our beachside homes.

"We have a new development of bungalows in the Outer Lands, with both electricity *and* indoor plumbing. Are you looking for a large home?"

He blushed. "I don't have a family of my own—not yet anyway."

His vulnerability endeared him to me.

"Is there a certain neighborhood you like?"

He grinned. "I'd love to stay in North Beach. I'm a supervisor at the Del Monte canning factory. I like being close to the water, and being able to walk to work."

Smiling, I thought about how I liked both of those things too. So many people were in a rush to get somewhere; they failed to appreciate the beauty found in small details, like poppies growing by the roadside, or the smell of the ocean. I searched through our listings. North Beach was also one of my favorite neighborhoods—my boardinghouse on Jackson Street in the heart of Little Italy was walking distance from several wonderful restaurants and cafés.

"Let me show you what we have available. Unfortunately, we don't have any single-family homes for sale, but we do have some nice flats."

He extended his hand. "My name is Ed. Ed Thompson."

His lovely, large hand was warm and dry, and I liked the way it felt wrapped around mine, like a gentle embrace. "Iris Eaton. Pleased to meet you."

Ed looked into my eyes, and for a moment I feared he'd recognized me from the Ziegfeld Follies. Men traveled across the country, after all. But he only smiled in his sweet, boyish way, and I showed him the apartment listings. Ed admitted he was a man of modest means who had saved over the years for a home of his own.

He was so full of warmth, with such an easy manner, that he made me feel as though we could become friends. We laughed while we talked, and Ed got excited about an apartment that I loved—one I would have picked for myself if I had more savings. It was in an Edwardian building on Columbus Avenue, above an Italian restaurant, with far more character than the stucco bungalows out in the avenues.

Ed rubbed his neck, his eyes sparkling. "Say, have you been to Fior d'Italia yet? They have the best real Italian food in San Francisco."

I shook my head. "Not yet, but I love Italian."

He laughed nervously. "I hope this isn't too forward, but I'd like to take you out to dinner, to thank you for all your help."

He held his hat in his hands, bracing himself for a rejection. I had been about to say no, but my heart spoke to me then—*say yes.* I paused, fiddling with a button on my sleeve. There was something about this man—his humility, his humor, his smile— that made me feel safe. He was the opposite of John, gentle and unpresumptuous, and his kind eyes had already told me everything I needed to know.

"Yes." My heart fluttered. "I would like that very much."

Chapter Twenty-Five

Ellie

Ellie brought her fingers to her lips, the halcyon days of her early childhood playing before her eyes like a Technicolor movie. She could remember being a little girl, Iris's hands around her waist, both of them shrieking with laughter as organ music played and wooden horses on poles moved up and down. "I loved riding the carousel at Playland with you. That's one of my favorite memories."

Iris's eyes twinkled. "Mine too."

Ellie shook her head. "Do you remember when I fell in the ocean with my clothes on, and we went back to your apartment until they dried, so my mother wouldn't find out?"

Iris chuckled. "You ran around naked like a little sprite!"

"And Uncle Ed called me Ellie-Belly, small and smelly!" Ellie smiled sadly. "I miss him and his sense of humor."

"So do I." Iris looked wistful. "But we had twenty wonderful years together, and for that I'm forever grateful."

"How did you know he was the one?" Ellie fiddled with a button on her cardigan, feeling a pang of guilt as she thought of Tom.

Iris smiled. "He took me to see the Seals play—I had never been to a baseball game before. We laughed so hard that day, I had tears in my eyes. Ed asked me questions, he valued my opinion, and I knew he was the one because being with him felt *so* right. I could simply be myself."

"That's wonderful." Ellie looked down at her hands, her finger bare where her diamond engagement ring had been. "Did you ever tell him about John? About what happened to you in New York?"

Iris blinked back tears. "No. I was afraid. He knew I had been through something terrible, but he didn't push me to name it. Our marriage wasn't always easy, but it was always worthwhile. Looking back, I wish I had told him."

Remembering how her uncle used to look at Iris like she was the most beautiful woman in the world, Ellie nodded. Uncle Ed probably would have accepted Iris exactly as she was, no matter her past. Ellie wanted a romance like Iris had—something real and lasting, full of laughter. Tom hadn't been the right person for her, but that didn't mean she would give up on love.

Ellie smiled at her aunt, remembering Iris's wedding. "I loved being your flower girl. The Palace of Fine Arts looked like a castle. And you looked like a princess. The memory of that day feels like a dream."

Iris's face lit up. "You ran around the colonnade like a whirling dervish. At four, you were a force to be reckoned with. It was a magical day."

In her hazy memories, Ellie had thrown rice at Iris and Uncle Ed, geese from the lagoon pecking at the ground beneath the rotunda. The venue, the Palace of Fine Arts, had originally been built for the 1915 Panama-Pacific Exhibition, but it was deemed too beautiful to be demolished, and still stood. Iris had worn a flowing white veil that swept the ground, and a silk sheath that fell just above her ankles.

It truly had been a gorgeous celebration. Ellie set down her empty wineglass, wondering if she'd ever have a wedding of her own. But becoming a wife was no longer an important goal. Yes, she was getting older, and she wanted to share her life with someone, but there was still plenty of time for that. Right now, she wanted to make a career out of writing, and pay her own way—just as Iris had.

Looking at her watch, Ellie frowned. "It's nearly time for supper. I ought to return home."

Iris met Ellie's eyes. "How is Clara?"

"The same . . . you know how she is." Ellie exhaled, surprised by what she was about to admit. "I don't think she's good for me."

Iris pressed her lips together, her features drawn. "Clara has her faults, but she parented you the best way she knew how."

Ellie looked down at her wineglass, a lump rising in her throat. "Thank you for being the mother I needed—the mother she couldn't be."

Iris's eyes glistened with tears. She reached across the sofa and gripped Ellie's hand. "You were a light in my life at the time I needed it most. And you still are. I love you."

"I love you too." Ellie warmed at her aunt's words—at being seen as a light, rather than as a burden. Since spending time together in New York, they'd grown even closer, and Ellie valued their special connection. She could be frank with her aunt in a way she couldn't with anyone else.

Ellie sighed, looking out the window at the shops below. "I don't think I can live with my mother anymore. I know I ought to take care of her, but . . ."

Iris shook her head.

"She's *my* sister. I can take care of her. It's your time to fly the nest."

Her heart filling with gratitude, Ellie smiled. "I want to stand on my own two feet—like you did. Thank you."

"I'm proud of you, and your father would be proud of you too." Iris winked. "And you never know—Mrs. O'Connell's home for unmarried ladies could still be taking applicants."

Ellie laughed, grateful Iris had lightened the mood. "If Mrs. O'Connell is still alive, and doesn't mind the sound of my typewriter, then sign me up."

As she stood to leave, she thought of Jack at the Delta Hotel and wondered if he could recommend a decent place to live. Hugging her aunt goodbye, Ellie sensed change in the air, carried on the ocean breeze. Her newfound freedom felt both frightening and exhilarating. But she was ready.

DEEP PURPLE SHADOWS stretched across the pavement as the sun set over the stately houses of Russian Hill. Ellie walked up Hyde Street, her muscles aching. She'd forgotten how Lombard's steep staircase caused her to pause and catch her breath every few flights. There hadn't been too many tourists on the steps, at least.

Trudging up to the front porch in the evening light, Ellie's eyes landed on her mailbox. A letter poked out of the metal container—the red and blue border of airmail paper causing her heart to stop. Ellie sucked air against her teeth.

Withdrawing the envelope, she looked at the name of the sender, *Marco Genova*. She didn't know of him, but she recognized her father's APO address in Italy, and her heart began pounding. *Was this man from her father's regiment?* Ellie tore the envelope open and began to read.

> *Dear Mrs. William Morgan,*
>
> *My name is Marco Genova. Your husband invited me to join his crew photo after I had flown with them a couple times. Here's the photograph we took together. I'm the guy farthest on the right, and I want you to have it now.*
>
> *First Lieutenant Morgan always treated me with respect, even though I was only a photographer. He said I fit in great, and he liked having me fly along. I want you to know, your husband was one of the best. Other lieutenants treated us like dogs, but he treated us like men. His crew would have moved heaven and earth for him.*
>
> *You see, I was supposed to fly with your husband on the morning of the crash, but I woke up with a bad fever that day. When Tommy Doyle was pulled from the wreckage, I couldn't believe what had happened. Tommy parachuted out as the plane went down, and then fishermen pulled him to safety near the island of Vis.*

Tommy died from his burns later that day. Before he passed, he told me Lieutenant Morgan put his crew ahead of himself, while everything went up in flames. I heard a few of the other men jumped too, but they were already on fire. Forgive me if this is too much—I've been at war so long, and I've seen such terrible things.

There was a loud bang as the plane exploded, and Tommy watched it go down with your husband still in the cockpit. Among the crew, there were no survivors. I'm so very sorry for your loss. If I'm ever out in California, I will come pay my respects. I thought you should know your husband was a hero.

> *Sincerely,*
> *Marco Genova*

Ellie's knees buckled beneath her, and the air was knocked from her lungs. She sank to the porch and covered her mouth with a trembling hand. The sounds of the city faded away, and in her ears she heard a monstrous buzzing.

Dead. Her father was dead.

A photograph had fallen from the envelope, and it lay on the porch. There was her father in his pilot's cap, its visor shielding his eyes from the sun while he smiled at the camera. He stood in the center, his men flanking him on both sides. They were no older than Ellie—just boys—and none of them were coming home. Ellie traced her father's face with her fingertip. And then she let out a wail.

Sobs racked her body. After the telegram, nothing had prepared her for the constant worry, the loss of appetite, the despair and the tears, the hopes and the disappointments she would experience throughout her search for her father. Ellie had felt panic and frustration and had suffered so many sleepless nights.

Now the painful journey had ended.

Her father was dead. There was nothing more she could do. His body lay at the bottom of a foreign sea, thousands of miles away. Ellie would never see him again, never hear his laugh or feel his arms wrapped around her in a bear hug. She would never listen to the deep timbre of his voice, hear his comforting words, or see the sparkle in his eyes. They would never share another donut at the Mayflower.

Ellie looked at the man in the photograph, Marco Genova, standing with his hands behind his back. He had strong Italian features; a young, kind face; and a head of thick, dark hair. He was the only person in the photo not wearing a cap, and by sheer coincidence, the only member of her father's crew still alive. His words meant more to her than he could ever know.

Marco had done what the army could not—he had brought Ellie the closure she so desperately needed. She hugged the photograph to her chest, weeping for the man she loved most in the world. Closing her eyes, she remembered summers spent camping in Lake Tahoe, the caws of blue jays, and the smell of the campfire. Her father had taken her out in his canoe, their paddles rippling the surface of the lake as fish swam in the crystal-blue waters below.

They had eaten smoked trout with their fingers, set up the tent together, not caring about the mosquitoes, and spent the night beneath the stars. Even Clara had laughed and smiled during those camping trips, more playful and relaxed than she ever was at home. In the morning, Ellie's father fried eggs and bacon, joking that he was a "modern man" who could cook just as well as Clara.

Ellie's heart bled memories—watching the streetcars pass by, crossword puzzles, rides on her father's shoulders, swimming in the lake, the way he looked holding his briefcase, dressed in his pilot's uniform. It bled for the wives and mothers of his crew members, for her own mother, for Lucy and Lillian.

Theirs was no longer a story with no ending. Ellie knew Marco's words were true because her father had always put other people ahead of himself, and it was exactly like him to go down with his plane. She cringed, thinking of the explosion, and prayed his death had been instant and painless.

Perhaps someday, far in the future, the army would find his remains and bring them home. Until then, the *knowing*, no matter how painful, felt like a small blessing. It was enough. Ellie picked herself up off the porch, wiped her eyes, and looked out at the bay. She drew in a deep breath, and then exhaled in a shudder. Then, turning toward the house, she walked inside.

Chapter Twenty-Six

Ellie

On the last Saturday in March, Ellie held her father's memorial service. It was unseasonably warm in Golden Gate Park, and cherry blossoms bloomed, their pink petals scattering to the spring breeze. Angler's Lodge felt as though it were tucked into the High Sierra, its mountain-style rustic cottage surrounded by tall redwoods, eucalyptus trees, and turquoise pools—a secret jewel of the park. Ellie's father had taught her to fly-fish here, and she'd chosen this place to pay tribute to him because it reminded her of Lake Tahoe.

Her mother had wanted to have the service at Saint Dominic's, but Ellie refused to be confined within the dark walls of the Catholic church. She felt closer to her father here, where the scent of pine needles and the sound of blue jays brought her back to nature. Taking a deep breath in, she looked out at the somber faces in the crowd gathered before her, and then down at her watch. It was nearly eleven o'clock in the morning, time to begin.

Iris sat at the front, her arm linked through Clara's. Ellie smiled at her aunt, grateful for all she'd done over the past few weeks, including helping to organize the memorial. As she scanned the sea of faces—her colleagues from the newspaper, her mother's neighbors and friends—Ellie's heart ached. Nearly everyone gathered before her today had lost a loved one to this war. Ellie's eulogy was dedicated to these families as much as her own. Clearing her throat, she began.

"Thank you for gathering here today." She glanced at the paper where she'd written down her thoughts, but decided she didn't need it. Instead, she spoke from the heart. "We're here to remember the life and service of my father, First Lieutenant William P. Morgan."

Her voice trembled, but it didn't break. "My father grew up on a small farm outside Boise, Idaho, and he is survived by his brother, John Morgan; his wife, Clara Morgan; and myself, Eleanor Morgan." She paused, thinking of Lillian and Lucy. It felt wrong not to mention them, but now was not the time.

"As a young man, my father saw a barnstormer come to town after the Great War. When he went up in that plane, the experience instilled in him a love of adventure and a love of flying." She took a deep breath. "He was strong, courageous, brave, and kind, a man who loved his family and his country."

Ellie blinked back tears. "My father told me our nation's future depended on command of the air. He fought for a future of freedom and liberty." She paused, looking out at the faces before her, solemn and drawn. "But when he wasn't flying, he loved crossword puzzles, fishing, and a nice glass of scotch."

This drew a few chuckles from the crowd, and Ellie smiled.

"After a career as a commercial pilot, he became a member of the Seven Hundred Eighty-Ninth Bombardment Squadron, and the Four Hundred and Sixty-Seventh Bombardment Group. He was deployed to the Mediterranean Theater of Operations on the first of July 1943."

She swallowed the hard lump in her throat. "No one is ever prepared to say goodbye to a loved one, even when we know the risks. My father, Lieutenant Morgan, was killed in action over the Adriatic Sea on the fourteenth of December 1944."

Ellie wiped a tear from her eye. "He gave his life in duty to his flag and country, but he also gave his life to his family."

Two families. A life split in two. And yet he had dedicated himself to all of them—Ellie, Mother, Lillian, and Lucy—flying across the country, sharing his love. And now she was filled with a complicated grief, mourning a complicated man.

Looking up, Ellie tried to keep her composure. Friends and neighbors blew their noses into tissues and wiped tears from their eyes. She took a deep breath.

"My father would not want us to be sad. He would want us to celebrate his life, to celebrate our country, to hope, and to fight for a brighter tomorrow. That is the promise I make to you today. I promise to live with the values he instilled in me, of courage, compassion, and selflessness; and I promise his memory will never be forgotten. Let us now take a moment of silence, to re-member the man we loved."

.   .   .

WHILE THE CROWD dispersed and entered the knotty pine interior of Angler's Lodge for food and drinks, Ellie felt her shoulders relax. She'd shaken quite a few hands and heard touching words from neighbors and friends, many of whom she hadn't seen in years.

It was wonderful how many people had fond memories of her father, and how they told her he had impacted their lives. Mrs. Cook, the neighborhood gossip, had surprised Ellie by wrapping her in a hug and telling her that her father was "a true gentleman." Of course, Mrs. Cook didn't know the half of it, but that was okay.

Iris approached with her arm linked through Clara's, both women wearing dark suit-dresses and pillbox hats, their makeup carefully applied. Though Ellie's relationship with her mother had only become more strained since Ellie had left home, Iris, true to her word, remained by her sister's side.

Clara gave Ellie a nod of acknowledgment and then turned on her heel and went to join their guests inside. Ellie felt the familiar pain of not receiving any validation from her mother—no pat on the back or affirmation she'd done well with her father's eulogy—but Ellie was learning to let these things go. Iris rubbed her shoulder. "That was beautiful. You did a great job."

Ellie smiled. "Thank you. I'm relieved it's over."

Shielding her eyes from the sun, Iris looked out at the turquoise ponds, where men practiced fly casting. "After listening to your tribute, I've decided something."

"What's that?"

Iris's eyes twinkled. "I'm going to write to the Ziegfeld Club, to tell them Stella Parsons is alive and well."

Ellie raised an eyebrow, grinning at her aunt. "You are?"

Iris nodded. "There's no reason I should hide my past anymore. I'm nearly fifty—far too old to be living with shame."

"Oh, Iris." Ellie was so proud of her aunt for embracing her past, including the dark parts. "That's wonderful. They'll be lucky to have you."

Iris chuckled. "Who knows, maybe I can reach out to some of the former Follies gals. We can't *all* have met tragic endings."

Smiling, Ellie agreed. "You must find the others who are thriving. And think of the stories you'll tell!"

Iris looked toward the lodge and then squeezed Ellie's shoulder. "I ought to join Clara inside. She's waiting for me."

Ellie exhaled, letting the familiar sense of duty binding her to her mother float away. "I'll join you in a moment."

Learning to let go of guilt was a process, but one Ellie embraced every day.

She had moved into a boardinghouse in the Fillmore District, where the beautiful arches that had once adorned the street with globe lights had been melted down for scrap iron, but a burgeoning jazz scene had unfolded.

Even during a time of war, people found ways to celebrate. Where Clara's home had been oppressively quiet, Fillmore Street was nothing but joyful noise. Horns blared from the nearby New Orleans Swing Club, buses rumbled past, and laughter emanated through the boardinghouse walls. Neighbors greeted Ellie by name at the grocer, the Laundromat, and passing by. In her new neighborhood, with a friendly smile and a simple hello, she made friends everywhere she went.

A warm hand touched Ellie's arm, and she turned around.

"That was a lovely service."

Seeing Anna's sweet face, Ellie pulled her colleague from the *Chronicle* into a hug. "You made it! Thank you for coming. You being here means a lot to me."

Anna smiled. "I'm sorry Frank wasn't able to join me. He had a prior engagement. But he sends his condolences."

Ellie hadn't expected Frank to come to her father's memorial service, but she'd developed a nice rapport with him since becoming a staff writer. She worked hard to make sure each article of hers was better than the last one, and she took Frank's constructive criticism to heart. Underneath his gruff exterior, he was passionate about his job. Both Ellie and Frank were delighted to see the readership "Tales from the City" had garnered. Readers wrote in regularly with suggestions, comments, and to express how much they loved Ellie's column.

Ellie gestured toward the wood cabin. "Would you like some tea or coffee? There's food inside the lodge."

"She's not one to turn down free food."

Ellie jumped, turning to see who had spoken. She *knew* that voice. It was as familiar to her as a dear friend. She looked up at the man beside Anna. He was tall, with dark hair and striking green eyes.

Anna nudged him in the ribs with her elbow. "Jack!"

She smiled at Ellie. "I hope you don't mind, I brought my brother along. He wanted to meet you in person."

Jack smiled, his cheeks dimpling. "Hey, kid. That was a wonderful tribute to your pops. I'm so very sorry for your loss."

Ellie's heart skipped a beat. *Jack.* Over the past year of their phone calls, she had joked about things like drawing on her calves with eyeliner to imitate the look of nylons and having garlic breath from eating the meatball sandwiches at the deli near the *Chronicle. Had she known he was so handsome, she would have kept her mouth shut.* Ellie's face flushed as he extended his hand.

"Thank you. It's—a pleasure to meet you."

As she felt Jack's warm fingers envelop her cold ones, a current of electricity ran through her. They locked eyes, and Ellie felt a mutual understanding pass between them, like a shared secret. They *liked* one another—there was no denying their chemistry. Ellie smiled, admiring the planes of Jack's face—his charmingly crooked smile, his thick, dark eyebrows, and his strong nose.

"You have dimples."

That had come out of her mouth? Her cheeks burned.

Jack and Anna laughed, their adorable smiles mirroring each other's.

"It's a Miller family trait." Jack's eyes sparkled. "What can I say?"

Anna grinned at them. "I'm going to step inside the lodge for some tea. Would you like me to bring you a cup?"

"No, thanks, Anna." Ellie smiled. "You aren't a secretary today."

Anna nodded and then slipped away, walking toward the lodge with a sly grin on her face. Ellie's heart beat faster. She and Jack were alone in the middle of the clearing, surrounded by redwoods and birds chirping.

"I'm sorry about your father." Thick, dark lashes framed Jack's light eyes, which were filled with compassion. "He sounds like an incredible man."

Ellie felt warmth pulse through her. They were standing so close, nearly touching. "Thank you, he was wonderful . . . but also complicated." Her cheeks warmed. "Forgive me, I somehow manage to say whatever is on my mind when I'm speaking with you."

"There's no need to apologize, kid." Jack smiled. "I enjoy talking to you."

Ellie smirked. "Even when I'm telling you about my girdle that's too tight or the runs in my stockings?"

"Especially then." Jack chuckled. "You said you were a sausage in a sausage casing, but I'd say you're more of a hot link. You've got some kick."

Ellie laughed. "I said I *felt* like a sausage in a sausage casing, there's a difference. And I'm not fond of hot links."

Jack gently nudged her. "I am. I like spice."

She nudged him back. "You're ridiculous."

"Ridiculously lucky."

"How so?" Her stomach fluttered.

Jack's eyes crinkled at the corners. "I'm lucky to know a gal so smart and so determined, she got her very own column with her *very own* byline." He placed a hand on her shoulder. Feeling the warm sensation of his touch, Ellie could barely breathe. Jack gave it a gentle squeeze.

"I knew you'd make a fine reporter, kid. Congratulations."

She smiled. "You're too kind. *You* got me to push beyond what I thought I was capable of."

Jack laughed, his dimples indenting. "Well, I *am* good at pushing people. Though usually I push them away." He ran a hand through his hair. "No one appreciates me except the alley cats, and that's because I feed 'em."

Ellie laughed at his self-deprecating sense of humor. "I don't believe that for one moment. You're a gas. Do you really feed the alley cats?"

Jack nodded. "Absolutely. Half my salary goes to cans of tuna. I've named them too. My favorite is an orange tabby with a broken tail, Mr. Baggins."

"Like Bilbo Baggins from *The Hobbit*?"

Jack smiled. "Yes, exactly. Do you like Tolkien?"

Ellie shook her head in disbelief. "I do. *The Hobbit* was my favorite book when I was a teenager. Now it's my younger sister's favorite."

Ellie's stomach clenched, realizing her gaffe.

Jack frowned. "I didn't know you had a sister. Is she here?"

Ellie felt panic rising inside her, but then she remembered she could tell Jack anything. He had never once judged her. She pressed her lips together, and then spoke. "My father has another daughter, Lucy. I met her for the first time while I was in New York. The reason I took that trip was to meet his mistress."

Jack's eyes widened. "Miss 'rhymes with . . .'"

Ellie smiled, grateful he could find humor in the situation. "I told you my father was a complicated man."

Taking both her hands in his, Jack gave her a meaningful look. "But he loved you. What you did took bravery and courage— traits he passed on to you. And your sister told you about her favorite book . . . that's a good sign. Right?"

Ellie nodded. "We're getting to know each other. And Miss 'rhymes with stamp' isn't so bad either. In fact, we shouldn't call her that. Her name is Lillian."

Understanding crossed Jack's face, not judgment.

"Lillian it is, then."

They grinned at each other. Talking with Jack felt so natural. After all, they had spoken on the telephone for a year, without any expectations. And now standing together in person, it was as though they'd known each other forever.

Ellie noticed the cluster of people gathered in front of Angler's Lodge, eating scones and sipping tea. She would thank each one of them for attending the memorial service before she could leave the park. *Would Jack be willing to wait around?* With nerves in her stomach, Ellie looked into his eyes.

"There's a special place downtown I used to go with my father. It's nothing fancy, just the Mayflower coffee shop. But if you'd like to come . . ."

"I would love to." Jack's eyes were kind. "They've got great donuts."

Ellie smiled. "You know it?"

"Of course." He laughed. "I like to sit and watch the trolley cars pass by. It's where I go to write."

Ellie's throat tightened. She hadn't been to the Mayflower in years because the thought of going without her father made her too sad. But now she could share that special place with Jack, and her memories of her father, both good and bad. Ellie tilted her head toward the group of guests.

"I'll just be a moment. I'm going to thank them for attending."

Jack nodded. "Take your time. I'll be right here."

Sunrays filtered through the canopy of trees, and Ellie breathed in the warm spring air, carrying the scent of pine needles. Walking away from Jack, she felt lighter than she had in years, her heart filled with hope for the future. She closed her eyes, taking a private moment to speak with her father.

"I miss you," she whispered. "And I love you so much. I know you tried your best to come home. I promise I'll take care of Lucy."

Opening her eyes, Ellie felt calm. Though her father hadn't answered her in a booming voice from heaven—something that would happen in the movies—she felt his presence. A blue jay had landed on the tree branch above her. It cocked its head, eyeing her carefully. Her father had always loved the cheeky jays; they made mischief at the campsite in Lake Tahoe, trying to steal pieces of bacon.

So much was changing, both in her life and in the world at large. Ellie paused, thinking of this morning's newspaper headline. The Allies were advancing, and it looked as though the war was finally coming to an end—a bittersweet victory. Ellie had phoned Lillian and Lucy about Marco's letter after receiving it, and they'd wept together for the man they loved, who had sacrificed his life for his country.

But then Ellie had received the most precious gift: a letter from her sister, her first piece of personal mail at her new address. In Lucy's looping cursive, she'd revealed her hopes, her teenage dreams, and her crush on a boy from math class. Ellie's heart swelled. Though she had lost a father, she'd gained a sister. Ellie had written back, with book recommendations and advice

about the boy, not that Ellie knew a lot about men, though perhaps she knew more than she thought.

These days, in spite of her grief, Ellie felt happier than she
had in years. Her room in the boardinghouse wasn't much, but it
was her own. She'd sewn cheerful yellow curtains for the windows, found a lovely antique desk at a secondhand shop, and set
up her typewriter against the wall. She always kept a vase full of
fresh flowers—daisies, sprigs of lavender, poppies, and lilies—
the kinds she loved. But most importantly, she kept a trundle bed
tucked beneath her twin mattress, made up with sheets, ready for
Lucy's visit, whenever she decided to come.

Ellie felt Jack's eyes on her, and a shiver of excitement worked
its way down her spine. He waved, and she waved back. There
was no need to rush anything—Ellie could already feel they
were destined to become more than just friends. Like Iris and
Uncle Ed, she and Jack had an easy way with one another, and
Ellie couldn't wait to see where their relationship was headed.

She looked up at the redwood trees before her, stretching
toward the heavens. They had sprouted from the roots of a
fallen giant, creating a near-perfect ring—a new generation—
encircling the old stump. Ellie smiled at nature's magic. She and
Lucy would carry on their father's legacy, just like these mighty
trees, overcoming hardship, growing roots, and reaching higher,
toward the sky.

Author's Note

Inspiration for this novel came in many forms. It was both conscious and unconscious, stirred by art, movies, novels, and music, and by memories of the past. Like Owen Wilson's character in *Midnight in Paris*, I am hopelessly nostalgic. I feel drawn to the glamour and recklessness of the Jazz Age and to the long echo of grief suffered by families who lost loved ones during World War Two.

Losing my own father as a teenager has shaped who I am, just as it shapes Ellie. The art I consumed during the depths of my grief made a lasting impression on me. Fitzgerald's *The Great Gatsby* captivated my broken heart in the same way Baz Lurhmann's *Romeo + Juliet* did. In both works, the coexistence of beauty and sorrow spoke to me on a personal level. Listening to the Smashing Pumpkins in my childhood bedroom, I found solace in the orchestral strings of "Tonight, Tonight."

I was mourning my father, but I was also mourning what might have been and what never was. I recognized my longing for another time and place in the music, books, and movies I loved. The illustrations of John Craig, the cover artist for *Mellon Collie and the Infinite Sadness*, have stayed with me all these years. They are striking, celestial, and mysterious, just like the black-and-white photographs of the Ziegfeld Follies girls taken by Alfred Cheney Johnston.

My father's death from cancer in 1997 was painful, but it was definitive. To explore Ellie's journey, and the generational trauma experienced by MIA families, I read the book *Vanished: The Sixty-Year Search for the Missing Men of World War II*, by Wil S. Hylton. It inspired the letters between the war widows in *The Pilot's Daughter*, women who desperately want to keep hope alive.

In my research, I learned of Dr. Pauline Boss, who coined the term "ambiguous loss" in the early 1970s, when she interviewed family members of pilots who were missing in action during the Vietnam War. Ambiguous loss differs from ordinary loss in that there is no verification of death, or no certainty the person will return to the way they used to be (think Alzheimer's). The Defense POW/MIA Accounting Agency (DPAA) reports that there are 73,515 American soldiers still missing from World War II.

The story of Ellie's father was inspired by the *Tulsamerican* B-24 Liberator bomber and Army Air Forces 1st Lt. Eugene P. Ford, whose plane was shot down in 1944 over the Adriatic Sea. PBS *NOVA* joined the US Department of Defense, the Croatian Navy, and an elite team of underwater archaeologists and technical divers to excavate the plane's wreckage in 2017. It took seventy-three years and extensive DNA testing to bring closure for the families of the missing airmen.

Eugene Ford's daughter, Norma Beard, made a promise to

her mother and brother that if her father's remains were recovered during her lifetime, she would make sure they were interred at Arlington National Cemetery, which they have been. I highly recommend watching this PBS documentary, *Last B-24*.

Further research for Ellie's story came from a vintage copy of the *The Writer's Yearbook 1944*, Volume 1, gifted to me by my mother, which I found very useful when writing Ellie's character and learning about the writer's market in the 1940s. I also found inspiration in the atmospheric photographs of Fred Lyon in *San Francisco Noir*, depicting San Francisco in the 1940s in all its foggy mystery. Along with Alfred Cheney Johnston's photographs, these black-and-white images provided wonderful visuals for the novel.

Through my character Iris, I was able to explore America's cultural infatuation with wealth and power and the dangers that lie there. The tragic murder of Dorothy King, otherwise known as "the Broadway Butterfly," is real, though it remains unsolved.

Born Anna Marie Keenan to poor Irish immigrants, she married a chauffeur named Eugene Oppel at age eighteen, but later divorced him and moved to Manhattan, where she reinvented herself as Dorothy King. In historic newspaper articles, King is described as a cabaret "butterfly" and an acquaintance of the famed Ziegfeld Follies girl Hilda Ferguson. King was really the mistress of John Marshall, the alias of John Kearsley Mitchell, millionaire husband of Frances Stotesbury, and son-in-law to E. T. Stotesbury. Ostensibly, she met Mitchell at the Brevoort Hotel, and then later accepted his gift of the apartment at 144 West 57th Street. I took artistic license in portraying Mitchell as an abuser, but he was a suspect in Dorothy King's murder. There's a 1932 book about him titled, *John Kearsley Mitchell, III, Million-aire Murderer: "Sweetheart" and Slayer of Anna Marie Keenan, alias "Dot King"* by John C. Hackett, available at the University of Pennsylvania Van Pelt Library.

Mitchell is also allegedly the reason the term "sugar daddy" was coined. The cultural reference appeared alongside an image of J. Kearsley Mitchell in the *Evening Times* (Sayer, Pennsylvania) on March 28, 1923, with the following text:

> John Kearsley Mitchell, son-in-law of E. T. Stotesbury, multimillionaire of Philadelphia, has been revealed as the mysterious "Mr. Marshall," who was the "heavy sugar daddy" of Dorothy Keenan King, New York model, who was chloroformed to death in her New York City apartment.

For additional information on the Dot King murder case, I scoured troves of digital newspaper archives and read excerpts of books such as *Cop Knowledge: Police Power and Cultural Narrative in Twentieth-Century America*, by Christopher P. Wilson; *Memoirs of a Murder Man*, by Arthur A. Carey; and *Wicked Philadelphia: Sin in the City of Brotherly Love*, by Thomas H. Keels. I also discovered much useful information in Brooks Peters's, "Death of a Flapper: The Dot King Scandal," *Open Book* (blog), and found inspiration from Stewart Jackson's article "'Spotters' Pick Girl Victims in Gem Robberies," in the *Santa Cruz Evening News*, March 1, 1924, in which I learned about girls who befriended wealthy women, learned about their jewelry and addresses, and then passed that information along to robbers. Reports of a dumbwaiter in Dorothy King's apartment allowed me to speculate about a plausible means of entry for the burglar.

I took liberties with constructing Dorothy King's personality, such as her custom-made perfume and her desire to become a Follies girl. (I have also included fictional Follies performers alongside real ones, and I have taken liberty with the timeline of events in order to enhance the plot. For instance, the Panama Pacific Line did not launch the cruise ship SS *California* until 1927, and Eddie Cantor did not perform in the Follies of 1922.)

However, in *Making the Detective Story American: Biggers, Van Dine and Hammett and the Turning Point of the Genre, 1925–1930* by J. K. Van Dover, Dorothy King is described as having "claimed to have danced in the Ziegfeld Follies." Therefore, I took the liberty to say she had auditioned for the Ziegfeld Follies, to enhance the plot of my novel. I sincerely hope Dorothy King's murder is solved one day, so her mourners may receive closure, like Ellie and Iris did.

A number of articles were useful in bringing the Ziegfeld Follies to life, especially "Doris E. Travis, Last of the Ziegfeld Girls, Dies at 106," by Douglas Martin (*New York Times*, May 12, 2010); "Ziegfeld Girls Recalling the Glitter of an Era," by Judy Klemesrud (*New York Times*, April 25, 1975); and "The Ziegfeld Midnight Frolic," by Nimisha Bhat (Museum of the City of New York, July 1, 2014).

Though I was unable to travel to New York for research (writing a novel during a pandemic was both a challenge and a welcome distraction), I read several notable books, including *You Must Remember This: An Oral History of Manhattan from the 1890s to World War II*, by Jeff Kisseloff; *Ziegfeld: The Great Glorifier*, by

Eddie Cantor and David Freedman; and *Ziegfeld: The Man Who Invented Show Business,* by Ethan Mordden. I also lost myself to hours of YouTube, watching footage of everything from the New York subway to the restoration of the New Amsterdam Theatre.

I sit here wearing my favorite old sweatshirt printed with the original 1925 *The Great Gatsby* jacket art by Francis Cugat, and I hope those of you reading this enjoyed *The Pilot's Daughter* as much as I enjoyed writing it. Thank you for your support!

Acknowledgments

When I began this novel, I had no idea I would complete it during a global pandemic. Instead of writing distraction-free in a quiet neighborhood café, I was forced to hunker down in my driveway, where I learned my Prius could double as an office, or in a folding chair in my backyard. I snuck in as many words as I could while hiding from my preschooler. Writing *The Pilot's Daughter* gave me a means of mentally escaping 2020 while doing something I love, and for this I'm immensely grateful.

I'm indebted to my brilliant agent, Jenny Bent, who never lost enthusiasm for this book, even during such an uncertain time. What began as the spark of an idea about the Ziegfeld Follies and an unsolved Jazz Age murder morphed into a deeper story about grief, World War II, and our individual ability to heal from trauma. I'm so grateful to Jenny for her hard work and careful edits, which make my novels stronger. Thank you also to the amazing team at the Bent Agency, including Victoria Capello and Kasey Poserina, who worked so quickly on my contracts.

Thank you to my fantastic editor at Dutton, Stephanie Kelly, whom I could not be more thrilled to collaborate with. From the moment we first spoke on the phone, I knew Stephanie recognized my vision for this novel. Her insightful edits have made Ellie's and Iris's stories shine brighter. I'm also thankful to my copy editor for helping with so many historical details, to Lexy Cassola for checking permissions, to my cover designer for their beautiful artwork, and to the sales, marketing, and publicity teams at Penguin Random House for getting my book into the hands of readers.

I am grateful to my writer friends, especially for their support during this past year. Thank you to Sally Hepworth for reading the first fifty pages of an early draft, and to Samantha Bailey, Elise Hooper, Jillian Cantor, Anna Vera, Jennifer S. Brown, Joy Calloway, Meg Donohue, Allison Larkin, Lori Nelson Spielman, and Cristina Alger for your messages of encouragement (or commiseration!). You made a difficult and lonely time feel less frightening and more connected. Thank you also to Andrea Katz, who does so much for the writing community, and to the many bookstagrammers, book bloggers, booksellers, and librarians who have supported my career over the years. I appreciate you so much!

Thank you to my family. Without you, none of this would be possible. Mom, I cannot thank you enough for the hours of "grandma camp" you put in while schools were closed so I could write and edit. This book is dedicated to you for a reason! Carolyn, you are always so supportive of my creative dreams and I support you equally in yours. Hazel, I love you so much. You make me laugh every day and you are the light of my life. Will, with every hardship thrown at us, we only grow stronger. You are the rock of this family and I love you so much. Thank you for doing all the responsible, boring, and necessary adult things, like filing our taxes, while I write the books.

To my friends, you made the last year survivable. I miss hugging you. And to my readers—you are the reason I have the best job on the planet. Thank you from the bottom of my heart.